JUSTICE SERVED

By

Joyce Dudley

Copyright © 2004 by Joyce Dudley

ISBN 0-7414-1981-5

Many of the quotations used at the beginning of each chapter were adapted from <u>Black's Law Dictionary</u>, by Henry Campbell Black, M.A. West Publishing Company.

Cover Design by Debra Geiger, Jim Kreyger, and Chris Master
Cover photo by Jim Kreyger
Back cover photo by Denise Retallack

Published by:

INFI⚭ITY
PUBLISHING.COM

1094 New Dehaven Street
Suite 100
West Conshohocken, PA 19428-2713
Info@buybooksontheweb.com
www.buybooksontheweb.com
Toll-free (877) BUY BOOK
Local Phone (610) 941-9999
Fax (610) 941-9959

Printed in the United States of America

Published April 2004

DEDICATION

For my mother Norma for inspiring me, my husband John for believing in me, and my four sons Chris, Matt, Mike and Sam for letting me play "Mega Mama." You have all brought so much joy into my life.

ACKNOWLEDGEMENTS

I began this book on January 11, 1999 while hiking with my husband John, on a ridge 10,000 feet above sea level. "I want to write a book," I announced. "Why?" he asked. John has always been a man of few words. When I gave him a list of *good reasons*, he wasn't impressed. "Seems to me," he offered, "you should only write a book if you have something to say— something that, if you had the attention of the world, you'd say it." Hmm, I thought, quite the mandate. I had no quick response, so we hiked on in silence. Several miles later, I told him about my ideas behind <u>Justice Served</u>; he listened intently, actively and with great encouragement. I went home after the hike, and called my reporter friend, Rhonda Parks-Manville. Rhonda advised me to start writing, and so I did.

Not knowing how to type, I wrote for 10 days and nights. On day 11, the book was *done*. However, I spent the next 5 years constantly rewriting while simultaneously embracing what I learned from the following extraordinary people.

First and foremost, there was my very close friend, Debra Geiger. Debra knew my heart, and with great talent and sensitivity, spent the last several years fixing my words to match. She and I both learned at the feet of Shelly Lowenkopf, who would delight and excite us with his knowledge and expertise in the art of writing. Shelly's guidance proved to be invaluable. Early on, Sue Grafton, Jerry Freedman, Vicki Allen, Duane Unkefer, Emily and Buzz Blair, and Fred Klein, all excellent writers and artists in their own right, gave me just what I needed to continue rewriting.

Once the book was underway, the following precious friends and relatives offered me their insight and expertise. At the very beginning and throughout, there was my mother, Norma Allerhand. Then, there were the rest of my family: Cathy Collins, Judy and Paul Willis, Aunt Millie Kuelling, cousins Jean and Amy Bass, Joan Abe, Chris D'Arco, Jim Romeo and, of course, John. Adding to that list are my P.M.C. pals, Joan and Dave McCoy, Pam Denny, and Sid Neal. Back at home there were Lana Shane, Sherrie Adler, and Judge James Slater.

Most recently, I was greatly aided by my munificent colleagues, DDA Ann "Sully" Sullivan, Kathryn Henebry, from the Santa Barbara Police Department, and my attention-to-detail-pal – Victoria Adair.

My final editors and purveyors of magic were Maralyn and Norm Hill.

Aside from the above, there were those who patiently expanded my knowledge in this critical area of social and criminal justice: Marshall Abrams, Jaye Adams, Jan Bullard, Dr. Elliot Schulman, and my esteemed partner, Ron Zonen.

Finally, none of this would have been possible if Santa Barbara District Attorney Tom Sneddon hadn't had both the courage to hire this middle-aged mother of four, freshly out of law school, and the integrity to demand that all of his DDAs work hard, know the law, and always strive to do the right thing.

Having written this book, my life is richer, in part because of the product, but much more because of the process. Each of the people mentioned above really cares about kids, and their overwhelming concern for them, fills my heart and these pages.

1

Equal Protection—The Constitutional requirement that persons under like circumstances be given equal protection in the enjoyment of personal rights and the prevention and redress of wrongs.

Jordon Danner concentrated on the long yellow pad in front of her. While everyone else waited, she ticked off each question she'd intended to ask. Certain they'd all been presented, she slowly moved her hazel eyes up toward Judge Thomas and smiled.

She was finally at the top of her game. She'd always been attractive, but now having reached middle age, experience, confidence, and poise further enhanced her beauty.

"No further questions, Your Honor."

No more questions were necessary. Police Officer Paul Howe had been a perfect witness. With his help, she'd finally nailed Marshall Riverstone, and from the expression on the face of Bert Feller, the District Attorney for Santa Barbara County, she knew he thought so too.

Sitting there, anticipating the defense attorney's cross-examination, she overheard Feller telling his two new female prosecutors, *"That's* how to handle a Defendant's Motion to Suppress. And *that's* how I want you to perform when you work for me."

Although Jordon knew her boss personally disliked her and her politics, his comments still added to the adrenaline rush of pleasure. Her mother had always taught her to embrace approval only from those she respected, but to enjoy whatever appreciation came her way.

Alan Stern, the defense attorney, scraped his chair back in an attempt to stand up. The screech of the chair made Jordon cringe. Stern looked down. It appeared as if he had to make sure he'd cleared enough room for his button-straining midsection. Upon rising, he shifted his weight onto his hands, and tilted his torso toward her. "Sorry," he whispered. "Sorry to do this."

She thought his breath smelled of too much coffee, and his comment concerned her. He knows merely puffing at this late date isn't going to affect me; so what's he got in mind? Jordon crossed and uncrossed her legs. She had to stay ready.

Before beginning his questioning, Stern rocked and pushed the podium forward until it was exactly five feet from Officer Howe. Jordon was sure he understood if he'd moved it any closer, she'd object, and the judge would sustain her objection. Jordon was convinced both Stern and the judge were well aware of her much-acclaimed law review article on the subject of witness intimidation.

Officer Paul Howe, however, didn't look intimidated. He looked like a handsome blonde water polo player, ready to endure whatever Stern served up. Jordon had known Paul for years, long enough to understand that, to him, his good looks were inconsequential. He simply hadn't earned them the way he had his impressive reputation. Jordon was glad it was Paul who'd made this monumental bust; not only because of his competency, but also because he was fun to look at—*eye-candy*, as one of her single friends would say.

Judge Thomas sat back, turned his head and scratched his neck; the gesture made most of his wrinkled neck skin move. He appeared disinterested, as if he'd already made up his mind; and resented having to sit through Stern's cross-examination.

A small crowd of prosecutors, defense attorneys, and on-lookers were scattered in clusters throughout the courtroom. Amid the usual murmur, Stern began his cross-examination of Howe, and Jordon began to doodle. She wanted to make it obvious to everyone she had nothing to worry about. In reality, she was, as always, extremely anxious. Experience had taught her to consider carefully the ramifications of everything Stern said and did.

"According to your testimony," Stern began, "you ultimately found all of this compelling evidence as a result of merely seeing a man weave his car in and out of a traffic lane?"

"Yes, sir," Officer Howe answered. "Except, I believe I said he was weaving all over the road."

Alan Stern didn't appear to pay any attention to Officer Howe's correction. "And by 'all of this compelling evidence,'" Stern continued, "I assume you understood I meant the alleged child pornography—photos and videos, the two child actors themselves, the contracts, and even my client's alleged partner?"

Jordon feared her olive skin was now taking on a pinkish hue. Why would Stern be reminding the judge of all this damaging evidence? Unless...

Stern didn't wait for Howe's answer; he obviously didn't want his rhythm disrupted again. Instead he began pacing behind the podium and avoiding any further eye contact with Paul Howe. "And you discovered all of this evidence because you just *happened* to see a man weaving his car?" Stern stopped pacing and looked directly at Howe. "Remarkable," he exclaimed, but he was clearly implying the opposite. "And just prior to observing him drive, did you see where he came from?"

"No, sir, not that I recall."

"And what were you doing at two a.m., just before you saw him?"

"I was patrolling Haley Street."

"That's your assigned area." Stern didn't bother to wait for Howe's concurrence. "And at precisely two a.m., all the bars in your assigned area close, at which time you and the other officers are told to sort of," Stern raised his voice, "lie in wait; that is, watch people as they leave the bars and then *pounce* on them when you see them commit a minor traffic infraction?" As if to add drama to his question, Stern took a quick step away from the podium as he emphasized the word *pounce*.

The courtroom chatter softened. Jordon considered objecting to the word *pounce* as argumentative, but knew Judge Thomas, with his usual 12:15 tennis match, would only tolerate a minimum number of objections. So, instead she sat back and slowly pressed the side of a knuckle against her full lower lip.

"...Well Officer, might that be what you were doing on April fifth at two a.m., lying in wait, ready to *pounce*?" Stern asked.

"I call that protecting our community from drunk drivers," Howe answered.

"Ah, I see, so then am I to assume when you saw my client weaving 'all over the road' as you phrased it, you were just assuming he was drunk?"

"I thought he might be."

Where the hell was Stern going with all of this? Jordon was baffled. Suddenly she felt as if she were back in law school, sitting there trying to understand what had just been asked, while others were already raising their hands ready to respond.

"And then what did you do?" Stern asked.

"I called in a description of him to our dispatcher."

"Officer Howe, tell the judge how you described my client to your dispatcher."

"I don't remember exactly—the exact words I used." Howe's voice began to soften and his words started running together.

What's Howe hiding? Jordon's eyelashes fluttered. A few of the other experienced prosecutors in the courtroom looked up. It appeared they too could sense that something was about to be surgically revealed.

"Well, I just happen to have a copy of the Santa Barbara Police Department dispatch print-out. It says here the very first thing you said to the dispatcher about my client was that he was a Caucasian male."

"Yeah, so, OK; that's what he is."

"It's somewhat unusual to see a Caucasian male in that part of town, that time of the morning, isn't it, Officer?"

Oh shit, thought Jordon as she recalled this judge's campaign promise—"To rid our community of every single aspect of insidious racial profiling." But Stern's got nothing—

"No, ah, it's not that unusual," Howe answered, but the break in his voice betrayed his words.

"Oh, really," Stern continued, "but citizens of our community have accused you of racial profiling before, haven't they?"

What the …Jordon began to worry.

"Yeah, I've been accused of it, but nothing ever came of it."

Jordon now knew she'd been sandbagged, she didn't know anything about these citizen complaints. She couldn't defend him against something she knew nothing about. If only he'd mentioned this to her….

"Isn't it true your office had to investigate three separate citizen's complaints regarding your stopping cars for no reason other than what's known in your business as *race out of place*?"

"Sir, each complaint was fully investigated and there wasn't enough evidence to prove any of them."

"But, Officer Howe, wouldn't you agree that, collectively, they prove a sort of pattern or practice on your part?"

"No, I wouldn't."

"Well, would it surprise you if I told you only one out of every twenty-five people driving down Haley Street, that time of the morning, is Caucasian?"

The courtroom was now quiet.

Jordon finally found something she could object to. "Object!" She shouted, shattering the silence. "Irrelevant, and Mr. Stern is not on the witness stand, therefore, he shouldn't be testifying." Jordon wanted to give Paul time to regroup; she still believed in him. She also wanted to give herself an opportunity both to disrupt Stern's rhythm and to display her indignation at the inferences being drawn by him.

"Overruled." Judge Thomas stared at Jordon. "Mr. Stern just asked the officer if it would surprise him."

Jordon knew the judge wanted her to back down, but she refused. She was now certain the fate of her case depended upon her perseverance.

"Well, then it's irrelevant," she argued, but she could tell it sounded more like a whine.

"Madame Prosecutor," Judge Thomas responded, "it doesn't sound irrelevant to me." After staring at her for an extra moment, he turned his attention to the witness. "Officer Howe, you are directed to answer the question."

After this exchange, all the other experienced attorneys looked up from their morning papers.

Shit, Jordon thought as she clenched down on her teeth, Thomas is actually buying what Stern is selling... My God, he *can't* let Marshall Riverstone go free.

"Would it surprise me?" Officer Howe finally replied. "No, I don't think so—"

He's hedging, she thought.

"...But I never really notice the race of a person I'm arresting anyway."

And now, she concluded, he's just lost credibility.

"Oh really," Stern said. "Well, would it surprise you if I told you that the very first words that came out of your mouth when you approached my client's car were, 'What are *you* doing *here* this time of night?'"

Jordon was now certain Stern had successfully manipulated the judge by raising the politically-charged issue of *racial profiling*. She wanted to rescue Paul because she cared about him and her case, but feared if she did so, she'd be accused of condoning behavior that many, especially Judge Thomas, consider unconstitutional, if not worse. She decided she had to wait.

"I always," Officer Howe responded, "ask them *something* in order to get them to talk." He turned and looked toward the judge. "That way, I can see if they have any alcohol on their breath."

"Oh," Stern retorted, "so saying what you said was just a ruse? Just something you uttered, but didn't mean. Just something you said that was meaningless and you said it just so you could determine if there was any alcohol on my client's breath?"

Stern's clear, carefully crafted words and tone, echoing in a silent courtroom, made Paul Howe seem less than truthful.

"Yeah, something like that."

"And, could you?" Stern asked, as if he expected a yes or no answer.

Jordon shifted her weight and thought, Stern knows *exactly* what Howe's going to say.

But Howe didn't immediately respond.

Stern raised his voice. "Well, could you smell any alcohol on my client's breath?"

"I don't remember."

"So you asked my client a question, hoping he'd incriminate himself, and now you can't even tell Judge Thomas if he did?"

"Object. Argumentative." Jordon announced.

"Sustained," ruled Judge Thomas, "but tell me, Officer, why can't you say whether you smelled alcohol on his breath or not?"

Jordon sat back. She knew the judge shouldn't have asked the question after he sustained her objection, but, given the way he rephrased it, she thought it now gave Howe the opening he needed to save himself. She just hoped he'd embrace it.

Officer Howe paused, exhaled, and looked directly into Judge Thomas' eyes, "Because, Your Honor, at the same time I asked him that question, I saw one of those photographs with the kids in them, and, to tell you the truth, Judge, the photograph made me sick, and I just about lost it. After seeing that," Howe swallowed, "the whole focus of my investigation changed."

All right Paul, thought Jordon.

"Well then, Officer." Alan Stern interrupted, "let's go back to the weaving you allegedly saw. How much time went by from the time you last saw him 'weave all over the road,' as you phrased it, until the time you pulled him over?"

"Not very long. Couldn't have been more than fifteen seconds."

Stern lowered his head, looked down at his notes, and whispered, "Gotcha." When he looked back up again, he was smiling. "No further questions, Your Honor."

After Jordon indicated she had no re-cross, Paul Howe slowly rose from the witness stand and walked toward the courtroom exit.

Jordon followed him with her eyes; he never looked up. As she glanced over those who remained in the courtroom, she caught a glimpse of the defendant.

Riverstone was leaning his chair back. He seemed to be straining to see a photograph on the courtroom clerk's desk. In response, the clerk rotated the framed photo of her children inward. Jordon shuddered. This man is shameless. He's got to be stopped!

Judge Thomas gazed up at the clock and down under his bench at what Jordon assumed was probably his tennis racket. "Ms. Danner," he asked, "do you have any other witnesses?"

After Jordon said she didn't, Stern called Clyde Smith to the stand. Jordon looked over at her DA investigator, Rose Torres. Rose turned and immediately left the courtroom.

As Clyde Smith walked by, Jordon caught a whiff of the combined stench of urine, cigarettes and wintergreen mints.

Once sworn in, Stern elicited that, on the night in question, moments before 2 a.m., Smith had been standing on Haley Street, just outside the Condor Club, when he saw a police car, "headlights off, dome light on low, parked about a block away." Having made this observation, Smith decided to "lay low and watch." He wanted to see which "poor son of a bitch was gonna get popped."

"And did you have to wait long?" Stern asked.

"Nope, I saw this here white guy come out of the club, get into his car, and start to drive away. About a block or two later, sure as shit," Clyde quickly looked up at the judge, "I mean sure as shootin', the cop pulled him over." Clyde smiled, displaying teeth the color of deli mustard.

"And do you see the driver of that vehicle in this courtroom?"

"Yeah, that's him over there." Clyde pointed to Marshall Riverstone. In response, Riverstone turned his head slightly and ran his fingers through his thick gray hair.

He looks harmless, even grandfatherly, Jordon thought. If only he looked more like Clyde Smith, then kids would never go near him.

Next, Stern established that from the time Riverstone left the bar, until the time he was stopped, Smith never lost sight of Riverstone, and never saw his car weave.

"Mr. Smith, do you know Mr. Riverstone?" Stern asked.

"No, but I've seen him around."

"Have you ever talked to him?"

"Nope."

"No, why not?"

"Because he's a sleaze bag."

A trace of laughter wafted through the courtroom.

"So you wouldn't lie for him, would you?"

"No way! I heard about what he does with kids."

Nice touch Stern, thought Jordon, but it's not over yet.

"Thank you Mr. Smith. I have no further questions."

Jordon began her questioning before she even reached the podium. "Mr. Smith, you wouldn't lie for this so-called sleaze bag," her voice now took on a quick-paced angry tone, "but you'd lie about a cop, wouldn't you?"

"I'm not lying."

"Oh come on, Mr. Smith, you'd jump at a chance to make a cop look bad—wouldn't you?" Jordon leaned forward and rested her weight on her forearms.

"Maybe."

"Maybe, huh?" Jordon nodded, stood up and turned her back on their witness. She was sure Rose Torres would be there; she didn't disappoint her. Jordon put her hand out. Rose gave her the document with a triumphant smile. Jordon briefly looked at it, and then flipped it over to Stern. She was sure in so doing the multiple page document would dramatically unfold. It did, reaching most of its way to the floor, but still Stern didn't react. Jordon continued.

"Mr. Smith," she said, "I've just handed your lawyer your rap sheet." She paused until Stern handed it back to her. "It looks to me as if you've had a long history of run-ins with the police."

Clyde took on a defensive but unwavering tone.

"Look, lady, I *know* what I've done in the past, and I *know* what I saw that night."

Concerned that the crook actually sounded credible, Jordon decided to approach her impeachment from another angle.

"But, Mr. Smith, do you really *know* what you saw that night? You *were* drunk, weren't you?"

"No, well, sure I'd been drinking. I always drink, but I wasn't drunk."

"Your Honor," Jordon said, infusing indignation into her voice, "I have no further questions for *this* witness." Jordon felt she should stop while still having something left to argue.

After Stern indicated he had no need to re-cross Mr. Smith, Judge Thomas told Smith he was excused.

Clyde stepped down from the witness stand and smiled at Alan Stern. Stern did not respond. Clyde shrugged his shoulders and left.

Judge Thomas glanced up at the clock; it was 11:50. After determining neither side had any more witnesses, he requested each attorney make a *brief* closing argument. Jordon was first. Although she was extremely worried, she employed her most confident voice.

"Your Honor, this morning a police officer of the Santa Barbara Police Department took the stand and swore he saw the defendant violate the law by weaving all over *our* roads." She paused to let the significance of that statement sink in.

"After lawfully stopping the defendant for this violation, the officer had an absolute right to shine his flashlight into the car. When he did so, he saw, in plain view, the horrifying photograph, which in turn gave him *reasonable suspicion* to detain him and search the entire vehicle. This search ultimately gave him *probable cause* to enter the defendant's studio."

Jordon then went on to list, in detail, all of the graphic, incriminating evidence found at the studio. She then explained how each piece was lawfully seized. "...In conclusion, Your Honor, what you have here is excellent police work, which resulted in getting a child pornographer, and therefore child molester, off our streets." She hoped if her legal reasoning didn't sway him, the potential public outcry would.

Judge Thomas showed no reaction. Instead, he replied, "Thank you, Ms. Danner. OK, Mr. Stern."

"Quite frankly, Your Honor," Alan Stern said as he slowly rose, "I am shocked by Ms. Danner's characterization of this as *excellent police work*." He turned toward Jordon and feigned personal indignation.

Oh come on Stern, she thought, give me a break.

"The stop of my client's vehicle was nothing more than blatant racial profiling. More than likely Officer Howe saw a white man in a predominantly non-Caucasian neighborhood, figured he was up to no good, and so stopped him. This stop violated both my client's Fourth and Fourteenth Amendment rights."

Stern paused; Jordon was sure he was doing it for effect. Every lawyer in town knew Judge Thomas considered himself to be a strict constitutionalist.

"Either way, the bottom line is Officer Howe had no legal right to pull Mr. Riverstone over. It doesn't matter what he claims to have found. Since his initial stop was unlawful, whatever he might have come upon is merely *fruit of the poisonous tree* and must, as a matter of law, be deemed inadmissible. Thank you, Your Honor."

As soon as Stern sat down, Jordon immediately shot up. She hadn't yet formulated what she'd say, but she knew she had to show she was ready to react to Stern's outrageous assertions. "Your Honor," she began.

"Sit down, Counsel," Judge Thomas ordered. "I've heard enough. I'm ready to make my ruling. The only reason I can say, with any certainty, that this defendant was pulled over, was because of the color of his skin—"

"Your Honor," Jordon interrupted, "he was pulled over because he was seen weaving."

"No, Ms. Danner, not according to an unbiased eyewitness."

"Your Honor," Jordon interrupted again, "Clyde Smith was a drunken, *bleary-eyed* witness, who's not the least bit unbiased. He hates the police; he has a rap sheet longer than my arm and—"

"That's enough, Ms. Danner. I heard the evidence. Mr. Smith may have a record, and he may have been drunk, but he was not motivated to lie for Mr. Riverstone."

"Your Honor, if you deem the stop illegal, all of the People's evidence will evanesce."

"I understand, Ms. Danner, but under these circumstances I'm powerless to do anything else."

"Your Honor, I respectfully disagree." But Jordon didn't sound respectful. "You have the power both to determine witness credibility and to dispense justice." To emphasize her last point, Jordon lifted up the penal code and dropped the hefty publication on counsel table.

The boom resounded throughout the courtroom. Everyone but Jordon froze. Jordon didn't miss a beat. "Your Honor, if you rule the 'stop' to be illegal, then I can't proceed, and a child abuser and molester *will* go free."

"Ms. Danner," Judge Thomas responded, after barely recovering from the earsplitting intrusion, "I understand both my authority and the ramifications of my decision. Now, if you say another word, or do *anything* else to disrupt my courtroom, I will hold you in contempt."

"Your Honor, if you decide to let this monster go, you will be making a contemptible decision." Jordon froze; she knew she'd just gone too far.

"That's it, Ms. Danner. I now find you in contempt of court and I fine you one hundred dollars. I've made my ruling. By overwhelming evidence, I've determined that the stop was based upon nothing more than racial profiling and prejudice. And Ms. Danner, unless you were being disingenuous with this Court, you no longer have any admissible evidence, so I suggest you move this Court to dismiss these charges at once."

"I won't, Your Honor."

"Then let's begin the preliminary hearing right now. Bring in your first witness."

"I can't, Sir, *you've* successfully gutted my case."

"Your Honor..." Alan Stern now soundlessly stood and announced with great fanfare, "I hereby request that this court now dismiss this case, on its own volition."

"Ms. Danner, you have left me no other choice."

"Your Honor, please don't do this!"

"Case dismissed. Bailiff, be sure to collect the one hundred dollars from Ms. Danner or, alternatively," he now raised his protruding eyebrows, "take her into custody."

The Bailiff, Deputy James Herrera, a rugged and handsome former marine, shot the judge a fleeting glare. Jordon and James were longtime friends. She knew he both despised child molesters and admired her. Still, she was certain, at that moment, he was just hoping she wouldn't do anything to aggravate the situation further.

Jordon couldn't help herself.

"Now, there's justice for you," Jordon mumbled while forcefully slamming her briefcase shut. "The child abuser goes free and the Prosecutor, who's trying to stop him from abusing more children, is threatened with being thrown in jail."

"I heard that, Ms. Danner!" Judge Thomas stood up. "Bailiff, take her away *and* increase the fine to one thousand dollars!"

Judge Thomas then grabbed his tennis racket and left through the door directly behind him.

***

Alan Stern quickly gathered up his papers and rushed out. He never said a word to his client.

Moments later, he caught up with Jordon and the deputy in the near empty hallway. "Bailiff, please wait." Stern handed her his card. "Call me, I'll be glad to help you out. What happened to you, in there just now was bullshit. You were just doing your job."

***

Jordon didn't respond, but in an effort to get Stern away from her as soon as possible, she took his card. As she turned back to face James, she saw the DA across the hall. It was impossible to misread the expression on his face.

***

An hour had gone by before James could come back and check on her.

She was seated on a bench, jacket off, eyes closed, long legs fully extended, delicate ankles crossed. Only her head and bare shoulders touched the cell wall. Jordon looks completely out of place, James thought, sort of like my daughter's *Career Barbie* doll, now abandoned on the floor of her cluttered closet.

Jordon opened her eyes and looked up at him. Her colorful eyes and flawless skin stood out in stark contrast to the cracked and peeling gray paint which surrounded her. They each smiled. She spoke first, "You know that judge of yours can be a real schmuck."

"Yeah, so, *you* knew that before this morning and still you chose to piss him off."

Jordon didn't respond.

James' smile broadened. "And I, for one am glad you did. So, are you OK?"

"Marvelous," she said extending her trim and muscular arms outward. They both laughed in response to her grandiose gesture. James then told her he had to go, but he'd come back as soon as he could.

"Hang in there," he said.

"I've got no choice," she replied.

***

Another hour had gone by and James had not returned.

"Tell me, Deputy Herrera." Suddenly, Jordon heard a familiar voice.

"Which pond did you put my little lost duckling in?"

"If you are speaking of Ms. Danner, sir, she's in the next holding cell." Jordon knew James didn't like Bert Feller any more than she did. "And if you don't mind my saying so, sir," James continued, "I think the judge gave her a pretty rough go of it in there today."

"Well, Bailiff, that's why she gets paid the big bucks," DA Feller responded. "Only after the stunt she pulled in court today, I think I'll have to take a few of those big bucks away. It's OK, Deputy, you can wait here, I just need a moment alone with her."

"Ah, Ms. Danner," he said as he approached her cell. "How fitting to see you behind bars; stellar performance in court today. You not only managed to get the case dismissed and the repeat offender released, but you also succeeded in getting one of our more mild-mannered judges enraged at you, a member of *my* office."

He stopped directly in front of the cell. Jordon focused on the protrusions from his hair weave. You're such a pompous asshole, she thought. You wouldn't have lasted 5 minutes in the New York neighborhood I grew up in…

"Jordon, are you listening to me?" he asked. "How dare you lose that case? And how dare you embarrass me in front of my *newbies!* Have you lost sight of what you've been hired to do? You are supposed to represent me. Instead, you gave the most arrogant defense attorney in Santa Barbara County a glorious win!"

"Bert, I believe my job is to represent the People of this county, not you. I've taken an oath to protect them—" She hated defending herself to someone she didn't respect.

"Ah, but Ms. Danner, that's just it, you failed to protect *them*. The child pornographer's been released, and you're the one impotently sitting in jail. So, now it's *my* job to protect them. Therefore, I've decided to reassign a few of your more high-profile cases, and give you a week off—and that's without pay."

Feller's eyes glistened. Jordon thought he now no longer even resembled a poised politician; he now just looked like the thug that he was.

Feller continued. "Consider yourself lucky. If you weren't such a goddamn hero in this town, I'd fire your ass right now. But make no mistake about it," he threatened, "embarrass me again by letting another repeat child molester go, and your career as a prosecutor is over. Have I made myself perfectly clear?"

"You always do," she responded, glaring right back at him.

"One week from tomorrow you can return to the office and reimburse me for paying your bail. Meanwhile, don't you dare set foot in my building!"

2

364 Days Earlier—March 3, 2001
EMILY SCOTT

Statute of Limitations—A law declaring that no criminal charge shall be filed unless brought within the specified period of time.

When the black BMW pulled up in front of the Santa Barbara Police Department, Emily flung open the passenger door and swung her legs out. The driver reached over and grabbed her hand. "Em, wait, are you sure you don't want me to go inside with you?"

"We've already discussed that," Emily replied.

"But I want to be there for you." He looked sincere. "I want to help you get past all this."

"Oh, bullshit." She stood outside the car. "You just want to make sure you get laid again some time soon."

She slammed the car door and attacked the concrete stairway. At the top, she yanked on the thick glass door with one hand and clutched that day's newspaper with the other. Upon entering the building, she found herself standing in the middle of a small, noisy lobby, just opposite the Station Officer.

***

The Station Officer looked up. As his eyes rose to meet hers, he noticed how perfectly she filled out her sweater. "Can I help you?"

"I want to report a crime."

"Then you've come to the right place." He smiled; she didn't.

Without changing the direction of his focus, he pulled out a blank report form from the shelf under his desk. "What kind of crime?"

"I was molested."

His smile vanished. He removed a pen from his uniform shirt pocket and looked down at the form before him. "When?"

"About twenty-five years ago."

He looked up. Although his pen was poised, he wrote nothing down. "Excuse me?"

"About twenty-five years ago."

"And *this* is the first time you're reporting it?"

"Yes." Her gaze bore straight into his.

"OK, well then, let's see, do you happen to know who it was that allegedly molested you?"

"He didn't *allegedly* molest me. He *molested* me. And of course I know who it was." She unrolled that day's newspaper. "It was him!"

3

March 2, 2002-5:45 p.m.
JORDON

Prosecutor—An attorney who performs functions on behalf of The People.

The rat-infested bushes behind the courthouse periodically served as a bathroom for the homeless. As Jordon pushed her way through this vegetation she held her breath and kept her eyes forward. When she finally reached the old basement windows, she applied her weight to the center of the glass. The window squeaked open; she crawled through. As soon as her feet found the floor, she moved swiftly, but softly. Her early years as a tomboy, followed by her later years as a dancer, both paid off.

She wasn't supposed to be there. Just that morning, Bert had ordered her to stay away from the office for a week, but Jordon felt she had no choice. She had to leave directives for the substitute prosecutor. She needed to tell him exactly what to do with each of her cases. She couldn't stand the thought of any other child molester going unpunished or, worse yet, any victim feeling ignored.

Before arriving at the courthouse she'd already written the directives. Now she just had to get them into her files. She ran up the back steps and paused on the ground level. Peering through the small window on the stairwell door, she expected to be looking at Feller's closed door. Instead, his door was opening.

Jordon raced up the remaining two flights, got to the second level, slipped into her office, and, locked the door behind her. Her bravado had suddenly turned into fear. She knew she'd just given Feller the excuse he needed to fire her. Jordon desperately wanted to hang on to her job; she not only loved working as a prosecutor but also believed that, and being a mother, defined who she was.

A moment later she heard the sound of something being dragged. She listened intently, exhaling only after deciding it was just the janitor moving a trashcan. Surely, she rationalized, it was he who'd come out of Feller's office.

She put the notes inside the files, grabbed her mail, and waited until the hallway was silent. Slowly she stepped out of her office and slipped back down the stairwell. Upon reaching the ground level she turned to her right. All at once her shin collided with the metal waste can. The sound was deafening. "Fuck!" she whispered loudly while clutching her calf. Having no time to spare, she sprinted down the last flight and headed directly for the window. She quickly went through.

Once outside, she ran across to the parking lot where her husband Greg was sitting in their Toyota. He was tapping his fingers on the steering wheel. She got in and slammed the door.

Earlier that day, she'd called him and told him most of what had happened. He told her how sorry he was, and suggested she literally leave her work behind, and they go off to their mountain cabin. Jordon had agreed.

While she was fussing with her seatbelt, he pointed to a large brown envelope she'd placed on her lap. "I can't believe you brought work with you."

"It's just my mail."

"Personal or work-related?"

She knew it was work-related, but didn't know what it was, nor did she volunteer the fact that Feller had ordered her to stay away from the office. She wasn't always forthcoming with Greg. More often than not, it was because she wasn't interested in rationalizing her own irrational behavior, especially not to someone who knew her as well as he did.

Greg was still waiting for her answer.

Jordon looked down at the large brown envelope. "This? Oh, it's probably just my copy of the photographs I ordered for next month's trial." She pulled the documents out of the envelope. "I'll just take a quick peek at them, make sure they're all here…"

"Did I," Greg began to ask, as he abruptly pulled out of the parking lot and into the stream of traffic, "misunderstand you earlier today? Haven't you been placed on a leave without pay? JoJo," he said, looking over his shoulder at the merging lane, "ego aside, aren't you off the clock?"

Jordon leaned forward, ready to tell Greg to back off, when suddenly she caught sight of the suspect's name at the top of the report. Her retort died in her throat; she sat back.

She put her left hand over her mouth, and used her right one to bring the cover letter into focus. Vanity be damned, she thought,

I've got to buy myself some reading glasses. She then began to read...

Jordon—

Attached are some related reports. The victim is Emily Scott. The original report was taken almost one year ago by one of our former station officers, who handed it off to the Detective Sergeant, who then assigned it to a detective. The only thing the detective remembers the station officer saying about her was that she was "an attractive nutcase with a major attitude." Anyway, the report quickly made its way to the bottom of that detective's pile. Don't ask me which detective; I've already spoken to him about this.

Apparently, the detective thought since it happened so long ago, you wouldn't be able to file any charges, so he wouldn't investigate it. Well, that's where the report stayed until a couple of days ago when he brought it to me and asked me where I wanted him to file it. He was thinking that even though we couldn't file this old charge, the information in the report might be useful to us. I took one look at it, recognized the name of the suspect, and then gave it a careful read. I guess both the station officer and the detectives were too young to remember him.

After reading it, I thought that this one just might fall under that Penal Code section 803(g) and the normal statute of limitations would be tolled. Assuming it was at least possible for you to file the old charge, I called the victim.

Miss Scott is now thirty-one and didn't seem the least bit nutty to me. Anyway, when I got a hold of her, I told her about the new law and explained the possibility of your filing the old charges as long as certain criteria were met and you filed it within one year from the date she reported it to us. I hope I got that right.

After that, I asked her if she wanted the charges filed. She said it was up to us, but that wasn't why she came in last year to report it. She said she reported it because her therapist told her to "seek closure."

So that's it. Let me know what you decide. Thanks and sorry for the screw-up and the late notice—Ted

"Screw-up?" Jordon blurted out. "Major fuck-up is more like it!" She crumpled the note and threw it at the windshield. It bounced off the window and landed in Greg's lap. Jordon hurled herself back onto her seat and placed both hands over her face.

As she began to rub her eyes, an image of the suspect arose. Why *him* and why *now*?

Greg remained silent until she took her hands off her face and placed them on the dashboard. She looked at her image in the outside mirror. Her eyes were red and her face was pale. Greg finally spoke. "Are you OK?"

"Do I *look* OK?" Jordon glared at him. "Pull over!"

"Are you going to get sick?"

"No, I'm going to drive."

"You hate driving, especially on Highway one fifty-four."

"No, I *dislike* driving. I *hate* incompetence."

Jordon took out his CD and put in hers. Greg pulled over to make the switch. He stepped out of the car. She crawled over into the driver's seat and barely gave Greg enough time to get back in before she peeled away.

Jordon then cranked up the volume of Aretha Franklin and began to drive too fast. She hit a series of divider bumps so hard the CD skipped. Greg let a few moments pass before he tentatively lowered the music.

"Any chance I could get you to slow down and talk to me?"

"Why? You never want to hear about the details of any of my kid cases. The six o'clock news version has always been good enough for you. Why now all of a sudden?" Jordon knew she was out of control, and could hear herself attempting to start a fight with the one person in her world she felt least deserved it.

Jordon grew up hearing that girls shouldn't curse or fight, but one of the things she loved about being married to Greg, as well as being a member of a law enforcement team, was that she was now encouraged to do both.

"Wait a minute," Greg interrupted, "that's not fair. I want to hear about anything that upsets you. But you're right, I don't want to know about the new and different ways the perverts you prosecute have found to torture children." He put his hand on her thigh and looked over at her. "Come on, Jo." He took a deep breath and waded in. "Remember, it's only a job, and, at the moment, one you're not even getting paid to do."

She snapped her head in his direction. She could tell he already regretted saying that. He turned his body toward her. He looked helpless. "Jordon, I love you." There was no doubt in her mind he did. "Please talk to me."

She exhaled and started off in a calmer voice. "Twenty-five years ago, a kid named Emily was allegedly molested by someone I know, and now it's up to me to decide, by tomorrow, what the hell to do about it."

"You're gonna work up there tomorrow?" he asked.

She swerved hard and barely missed being hit by an oncoming car.

"Jordon, how 'bout I drive?"

"No, I've got a better idea. How 'bout you try and understand? I've got an envelope full of accusations and I've got hours, literally hours, to decide whether to turn them into a filed case. And you—"

"And me?" Greg began.

"Yeah, you, all you're thinking about is whether this is going to interfere with your vacation."

Greg stared straight ahead. "Jordon that's not fair; and that's not what I was thinking."

Oh bullshit, she thought.

"I was thinking," he continued, "about what a bad day you've had, and I was hoping our time away together would make you feel better."

Jordon immediately felt guilty for her behavior toward him. Still, she went back to worrying about her dilemma.

After a few more minutes had gone by, he removed her Aretha CD and put in his Nitty Gritty Dirt Band. She didn't care; she really wasn't listening to it anymore anyway. Now she was just trying to assimilate what she already knew about the suspect, with what she'd just found out.

Shortly thereafter, she pulled over at one of their favorite viewing spots. Looking straight ahead, she quietly asked him if he'd mind driving the rest of the way. She wanted to use what daylight still remained to read the other documents in the envelope.

They both stepped out of their sides of the car. When they met at the back bumper, they came together like magnets and wordlessly hugged.

Once they settled back into the car Jordon reached over and placed her hand on his thigh. "I'm sorry," she said. She'd always hoped that because they were both so educated and respected each other so much, they'd never fight. But Greg taught her early on, letting off steam with each other was a testament to how strong their relationship really was.

"I know," he said. "You just had one of those no good, very bad days."

He was quoting from one of their grown son's favorite children's books, which made them both smile, but only for a moment. Soon Jordon turned her attention back to the contents of the brown envelope.

***

By 8:30 they stepped out of their car and into a majestic grove of tall pine trees. Usually, upon their arrival, the grove's familiar splendor and strong perfume coaxed Jordon into taking her first deep breath of the day. But this evening she was oblivious to it all and just mechanically gravitated toward their log home.

Once inside she created a meal out of cheap canned beef stew, mixed with good red wine.

An hour later, while silently staring into the flames of their stone fireplace, she concluded: This is huge; it can't wait. I have to start working on it now, but that's so unfair to Greg.

Once again, she put both her hands over her face and rubbed her eyes. It was then that the thought of ignoring the whole thing first occurred to her.

After all, she considered, no one except Greg actually saw me take the envelope. They'll all just assume I didn't get it until I got back, and by then, the Statute of Limitations will have already run out…

She stepped away from the warmth of the fire and put her hand, followed by her forehead, on the cold glass of the living room window. The moon was rising over the nearby hilltops. She exhaled, fogging the pane and her view. The only sound she heard was the crackling of the fire.

Who am I kidding, she thought. I can't do that; I can't let another known child molester get away. She struck the double-paned window with her opened hand. "But damn it," she said out loud. *I've* been put on a forced leave. *I* shouldn't have to do this tonight. Hell, *I* probably shouldn't do this one at all.

Jordon walked back over to the fire, knelt down and started snapping twigs from the firewood box. Greg entered the living room; he looked worried. She knew as a geology professor he'd seen scores of faculty and students get riled up, but he himself rarely did. Greg now stood by her, and put his hand on her lower neck. She looked up at him.

"Talk to me," he offered, letting his hand rest on her shoulder.

"I hate this. The whole thing stinks. I know *I* have to make this call. No one in my office understands these particular people the way I do, but at the same time, no one more than me will be as personally affected by whatever it is I decide." She ran her fingers through her soft-cropped hair and grabbed a fistful of curls. "What I need is time, time to think about all the possible ramifications of my decision, but time is the one thing I don't have."

She let her hand drop down to her shoulder and squeezed Greg's hand. Seconds later she stood up and stepped away. She returned to the imprint of her hand on the window and placed her hand over it. She didn't want to face him when she gave him the news.

"Greg, I'm going to have to start dealing with this thing now. As it is, I can't stop thinking about it, and, if I run out of time, I'll never forgive myself." She looked up at the sky. "This decision will be made with or without me, as a matter of law, by 4:45 p.m. tomorrow and I can't just stand by and let that happen." She glanced over at him. "Does any of this make any sense to you?"

"No, nor do I think you owe me an explanation. Just do what you gotta do." Greg shrugged. "We've been here before. We both know you'll make the right call, and you won't," he said with a big smile and a small wink, "be any fun until you do."

Jordon looked into his eyes and took a step toward him. He wrapped her in his arms. She rested her head against his chest, but only for a moment. She then patted his lower back and headed toward her old filing cabinet. She needed to find those two case files.

Those two files were amid the 20-odd cases she'd copied and brought up to their mountain retreat. They were the cases she occasionally went through because she felt they still had something to teach her. The two she was now looking for were among the ones she'd looked at most often. Jordon found them frayed and pressed up against each other along with a large envelope filled with audio and video tapes. As she retrieved them, disturbing images of Marcos, Sophia, Pat and Colin began to come into focus. Momentarily overwhelmed, she stood silent. "Greg," she finally said, "You know this isn't my idea of a good time. I ..."

"I understand," he said. "Really, I do."

Brows furrowed, head cocked, she continued to look at him; she was seeking even more reassurance.

"Really," he said in a softer and more deliberate voice. He then turned, gathered up their dishes and brought them into the kitchen. Jordon watched him leave and thought about how well he knew her, and how much she loved him.

She took the files and envelope over toward the woven Navaho rug in front of a small entertainment center and settled in. A few minutes later Greg emerged from the kitchen and gave her a prolonged kiss on the top of her head. She felt herself momentarily respond and was temporarily distracted.

"I love you," he whispered.

"Still?"

"Always."

"Thanks, I needed that."

"Then there's more where *that* came from when you come to bed." Greg smiled one last time and headed off in the direction of their bedroom.

If I come to bed, she thought.

Now she just hoped she would eventually find the answers she was seeking somewhere within the files of Marcos, Pat, Colin or Sophia. She gazed at the cover of Colin's file and the note her Wisconsin colleague had attached. "Hope you find what you're looking for—Jerry." Jordon thought those words were never more meaningful. Still, she decided to start with Marcos' file. From the moment she picked it up and read the first sentence of Father Albert's letter, she was transfixed.

> Dear Honorable Judge,
>   To understand Marcos, you must first imagine the unimaginable.

4

May 3, 1969
MARCOS ESTRADA

Sexual Assault in Concert—A person is deemed to have committed a sexual assault in concert when he acts with others.

Two kindly priests knelt down near the young boy. He was lying upon a forgotten horse blanket on the cold floor of the old meeting hall. The coarse blanket smelled like the horse it used to protect, and would have been unbearable to lie upon, had the boy been conscious.

The boy involuntarily cringed and cried out in his sleep. Father Albert picked him up and was surprised by his lightness. As he carried him into the small rectory, he saw that his handsome face was flawless; yet it was his frail body and the freshly formed bruises around his neck that told his story.

The room was silent except for the sound of Father Dennis dragging in an old mattress and then letting it fall, with a whoosh, onto the rectory floor. Father Albert gently laid the child upon it. Marcos didn't react. As Father Albert moved his legs over to the center of the mattress, he noticed that the inside seams of the boy's pants were caked with blood.

For several moments Father Albert's sadness and conflicting concerns rendered him silent. Father Dennis, the new recruit, interrupted his thoughts.

"Do you recognize him, Father?"

"His name is Marcos Estrada. A few months ago I presided over his father's funeral. Before his father's death his parents brought him here for Mass every Sunday." Father Albert paused as he pictured the robust and beautiful boy of days past walking into church, holding both his parent's hands. "After his father died, he and his mother just couldn't get by. Eventually, his father's brother took him in, but he wouldn't take them both, so the mother abandoned him and went off to America." Father Albert shook his head and looked down. "He must be about eleven years old by now, and he must've walked here last night, all the way from his uncle's farm. He's a brave one, that's for sure...Father Dennis, please bring me a bowl of water, some clean rags, and a sheet. I have to tend to him."

Father Albert took a deep breath, clenched his teeth, and bent down to examine Marcos. After Father Dennis returned with the requested supplies, Father Albert began to clean him up. Marcos' injuries shocked and disgusted him. Marcos remained motionless.

Once he completed this task, Father Albert carefully covered Marcos with the freshly laundered sheet. As he started to stand up, he felt woozy.

"Has the bleeding stopped?" Father Dennis asked.

"Yes, just."

"Will he be OK?"

"This time, but we can't send him back. By the looks of him, he was violated by more than one—" Father Albert stopped speaking; he didn't want to give any more voice to what he was sure had occurred. He knew he couldn't send him back, but he was also sure Marcos wouldn't be welcome anywhere else; from now on, Marcos would be considered an outcast.

He turned to Father Dennis. "We must get word to his uncle and tell him the boy will stay here with us." He then reached down and began to tuck Marcos in. "He won't have much of a life here," he muttered, "but at least he'll be safe." Shaken, Father Albert struggled back up to his feet. "Come," he announced, "let's leave him in peace. For the moment, the two things he needs most are his rest and our prayers."

***

Jordon decided it would be most helpful to read the files in segments. She closed Marcos' and moved on to Pat's, so different and yet so similar.

Although Jordon could practically recite the contents of Pat's file from memory, she continued to believe that the more she read through the details, the more likely she'd find something new, something useful, something to help her understand why child abusers were driven to do the things they did.

She started by re-reading the previously highlighted notations made by Pat's psychologist.

***

"Note to the file: Female perpetrator-Psychotic/Multiple abuser-spousal/child/alcohol—Manifest behavior not rare, but infrequently reported. Dearth of significant scientific research and literature. Existing literature un-contradicted—the resulting psychological and perhaps physiological damage to the child is pervasive.

"The patient remains reluctant to discuss any aspect of his childhood. However, today, he referred to his mother as 'The Kettle'.

"For as long as Pat could remember, his mother Alice reminded him of their steaming, hissing, kitchen kettle. At her best, she merely simmered, teetering constantly on the point of boiling. At her worst, she boiled over, which resulted in her yelling, screaming, and beating him with whatever objects she could grab.

"Pat's worst memories were of the days she also physically abused his father. Not only were those episodes painful, but also extremely humiliating. Early on, his father had taught him never to tell anyone about those times, to always hide his bruises, and to lie about the bruises he couldn't hide.

"During this particular session, the patient, under the effects of hypnosis, was able to articulate some of the details of the events surrounding November 4, 1962, a day he has always revered."

5

November 4, 1962
PATRICK MacMILLAN

Child Abuse—Any form of cruelty to a child's well being.

Pat's father Richard emerged from the bathroom. The angry, red scratch marks on his neck had finally stopped oozing. "OK Pat, I'm out of here. I've got some errands to run." Richard gingerly pulled on the familiar black turtleneck. "Just lay low. I'm sure your mother'll be calmer when she gets back from church."

Pat, even at age 13, knew she hadn't gone to church and his father didn't have any errands to run. He just hoped they didn't end up at the same Brooklyn neighborhood bar. Pat wasn't angry; he was just envious. He wished he had some place to escape to. Instead he went into his room and leaned the usual scarred chair up against the doorknob.

It hadn't always been this bad, Pat thought. When he was still in elementary school his father would at least try and distract him from their miserable existence by planning exciting adventures, where together, and without *her,* they'd travel happily throughout the world. But none of those dreams ever materialized, and now that Pat was in 7th grade at St. Mary's, even the planning had stopped. Richard had by then slipped away from Pat, and concentrated instead on nursing his own wounds and whiskey.

Just before dawn his mother returned home. Pat was awakened by the sound of her ear-splitting voice. "Pat! Where-the-hell-are-you?"

Pat immediately sat up, even before he was fully awake. He then grabbed his blanket and brought it up to his chin.

"Don't you dare make me come in there after you!"

Pat could tell from her slurred tone that things were about to get worse. He couldn't bear the thought of another beating, so, for the first time in his life, he decided to run away. He threw on his clothes, opened his window, and climbed down the fire escape.

Once outside the apartment building, he froze—he had no place to go. Still, he knew he'd better start running. He was sure in a matter of seconds she'd be right behind him. He decided to head toward St. Mary's.

Pat had always thought of St. Mary's as a dilapidated old building located on a filthy section of Fulton Avenue, but as he ran toward it that morning he saw it as a thing of beauty. It seemed to welcome him.

Just before entering, he stole one last look behind him. She was nowhere to be seen. He pulled hard on the heavy wooden portal and ran into the church's smallest confessional.

Once inside, he grabbed hold of its flimsy door and shut it. Standing there, still gripping and pulling on its tiny knob, he could feel his pulse thunder throughout his body. He was certain at any moment he would be standing face-to-face with her.

When time passed and she still hadn't appeared he slowly stepped back. As soon as his sweat-streaked shirt touched the confessional's rear wall, he slid down to the floor and began sobbing.

***

Just beyond the confessional, someone heard Pat sob: "Please, Dear God, don't let her find me…I beg of you, strike her dead!"

***

Jordon closed Pat's file and reached for Colin's. She wanted to move through this process quickly but deliberately. She felt that proceeding this way provided her the only chance she had of making a judicious decision by morning.

Paper-clipped inside of Colin's file was a copy of the probation officer's report. There, under the section Victim Interview, the probation officer had written the following:

"I asked him how it was he came to be alone with the perpetrator that night. He looked down, appeared embarrassed, and then explained…"

The probation officer's description, which followed, was so vivid, Jordon felt as if she were standing in Colin's shadow.

6

Grooming—The actions of a child's sexual abuser who uses friendship rather than force.

The candlelit room was still, except for the occasional bursts of vagrant air. These cold gusts played havoc with the spineless flames. Colin continued to perspire.

Moments later, he decided he couldn't possibly stay. He stepped outside into the dark hallway and looked around. Elongated shadows from the candles appeared on the opposite wall. Colin shuddered. He walked over to the main chapel and peeked in. The pews were empty; the room was silent. He stood motionless in the doorway. He'd never before been alone in the church at night. He looked toward the platform in the front and up at the enormous pipe organ. He remembered back to a Sunday when he was 5 years old...

It was the Sunday he'd finally convinced his parents to let him sit with them during the services. Each preceding Sunday, he'd always dreaded the moment when the woman, who smelled like raisins, took him and the others into the noisy child care room. But, on this particular Sunday he remained seated while the other children were ordered to rise. And as they were forced to line up, he triumphantly watched from his position of power and safety— right between his parents.

When the other children had finally left the organist executed a deafening chord. Colin sat upright and gasped. The music began. Suddenly, Colin felt the music from the church's grand pipe organ mix with the beating of his heart and cause a rumbling in his chest. When he started to explain this sensation to his parents, his mother Cathy shushed him, but then smiled and tapped her heart, as if to tell him she understood. After that, his father Dwight took his hand and discreetly moved it in time with the music.

As Colin stood there now, some 6 years later, he thought about how good it felt to see his mother's smile and to conduct the music with his father's hand. All at once, he was anxious to go back home, but he hadn't yet accomplished what he'd set out to do. He stepped away from the doorway and looked for the priest.

He walked over to the double glass doors, cupped his hands along the sides of his face and looked outside. Bright lights surrounded the sign, *St. Anthony's of Madison*. The lights were strong enough to illuminate the entire church property. It was a sprawling red brick building surrounded by a vast and immaculately groomed lawn. The idyllic view was obstructed by the name painted in black letters on the door itself, *Father Williams, Presiding*. When Colin realized his hands were pressed up against *that* name, he quickly pulled away and wiped his hands on his jeans.

Father Williams was the head priest, the man who delivered the sermons. Colin felt he preached too much about hell and how easy it was to get there. Beyond that, whenever Colin saw him, Father Williams was always rushing about, but still managed to find the time to reach out and squeeze Colin's elbow. Colin hated his touch and wanted to pull away, but he never did. Colin had always been taught he should never be disrespectful to a priest.

After stepping back from the glass doors, Colin returned to the main chapel and peeked in again. This time, as he looked toward the platform in the front, he thought of the first time he sang with the church choir; it was only a month ago. He loved everything about singing in the choir. Not only was he finally able to make music along with the grand organ, but he also found a friend in the choir director; he too was a priest, but one who shared Colin's passion for music. He was nothing like Father Williams.

Colin's disdain for Father Williams was the reason he'd come that night; it was because of what Father Williams had done the night before.

It was near the end of choir practice, and Colin had seen Father Williams peering at him from the darkened audience. As soon as rehearsal ended, he walked over to Colin, took hold of his elbow, separated him from the others, and told him he wanted Colin to become an acolyte. Then in whispered, alcohol-drenched tones, he explained to Colin just what being an acolyte would entail. Colin didn't like what he heard, and, worse, what he felt. He didn't want to spend any time alone helping the man he thought of as—the creepy priest. Still, in an effort to get Father Williams to release his elbow, he promised to discuss the priest's proposition with his parents. As soon as he got home, he did. His parent's excited response was to insist he accept Father Williams' ethereal offer. Colin hardly slept that night.

By morning, Colin was completely distraught. He decided he couldn't go through with it; he'd have to defy both Father Williams and his parents. Immediately after dinner he got on his bike. As he peddled over, his pace slowed as his determination wavered. He was certain he didn't want to be an acolyte, but neither did he want to disappoint his parents or confront—the creepy priest.

Colin was now sure of what he had to do, but with his head down and his hands sweating, he had trouble even reopening the door. When he did, he stood temporarily frozen on the threshold of the room lit only by candles.

7

Nonfeasance—Nonperformance of some act, which ought to be performed.

"Stop! Enough!" Jordon cried. She put the papers down and stood up. "I don't want to read any more."

If only, she thought, she could leave Marcos, Pat, and Colin just where they were in the pile of papers in front of her—still safe within their churches, never to experience what was about to occur.

What she wanted to do was change the course of their lives, and she wanted to do it by simply throwing the rest of their files into her fireplace.

As a child, she believed she *could* magically change things. She thought if she turned the TV off just before the woeful scenes began, the trouble brewing in front of her would necessarily end. The result of these grandiose illusions was that on Sunday nights she actually believed it was she who saved Lassie, or that week's victim, by valiantly and swiftly getting up and proudly turning the TV off the moment the sad music started.

And here it is, she thought, some forty years later, and not much has changed. I still want to swoop in and rescue the defenseless. And, I still hold myself personally responsible if I can't.

I've got no choice, she decided, I've got to keep going, and I can't be distracted by Feller's threat.

She rubbed her face with her hands, exhaled deeply, and picked up the final folder. She gazed at it for a moment, while the image of a very young Sophia started to emerge. Don't get stuck there, she cautioned herself. She sat back down and began to read the document on top—it was a transcript of an interview with Sophia's perpetrator. It was made about a year after the offense had occurred.

8

Abused and neglected children—Those who have suffered as a result of physical or emotional injury inflicted upon them.

"So, now I want you to tell me everything you *do* remember about that night and I won't interrupt. You just tell me when you're done. OK?"

"OK. Well, it all started when I was sitting alone at the kitchen table. I remember I was really tired and I had my head down on my arms. Then I started staring at some crumbs, and I started thinking I should wipe them off the table, but I knew it wouldn't make any difference, so I didn't move.

"By then, I'd been living in *that* apartment for about three months and the stench was really getting to me. No matter what I did, everything still smelled bad. It was the odor of rot; rot in the walls, in the cabinet, and even between the cracks of the linoleum floor. It felt like everything including me was rotting away and, on top of everything else, now *she* was driving me nuts.

"She wouldn't stop calling out for me. I tried to ignore her. I even tried to put my hands over my ears, but I could still hear her.

"I remember thinking I just wanted her to stop. Stop yelling my name, stop crying, stop whining, and stop begging. But she didn't stop; she just got louder. Finally, I banged the side of my fists on the table. I banged them so hard the crumbs actually sprang into the air and onto the floor. Suddenly, she stopped.

"I got up, went to my room and threw myself on my bed. As soon as I landed, I went for the copy of *Playboy*, which I'd stashed under my mattress. At first, I tried to look through it, to see if I could distract myself, but I knew I couldn't; they were just pictures, she was real. Then I heard her start up again.

"'Please just come here, just for a minute,' she begged.

"I figured then if I didn't go to her, she'd just keep calling me, and then neither one of us would get any sleep. So I decided I'd go in there, but only for a minute.

"The next thing I remember is sitting up slowly, as if I'd been hypnotized. I was already turned on, if you know what I mean, but I was still trying to stop myself. Even when I came to her room, I stuck my hands on each side of her doorway and just stood there. 'Look,' I said, 'I can't stay in here with you. I have to sleep in my own bed. Now please, just try and go to sleep all by yourself.'

"'But can't I just cuddle with you?' she asked.

"That's where things start getting a little fuzzy. I remember thinking that her room felt like another world and that that other world was calling me. The next thing I remember was walking in and I wasn't thinking, not for a minute, that she was my five-year-old sister and what I was doing was wrong. All I cared about was the way her long curly black hair looked pressed up against her soft white nightgown.

"As I got closer, I saw that she was trembling, probably from the cold, but in my own sick mind I thought it was because she wanted me. Then she moaned, 'Pleeeease get into bed with me and make me cozy'. 'OK, OK,' I said out loud, but I still kept promising myself I'd just lie down for a minute, but a part of me knew better.

"So, I lay down next to her. At first, I was just on my back with my arms planted at my sides, but when she put her soft face on my chest; I just lost it. She smelled so good after her bath and she was so warm and tender. And I knew she loved me. I remember thinking then that I could probably just come with her lying next to me. Or if I just rubbed her back…her bottom. And all the time I was thinking these things, I was getting harder and harder.

"Then, I laid her on top of me, closed my eyes and began moving her up and down. The next thing I knew she was yelling—but I don't remember what. What I do remember was that it made me mad, and I thought, just a few minutes ago she was begging *me* to come into *her* bed, and when I finally do, she just starts screaming at me…"

"And what happened after that?" the interviewer asked.

"I don't remember exactly, except I know I came… and I guess after that I must've fallen asleep for a minute because I woke up to her crying.

"She said she was wet and sticky and she wanted me to clean her off. All I was thinking then was—why doesn't she just roll over? Why do I have to get up? Why do I have to clean her off?

Why do I have to do the laundry? Why do I have to do everything? Why do bad things always happen to me?

"And then I started thinking about all those bad things that had happened to me, and I could even hear my uncle's voice, just like he sounded 8 years ago. 'Cry all you want, nobody here gives a shit.' And I almost said that to her, but I knew it wasn't true. I knew I cared about her. I cared a lot, especially when I heard her groan, 'Marcos, you hurt me. You really, really hurt me.'"

***

Jordon's pager vibrated rapidly and then fell off the kitchen counter. Her hands flew back and she dropped Sophia's folder. Disoriented, but only for a moment, she walked into the kitchen. She picked up the pager, saw the familiar number, and immediately returned the call.

9

March 2, 2002—11:40 p.m.
JORDON

*California Health and Safety Code Section 11360 (a)—Every
person who transports more than 28.5 grams of marijuana, is
guilty of a felony and shall be punished by imprisonment in the
state prison...(b)...transports not more than 28.5 grams, is guilty
of a misdemeanor and shall be fined $100.00.*

"Santa Barbara Police Department, Watch Commander's office.
Sergeant Olsen speaking."

"Ted, Jordon Danner here. Did somebody just page me?"

"Sure did. Hey, how are you? I hear you had a pretty rough day
today both in and *out* of court."

"I'm OK, thanks for asking." Jordon had always liked Ted, and
under normal circumstances would have indulged in his empathy,
but tonight she was pressed for time. Still, his concern felt good, it
always did. "So," she asked trying to move the conversation along,
"what's up?"

Ted sounded excited. "Paul Howe called from the field and
asked me to page you. He's got some news for you, the kind that's
sure to cheer you up. Hang on I'll connect you. Take care and
don't forget—we're all on your side."

Jordon smiled; Ted often had that effect on her. Damn, she
thought, I could use some good news.

The line went dead for a moment. Then she heard, "Jordon,
I've got him. I'm looking at his sorry ass right now. He's cuffed
and sitting on the curb about twelve feet from me."

"What happened?" She asked.

"I saw him driving along without a seat belt, pulled him over,
and found a baggie of marijuana between him and the passenger
seat."

"That's it?" She stepped back and tried to brace herself on the
kitchen counter. Instead she almost knocked over the opened
bottle of wine.

"Well, yeah, but that's enough. He was transporting, and you
know he was gonna give it to some kid, and you know what for—"

"Still, it probably doesn't even weigh more than an ounce."

"Well, it might be, it could be; I mean, I don't carry a scale around—"

Jordon grimaced and tightened her grip on the phone. "Come on, Paul," she interrupted him, sounding angrier than she intended, "he's carrying a sandwich bag of grass, a misdemeanor. If you caught someone else walking down the street with it, you'd grab it, give him a citation, and send him on his way."

"But *he's* not someone else and he *wasn't* walking down the street with it. He was driving, so I got him on a transportation charge, which is a felony! Shit, I thought *you* knew the Health and Safety Code better than that."

"Hey, Paul," Jordon said, "lighten up. You know we're still on the same side." She paused, hoping he'd ease up and she'd calm down. "So, I gather he's not under the influence, right?"

"Not that I can tell." His tone remained unchanged.

"Let him go, Paul."

Paul was momentarily speechless. "Jordon, that's bullshit, and I'd think after spending your day in a cell, you'd be looking for a little lawful revenge, which is precisely what I've brought you. This, my learned friend, is a righteous bust."

"Come on, Paul, it may be lawful, but that doesn't make it righteous. You and I both know if he were anyone else, you'd cite and release him. Those kind of transportation charges always get reduced. And I don't want to bring him back into court again until we've got him by the balls."

She took a deep breath and softened her voice. "Look, I appreciate what you did, and why *you did it*, but the next time we charge him, we've got to make it stick."

Jordon paused, hoping Paul would say something that sounded like he agreed with her. He didn't say a word; still she could hear his heavy breathing.

"Let him go, Paul," she said using an even softer voice, "he'll screw up again, and when he does, we'll be ready for him."

"*I'm* ready for him now; if we wait until he screws up again, another kid'll be hurt. *I'm* trying to stop that from happening."

"So am I, Paul," she began to feel defensive, "but your bust will at best keep him in jail for a few hours. Then he and his asshole lawyer will be back in court accusing you of harassing him and me of malicious prosecution."

Paul didn't respond. Jordon knew he wasn't thinking clearly. He was driven by guilt and frustration over what had happened in court earlier; she was sure about that, because she felt the same way. But she was also certain his questionable arrest would only make things worse.

"Look, Paul, you didn't have to call me before you arrested him, but you did, so I assume you wanted my blessing or at least my advice. My advice is cut him loose with a citation. Then go home and get a good night's sleep. If you feel like it, give me a call in the morning and we'll talk more about it. For now, we're both stuck with what happened in court today—and that definitely sucks." She added the last part to make him smile, and she sensed she was successful.

"Well," Paul said, "at least, we agree about that. OK, Jordon, sorry to have given you such a hard time; it's just that this whole thing really pisses me off."

"I know, me too, and as a mother of four, I'm sure glad you're out there protecting them." She wanted to make Paul feel better. She knew his heart had always been in the right place, and she was sure he never knowingly engaged in racial profiling.

Soon after that, they hung up; there was nothing left to say. She was right as a matter of courtroom dynamics, and he was just trying to do the right thing.

She looked up at the kitchen clock. "Shit," she said out loud. It's almost midnight, and there's still so much more stuff to go through. She stood in the middle of her kitchen and was momentarily tempted by the open bottle of wine, but decided instead to return to her files.

As she picked up Pat's, she remembered she'd left him sobbing on the floor of the confessional, fearing his mother would burst in at any moment.

10

In loco parentis—In the place of the parent.

Time had passed and still his mother hadn't come. He slowly opened the door and walked out. The lights outside the confessional were bright. Squinting, he saw Father Romero sitting in the back pew. Embarrassed, he quickly turned toward the altar and dropped down to his knees. He wanted to appear as if he were praying, when in actuality, he was trying to plan his escape.

It wasn't as if he didn't like Father Romero. After all, he thought, everyone liked Father Romero; he was always friendly and continuously walked around with a sparkle in his eyes.

That sparkle amazed Pat. He didn't know how someone could still sparkle after going through everything Father Romero had.

He'd heard from the other kids that the Father was a tank sergeant in World War I, and, by the time he was 19 he was already in charge of 25 other boys. Pat also understood that throughout the course of the war most of those other boys had died. Pat knew Father Romero didn't talk much about their deaths, but he often told the kids at school about what it was like when he returned home from his tour of duty. He said he wasn't sure at that point whether he should thank God for his mercy or curse him for his cruelty, but after he thought about it awhile, he decided the best way to honor his comrades was to try and change the world— one kid at a time. Pat always admired him for that.

Finally, Pat accepted the fact that he'd have to get up and go. Unfortunately, the only way out was past Father Romero. Pat pulled up his jacket collar as high as it would reach. He didn't want the priest to know about his injuries or his scars, and so far he thought he didn't.

***

Over the years, Father Romero had learned to keep a mental note of those boys he thought were particularly vulnerable, and Pat had quickly made it to that list. Early on he'd attempted to get to know

Pat, but his efforts had always been rebuffed. Not wanting to alienate Pat forever, he knew he'd have to wait patiently for just the right moment.

When he first observed Pat sprinting into the church that morning, he thought their moment had finally come. However, when he saw Pat frantically rush into the confessional and hide, he decided he'd have to wait a bit longer. Fearing Pat might once again slip away, Father Romero entered the church, sat down in the pews, and tried to read his bible.

Now that Pat was finally about to walk past him, he stood and smiled.

***

"Good afternoon, Pat."

"Good afternoon, Father Romero."

"Taking up track, are you?"

"No, Father."

"That's funny, because I could have sworn I saw you run in here at breakneck speed, and priests aren't supposed to swear."

Pat felt trapped and confused. He didn't know if Father was giving him a hard time or just making a joke. Either way, he knew he shouldn't lie to a priest. "I'm sorry, Father."

"Please don't apologize. I wish more young men showed your exuberance for getting to church so quickly." Father Romero smiled as his eyes twinkled. "You know Pat, you and I have never really had much of a chance to talk. Care to join me for afternoon tea?" Pat didn't respond. Father Romero continued, "You see, I have this new package of Oreos and I've been looking for an excuse to open them. Your joining me would give me just that excuse."

The mere mention of Oreos reminded Pat he hadn't eaten all day. He was starving and certainly in no rush to get home, but he was also fearful—he knew the longer he stayed away, the worse the punishment would be.

"Father Romero, I'd like to, but you see, my mother..." He had trouble going on. Father Romero finished his sentence for him.

"Your mother doesn't know where you are. You were actually running away from home?"

Pat took a step back. "How'd you know?"

"Believe it or not, I was once thirteen, and you seemed pretty upset when you first got here. Listen, I've got an idea, join me for tea and Oreos and then, when you get home, just tell your mom you were at church praying you'd become a better son. Mothers love that line. I used it once or twice myself when I was your age." Father Romero reached out and placed his warm hand on Pat's shoulder. Pat liked the way it felt. "You'll see," Father Romero continued, "not only will she believe you, in part because it's true, but she'll also *praise* you for your insight."

Pat was sure she wouldn't praise him, but eating Oreos with the kindly priest sounded much better than what he knew awaited him at home. Pat nodded in agreement and followed Father Romero to the sunny back deck.

Tea was served from Father Romero's cracked teapot, which he placed upon an ornate, wrought iron table for two. Pouring the tea, he proudly told Pat he'd recently repainted the table with some leftover pink paint. Pat thought the table looked like it belonged in a cartoon.

Within moments, and with great ceremony, Father Romero began to open the new package of Oreos. After gingerly separating the wrapping, he put most of his face inside the bag and breathed deeply.

Pat laughed.

"What are you laughing at?" Father Romero asked, emerging from the bag.

Pat wasn't sure how to respond, so he just looked down.

"Oh, don't get all quiet on me again. I really want to know what made you laugh. I like the sound of your laughter, and I can't recall ever hearing it before."

Pat was stumped. He didn't know what he should say, but, once again, he knew he had to tell the truth to a priest.

"It's just that, just now, with your face in the Oreo package, you sort of looked like a horse with a feed bag on."

"So I did, so I did," Father Romero chuckled. "Well, I've been accused of being a part of a horse's anatomy before, but the head definitely wasn't it." They each exploded with laughter.

After their laughter died down, Pat felt, for the first time he could remember, somewhat relaxed.

"So I looked a little silly, eh?" Father Romero said, rubbing his chin. "But you know, you really shouldn't knock it until you've tried it." He gave Pat the Oreos and an encouraging smile.

Pat put the tip of his nose into the bag and sniffed it, like a timid rabbit.

"No, no, no, that's not the way to do it. You must let the fragrance enter your very soul," he said, opening his arms wide, and dramatically extending them toward the heavens. "You must," he emphasized, beaming directly at Pat, "put your *whole* face in the bag!"

This was definitely not the way people in Pat's house behaved, nor how Pat expected a priest to behave. But Pat was good at following orders, so he did just as he'd been directed.

Suddenly, his head was spinning and he began to salivate. The smell and taste of fresh cookies and cream were everywhere. Never before had he experienced such pure joy. Father Romero interrupted his rapture by smiling broadly, shaking his fists and bellowing, "See, see what I mean? Great stuff, huh?"

"Smells pretty good," was all Pat would allow himself to say.

In an obvious effort to keep Pat's joy alive, Father Romero announced, "Well, after that exciting opening ceremony, I say, 'let the games begin.'" First Father Romero, and then Pat, grabbed a handful of the creamy chocolate treats and started dunking them in their respective beverages. Pat was cautious at first; never having had tea, he filled his cup to the top with cream.

Once they had their fill, Father Romero asked Pat what his favorite class was. Pat told him it was history. The priest nodded in agreement and commented that, at his age, he felt the same way, which was why he enlisted.

Pat soon felt as if he were in heaven; warmed by the early afternoon sun, the culinary treats, and, best of all, by Father Romero's war stories.

As Pat watched him speak about The War, he became fixated on his eyes; they were the most expressive Pat had ever seen. Never before had Pat seen anyone's eyes show how they truly felt. Nor had he ever experienced anyone's gaze register an understanding of Pat's own unspoken words.

All too quickly an afternoon chill started infiltrating their world, and dusk began to settle in. As much as he tried to fight it, Pat knew he had to go home. Reluctantly, he said good-bye to Father Romero, and promised he'd come back soon.

At first when Pat left the churchyard, he strutted away with an afterglow of confidence and good cheer. But as soon as he turned onto his street, his old gait returned, and his joy transformed to dread.

By the time he got to his apartment building, his body was rigid with anticipation.

When he opened the apartment door, he immediately smelled the strong odor of burnt liver and onions. Waves of nausea took over. He now tasted his mostly digested Oreos and milk. He swallowed hard.

Alice looked over at him. Her eyes were ablaze; she looked possessed. She came toward him while clutching an onion-draped spoon high above her head. A few slimy onion pieces slid off as she approached. A moment later the beating began.

Pat tried to speak out, but her precise and practiced aim made that impossible. Suddenly, she smashed the spoon into the side of his head. He heard a soft pop and liquid began to ooze out his ear and down his neck.

He said nothing. He had experienced enough beatings to know that screaming he'd been hurt only seemed to provoke her. The whacks continued.

Eventually, she collapsed onto the couch, and he started to slink off to bed.

"Where do you think you're going?" she shouted. "You made me run all over town looking for you. Where the hell have you been, anyway?"

Pat didn't answer. He didn't want to sully his memory of the time he'd just spent with Father Romero. He stood perfectly still, with his head down, and concentrated instead on the yellow fluid seeping out of his ear and running down the front of his shirt.

Alice appeared to have lost interest in her own question. Without moving from her prone position on the couch, she yelled, "You sit your ass right down and eat every bit of the dinner I made you."

Pat sat down, stared at his plate, and kept swallowing his repugnant saliva.

He remained that way until he heard the liberating sound of her drunken snores.

***

The following week at school he dressed to hide his injuries and managed to avoid Father Romero, until Friday.

As he was leaving school on Friday, he stopped on the outdoor steps when he saw Father Romero struggling to open his rickety office window. Father then reminded Pat to stop by soon. Pat assured him he would, but he knew he never could, at least not until all of his external bruises had once again faded.

The next day, Alice woke Pat with a violent shake and the pronouncement that she'd found him a job cleaning up at the corner market. Her only explanation was, "If you're old enough to run away, you're old enough to work."

From then on, Pat spent all of his after-school hours and weekends at the market. Sadly, his new schedule left him with no time to visit Father Romero. On the other hand, it also kept him away from home, and out of harm's way.

***

The day before their Christmas break, Pat's teacher received a note directing him to have Pat report to Father Romero's office. Pat left right away. Anxious and confused, his walk to the office seemed eternal. When he finally arrived, the priest looked very proud.

"This, my fine young man, is for you." He handed Pat a colorfully wrapped gift.

Pat froze; he didn't know what to say or do.

"Go ahead, open it. I'm hoping it'll make you smile."

Bewildered, he opened his present. It was an album of Christmas carols sung by the Vienna Boys' Choir and a Rosary with olivewood beads. Pat smiled and then he quickly looked away. "I didn't get you anything."

"Well, of course you didn't, and I certainly didn't expect you to. I heard you singing last week during services, and I thought you were quite good. It occurred to me then that you might enjoy this album. These beads are a different story, they are a token of our friendship, something to remind you that both God and I are always with you."

Pat didn't know how to respond; nothing like this had ever happened to him before. Now, more than anything, he wanted to hug the munificent priest, and much to his own amazement, he did.

"Why, thank you, Pat. Those were the best Christmas gifts you could have given me—a smile and a hug. And, Patrick, if I'm not mistaken, I also think I might have seen some unshed tears in your eyes."

Father Romero paused and placed both his hands on Pat's shoulders. "Son," he said, looking right into Pat's soul, "never be afraid to share your feelings or your love, for the Lord giveth and the Lord taketh away. And you never know when the good Lord will call you home."

Father Romero looked sad. Pat had never seen him look that way before. He assumed he was thinking about all his young comrades who had died. "Father, are you OK?"

"Yes, yes, I am. I'm sorry." Father Romero let out a breathy sigh, shook it off, and continued, this time using a lighter tone. "Well, I guess it's time for you to hurry back to class and for us to plan on meeting again for Oreos, right after the holiday recess."

Father Romero tousled Pat's hair and turned away, but Pat didn't move. Instead, he spoke, "Thank you, and err, God bless you, Father Romero. I'm really looking forward to our date." Father Romero turned his head and smiled; once again, his eyes twinkled.

As Pat turned away from Father Romero's closing door, he noted that the long hallway was completely empty, and so he began to skip back toward class.

Suddenly, Pat stopped and grinned. All at once, an image of the gift he'd give Father Romero emerged. Pat was elated.

***

During his Christmas break Pat worked extra hours at the market. With his additional earnings he bought Father Romero the only thing he knew he needed.

***

When the first day of classes resumed, Pat arrived at Father Romero's office early. With his present proudly tucked under his arm he knocked on the inner office door.

"Can I help you?" Mrs. O'Malley, the church secretary, answered the door. She looked pale and her makeup was smeared.

"I'm looking for Father Romero."

"Oh, well... I'm sorry to have to tell you this..." Mrs. O'Malley said, pressing and then rubbing her fingers under her bloodshot eyes, "but Father Romero passed away." Suddenly, she began to speak very quickly. "It was on Christmas Eve, while he was walking toward his family's church, somewhere in the Midwest. Blessedly, he died in God's presence."

Pat dropped his gift. The teapot cracked loudly.

Mrs. O'Malley briefly flinched, but then repeated, "He died peacefully." She looked down at the package. Neither of them moved toward it. "Father Gabriel will be here soon; would you like to speak with him?"

Pat turned and ran. He sprinted as fast as he could, back to the smallest confessional, the same one he took refuge in before. Devastated, he was once again cradled up on the floor, crying.

Before that moment, Pat was sure he and Father Romero were going to have many more talks; now he just desperately wanted to be with him one more time. He wanted to see his face when he opened Pat's present. He wanted to sit opposite him at his table, and watch him pour tea from his new teapot. He wanted to tell him how terrific he thought the album was, and how much the beads had come to mean to him. But above all else, he just wanted the chance to *be* with him one more time.

Pat felt himself fading away, and he never wanted to come back.

He hovered in the small confessional for the rest of the day, sobbing, rocking, and rubbing his rosary beads. When he finally emerged in the late afternoon, he couldn't stop himself from looking in the pews for Father Romero. As soon as his brief search ended, he felt as if he'd been stabbed in the heart. It was the worst physical pain he'd ever known. He stood there, unwilling and unable to breathe.

Moments later, he gasped for air. The stabbing pain started to subside; in its place, he felt an icy chill, and then—nothing.

***

The psychologist's notes indicated that Pat never got over the loss of Father Romero, nor did he befriend anyone else. To console himself, he spent as much time as he could at the church. Throughout his years in high school Father Gabriel saw him sitting alone at Father Romero's fading pink table, but he never knew, until decades later, just how much the old priest had meant to Pat.

***

After high school, Pat attended Brooklyn College, where he decided he'd become a priest. It was a decision based upon memories and loneliness, rather than divine inspiration. Although he was forced to live at home while attending college, he was finally able to escape when he began his studies at St. Joseph's Seminary in Westfield, Massachusetts.

Once he arrived in Massachusetts he never went back to Brooklyn again; and his years at St. Joseph's, although intensely solitary, were nonviolent, and, therefore, the best years of his life.

By the time Pat was ordained, he had befriended no one, and had reduced his contact with his parents to an occasional Christmas card.

On June 1, 1974 he quietly left St. Joseph's and joined a foreign ministry. He never intended to see anyone from Westfield or Brooklyn again. Instead, he anticipated beginning his long overdue adventures.

His first missionary assignment was in Mexico, where he was expected to teach young children in a destitute orphanage. Prior to his coming to Mexico children had never been a part of his world. Once he arrived in Mexico, he worked very closely with them and delighted in their non-judgmental and adoring gazes. Soon thereafter he was often seen with a small group of boys accompanying him wherever he went.

After a few months, he started to feel strangely drawn to the boys. At first, he believed his interest in them was tied to his excitement about his new surroundings, but then he began thinking about them in ways he knew were wrong. Most of the time these thoughts only came to him late at night, when he'd quietly touch himself, and then fall asleep. For a while, this routine enabled him to wake up in the morning and rationalize that his memories of the night before had only been a dream. But, as time went on, merely thinking about the boys and touching himself wasn't enough. He soon indulged in a daily, carefully calculated, but by all appearances, inadvertent graze against their perfect skin. Then, at night, he'd review in depth the wonder of that touch. Soon, he was obsessed with these moments and they became the focal point of his day. In time, the grazes weren't enough so he'd go down to the swing set. There, each morning, he'd swing the little boys on his lap, until one day he went too far…

***

He stood back watching the three little boys run around the church's swing set. He could feel himself getting aroused. He picked up the smallest of the three; his name was Juan. He spun

Juan around in the air, and then put him on his lap. Pat then began to swing.

This feels so good, he thought. Soon, Juan started wiggling around, and *that,* even better. Pat closed his eyes and started to breath heavily. His hot breathe streamed down Juan's neck. As Pat's excitement increased, his grip on Juan tightened. Finally, Juan wiggled off his lap and left, but not before stopping and turning around to glare at Father Pat.

That night, as Pat relived the details of his erotic experience, instead of becoming aroused, he became worried. He kept seeing Juan's face as he glowered at him. The next morning he requested a transfer.

***

Over the years, Father Pat asked to be transferred on several occasions. Each time he arrived in a new country he hoped things would be different, but they never were.

By the time he was 29, he was beginning to feel that *things* were getting out of control. This scared him, but not enough to risk directly divulging his secret to anyone. When he occasionally tried to hint at it to the other priests, they gave him the very clear message that things like that just weren't discussed. In the end, he dealt with those feelings the same way he'd dealt with all the other pain he'd ever experienced—he became numb to it; he had to in order to survive.

Just before his 30th birthday he was told by the church liaison that both his parents had died. Although he appeared to be listening intently to the details of their car accident, he was certain, that no matter what the police report said, one or both of them were drunk, and the accident was all his mother's fault. His only question of the liaison was, "Where will my next assignment be?"

The baffled-looking liaison's response was, "San Carlos."

***

San Carlos was the poorest country he'd been to thus far. In the majority of its villages parental supervision was a luxury most people couldn't afford, and its police departments were jokes. In short, this environment was a child molester's paradise.

It was in a small village in San Carlos that Father Pat molested the greatest number of boys. It was also there that, after several years, the local parish could no longer turn a blind eye to his predilection. Ultimately, they sent him back to the States, but they never gave the Board of Ministries any explanation. They didn't want to offend their generous American neighbors.

Father Pat was 31 years old when they told him they'd be returning him to his homeland. His only response was to request he be sent to Madison, Wisconsin. His sole explanation was that he'd hoped he'd always end up there.

***

At first, Father Pat loved Madison, so much so he was able to control himself by merely staying away from little boys. However, that became untenable once the resident parish priest insisted he become director of the boys' choir.

11

"But for" Test—Legal test used in determining whether someone would have suffered a wrong, " but for" the actions of another.

Jordon closed Pat's file as if she were sealing a casket. After years of being abused and neglected, Pat had finally snapped. *But for* the death of Father Romero, Jordon considered, perhaps Pat could have been saved; instead, his death was Pat's last straw. There's no question about it, she concluded, being abused as a child affects that child for all of the rest of his or her life. But, does it always have to end badly? Can a child recover? Can a molester change? I need those answers tonight.

Jordon sat back down and picked up Sophia's file. She began to page through it, eventually she found what she was looking for. It was the handwritten pages from the journal of Sophia's pre-school teacher, Mrs. Tollson. It had been written the evening after Sophia's assault. It included both the teacher's description of the events as well as her thoughts and feelings. The journal entry was something Mrs. Tollson had written to record the details of what had happened. She later told Jordon she wasn't sure at the time, but she thought she might also need it for testifying in court. Hence, she put in as many quotes as she could remember.

12

March 5, 1977
SOPHIA

Forensic Interview—A discussion in which potentially admissible evidence is gathered.

"Just after *snack-time,* I looked up and saw 5-year-old Sophia and her little neighbor friend go off to the bathroom. Moments later, her friend came out and whispered to me, 'Sophia's crying. When she wiped, we saw a little blood.' Just then, Sophia slowly wandered out onto the playground. Her eyes were red, but she wasn't crying. I walked over to her and asked her to please come with me. Sophia took my hand and we walked together over to the picnic table. Once there, I told her she seemed unhappy and asked her if something had happened. At first, she didn't answer; she just looked up at me wide-eyed and fearful. So, I asked her if she knew the difference between a *good touch* and a *bad touch.*

"'Yes,' she said, 'a good touch feels good and a bad touch feels bad.' I thought then she might only be parroting the words we'd taught her during our *personal safety* lessons.

"'That's right,' I said. 'So, I'm wondering if anybody has recently touched you, in a way that made you feel good or bad?'

"Sophia didn't immediately respond. I knew I had to be patient and only ask *open-ended,* rather than *leading,* questions, so I waited. Finally, Sophia looked down and said, 'Bad. My brother gave me a bad touch. He hurt me.'

"'When did he hurt you?' I asked.

"'Last night,' she said.

"And the only other question I asked was—'How did he hurt you?'

"'He poked me where I pee,' she whispered.

"After that, I knew I shouldn't ask any more questions, so I called Child Protective Services."

***

Many years later, Sophia herself recalled for Jordon her memory of what had happened next. At the time Sophia described it,

Jordon was dumfounded by the images, which stuck with the then 5-year-old girl.

Also, within the file, Jordon found Sophia's medical report and a copy of the Sexual Assault Response Team (SART) videotape. Jordon reviewed it all, as well as her own notes. When she was done, she felt she could see it all through the eyes of the very young Sophia.

***

It was still *naptime* at the pre-school when Sophia was awakened by the sound of her mother sobbing. Next to her mother stood a very sad looking Mrs. Tollson and a stranger. As soon as Sophia woke up she asked, "Where's Marcos?"

No one answered her. Her mother, Margarita, just shook her head and cried. Eventually, Mrs. Tollson offered, "Marcos isn't coming for you today, honey. Today, you're going to leave here with your Mama and Laurie. Laurie is a nice lady whose job it is to protect children. She's going to take you to a place called The SART house."

***

Sophia liked the SART house from the moment she walked through its light purple doors. Once inside, she saw many things that were her favorite colors and just her size. As she was escorted farther in, she was introduced to someone named *Anna-the-forensic-interviewer*. Sophia didn't understand her name, but she thought she was pretty and smelled like Christmas. She liked that Anna was small for a grown woman and that she had pretty eyes, a nice smile and silver hair. She noticed too that Anna was wearing slippers instead of shoes, and a very long skirt, which reached the tip of her toes and went *swish* when she walked.

Soon after they met Anna took them all to the back of the house to the *Interview/Playroom*. When she got to the door of the room, Anna said that Margarita wouldn't be going in with them. "This room is just for me and kids," she explained. "This is the room you and I will go into, and while we're in here, your Mama will wait for you in a room we call the *Waiting Room*, OK?"

"OK," Sophia said. But, she wasn't sure if it really was OK. Still, she saw that the playroom had some toys and magic markers in it, so she turned, gave her still crying mother a hug, and walked in.

When she entered the room, she saw one side had a big mirror on it. Anna quickly told her the mirror was actually a window, which made it possible for others to watch them play. All Sophia could see was a mirror. Next, Anna pointed out the video camera attached to the wall, and explained she was going to make a videotape of their time together so she wouldn't have to write everything down. Sophia saw the camera light was already on. She didn't understand why people would want to watch them, or why Anna might need to write everything down. But Anna seemed nice, the toys looked like fun, and she was ready to play.

As soon as Sophia sat down, Anna started asking her questions, which Sophia worked very hard at answering. A few of the questions had to do with the toys they were playing with, but most had to do with things that had happened to Sophia and how she felt about them.

Sophia thought some of the questions were hard to answer, while others were easy. One of the hardest questions Anna asked her was if anyone had ever touched her in a way that made her feel bad. Sophia remembered that was the same question Mrs. Tollson had asked her, and she gave Anna the same answer.

"Yes, my brother."

"Can you tell me how he touched you when he made you feel bad?"

Sophia didn't want to tell her, because she thought she'd get in trouble for asking Marcos to get into her bed, so she just shook her head no.

"You don't want to tell me what he did?"

Sophia looked down and once again shook her head no.

"You know it's my job to listen to kids, but sometimes they don't want to tell me things. Sometimes, the reason they don't want to tell me things is because they think they've done something wrong. Do you think you've done anything wrong?"

Sophia continued to look down, but now nodded her head yes.

"Sophia, this is important. Do you believe that whatever it is you *think* you did wrong might have made your brother hurt you?"

Sophia was amazed Anna had figured that out. She nodded yes and slowly began to look up.

"Well, I don't know what you did, and I don't know what your brother did. I do know that whatever *you* think you *might* have done, didn't make it OK for your brother to hurt you, because big brothers are *never* supposed to hurt little sisters, no matter what. Do you believe that?"

Sophia nodded yes. Anna continued speaking very slowly. Sophia could tell Anna really wanted her to believe her.

Anna went on. "Now, maybe your big brother didn't mean to hurt you, but if you tell me what he did, then I can help make sure he never does it again. Do you want me to do that?"

Sophia's eyes filled with tears as she, almost imperceptibly, nodded yes.

"OK then, will you tell me what he did?"

Once again, Sophia motioned yes, this time with slightly more energy, and finally, she told Anna what had happened the night before. As she did, Sophia thought Anna looked sad.

Midway through her explanation, Sophia also wanted to tell Anna how some of Marcos' touches actually felt good, but she wasn't sure if she should tell her that. She could tell everybody thought Marcos was bad, and she didn't want them to think she was bad too.

"Sophia," Anna next asked, "after he did this to you, did you say anything?"

"Yes, I said, 'Marcos, you hurt me'." Sophia felt proud.

Anna looked pleased, but then continued to ask Sophia more questions. Sophia liked Anna and wanted her to be her friend, but she didn't want to answer any more questions about Marcos. She didn't want Anna or anybody else to be mad at him. She wanted to go home and see him. She wanted to tell him all about Anna and the questions she'd been asked. She started rubbing her eyes and looking around. "I want to go home now," she finally announced.

"OK, and thank you for telling me," Anna said, "but do you think I could just ask you a few more questions?"

"I'm really tired." Sophia began to wiggle in her seat.

"All right then, I'll stop, but there's one more nice person I'd like you and your Mama to meet before you go home. I'll go tell him you're ready. Meanwhile, can I bring you some juice?"

Sophia licked her obviously dry lips. "Yes, please."

After Anna brought Sophia a can of apple juice, she took her and Margarita into another room, where they were promptly introduced to a smiling *Doctor Elliot*.

Elliot Salzman didn't look like a doctor. He was wearing baggy clothes and a tie with children on it. He reminded Sophia of a cozy teddy bear whom someone had dressed up for a party. Because of the way he was dressed and his gentle manner, Sophia liked him right away.

When they walked into the room, Dr. Elliot was already sitting on a chair with small wheels on it. After motioning to Sophia to sit in a nearby chair, he rolled over to her, looked into her eyes, and gave her the best smile she'd ever seen. Then he placed both his elbows on his knees, leaned a little closer to her and said, "Anna's already told me that you were touched in a way that made you feel bad. So now it's my job, along with some others, to help you feel good again. For me to help you, I have to look at your body. I have to examine you. Have you ever been to a doctor before?"

"Yes," she said, happy to answer a question which didn't make her sad.

"And did he examine you?"

"Yes."

"And did he make you feel good again?"

"No, he told my Mama that I had a tummy ache, and that we had to go buy some pills. And then, after I took the pills, I felt all better."

"Wonderful, I'm so glad the pills he told your Mama about made you feel all better. And since you understand what an examination is, is it OK if I examine you?"

"Oh, yes!" Sophia said, trying to sound very grown up.

"Good," Elliot said. "Then I'll be able to see if there's anything wrong with you, and if there is, I'll give you some pills or some other medicine to make you feel all better. But if I see that there's nothing wrong with you, then I'll just tell you and your Mama, and you can just go home. OK?"

Sophia smiled and said, "OK."

"Now," Dr. Elliot continued, "in order to examine you, I have to look at your whole body—inside and out, and I won't do that unless you tell me that's OK with you. So, may I examine you inside and out?"

"Will it hurt?"

"No, I don't think so, I examine kids all the time and not one of them has ever told me I hurt them. But, I'll make a deal with you. If anything I do hurts you, you tell me and I will stop right away. OK?"

"OK." Sophia nodded her head yes.

A short while later the examination was over, and Sophia felt it hadn't hurt at all. During the exam Doctor Elliot talked to her and showed her on a small TV what he was doing and why. Sophia liked his voice, even if she didn't understand much of what he said.

Afterward he told both her and her mother that she was just fine, and didn't need any medicine.

"But, did you know that my brother poked me where I pee?" Sophia asked with a quiet but serious voice.

"Yes, I heard about that," Dr. Elliot responded.

"And did you check there?"

"Yes, yes, I did."

"And I'm OK there, too?" she asked, biting her lower lip.

"Yes, you're OK there too," he replied, once again looking directly at her.

Sophia turned to Margarita. "See, Mama? I'm OK; you don't have to buy me any pills that cost you a lot of money. And you don't have to cry anymore."

Margarita didn't speak. She remained pale and continued to cry.

***

On the video, Jordon could hear Dr. Salzman quietly tell Margarita that Sophia was still a virgin. He then turned back to Sophia and asked if she had any more questions. When she didn't, he walked them into another room. This room had a long shelf full of new stuffed animals.

"Go ahead," Elliot said, "pick one out. They each need someone to love and take care of them."

Sophia picked out a soft brown teddy bear with shiny black eyes. Elliot smiled, gave her his phone number, and told her to call him any time if she ever had any more questions. Sophia thanked him and soon after they left.

Meanwhile, the professionals on the Sexual Assault Response Team remained seated on the other side of the interview room's one-way mirror. The team was composed of Jordon, the investigating detectives, Sophia's soon-to-be counselor, and Mrs. Fairway a victim/witness advocate from the DA's office.

Once Elliot and Anna joined them, the air in the already crowded observation room became thick with sadness and anger. Although the team wanted to *debrief*, everyone agreed there just wasn't time. All of them were anxious for the detectives to leave and secure the necessary warrants. In a matter of moments, the room was empty.

***

As soon as Sophia got home, she called out for Marcos, even though she sensed he wouldn't be there.

"Mama, where's Marcos?" she asked. "When's he coming home?"

Margarita didn't respond; instead she sat down on the couch, grabbed a pillow, brought it up to her face and continued to cry. In response, Sophia picked up her bear, which she promptly named Elliot, scooted next to her mother, and stared at the front door.

***

Jordon could now picture Sophia sitting there, clinging to her bear, as well as the hope and fear that Marcos would soon walk in.

Meanwhile, Marcos was at school, undoubtedly oblivious to what Sophia had reported.

And what about poor Colin? When she last read about him, he was waiting in the small room just outside the chapel. Both he and Marcos were completely unaware of what was going to happen next.

Colin first, she, thought. Jordon reached over and picked up several pages of notes from Colin's file. She still believed that by continuing to break down their pasts in this manner, she'd at least have a shot at understanding their futures.

13

Pedophile—An adult with a sexual predilection for children.

Father Pat walked by and saw Colin sitting alone in the candlelit room. "Colin, is that you? Are you all right, my son?"

Colin turned toward Father Pat and appeared surprised to see him. "Father Pat, I'm here to see Father Williams; he wants me to be an acolyte, but I don't want to be one."

Father Pat sat down next to him. Colin leaned forward and cried into his hands. Suddenly, Colin threw his arms around Father Pat and pressed his small face into his stomach. Pat instantly reacted. Oh no, not again, he thought, I've got to push him away. But, this feels too good. I'll just let him keep his face there for a moment. I haven't felt this good for so long...

Now what's he talking about? Pat wondered. His family, Father Williams, his confusion about the church, how hard it is to be 11 years old... I can't keep track of his words, but his warm face so close to my groin... I have to get away. I've got to tell him Father Williams isn't here. I've got to insist he go home at once.

But Pat didn't say any of those things. Instead, he replied, "I know exactly what you're going through, my son. When I was your age, I felt the same way. I know it's hard to believe I was ever your age. Come on back into my quarters, and I'll show you some old photographs."

Slowly, they walked across the courtyard. Silently, Colin followed him into the room. Carefully, Father Pat shut and locked the door behind them. What am I doing? Pat thought. I *have* to tell him to leave! But, the next thing Pat heard himself say was. "Come sit here, by me."

Father Pat began negotiating with himself again. I'll just open the photo album and rest my hand on Colin's leg. I won't do anything else.

Pat placed the back of his hand on Colin's upper thigh. He could no longer hear what Colin was saying. Colin's leg began to tremble. Pat could see Colin was getting hard. I *have* to touch him.

I'll just brush the back of my hand up against it as he turns the page.

Colin grew harder and gasped.

He wants me, Father Pat concluded. Pat laid Colin down and took his pants off. Colin kept his eyes closed and lay perfectly still. Pat took him in his hand and then his mouth. My turn, Pat thought. Pat took his own pants off and straddled Colin's face. Colin clenched his jaw and tossed his head from side to side. Pat kept forcing himself on him. Colin opened his mouth and gagged. Moments later, Pat climaxed.

Seconds later, Pat's mind filled with images of what he knew he'd have to do next.

***

A half-hour later, Pat walked into Madison Sports, a large sporting goods store on State Street. There, he engaged the owner, Ron Dent, in a conversation Dent subsequently claimed he'd never forget.

***

"Good evening, Father Pat. You're here rather late, but it's always a blessing to see you." Ron smiled at his own pun; Father Pat didn't. Ron continued, "So, are yah here to buy some equipment for the church?"

"Yes, matter of fact, I am. We're thinking about taking a few of the older boys out of town to do some backpacking in the forest, and Father Williams thought it might be a good idea if we took along a small handgun, in case of an emergency."

"Well, as usual, I think Father Williams is right on the money. Between the bears and the bums, you're just not sure what you might run into out there. What kind of gun were you gentlemen thinking of?"

"Well, we're not sure," Father Pat, said. "We want it to be small enough so we can pack it away without alarming the boys, but we also want it to be large enough to accomplish the task at hand. I mean, if I shoot to kill, then I've got to be able to do what I set out to do, right?"

"Right again. Come with me, I'll show you what I've got. Now the only thing I *can't* do—" As soon as Dent uttered those words, he noticed Pat suddenly looked worried—"...is sell you the will to use it. Now, have you ever honestly asked yourself, if it really came down to it, could I pull the trigger?"

"Asked and answered," Pat said exhaling. "That's why I'm here." And, in a softer voice, he added, "Sometimes, things can get so far out of control, you have no other choice…"

***

Jordon stood up and walked onto their deck. She looked up at the vast sky. Moments later, she felt small and very much alone; probably the way Marcos felt the instant of his arrest.

A few minutes later Jordon went back inside and reached for Marcos' file. Once again, she picked up several documents, a microcassette tape which a detective had hidden in his breast pocket, and a videotape of Marcos' interview. She reviewed them all.

14

March 5, 1977
MARCOS

Santa Barbara Police Department's motto—Dedicated to Serve.

Marcos heard the classroom buzz before he looked up and saw them. "Why're the cops here? Who'd they come to bust? What'd someone do?"

The principal went directly to their teacher, turned his back to the class, and spoke in hushed tones. Their teacher lowered his head and shook it from side to side. When he looked up, he said, "Marcos, grab your things and go with Principal Brey to his office." Marcos gathered his books, stood, and walked out. He never looked back.

En route to his office, the usually chatty Mr. Brey was uncharacteristically quiet. Marcos was told to walk behind him, an officer walked on either side.

Marcos wasn't sure what was going on, but his insides were churning and his palms were sweating. The hallway was eerily silent.

As soon as they arrived at the door to Mr. Brey's office, Marcos was introduced to Detectives Greene and Alexander. "Marcos," Detective Alexander said, handing him a piece of paper, "this is a warrant for your arrest. We're going to be taking you in now, so gather all your possessions. Once we get somewhere more private, we'll tell you what this is all about."

With mounting dread and total bewilderment, Marcos left the school building. When he crossed the wet grass of the abandoned football field, he focused on the droplets of water bouncing off his shoes, but he felt the eyes of the entire school focused on him. He had no idea why the police were taking him away, but he assumed it had something to do with his immigration status.

Once they placed him inside the police car he heard a soft click. He later learned it was the sound of Detective Alexander starting his tape recorder.

"You're 18, right?"

"Si, I mean yes."

"Do you need an interpreter?"

"No," Marcos lied. He did speak enough English to get by, but not enough to communicate effectively with them. Still, he didn't want to admit that to them, for fear it could affect his citizenship.

"OK, well, for now, I just want to make sure you know you're under arrest. Later, if you want to, we can talk."

Believing that in Guatemala, once you were taken to jail you were never seen again, Marcos first felt terrified, and then he felt his bladder give way.

After driving in silence for a few, seemingly eternal minutes, Detective Greene finally told Marcos why he'd been arrested.

"We just got finished observing an interview of Sophia." Detective Alexander glanced up at Marcos in the rearview mirror. Detective Greene continued, "… She told someone that you sexually assaulted her."

Marcos wasn't sure he knew exactly what 'sexual assault' meant, but he knew it sounded bad. He was now having trouble breathing, and his stomach was starting to cramp.

"Now, if you want to, we can take you to the police department where you can tell us your side of the story. Alternatively, we can take you to jail. So, what'll it be?"

Marcos didn't want to go to jail, especially in his current condition. After the question was repeated again, and he was once again offered an interpreter, he finally said, "Take me to the police station. I don't need no interpreter."

Once inside the station, they brought him into an interview room. It didn't look anything like the ones he'd seen on TV. It was clean, but extremely small and drafty. Marcos' wet pants, combined with the cold environment, sent a chill throughout his body.

"Want a soda?" Detective Greene asked.

Marcos shook his head. The detective's behavior baffled him. Marcos didn't understand why Detective Greene was going through the motions of being so nice, but wouldn't look directly at him when he spoke.

As Marcos sat shivering, both detectives whispered back and forth. Suddenly Detective Alexander noisily shoved his chair back, stood up, gave Marcos a scornful sneer, and left. Marcos was glad to see him leave. He looked over at Detective Greene; he didn't seem angry or disgusted. He seemed like a nice guy.

***

Detective Greene, however, was filled with anger and disgust. He had a daughter the same age as Sophia. Still, he knew he'd have to play the *good cop*, to Detective Alexander's *bad cop*, in order to get Marcos to tell him the truth.

***

Initially, Marcos denied that anything had happened. Instead, he insisted Sophia made the whole thing up. Still, Detective Greene was steadfast.

"Marcos, there's just something I don't understand. Why would she say you touched her like that if you didn't?"

"I don't know."

"I mean, does she hate you?"

"No."

"Did you ever do anything to her that made her mad at you?"

"No. Well, yeah. I wouldn't let her watch too much TV. She probably made this up, 'cause she was mad at me for that."

"Does that sound like something she'd do?"

"No, not really."

"Anyway, how would a five-year-old girl learn about that kind of touching if it didn't really happen to her?"

"I don't know, maybe from TV."

"But I thought you just said you didn't let her watch too much TV?"

Greene's questioning continued for close to an hour. Before long, Marcos' wet pants were sticking to his skin, and he was getting lost and confused in his own lies.

Maybe it would just be easier, he thought, to tell the truth and get it over with. They're never going to take my word over hers anyway. But I'll bet she never even told them it was all her idea, or that she actually begged me to get in her bed. Yeah, I'm sure she left that part out…

Having concluded that his situation was now hopeless, Marcos responded truthfully, and temporarily stopped caring about what would happen next.

***

Trying to stick with her plan, Jordon closed Marcos' file and went back to Colin's.

15

January 22, 1981
COLIN

Mental Anguish—The resultant mental sensation of pain, also includes the accompanying feelings of distress, fright and anxiety.

Moments after Colin arrived home he couldn't remember how he got there. He assumed he rode his bicycle, because he was home and so was his bike. The only thing he knew for sure was that he still felt sick. He walked over to the side of his house and dropped down to his knees.

Father Pat's words kept screaming in his ears—"Colin, get dressed. Go home. And don't tell anyone about this. You know you wanted it as much as I did." Colin threw up and then stayed there on the moist grass until he began to shiver. By the time he made his way inside his house, he was certain of only one thing— he could never face anyone, ever again.

He felt woozy going up the steps. One step at a time, he thought; tonight, up the stairs, yell goodnight and go to bed. Tomorrow, I'll fix everything...

***

The next day, Dwight left before Colin came out of his room. When Colin walked into the kitchen, he was sure he looked pale, which made it easier for him to convince his mother he was too sick to go to school—but not so sick she should stay home with him.

Cathy took his temperature, and of course, it was normal. Colin assured her all he needed was rest.

Just before leaving, Cathy kissed him behind his ear and whispered, "Love you." Colin felt a sharp stabbing pain in his chest, but said nothing. Cathy walked out the front door, got into her car, and waved goodbye one last time. Then she turned around and backed out of their driveway.

Colin stood in the doorway, and watched her leave. "Love you too, Mom," he whispered back. He turned away. He couldn't risk the possibility of her seeing his eyes. One step at a time, he reminded himself. Then he dragged himself back upstairs, and collapsed on his bed. He was too sad to do anything but cry.

When he thought he was all cried out, he began to formulate a plan. Dazed, but driven, he got up and began his fruitless search for a rope. He remembered seeing one recently, but at first he couldn't remember where. All at once the image became clear. The rope was in his best friend Tom's backyard.

Confounded but focused, he walked over to Tom's house. When he arrived, Colin saw the rope just where he knew it would be—still attached to the little red wagon. Spotting it, he remembered how Tom had called him a chicken, when Colin refused to barrel down the hill, holding on to nothing but that rope.

"By this afternoon," Colin said out loud, "Tom won't think I'm a chicken anymore."

***

What the hell is Colin doing? Tom wondered, as he watched from his upstairs window. Once again, Tom was home, smoking marijuana and playing hooky from school.

When the rope finally came loose from the wagon and Colin started to leave, Tom wanted to yell out to him, but didn't. He knew Colin would give him hell for skipping school and smoking grass, and he wasn't in the mood for one of Colin's lectures.

***

As soon as Colin got home, he carried the heavy rope up to the attic. His heart was pounding. The thought of doing what he was about to do had never occurred to him before, but after last night he felt he had no choice.

Still, in the back of his mind, he kept hoping that the whole thing was just a bad dream, and soon he'd roll over and wake up. However, by the time he got to the attic and sat down in his father's old chair, he was sure it wasn't a dream. Caressing the chair's worn armrest, he thought about his father.

Finding me will be very hard on him, Colin lamented. But if he found out about what I did with Father Pat, that'd kill him. At least this way, he'll never find out about that.

Colin walked over to an abandoned nightstand, picked up an old pencil and wrote them a note.

"I'm sorry. I love you. Colin."

Once again overwhelmed by sadness, he started to sob. He didn't want to die.

***

Tom had just made his way to Colin's house, and somehow managed to crouch behind the backyard bushes without falling over. Given his marijuana-altered state, he thought he'd stay there, until he was sure no one besides Colin was home.

After waiting a few minutes, Tom started throwing pebbles at Colin's window, but none hit their mark.

***

Colin heard nothing out of the ordinary; he was trying to prepare the rope, but was becoming frustrated in the process. "Damn it!" he yelled, throwing the rope at the curtain.

***

Tom saw the attic curtains move. What the fuck...?

***

Frustrated, Colin retrieved his thrown rope. It turned out everything he knew about hangings he'd learned from watching cartoons. Now he discovered, the hardest part was making the right kind of knot.

***

Tom was getting bored, and decided to head home. As he turned onto his street, he again worried about Colin, but decided the marijuana was just making him paranoid.

***

Colin's frustration was increasing. He'd been trying to make a noose for several minutes and was beginning to feel like a failure at that too. He slapped the hardwood floor with the rope. Suddenly, he remembered something his father had shown him when he was little. It was a book about knots; one his father had from the Navy. Colin remembered how he used to sit next to his father as they poured over pictures in that book. It was a wonderful memory, but only until the same image reminded Colin of what he and Father Pat had done last night.

Colin rushed down to the bathroom and got sick all over again. When he emerged, he wiped his mouth with the back of his hand. I can't live like this, he thought. I *have* to find that book.

Colin headed toward the old bookcase. The first book he pulled out was filled with photographs from his second birthday party. As he looked at one picture, Colin wasn't sure who looked prouder, he, for owning the new toy truck, or his mom, for giving it to him. Colin yearned to escape by jumping into that picture, but he knew his only real chance of escaping was to find his Dad's old book with its directions for making a slipknot.

Once he found the book he returned to the attic and created the knot and noose. He then tossed the book onto the floor and the rope over a rafter. Next he got out an old stool, took a deep breath, stepped up, and put the scratchy rope around his neck.

Collin's mouth went dry, and his limbs felt heavy. He was sure there was no other way.

***

"What the hell are you doing?" Tom yelled, as he grabbed Colin and yanked the rope from around him. "What's this, some kind of stupid fucking trick to get me to quit playing hooky and go to school? This isn't funny, you could have gotten hurt. What if I didn't come back? This is bullshit!"

Tom was ranting and raving. He was confident Colin's antics were all about him. Meanwhile, Colin stood there with his head down. Suddenly Tom grew quiet; things weren't adding up.

Tom spied Colin's note and read it aloud. " 'I'm sorry.' You're sorry? What?" Tom searched Colin's eyes for answers. Finding none, he read on, " 'I love you. Colin.' "

"Colin, what the fuck is going on here? What are you sorry for?" Tom stood there, demanding to know.

Colin was pale and completely overwrought. Exhausted, he sat down and told Tom what had happen, but he never once looked up at him. Meanwhile, Tom stared at Colin in abject disbelief, only periodically interrupting him by saying, "No shit."

When Colin finished, Tom paused for a moment to let it all sink in, and then he exploded, "That fucker!"

Colin looked confused. He tried to explain to Tom that it was his own fault, and not Father Pat's, but Tom was indignant. "Bullshit, that guy raped you. I mean, I know he didn't rape you, but it's the same thing. Colin, don't you get it? Father Pat is one of those fucking child molesters!"

Now Colin looked shocked. "But, don't you—don't you think all this means I'm a fag?"

"What?" Tom was taken aback. "Well, are you?"

Colin paused, and then he shook his head, no. "Tom," he said, "I'm all confused. No, 'course I'm not."

"Then, I'm telling you man, you were raped. And Father Pat's a horny child molester and now we gotta tell someone."

"No!" Colin replied with a panicked pitch. "We can't tell anyone, not now, not ever! I shouldn't have even told you!"

Tom spent the next few minutes trying to talk Colin into telling someone, anyone, but Colin refused to listen. Finally, Tom said something he was sure Colin couldn't ignore.

"Come on, Col, what about the other kids in the choir? What about the kindergarteners he sings with on Tuesday afternoons? What about them? How'd *you* feel if he messed with one of them?"

"How do you think I'd feel? I'd feel like shit," Colin said. "But I still can't do it." Colin let his eyes shift downward and shook his head. "I'm sorry," he said, avoiding all eye contact with Tom. "I just can't do it." Suddenly Colin looked intently at Tom, adding "and you gotta promise me *you'll* never tell anyone, either."

All morning, Tom tried to change his mind, but Colin wouldn't budge. Eventually, Tom gave up and promised he wouldn't tell anyone, if Colin promised he wouldn't try to kill himself again. They shook on it.

Now, desperately trying to bring some lightness or at least closure to the morning, Tom awkwardly asked, "So, what do ya think, Col? You think one day we'll look back on all of this and laugh?"

"No," Colin said, looking down. "Not ever."

"Oh yeah, right, that's what you said last week after I untied the red wagon from your bike and went flying down the hill. Boy, you were pissed off that day. And the way I remember it, you said you'd never talk to me again. Then the next day, when I saw you at school, you cracked up laughing. We both did."

Colin smiled, but not for long. "Tom, look, I'm really tired now. I'm gonna go lie down." Colin started drifting toward the couch. "Thanks for coming over."

Tom refused to be dismissed. "I'll just stick around for a while and watch some TV while you catch some zzzs." Tom was worried Colin might not hold up his part of their agreement.

As Colin fitfully dozed off, Tom's mind spun. He was disgusted by what had happened, and incredibly angry that someone had messed with his best friend. Beyond that, he was also worried Father Pat might strike again. He had to stop him, but to do that he knew he'd have to tell someone. But if he did, he'd be breaking his promise to Colin, and then Colin might...

By late afternoon, Tom's agonizing finally ended; he telephoned 911.

***

Jordon knew she *should* go back to reading about Pat, but, instead, she continued through Colin's police and medical reports.

16

January 23, 1981
The Dane County Evidence Collectors

Tangible Evidence—Physical evidence; evidence which can be seen or touched.

"Wake up, son, wake up."

Colin thought he was dreaming. Why is somebody shaking me so hard? Who is this guy? What's going on? He squinted. Why are the police here? Why is a policeman shaking me? He opened his eyes, looked straight ahead, and saw Tom. Suddenly, he understood everything. He glared at Tom; his eyes screamed, "How could you?"

Tom looked away.

The policeman began to ask him questions about Father Pat, but Colin just kept glowering at Tom. Soon he heard his parents arrive, but before Colin could talk to them, he saw one of the policemen take them into the living room. The other policeman stayed with him and kept asking him questions, questions Colin refused to answer.

Colin even refused to acknowledge the policeman's presence. The policeman kept calling him *Son*. Don't call me *Son*, Colin silently demanded. You're not my father or my priest. The thought of his priest made him want to rush out and throw up again, but instead, he stayed and swallowed the vile taste down.

"Son," the cop continued, "your friend here, Tom, is that your name? Todd? No, Tom. Tom tells me that Father Pat, er-uh, touched you and there was also some kind of oral copulation going on. Is that what happened, Son?"

Colin still refused to respond. Oral copulation, he thought, is that what it's called? What a stupid word that is. He kept silently repeating those two words over and over again, oral copulation, oral copulation... After awhile the two words actually began to sound funny to him, and he began to laugh. The laugh started off as a smirk and then turned into a giggle. All at once, Colin heard himself getting louder and louder and knew he couldn't stop. Suddenly his laughter turned to crying and then back to laughter.

Through his hysteria Colin heard someone say something about a doctor, and he thought that was pretty funny, too, until the ambulance actually arrived to take him to the hospital. He didn't want to go to the hospital, but the more he complained and fought back, the more they talked to him as if he were back in kindergarten. Ultimately, he decided it would just be easier to shut up and shut down.

***

As Tom watched the ambulance pull away, he felt as if he'd lost his best friend, and wondered if he'd made the right call.

***

When they got to the hospital Colin was immediately taken to an examination room where the nurse and doctor started asking him the same questions the policemen had. Again, everyone kept calling him *Son*.

I'm not any of their sons, he thought. The only people who get to call me son anymore are my parents, and they didn't even want to come in the ambulance with me. Finally, the doctor started asking him the kind of questions he could answer.

"Do you know where you are?"

"Yeah, I'm at the hospital."

Touching Colin's throat, he asked, "Does that hurt?"

"No."

He turned and took a long wooden tongue depressor out of a glass jar. Colin's eyes grew big.

"Open your mouth, wide."

Terrifying flashbacks from the night before suddenly overwhelmed Colin. He clenched down on his teeth.

"You're going to have to open your mouth."

Colin couldn't, and the awful smells of the emergency room were starting to make him dizzy.

The doctor thrust the tongue depressor into Colin's mouth, pried open his teeth, and pushed down on his tongue. Colin gagged.

"Son, I'm going to need your cooperation here. Now, take it easy, it's only a tongue depressor."

Colin couldn't stop gagging. In between coughs, the doctor scraped the inside of his mouth. "Now," he said, "I'm going to have to ask you to take off your pants."

"What?" Colin asked.

"Son, we need you to take off your pants; if you can't do it, someone will do it for you."

Colin was astounded by what the doctor was doing. It's just what Father Pat did to me last night. He called me *Son*, took off my pants, and jammed something—his thing—into my mouth. Well, I didn't have the guts to scream last night, but I do now. "No," he roared, "no, no, no, no, no!"

At first the doctor looked shocked by Colin's outburst, but then he just ignored him and started to pull his pants off anyway.

Colin's screams grew louder. Once he started kicking the doctor stopped. Colin was glad he'd won this time.

But he hadn't. The doctor gave his nurse a nod, and the next thing Colin felt was a sharp prick to his upper arm. Before long he was too weak to fight, but not too weak to care, or too feeble to know exactly what the doctor was doing. He watched, powerless, as the doctor pulled down his pants. Then Colin threw up.

"Probably just a bit of a reaction to the medication," the nurse opined. But Colin knew that wasn't it at all; he knew it was all about the night before. Dazed, Colin looked on as the doctor held and examined his penis. When he finished, he turned Colin over.

Helpless, Colin felt like a chicken on his mother's cutting board. First he grabs my private parts and then he flips me over. He probably thinks I'm chicken too…Colin felt lightheaded.

Next, the doctor pushed Colin's knees up under his belly and looked inside his rectum.

I can't believe he's doing all this to me and in front of the lady nurse. And he isn't even talking to me anymore? It's like he thinks I'm dead…

When the doctor swabbed Colin's testicles, the nurse smiled. Colin didn't know why she did that, but he thought she was laughing at him. The only thing he was sure of was that, as bad as last night had been, today was worse. While continuing to stare down at the floor, he mourned, if only Tom hadn't stopped me…

Colin lost track of time. At some point he heard the doctor say, "OK, Son, we're all done. Now you can slowly get up, get dressed, and go home."

Get up, get dressed, and go home, Colin thought—*just* like last night. In his still drowsy state it took him awhile to get dressed. When he finally did, he walked out of the room and kept his head down.

As soon as he entered the emergency room lobby, Cathy ran toward him and started to cry. When she reached him, she gathered him up into her arms and held on. Colin tried to keep his head free; he was looking for his father.

When Colin spotted Dwight, he was standing with his back against the wall, his hands firmly affixed in his pant's pockets. As Dwight slowly looked up, Colin could tell he'd been crying. Oh Dad, he thought, I'm so sorry.

During the drive home, no one spoke, no one even tried. When they got home, they drifted in and went right to bed. Colin's last thoughts were—I've never seen them so sad; this is all my fault, mine, and that Goddamn Tom!

***

Very early the next day, Colin awoke to a bleary-eyed Dwight walking partway into his room. Colin raised his head. Dwight cleared his throat. "Hey Col, how 'bout breakfast, and then maybe a drive in the country?"

Colin sat up. For a moment that sounded like a good idea, but then nausea, along with the memory of the day before, returned. He lay back down and pushed his face into the still warm pillow. His breath smelled like vomit, he didn't want to go anywhere, but feared if he didn't get up, his father would come back and want to talk about *it*. He didn't want to talk about *it* anymore; he just wanted *it* to go away. Finally, he forced himself to get up.

Moments later, Colin walked past his parents' room and briefly looked in. His father was nowhere to be seen. His mother was rolled up into a ball, her face pressed up against her pillow. He could hear her muffled sobs. Colin walked out the front door and let the screen door slam behind him. Dwight was already sitting in the car, his head pressed against his hands. Colin opened the passenger door and got in. Dwight quickly sat up. Neither said a word. Dwight started the motor and stared straight ahead.

***

Twenty minutes later they were seated in a booth at the pastel-colored Pancakes Plus, where they remained pale and silent. Just when Colin was beginning to wonder if his father would ever talk again, Dwight shattered their silence by quietly stating, "Colin, I'm sorry. I'm so very, very sorry."

Colin thought his father's eyes looked hollow and murky. He'd never seen them look that way before, and he wondered if his father was still inside.

"Why are *you* sorry, Dad?" he finally asked.

Dwight answered without hesitation. "I'm sorry because I trusted Father Pat, and told you to sing in his damn choir. And I'm sorry because if I were the kind of father I thought I was, you'd have come to me the moment you came home from church two days ago. And, I'm sorry because I didn't know what to say or do when I finally heard what happened." Dwight shook his head, "I didn't even raise a fuss when they wouldn't let us go in the ambulance with you." Dwight's eyes began to tear up. "But, most of all," he continued, "I'm sorry because I almost lost you." Tears began to roll down Dwight's face and onto his collar. Colin wondered if he was going to wipe them away; he didn't.

"Dad," Colin said in a barely audible voice, "don't be sorry; it wasn't your fault." Dwight leaned forward in an obvious attempt to hear anything Colin had to say. The boy continued, "It was mine." Dwight suddenly pulled back. A moment later he reached across the table, and took hold of his son's hand.

"Colin, don't say that. Don't ever say that. More importantly, don't think or feel that. This was *not* your fault." Dwight stopped for a moment as if he were gathering his thoughts. "It was Father Pat's because he hurt you, and ours because we failed to protect you. We should've known better. We should've been paying closer attention…" Dwight shook his head. Once again, his eyes reddened and he couldn't go on.

Colin didn't know what to say. Everyone kept telling him it wasn't his fault, but he knew better, he was there.

They finished breakfast, just as they started—in silence.

Driving home, Colin asked, "Dad, where's Father Pat now?"

Dwight clamped down on his jaw. Through clenched teeth he replied, "Where he can't hurt anyone."

***

Well, *that* wasn't exactly true, Jordon thought, as she reached over and picked up Pat's file once again.

17

Hostage—One who is held captive.

Pat felt the vibration of the officers' steel-toed boots hitting the floorboards at the same time as he heard them storm in. From inside his tiny room he could feel and hear everything.

Moments earlier, he'd heard the Monsignor receive the call from the police, and immediately afterward heard him call the church's lawyer. Pat knew they'd all be there momentarily, but he was sure he'd never see any of them again.

As soon as the officers stopped near his door, they ordered him to come out. Pat laughed and warned them he had a gun. They kept insisting he exit with his arms up or they would come in and get him. Pat told them if they did, he'd kill himself. They began to whisper among themselves; Pat listened.

"He's a fucking child molester. He *should* die. And if it saves the taxpayers some money on a trial, even better."

From where Pat sat, it sounded like one of the other policemen agreed, but the remainder told their fellow officer to shut the fuck up. Suddenly, there was silence, and a new, authoritative voice was heard. Pat recognized it immediately as that of Joan Bullard or, apparently, Lieutenant Bullard, as she was officially referred to in *situations* like these.

"Has someone called in the negotiating team?" she asked.

"Called, but they are *unavailable*," was the answer.

"OK, I'll handle it."

Pat knew Joan from the church. He knew her as a single mother who worked hard and slept little. Within their community she had a reputation for being a clear thinker with a kind heart. Given everything he knew about Joan Bullard, he wished she were off duty that night. He didn't want her to be involved in what was about to unfold.

"Father Pat, it's Lieutenant Bullard, Joan Bullard. We know each other from church. Are you OK?"

Lieutenant Bullard was interrupted by a voice coming from behind her. "This is Angelo Bellfetto. The church has hired me to represent you. I am advising you not to answer that question. Am I making myself clear?"

Pat smiled.

Angelo Bellfetto slowly repeated himself.

Pat didn't respond.

Undeterred, Angelo Bellfetto repeated himself a third time; this time, he carefully enunciated each word. Pat finally responded.

"Angelo, I know who you are and who you're representing. Now stop talking and listen. I'm not an idiot; I'm an educated priest who grew up in Brooklyn. I understand my rights. Beyond that, I know what everyone's job out there is. You say you are representing me, but you're really representing the church. You've been hired by *them* to protect *their* interests. Don't worry, I'll take your so-called representation, but do not, under any circumstances, underestimate me. Now, Angelo, stop talking and step aside. I want to talk to Lieutenant Bullard."

"Fine," Angelo offered, "but I want you to sign a waiver, saying you're speaking to law enforcement against my advice."

A moment later, Joan Bullard told him she was sliding Bellfetto's waiver under the door. Pat immediately slid it back.

"Joan, please tell Mr. Bellfetto I'm not signing anything, but neither will I be around to sue him, or anyone else. Joan, you've done your job, you've given me my opportunity to speak to my so-called counsel. Now, please order him to back off."

***

Joan Bullard watched as Bellfetto rolled his eyes, stepped away, and immediately began dictating into his Dictaphone. As Bellfetto retreated, Joan briefly turned inward in order to muffle the click as she turned on her tape recorder. Ever cognizant of the alleged loaded weapon, she advanced cautiously. "So, Father Pat, how're you doing?"

"I've been better. Look, Joan, I'm sorry you were called out on this. I'd rather you were home with Jess."

Joan clenched her teeth as her eyes narrowed. Even though she was certain he'd never been alone with Jess, the mere fact that he knew her child's name upset her. Still, she responded in a tempered voice, "Thanks, Father, but we all have our jobs to do, and I'm just trying to do mine."

"Joan, please call me Pat. I don't feel much like a priest right now."

"OK, Pat. Now tell me, do you need anything: food, water, a priest?"

"I'll decline the latter, but I'd sure like the water turned back on. They turned off the plumbing a little while ago in an effort to, shall we say, coax me out of here."

"OK, I'll see what I can do. Don't go anywhere, and I do mean anywhere." Joan motioned to the custodian to turn the water back on. She then turned her attention back to her suspect. She had to get him out of that room, preferably alive, but under no circumstances was he going to take anyone else with him, not on her watch.

She was told that in his room there was only a bed, a chair, a table, and a sink. She could surmise by the sounds she heard that he seemed to be sitting on his chair, just behind the locked door.

As she spoke with him, she stood as close to his door as she dared, while most of the police officers involved stood a safe and respectful distance away. "OK, Pat, I'm all ears. Now, what can I do for you?"

"That's easy. Make everybody go away, and make me different."

"Why? What have you done that makes you want to be different?"

"Now, don't you go underestimating me, too, Joan. I know what you're doing. Remember, I'm in the business of hearing confessions, not giving them. Anyway, like I said, I'm not planning on sticking around for my trial."

Joan decided to take another approach.

"Pat, if you do kill yourself, won't you go to Hell?"

Pat laughed. "Haven't you noticed? I'm already there."

"Why do you think you're in Hell?"

"I'm in Hell because I have impure *thoughts*."

He's no fool, Joan thought, still, I've got to push it. If I do manage to get him out of the room, any statement he makes now could be admissible in court later. "Why, Pat?" she asked. "Why do you have impure thoughts?"

"Do you want the truth, or the answer you'd like to record?"

Joan looked down at her tape recorder and realized she had underestimated him. "The truth," she answered.

"The truth is, only society thinks my thoughts are impure. In truth, I love children and children love me."

"But, Pat, you're a very intelligent man. You must know the children only love you until you hurt them. Now, if you come out of the room peacefully, you can get some help and stop hurting children and then..."

"I've never hurt a single child in my life!" Pat exclaimed with great aplomb.

"But can't you see that you have?" Joan decided to agitate him momentarily, hoping it would unnerve him. "Pat I *know* you hurt Colin."

"I repeat, and for the last time," Pat said, with mounting anger in his voice, "I have never hurt a single child in my life!"

Joan was now sure Pat was not going to admit he'd done anything wrong, or acknowledge he'd ever hurt a child. He was, she concluded, in complete denial.

She then tried to remember some of the things she'd learned in her training about this type of child molester. She hoped it would help her figure out what to do next. First and foremost, she recalled, they do not view their own actions as hurting children. In fact, if one gave them a police report that discussed the circumstances of their own cases, blacked out their names, and slightly changed events, they'd not only be incapable of recognizing the perpetrators as themselves, but they'd also condemn the *unknown perpetrator* for committing violent crimes against children. No doubt about it, she silently resolved, Pat is this type of child molester, and I'm going to have to try another tactic. "Pat, I don't want to lose you."

"Joan, I'm of no significance."

"That's not true."

"Joan, please don't patronize me. Stop talking, I've heard enough. I now need time to think and maybe time to pray."

"Pat, you know as well as I do that I can't be silent. My job is to talk you out of there, and on a personal level, that's what I want more than anything."

"On a personal level," Pat responded, "I don't think you really care, although thank you for saying so. As far as your silence is concerned, I'm not asking you for it, I'm demanding it. If you continue to talk, I'll shoot."

"Pat, I know you *can* shoot. I'm just asking you not to. You still have so much to offer, and I want to get you some help—"

"Joan, stop!" Pat cut her off. "I'm done. Here are my rosary beads. Please give them to Jess." The beads appeared from under the door, but Joan didn't stoop to pick them up. Instead, she listened carefully as Pat began to sing.

"Amazing Grace, how sweet the sound..."

Pat began to sing in a voice that was eerie, in both its beauty and its pain. As he did so, she pictured him standing in front of the boys' choir, singing that same song on Sundays past. On those mornings her eyes would often be drawn to him, as he sang each note with great clarity and expression. When he sang, "Was blind, but now I see," in the last verse, he always closed his eyes. Joan knew what she had to do. She walked away from the door and met briefly with the congregated SWAT team. As she whispered, they nodded affirmatively.

"One last thing," she said, "if anyone uses poor judgment and unnecessarily injures Father Pat, I'll personally see to it that you're transferred out of SWAT." As soon as she made the blatant threat, she felt ridiculous. She knew they were the best, and could be counted on for their skill and judgment.

As they left, Joan prayed for their safety, and wished she could go with them. After years of being in command, it was still harder for her to order others into harm's way than it was to step into harm's way herself. She quickly returned to her spot near his doorway and listened carefully as Father Pat continued singing.

***

Joe McGrew was the well-respected SWAT Team Leader. He kept his eyes riveted on Lieutenant Bullard, while his team stood ready and focused on him. Everyone listened carefully while the priest continued singing Amazing Grace...

"I once was lost, but now I'm found ... w-a-a-s-s blind..."

***

Pat never even heard them bust in. Caught up in the words of his own song, his eyes closed, he was knocked off his feet and onto the ground. He didn't even realize the SWAT team had entered until after he found himself lying face down on the floor, with his loaded gun kicked several feet away.

As Lieutenant Bullard entered the room, he was being stood up and turned over to two waiting patrol officers, while Sergeant McGrew was carefully seizing the gun.

***

Once Joan saw everyone was safe, she gathered the SWAT team, apologized for her unnecessary admonishment, and thanked them for a job well done. Next she walked over to a waiting patrol car and saw Father Pat sitting in the back. He looked exhausted and forlorn.

"Why, Joan?" he asked.

"Because it was the right thing to do." She could have left it at that, but, for her officers' sakes, she went on. "Look, Pat, I don't know if you're guilty or innocent, but I owe it to you, Colin, his family, and our community, to see to it that you are treated fairly, and this case is thoroughly investigated. Letting you kill yourself would simply not have been fair or just."

"Joan, you have a perverted sense of justice," Pat responded.

"Maybe so," she replied. "Officers, he's all yours, I'm sure he'll be no problem now. Pat, I believe your lawyer will follow you to the police department; if you want to see him, just ask."

Joan then turned toward the church; she wanted to return in order to supervise the crime scene investigation.

As she walked away no one would have guessed she ached inside for all concerned, Colin, his parents, the parishioners, and even Father Pat. Over time she'd become adept at hiding her feelings, but she'd never become immune to them, nor did she want to. She firmly believed the moment law enforcement officers stopped caring, they should get the hell out of the business.

Hours later, she was the last to leave. Once she was alone in her car, she finally allowed her thoughts to turn to Jess. All objectivity now lost, she took a deep breath, let herself feel both pain and relief, and started her car for home.

***

Pat was taken to county jail and booked without incident. During the process he kept his eyes closed whenever he could, and distracted himself by singing songs he used to share with his boys. Once in his cell he refused to talk to either his lawyer or the police. Instead, he just sat, sang, rocked, and masterminded his next move.

***

Jordon closed Pat's file and returned to Sophia's file and videotape.

18

Best Interest of the Child—The legal standard used by Courts in child custody situations; a standard which requires Courts to make the good of the child their primary consideration.

The day after Sophia went to the SART house, Mrs. Fairway, from the District Attorney's Victim/Witness Office, called and spoke with Margarita. During their conversation, Mrs. Fairway explained both the criminal justice system process and the various free services that were now available to Sophia, the most important of which being counseling. Before they hung up, Mrs. Fairway emphasized to Margarita that the assigned DDA was deeply concerned about Sophia's welfare and felt if Margarita didn't take her to see a counselor, she wouldn't be acting in Sophia's best interest. Margarita felt as if she'd just been threatened. She already resented having Marcos taken away from her and didn't want to lose Sophia as well.

"Which counselor," she abruptly asked, "does the DDA think my Sophia should see?"

"I don't think she feels strongly about that, but I think Craig Petner's the best."

As soon as they hung up Margarita called Petner's office and made an appointment.

***

During her third videotaped session, Craig and Sophia sat in a pillow-lined playroom. While they busily put together a house of Lincoln logs, he asked her how things were at home.

"Mama still cries a lot," Sophia offered, as she forcefully chewed on her nails.

"How do you feel about that?" he asked.

"I hate it, and I ask her not to, but she cries anyway."

"Why do you think she's crying?"

"I don't know."

"But why do *you* think she's crying?"

"I think she's crying because she misses Marcos."

"Do you miss Marcos?"

Sophia looked down. "Sometimes." When she looked back up, she appeared guilty.

"Do you know where he is?" Craig asked.

"Mama said the policeman put him in jail."

"Do you know what jail is?"

"Yeah, it's a place where bad people go."

"So, how do you feel about his going to jail?"

"I-don't-know," Sophia shrugged.

"Do you know *why* he's in jail?"

"Mama says it's 'cause of what happened wit' me."

"And how do you feel about that?"

"I-don't-know." Sophia returned to chewing on her nails, only now she added wiggling in her chair. "Can we play at your sand table?" she asked.

"Sure… you know, Sophia, you can always tell me how you feel, even if it means telling me you don't want to tell me how you feel. OK?"

"OK."

"I just want you to know you can tell me *anything*, and you can ask me *anything*. In turn, I will always tell you the truth, as best I can. OK?"

Sophia bit her lower lip, looked down, and then around the entire room. When her eyes returned to Craig's, she asked, "Is it my fault Marcos is in jail?"

"No," Craig said shaking his head emphatically, "it's Marcos' fault Marcos is in jail."

"Is he ever coming out?"

"Yes, I think so."

"When?"

"I don't know."

"When he comes out, will he come back and live with me and Mama?" Her eyes widened.

"No, probably not."

"Where will he live?"

"I don't know, but it will be some place safe."

Sophia dropped her gaze again. When she looked back up, her eyes were red and full of pain.

"Will he ever come back into my bed and hurt me?"

"No, we won't let that happen ever again."

"OK," she said, nodding slowly, as if she were taking it all in. The room became silent and still. Moments later, her little chest rose and gently fell. As she exhaled, she again asked, "Now, can we go play at the sand table?"

***

When Sophia left Craig's office that afternoon, he thought she looked a little less worried, which made him feel slightly more optimistic.

***

During Sophia's sixth session they hardly spoke at all. Sophia wanted to play with the puppets and dolls. Craig watched in amazement, as she acted out scenarios that no 6-year-old child should have knowledge of. But he was encouraged by the fact that, more often than not, she brought in the little girl doll she'd named Sophie to save the day.

That afternoon he wrote in his notes, "Clearly, she's been traumatized, yet she is extremely intelligent and resilient. With sustained therapy she just might grow up to be a remarkable young woman."

***

Jordon was amazed at Craig's insight. As she returned to Colin's file she thought, if only Colin could have had Sophia's care and treatment.

19

January 25, 1981
COLIN

Subpoena—A command to appear in court to give testimony upon a certain matter.

Humiliated, Colin returned to school the Monday following the assault. He was certain everyone at school knew all about what he and Father Pat had done, and he was sure they all thought he was a faggot. One step at a time, he thought, as the days slowly passed and his sense of isolation grew.

***

Even months after the incident, Colin still felt spending time with anyone seemed uncomfortable, and at times, unbearable. In the end he decided it would just be easier to spend most of his time alone. Over the first few months, the only friend he saw at all was Tom, and he did so just to placate his worried parents. After Tom broke his promise by calling the police, Colin no longer wanted any part of their friendship.

Inside his home things were just as bad. No one ever mentioned either the assault or the conversation he and his father had at Pancakes Plus. It seemed to Colin as if he and his parents had chosen to say nothing, rather than risk upsetting each other.

The sounds and smells of the house had also changed. The exciting noises of a busy household had been replaced by sustained silence. Homegrown flowers were usurped by the synthetic fragrance of air fresheners. Although from the outside everything appeared the same, inside their home felt dry and barren. Yet its youngest inhabitant was drowning.

Colin's nightmares, which had begun soon after the assault, were getting worse, but he never told anyone anything about them. He often wondered what had happened to Father Pat, but he didn't know whom he could safely ask. He heard from kids at school that Father Pat had tried to kill himself and that Jess' mom had saved him. He wondered why she'd done that, and decided it was probably because she thought it was all Colin's fault, too. His parents never talked to him about that, and neither did Jess's mom. At times, it seemed to him that everyone just forgot about the incident, that is, everyone but him.

On June 1, 1981 Colin brought the mail into the house and found an envelope addressed to him. He wondered what it was, and thought it looked important. He hoped he'd won something; he opened it.

He read it several times, and finally concluded he was being ordered to go to the trial of Patrick MacMillan or they'd arrest *him*. The top of the document was labeled *Subpoena*. He didn't know what any of it really meant, but he feared he'd to have see Father Pat. Terrifying images started to take shape. Moments later, Colin's knees gave way and suddenly, his stomach hurt. He gathered himself into a ball and began to sweat.

***

An hour later, when Dwight entered their front door, he found his son still in this condition.

***

Poor Colin and his family, thought Jordon. At that point they were all lost and getting no outside help. Sophia, on the other hand, was receiving lots of outside help, but had lost her family. Jordon returned to Sophia's file.

20

Summer 1977
SOPHIA & CRAIG

Disclosure—To bring in to view by uncovering.

Over the next several months, through her counseling sessions with Craig, Sophia continued to improve; Margarita however remained morose. Although by then Margarita had stopped her incessant crying, she still wept profusely whenever Sophia referred to Marcos. Consequently Sophia stopped mentioning him at all, and the distance between mother and daughter grew.

The only person Sophia felt she could talk to about Marcos was Craig. She felt it was easy to tell Craig she was mad at Marcos, but not as easy to tell him that, at times, she actually missed him. She didn't miss his *bad touches*, as she'd learned to call them, she just missed Marcos.

On the August 18, 1977 video, it appeared she finally found the courage to bring it up.

"Craig," she said slowly, "sometimes I miss Marcos." She never took her eyes off Craig's for a moment.

Craig didn't flinch. He gently nodded. "Well, that's OK."

"But I think that's bad."

"Why?"

"Because everyone else hates him. They all think he's bad."

"Well, I don't know how other people feel, but, even if they do feel that way, you can still miss him. It's the way *you* feel, and so it's OK." Craig paused to make sure Sophia understood. She appeared to be listening intently, so he continued, "Sophia, what Marcos did to you was bad, but that doesn't mean Marcos is bad."

***

Sophia wasn't sure she understood, but she was glad to hear that Craig didn't think Marcos was bad. Sophia still thought about Marcos a lot; sometimes, she even dreamed about him.

At times the dreams scared her, while at other times they comforted her. Once in a while, she felt sad when she woke up and he wasn't home. Often, Craig asked her to tell him about the dreams. Sophia would try, but she couldn't always find the right words. Craig would then tell her, "Just draw it."

When she finished her drawings, Craig would ask her to tell him about the drawings and she did.

***

On the August 25, 1977 video, Sophia is seen pausing in front of Craig's easel. Having just painted a picture of one of her dreams, she asked, "Craig, does Marcos hate me?"

"No, I don't think so." Craig shook his head.

"Then why did he hurt me?"

Craig paused as if he were searching for an answer. "I don't *know,*" he finally said, "but I can *guess.* Do you want me to guess?"

"Yes, guess," Sophia said, putting her paintbrush down.

"OK then, my guess would be that it was because when he was a little boy, somebody hurt him, and nobody helped him the way I'm trying to help you."

"Oh," she said, looking sad and temporarily abandoning her drawing all together. "I wish I knew him when he was a little boy; I would've helped him."

"I'm sure you would have," Craig said, smiling.

"Craig," Sophia said, clearly interrupting his thoughts, "do you think he's mad at me?"

"Again, I don't know, because I've never talked to Marcos. But, why do *you* think he *might* be mad at you?"

"Because I'm bad," Sophia declared, sitting down and then looking down.

"Sophia, why do you think you're bad?"

Craig's notes indicated he tried not to look as shocked as he felt.

"Because I begged him to come into my bed," she said in a barely audible voice.

Craig let out a deep sigh and looked directly into Sophia's now reddening eyes.

"Sophia, listen to me. This is *really* important. When Marcos hurt you, you were little and he was big. But, you were *both* still kids. Little kids ask big kids to do all kinds of things. The difference between big kids and little kids is that big kids are supposed to know right from wrong and little kids are supposed to learn. You didn't know any better and Marcos should have.

Anyway, what you wanted Marcos to do was to get into bed with you and hold you. You didn't want him to hurt you. It's Marcos' fault he hurt you, not yours."

Sophia sat quietly. Craig later wrote he thought she was working very hard at trying to understand what he'd just said. Suddenly her eyelashes began to flutter, and tears rolled down her crimson cheeks. Craig sat still. More than anything, he wanted to take her in his arms and comfort her, but he held back. He knew he shouldn't touch her until she was ready.

Once again, she interrupted his thoughts. In a small, hopeful voice, she asked, "So, I'm not bad either?"

"No, you are not bad, Sophia. Matter of fact, I think you're wonderful," Craig said with a warm loving smile.

"I think you're wonderful too." Sophia then wiped away her tears, stood up from her seat, stepped toward Craig, and hugged him.

***

Later Craig told Jordon, in spite of all his professional training, his heart swelled and he was moved to tears.

Jordon decided now was a good time to return to Marcos' file. When she last put it down, he'd just been arrested and taken to jail. Picking up his "jail jacket" she read what had been written about him. She then considered those entries, as well as her own memories, and subsequent conversations with those involved...

21

Summer 1977
MARCOS

California Evidence Code Section 1360—Statements made to someone else, by a child under the age of 12 describing an act of abuse, can be admitted into evidence as an exception to the hearsay rule.

Marcos sat opposite his mother, watching her tears and mucus meet on the telephone's receiver. In spite of his telling her not to, she still came to visit every Sunday. He loathed those visits, because of how she looked, and what she said. Over and over again, she kept asking, "Por que, Marcos? Por que?"

Does she really think I know *why* any of this happened, he wondered. All I really know is that it wasn't my fault. She made me baby-sit, and Sophia begged me to come into her bed.

***

During the week, Marcos read, watched TV, did push-ups, and played cards. Time went by very slowly. The sole event that broke up his now monotonous life was that every few weeks he went to court. Although he appreciated getting out of jail, he dreaded those trips. He hated seeing the faces of people who knew what he'd been accused of.

Only one person treated him with kindness and respect, and that was his lawyer, Michael Carron. Although Michael was a very smart man, he told Marcos he wasn't a miracle worker, and Marcos would likely be convicted and sentenced to six years in prison.

***

Six years seemed like an unbelievably long time to Marcos, but when he listened to the prosecutor's arguments, he began to accept her inevitable victory.

When Marcos first saw the prosecutor, Jordon Danner, he thought she seemed very pleasant, someone whom everyone liked; everyone that is, except his lawyer, who'd warned him that Jordon was a highly manipulative actress. "And a dangerous one at that," Carron added, "because she wins most of her cases." What Marcos noticed about Jordon was that she seemed as fervent about convicting him as she was about taking care of Sophia. This confused him, because he wanted to take care of Sophia too, but he didn't think he should go to prison for her.

***

As the day of trial approached, Michael told Marcos that the first day would be full of pretrial motions. The motion he was most concerned about was the one that would admit Sophia's *hearsay* statements into evidence. Marcos wasn't sure why this was a problem until he heard Michael's explanation.

"You see, the deputy DA doesn't want your sister to come to court. Instead, she wants to show the videotape that was made of Sophia's interview at The SART house."

"So, what's wrong with that?" Marcos asked. He didn't want Sophia to come to court either; he thought her testimony would only hurt his case.

"I can't cross-examine a videotape."

"So, why is cross-examining her such a big deal?" Marcos asked.

"Because that's the only way I can get the jury to believe she's lying about what happened."

Marcos didn't respond. He knew Sophia wouldn't lie, but he also understood that convincing the jury otherwise was his only chance.

***

Jordon recalled her own state of mind during that time. She was convinced Sophia should not have to testify in person. She didn't believe it was reasonable to expect her to face her half-brother, and tell a courtroom full of strangers what he did to her. But, in order to avoid that, she first had to convince the judge that the law was on her side.

Jordon read the transcript, with her original argument:

"Judge, Sophia has already been traumatized by all of this. Testifying would only re-traumatize her. If we didn't have the videotape of her original interview, we wouldn't have a choice. But, we have the tape, and you have a choice."

In the end, she convinced the judge, and the videotape was played for the jury. Sophia never had to face Marcos that day; instead, she went to school and then on to one of Craig's counseling sessions.

Jordon sat back, still proud she'd won that one.

***

On some level, Marcos was also pleased by the judge's ruling. He felt even more certain of that, after seeing his mother testify.

At first, Margarita tried to answer each lawyer's questions evasively, obviously trying to protect both Sophia and Marcos. The result was she appeared untrustworthy and deceitful. Consequently, she incurred everyone's wrath, and left Marcos feeling abandoned once again.

After each side called a handful of other peripheral witnesses, the trial finally ended, and a guilty verdict came within 2 hours.

Marcos wasn't surprised. Although he thought his attorney put up a good fight, it was clear even to him, the evidence against him was, as the prosecutor argued, overwhelming.

***

Four weeks later Marcos was returned to court.

"Having read the Probation and Sentencing Report," Judge Ortega announced, "I am now ready to proceed to sentencing. Mr. Estrada, what you've done defies belief and common decency. You used a little girl who loved and trusted you for your own sexual gratification. And you did so without any regard, whatsoever, for how it would affect her and your mother. For that alone, I should sentence you to the maximum term of eight years in the state prison."

Margarita gasped. The Bailiff, Roberto Duarte, gave her a look of admonishment. The judge went on.

"But, because you are so young, and, according to the probation report, have been abused yourself, and have no prior record, I won't do that. However, I also won't place you on probation as your lawyer requested."

Michael Carron showed no expression, but Marcos knew he was disappointed. The judge continued.

"I will sentence you to state prison, but I will only sentence you to three years, the lowest prison term possible under the law."

Marcos dropped his shoulders and head. The courtroom was momentarily silent, except for the sound of Margarita's sobs.

"You are now at a junction in your life," Judge Ortega continued. "You are both young enough to change and young enough to become a real threat to society for many years to come. By sentencing you to only three years, I'm counting on your realizing that you've committed a grievous violation of our laws and giving you an opportunity to turn your life around."

Judge Ortega paused in an obvious attempt to make eye contact with Marcos, but Marcos kept his head down and mumbled. In response, Ortega added, "Mr. Estrada, one last thing. The sooner you take responsibility for your heinous actions, the better off you'll be. That's all, and good luck, young man. Court is adjourned."

Judge Ortega left the bench.

The judge doesn't get it either, Marcos thought. None of this was my fault. It's just that everything bad always happens to me. At least I only got three years, and they never brought Sophia or the neighbor girl in to testify.

***

Before Marcos was led away by the bailiff, his lawyer briefly patted him on the shoulder and said he hoped he'd get needed treatment while in prison.

Once his client was gone, Michael turned to Jordon and said, "And they call this a criminal *justice* system, but we both *know* the punishment he's likely to receive in prison will be anything but just."

Jordon said nothing in response; she just nodded. Soon they both snapped their briefcases closed, left the courtroom, and silently separated.

***

Jordon could now picture herself walking down the echoing hallway that morning, high heels clicking, thinking she didn't feel much like a winner, and hoping the three-year prison sentence would be Marcos' only punishment.

Still, Jordon thought, now closing his file, as bad as everyone's speculation of what prison life would be like for Marcos, no one could have imagined the horror of his actual experience. But I can't go there yet. Instead, she reached out and picked up Colin's file.

When she last read about Colin, he was lying on his hallway floor, having buckled after reading his subpoena. His father, Dwight, had just walked in.

22

June 1, 1981
The Dane County District Attorney's Office

*Deputy District Attorney—The name of the government employee
who is hired by the District Attorney to conduct criminal
prosecutions on behalf of The People.*

Dwight rushed over to Colin and helped him up. On the ground
next to him, he saw a document labeled *Subpoena*. Heartsick,
Dwight left it there, walked Colin over to their couch, and sat
down next to him.

Colin rolled up into a ball, but put his head on his father's lap.
Dwight began stroking Colin's forehead and hair, as Colin began
to mumble. He was saying something about being arrested if he
didn't go. Dwight told him not to worry, and placed his perspiring
hand over Colin's closed eyes. His son's breathing began to ease.

Once Dwight was certain Colin was asleep, he placed a couch
pillow under his head, got up, and took a closer look at the
apparent source of the boy's agony.

What he saw was the torn envelope from the Dane County
District Attorney's Office, and the subpoena that had once been
inside. He retrieved it all. Once he returned to the couch, he placed
Colin's head back on his lap. After carefully reading the
documents, Dwight rubbed his own forehead and helplessly
wondered—when will this nightmare end?

***

On June 12, 1981 Dwight and Cathy dutifully brought Colin to
court. The subpoena ordered them to arrive at the courthouse by
9:00 a.m. They arrived exactly on time, but no one was there to
meet them. Not knowing what to do, they sat on a wooden bench
outside the courtroom door.

As the morning progressed, their wooden bench felt harder and
the airless hallway got stuffier. Whenever anyone walked by or
opened a door, the Taylor family all simultaneously looked up, but
no one ever looked back.

***

Colin looked down at his father's watch. It was after 1:00, but still, no one had come to speak with them.

Just before 1:30 Colin saw someone quickly coming toward them. He heard the man speaking rapidly, but he couldn't understand all of his words. Moments later, Colin understood he was the Deputy District Attorney in charge of the case, but he didn't get his name. All Colin heard was, "Son, come with me."

He and his parents rose, but, when they got to the courtroom door, the Deputy DA told his parents that, as potential witnesses, they'd have to wait outside. Colin was shocked; he never imagined he'd have to go through this alone. Still, no one argued with the Deputy DA, no one said a word. His mother gave him a hug and his father rubbed his head. Obviously overcome by powerlessness, neither one of them looked at him; they just turned away and returned to the wood bench.

Stunned, Colin followed the Deputy DA into the courtroom. As soon as he walked in, Colin took a step back. He desperately wanted to return to his mother's arms, but the Deputy DA told him, "Stay close and follow me."

Colin continued to walk toward the front of the courtroom, but when they reached the swinging wooden gate separating audience from participants, he froze. To his immediate left was Father Pat.

It was the first time he'd seen him since the night of the assault. Colin was stunned at Father Pat's frightful appearance; he'd become very skinny and extremely pale. Colin tried to calm himself down by turning away, but that didn't work. The courtroom looked and smelled like an old haunted house, replete with high ceilings, long heavy burgundy curtains, and dark wooden furniture. Suddenly the uniformed man, whose badge said *Bailiff*, told him to *sit* in the witness stand. Colin looked for a stand, but saw only a chair. The Bailiff then pointed to that chair, and Colin headed toward it.

When he climbed in, the chair seemed too big, and the attached microphone too high. He didn't fit. He felt like an 11-year-old trying to play basketball with the University team. He looked over to his right. The nearest person to him was the judge, who, with his long black robe and angular nose, looked like the Grim Reaper.

As soon as Colin sat down, but before he took his first breath, someone else, in a bold echoing voice, asked him to stand up and swear on the Bible. Colin hesitated, which seemed to annoy everyone. Finally, the judge asked him why he wouldn't swear to tell the truth. Colin wouldn't answer, he knew he'd be truthful, but he didn't want to swear on the Bible in front of Father Pat.

"Oh, great," grumbled the prosecutor.

The judge turned back to Colin. "Son, we have to know if you're going to tell the truth."

"OK," Colin quietly replied.

"Well, will you tell the truth?"

"Yes."

"Do you promise?"

"Yes."

"OK, Mr. Radner, that should do, you may inquire."

The Deputy DA began, "Colin, how old are you?"

At first the questions were easy, and Colin felt somewhat comfortable answering them.

"What school do you go to?"

"Randall School," Colin answered.

"What grade are you in?"

"Sixth."

Colin was starting to feel more confident, but the Deputy DA's next question confounded him.

"Now, please tell the jury, in your own words, exactly what Father Pat did to you during the early evening hours of January 22,1981."

Colin couldn't believe it. He'd never told anyone *exactly* what Father Pat did to him. How could this man expect him to tell all that now, especially in front of all these strangers sitting in the courtroom, staring at him? He couldn't. Colin said nothing; instead, he just stared at the Deputy DA, as the now familiar taste of nausea started filling his mouth.

Meanwhile, Mr. Radner seemed oblivious to Colin's pain and discomfort. He just kept asking him the same question in different ways, but Colin wouldn't answer. He was afraid that if he opened his mouth he'd throw up.

Finally, the judge said they should take a break so the prosecutor could talk to Colin. He took him to the back of the courtroom.

"You have to tell the jury what Father Pat did to you. If you don't, Father Pat will get out of jail, and *that* would be really bad."

Colin didn't care and he didn't respond. Instead he thought, there's no way I'm telling all those eyes in there what really happened.

But then, Mr. Radner told him something that quickly changed his mind. "If you don't tell the jury today, you'll have to come back tomorrow and tomorrow and tomorrow, until you do tell them. Look," Mr. Radner said, his voice finally softening, "I don't mean to be hard on you, but we *can't* let this guy get away with doing what he did to you. Now can we?"

Colin was confused. As far as he was concerned, Father Pat had already gotten away with—doing what he did to him. But, Colin hated the thought of coming back to court, so he reluctantly promised to return to the witness stand and try again.

Once reseated, Colin stared at the back of the courtroom and told what Father Pat had done. At times, through the corner of his eye, he saw the priest shake his head in disagreement.

Finally, when Colin completed stating what had happened, he got up to leave, but the judge told him he had to sit back down.

"Colin, please sit. The defendant's lawyer, Ms. Alison, probably has some questions for you."

Ms. Alison's questioning took a very long time. Colin hated her questions, and felt many were the same ones as Mr. Radner had already asked. Colin didn't understand why he had to answer the same questions twice, or why some of her questions already had the wrong answers in them.

"This didn't really happen with Father Pat; it was actually something you did with your friend Tom when you played hooky that day, wasn't it?" Ms. Alison asked.

Colin had no idea how to answer that kind of question. Therefore, he just said, "No," but by the way she asked the questions, and how he answered them, Colin thought everyone believed her and not him. Colin also thought she seemed so sure about her questions, while he felt so insecure about his answers. The only thing Colin was certain of was that everything was coming out wrong.

Toward the end of the cross-examination Colin became so tired he couldn't keep his head up any longer. Finally he laid it down on his forearms atop the railing in front of him. Soon he began to wonder: Why does she keep asking me questions like I'm lying? That night with Father Pat was the worst thing, the most embarrassing thing that's ever happened to me. Why would I make something like *that* up? I never even wanted anyone to find out, and, if it weren't for Tom, no one would've...

Colin became distracted, thinking about Tom for a moment. When he looked back at the defense attorney, she was rolling her eyes at the jury. At that point, the judge finally told Colin he could leave. For the one-hundredth time Colin wished he'd never told Tom what had happened. Even dying, he concluded, would've been easier than coming to court.

As he began to stand up, he felt queasy. He took a deep breath and stood still. Using all his remaining strength, he got down from the witness stand and walked past Father Pat. By the time he reached the courtroom door, he was sure everyone thought he was a liar, and that it was all his fault.

Once on the other side of the heavy courtroom door, his knees gave way, and he let himself slide down to the floor. This time he only remained helpless on the floor for a moment, because his parents were right there to help him up.

The three of them then drifted out to their car, and drove home in near silence.

***

As Colin lay in bed that night, he started to relive the day, and the events that had brought him to court. Soon, he realized he was having another nightmare; but he wasn't sure if he was still awake.

23

June 12, 1981
DWIGHT & COLIN

Parentum est liberos alere etiam nothos—It is the duty of parents to support their children.

Upstairs in their bedroom, Dwight kept moving and shifting his pillow. He couldn't stop imagining how brutal Colin's time in court must have been. He'd almost lost Colin once, and after seeing what he'd looked like when he came out of the courtroom today, he feared another suicide attempt might be imminent. He had to do *something*. He got up out of bed and began to pace.

By 1:00 a.m. he had a plan, and went back to bed. "Cathy, are you awake?" He knew she probably was, although they hadn't spoken at all since he'd turned out the light.

"Yes," she asked without delay, "what is it?"

"I'm worried about Colin—"

"I know," she interrupted, and then rolled over onto her back. Now they both gazed up at the ceiling. A moment later Dwight took a deep breath and told her he'd decided to call in to work in the morning and take Colin on vacation. "Maybe I'll bring him to some of the National Parks." He waited a moment for Cathy to react, but she didn't. He continued, "I feel like I have to do this right away. With school out for the summer... I'm really worried about what he might do—"

"But Dwight," Cathy interrupted, "you don't have much vacation time left on the books."

"Then I'll take time without pay," he said, somewhat defensively. "Cathy," he continued in a softer voice, "we both know that what we're talking about here is a matter of life and ..." He didn't even want to say the word.

Cathy abruptly turned away and pulled the blankets tightly up to her neck. Moments later she started to cry. He reached over and began to rub her back.

"I'm just so scared," she said. "I've never been so scared in my whole life... I just want my baby back."

"That's what I want, too," Dwight tried to assure her. "That's what this plan of mine is all about." Dwight knew he was confused about many things, but at least about this, he was sure.

After awhile, Cathy offered, "I understand and of course, if you think it will help, take him."

"Cathy..." It was hard for Dwight to admit, even to himself, what he knew he had to say next. He was glad the room was dark. "I feel like a failure."

***

Cathy didn't argue with him; she knew precisely how he felt. Not a day went by when she didn't ask herself, what kind of mother lets her son be molested, and, even worse, didn't raise him to believe he could come to her if something like that happened?

Cathy wanted to say something to comfort Dwight, but couldn't. She was too paralyzed by her own guilt and self-loathing. Finally, she found the strength to take his hand.

***

Dwight held on tightly to Cathy's hand. In the stillness that followed, he became more confident of his plan. He and Colin had to get away. "You know," he said, once again shattering their silence, "before Colin was born, the only pain I ever truly felt was my own—"

Cathy finished his sentence. "And even though what happened to Colin months ago and in court today didn't happen to you, you've never been in as much pain as you are right now."

He laced his fingers through hers in order to tighten their grip. Still, he knew they were both incapable of being consoled. Their only child had been deeply hurt as a direct result of their negligence and blind faith.

Throughout the night they held on to each other, but still they drifted apart.

***

When Dwight woke up he immediately looked in on Colin. After assuring himself Colin was still breathing, he called his boss, Alan.

"...Bottom line, Alan, I'm going to take some time off, starting this morning."

"Now Dwight," Alan responded, "I understand how you feel. But, don't you think it would be better if you just sued the church? Then, with that extra money, you could afford to send Colin away. And, you could send him to a place where you know he'd be safe and get the right kind of help." The thought of either being away from Colin, or giving someone else the responsibility of helping him, mixed with the preposterous notion of bringing him back to court for any lawsuit, was inconceivable to Dwight.

"No, Alan, I don't think that's a *better* idea. Now, I'd like to use my vacation time, but if that won't work or there isn't enough, I'll take a leave of absence without pay. If that won't work, I'll just quit!"

"Dwight, hang on a second." Alan jumped in, "I didn't say it wouldn't work; I'll make it work. I was just telling you what I would do in your position."

"Alan, with all due respect, you have no idea what you'd do in my position and I hope you never find out."

Alan was rendered silent; seconds later he offered, "You're right, I don't know what I'd do, and I pray I never have to find out."

Dwight cringed at the thought of someone praying.

"Listen Dwight, I'm sorry. No question about it, the insurance industry can do without you for a little while. I'll have someone from Personnel figure this out and they'll be in touch. Meanwhile you just concentrate on taking good care of your family."

Moments later, when he finally hung up the phone, Dwight still didn't know how his boss really felt about his taking the time off, nor did he care. Instead he walked back into Colin's room, woke him and smiled. "Hey Col, we're going on vacation!"

"OK Dad," Colin said. Then he rolled over to face the wall.

"No Son, don't go back to sleep, we're leaving this morning. You need to get up now and pack."

"OK Dad," he softly responded.

Half an hour later Dwight reentered Colin's room. When he walked in he saw Colin's clothes scattered and Colin lying on the floor with his face burrowed in a pile of freshly laundered T-shirts.

Dwight panicked. He dropped down next to him to make sure he was still breathing. When he realized Colin was only asleep, he woke him a second time.

"Sorry Dad, I don't, I don't, I don't know, I don't know what to take. I don't know how much to take. I don't even know where we're going."

"That's OK Pal, Mom will help you pack and we're going to visit some National Parks."

Colin nodded and put his head back down on the T-shirts. Just then Cathy came in, helped him up, kissed him, and sent him on his way to the bathroom. While Colin showered, she packed everything she thought he might need, as Dwight loaded up the car with everything he thought they might want.

In the end, most of the room in the car was taken up by the food Cathy had gathered and prepared during her sleepless early morning hours.

***

Just before leaving, Dwight invited Cathy to come along. Cathy turned down his belated, but well-meaning, invitation. She told him she had too many things to do at home. She knew this was their journey and some day, under different circumstances, Colin might need her and if he did, she'd be right there for him.

Cathy stepped outside and saw Colin leaning up against their car door. She walked over to him, took him in her arms, and hugged him as tightly as she dared. When she finally released him, she brushed her hand against his still soft face and a memory emerged…

She recalled the first time she'd ever touched his cheek; it was just moments after his birth.

Before Dwight got into their car, Cathy embraced her husband and whispered, "Call me as often as you can, and let me know you're both OK. You know I'll be thinking about you guys constantly. In the last few hours I've come to understand why you have to go, so go in peace, and please do whatever you can to bring my baby back."

Dwight held her tightly. "I'll try, as God is my witness, I'll try." She cringed; neither one of them had mentioned the word God since they first learned of the assault.

As their car pulled away without her, Cathy felt as if she'd been punched in the chest and knew she'd made the first truly selfless decision of her life. Convinced she was right, but feeling painfully alone, she went back inside her now empty house.

She looked around, walked up the stairs, collapsed back on their bed and cried.

Throughout the last several months, she felt she had to be strong for the sake of her boys. Now, at last, she would let herself grieve. She buried her face in Dwight's pillow and let the house reverberate with her sobs...

***

Eventually she willed herself out of bed. When she first stood up she felt woozy, and so sat back down. Fearing if she lay down again she'd never get up, she went downstairs and systematically began putting her house in order.

Everything she saw, touched, and moved reminded her of them. She felt overwhelmed by sadness, but still she knew she'd find the strength to make it through the summer she had to, her boys depended upon her.

***

By late morning, Colin and Dwight were well on their way. Their first stop would be the Apostle Islands National Lakeshore, at Lake Superior, in northern Wisconsin. From there they had no plans except to visit as many National Parks and Forests as they could.

After their first day on the road, Dwight began to notice a change in Colin. Instead of leaning against the window in a semi-catatonic state, he began to sit up, take notice, and occasionally ask questions.

On the afternoon of their second day, they stopped and bought snacks, which they didn't need, and maps, which they did. They were now on an adventure, and they were in it together. When they got back on the open road Dwight started to relax and think about all the places he wanted to go.

"Dad," Colin interrupted Dwight's meandering thoughts, "when are we going back?"

"When we're ready," Dwight answered truthfully, "but certainly sometime before sweet corn season ends."

Dwight looked over at Colin and smiled. He wasn't sure how Colin wanted him to answer his question. He didn't want to mention school and he knew talking about sweet corn was safe. They both loved roasted sweet corn—paint-brushed with fresh Wisconsin butter, and Dwight knew they needed to enjoy this year's crop as a family. He desperately wanted some things to remain unchanged.

Once again, Colin interrupted Dwight's thoughts. "Dad, are we running away?"

His question surprised Dwight, "No," he quickly responded, "we're going on a journey."

"What kind of a journey?"

Dwight wasn't sure he could put his own chaotic emotions into words but he tried. "We're going in search of peace of mind." Dwight surprised himself with that answer and hoped it made sense to Colin.

"But Dad, where are we going to find peace of mind?"

"I wish I knew," he said, pausing only briefly to look up at the hills beyond the open road. "All I know for sure is that I just want to leave everything bad that happened behind us, and I want to show you some of the good this world has to offer..." Dwight's voice trailed off.

Colin looked down, and then, in a non-confrontational tone, he pointed out, "But Dad, you used to tell me church *was* good and that I'd find peace of mind there."

Dwight gritted his teeth. "I know. I was wrong." His eyes tightened with anger as he forced himself to look straight ahead. Dwight wanted to kill Pat MacMillan, but more than that, he wanted to protect his son from experiencing any more pain.

For the next few minutes, they drove along in unsettling silence. Finally, Dwight, in an attempt to abandon his anger and lighten things up, cleared his throat and asked, "So Col, where do *you* think we'll find peace of mind?"

Colin was quiet for a moment. "Maybe on some country road?"

Going for Sunday drives on country roads as a family was something Dwight always relished, but prior to that moment, he didn't realize Colin knew just how much those drives meant to him.

Colin looked back at his father, smiled, and continued his thought. "I just don't know which one."

Dwight smiled; he was deeply touched to see Colin reaching out to him. "OK Col, well with you as my copilot, I'm sure we'll hit quite a few great ones!"

"Sounds good," Colin said, nodding thoughtfully. He then reached into the glove box and pulled out a map. After a few minutes of study, Colin's eyes began to blink shut. "Hey Dad," he asked, "mind if I take a nap?"

"No problem." Dwight smiled again, reached out and briefly rubbed his son's knee.

"And if I fall asleep," Colin offered, "and you get lost, and you need help, just wake me."

Dwight nodded. He was too choked up to speak—if only his son knew just how very lost he felt.

Within moments Colin was asleep, and Dwight again reached over to touch him. This time he slowly brushed the back of his hand against Colin's cheek. That single touch brought back a memory of the moment he and Cathy had first touched Colin; it was on the day he was born.

Cathy, I promise you, Dwight thought with reddening eyes, I will bring your baby back.

It was a vow he viewed as sacred as the one he'd made the day he married her. He just hoped it wasn't too late to finally become the kind of father and husband his family had always deserved.

***

They ended up being on the road for five weeks. Much to Colin's surprise, they never once mentioned Father Pat or what happened at church, the hospital, or in court. Colin still thought about it every day, but as the trip progressed, he began to feel less possessed by it. By then he'd developed a deep affinity for all the National Parks and Forests they'd explored.

Colin knew their time together would have to end soon; still, before it did, he especially wanted to go to Bryce Canyon. All of the maps and books he'd been reviewing made that park seem like the grandest of them all. With very little prodding, Dwight agreed to take him there, but told him after that they'd have to head home.

The thought of returning home frightened Colin.

***

Two days later, August 24, 1981, they arrived at Bryce Canyon. Colin was certain that this was the spot he was destined to come to. He rushed out of the car and over to the rim.

***

Jordon closed Colin's file. Gotta stop here, she thought, I *need* a break. I've been going at this for hours. She stood up and stretched. She could have sworn she heard her back creak. She sat back down on the floor and started doing some of the yoga moves she'd excelled at in college. She immediately felt both stiff and old. Deflated, she decided instead to return to Marcos' file.

24

October 25, 1977
MARCOS

Cruelty—The intentional and malicious infliction of physical or mental suffering upon living creatures.

Five days after being sentenced Marcos boarded the prison bus to Stockton. Walking toward the back of the bus his limbs felt heavy, making even the simplest movements an effort. When he finally dropped into his seat, he let his head fall back and closed his eyes.

After a while he took a deep breath, exhaled, and put his head into his sweaty handcuffed hands. He wondered what life in Stockton would be like. While in county jail, he was told child molesters in prison were treated worse than the prison rats. From what he'd heard, it sounded like he could count on being raped. He'd also heard that sometimes people got *shanked*. He later learned that being shanked meant being stabbed with a weapon, usually hand-honed by another inmate.

His sweat increased as he sat there, thinking about all the things that might await him.

"It's all about respect," one of his fellow prisoners said as the long bus ride continued. "This is my seventh trip. You've never been up to The Joint before, have you?" The prisoner leaned forward, causing his muscular tattooed arm to swell.

"No," Marcos said, trying to wipe his now sweat-soaked eyebrows with his handcuffed wrist.

"Yeah, I figured as much. You look scared shitless. Well, you'll know the building as soon as we get there. It looks like a huge brick cage. It's in the center of a gigantic cement parking lot, right in the middle of fuckin' nowhere. There are no windows anywhere, but there's electric fencing everywhere. The good news is there's a big old exercise yard. The bad news is to get to the exercise yard, you gotta walk through—The Tunnel." He paused then, as if to make sure he still had Marcos' complete attention. "That tunnel is one scary mother-fuckin' place." He slowly shook his head from side to side. "I don't know how many people have died in that tunnel, but I've heard it's a lot. You gotta watch your fuckin' back in The Tunnel."

Marcos knew the guy was trying to freak him out, and it was working.

"At first," he continued, "the worst thing about the place is its stench. No one gives a shit about being clean, so the whole place stinks like your armpit; but after a few days, you get used to *that*." He slowly shook his head again. "It's all the other stuff that you can't never get used to, but you'll learn about all that shit soon enough."

In spite of understanding this storyteller's perverted motivation, Marcos was still hanging onto his every word.

"As soon as we get there, they'll bring us right into the mess hall. The food's not bad, but they don't give you much of it, so count on leaving hungry. After that, you'll get 'processed' and taken to your cell. After that, every day is just like the one before." He sat back and smiled. His upper lip curled up slightly, exposing a cracked tooth.

Marcos was clearly frightened, but he tried to appear cool. He knew his sweat was betraying him; he now frantically tried to wipe it from his neck.

"Kid, you look like you're gonna be sick so I'm gonna give you just one piece of advice. Don't let anybody 'diss' you. You let somebody diss you, you're dead meat. You understand what I'm talking about?"

Marcos knew 'diss" meant disrespect, but he wasn't sure he understood the rest; still, he slowly nodded his head yes.

***

The "dissing" began that night at dinner. Amidst the clamoring of dishes and the grumbling of restrained male voices, one of the Cons sitting across the table from Marcos asked, "Boy, you like to mess with little girls?" He leaned forward onto his skinned elbows and continued in a softer eerier voice, "Is that what you like little guy?"

Marcos' heart began beating so loudly he was sure everyone else heard it. He didn't answer the question or even look up.

Within moments others joined in, and the taunting began in earnest.

The insults quickly degenerated into a feeding frenzy. The less Marcos stood up for himself, the more people joined in. Each moment he sat there, he could feel his heart thumping from the top of his head to the soles of his feet. Suddenly, his hand started to shake. No matter what, he thought, I have to stop the shaking. I *can't* let them see they're getting to me.

At the end of the meal, the one with the skinned elbows reached over and took Marcos' dessert. "You won't be needing this, you fucking pervert. This ain't the kind of sweets you like."

Marcos kept his head down and let him take it.

***

Jordon took a deep breath, leaned back, and closed her eyes. She knew enough about prison life to recognize that from that moment the die had been cast. In prison, two things matter most above all else food and respect, and Marcos had just lost both. She thought about moving on to another file, but she couldn't tear herself away. In addition to the written material, she also had audio and videotapes that memorialized this portion of his life. She decided she needed to review it all.

***

After dinner that night Marcos was taken to be *processed*.

Being *processed* meant moving through a series of de-humanizing experiences. It began by turning over his clothes.

Standing naked in a crowded vestibule, Marcos had every part of his body examined by someone who made no secret of the fact that he enjoyed touching him. From there, he was given linens and a used prison uniform, but not enough time to dress. As he walked down the cold, filthy, and echoing corridor he could hear the catcalls and screams. He kept his eyes forward and his pile of clothes pressed up against his groin. His eyes filled with tears.

When he arrived at his cell, he heard a reverberating buzz, which startled him and caused him to drop his clothes. Laughter ricocheted off the walls. As his cell door began to slide open. Marcos rushed in.

As soon as he was dressed he dropped down on the only unmade bed and tried to will his heart to slow down.

Eventually, he forced himself to sit up. Looking around, he was astonished by how much stuff was already jammed into this one small space. The cell looked as if it was only about eight by ten feet, yet, it had beds for four prisoners, a miniature sink and a soiled toilet. He heard another piercing blare. This time, he only flinched and quickly inhaled. The powerful stench of the cell made him gag. He lay back down and put his hands over his face, squeezing shut his nose.

When he looked up he saw peeling pornographic posters and felt the low ceiling closing in on him. He turned over onto his side. He now noticed that each prisoner had a small plastic storage tub beneath their bunk, and that the areas surrounding their bunks and inside their tubs were filled. Marcos was sure if he had time to look at each of his cellmates' personal items he'd know which subjects to avoid and which were safe to talk about. He never got that chance; moments later three men in their late twenties were buzzed in.

From the instant they entered, they ignored Marcos. Taking his clue from them, Marcos just made up his bed and crawled into it. He knew he'd have plenty of time to get to know them, and he sensed they'd control how and when that would happen.

That night Marcos tried hard to concentrate on falling asleep, but the eerie sounds and putrid odors made falling into a deep sleep impossible.

***

At 4:30 a.m. the prison wake up siren shattered the night's near silence. Its abrupt high-pitched squeal instantly terrified Marcos. He lay motionless until he could calm himself down, still he secretly watched his cellmates slowly get up and waited for his opportunity to do the same.

As he put on his shoes he continued to watch them out of the corners of his eyes. All 3 were slight in stature and appeared so similar he thought they might've been related. Based upon their sporadic grumbling, he surmised they were all Mexican nationals. Although they spoke Marcos' language, they clearly had no desire to speak to him.

Just before they were released for breakfast, one of them took a step toward him and said through clenched teeth, "Listen you fuckin' scumbag, word's already gotten out about you. You stay the fuck away from us and we'll do the same. Any questions?"

"No," was all Marcos needed, or was expected, to say. The rules were laid out for him and he would obey them.

Over the next few days, his cellmates were true to their word, but the taunting and food stealing in the mess hall continued. The fact that others took his food was meaningless, he was just glad they only abused him verbally. All that changed on day four.

On Marcos' fourth day at Stockton, he was permitted to spend forty-five minutes in the weight room. While doing push-ups, someone walked past him and dropped a weight on his foot.

At first he just heard the sound, but then the excruciating pain ran through his foot, up his leg and into his temples. Sheer instinct stopped him from looking up or screaming. Soon his eyes widened and welled up with tears. Sweat beaded up on his upper lip. He thought he was going to pass out, but he knew, above all else, he shouldn't look at his assailant. "That one's for my little girl and all her little friends." Marcos continued to look down; he knew he'd be putting himself in even more danger if he were able to identify his attacker.

Fearing the retaliation for divulging the incident would be far worse than the occurrence itself, Marcos didn't risk going to the infirmary. He felt he had to suffer in silence; he believed his life depended upon it.

Marcos couldn't sleep that night. Early the next day he was in agony. His foot had swollen to three times its normal size. When he finally managed to get up, he hobbled slowly and painfully into the group shower. The next thing he knew, there was a cast on his foot, a bandage around his head and he was lying some place he'd never been before.

***

The prison investigation report Jordon now read indicated that when Marcos entered the shower he was hit over the head with a mop. Some unknown assailants then sexually assaulted him, after which he was shanked with the lid from a tuna can. By the time the guard found him, he was in a ball on the shower floor. The guard called for back up. Two guards tried to help Marcos up, but he couldn't stand. Each time they stopped supporting him, he fell back down and returned to the position they'd found him in. As the guards carried him to the infirmary he kept mumbling, "I wish I'd stop bleeding. I've got to get up and go." They all thought he was referring to the bleeding on his back and kept assuring him it had stopped. Moments later, they discovered his back wasn't the only place dripping blood.

What the guards had no way of knowing, Jordon thought, was that at that point, he'd probably reverted back to his childhood. In his mind he was now lying in the old barn in Guatemala, the place where that bleeding had begun.

***

According to the medical file, the doctor at Stockton insisted the prison administration transport Marcos to the local hospital immediately, but the prison officials refused. Jordon was sure that was because they didn't want anyone on the outside to know what'd happened. It appeared all the powerless physician could then do was make a note in his file, patch him up, fill him with narcotics, and put him to bed in the prison infirmary. Reading between the lines, Jordon could tell he didn't even expect Marcos to make it through the night.

***

By morning Marcos was still alive, but completely delusional. In his own mind he was back in the barn and struggling to survive.

Marcos continued in this delusional state for several days. When he finally spoke, he mumbled incessantly about finding the strength to get up and walk over to a church. According to his chart, none of the prison infirmary orderlies understood what he was talking about, nor did they appear to care.

By the end of his fourth day it appeared the warden started to worry. He likely feared if Marcos died now his death could not be easily attributable solely to the assault, but also to poor post-assault care. On the morning of his fifth day, the warden decided to let Marcos become someone else's problem, and requested an ambulance temporarily transfer him to California Men's Cooperative or CMC.

25

November 4, 1977
MARCOS

Rehabilitation—Regaining a useful and constructive role in society.

The pamphlet Jordon picked up from Marcos' file made CMC look like a sprawling college campus; replete with small flower gardens strategically planted in between each single-storied cement dorm. According to the small print, it was thought that this "soothing" environment would help keep their population of prisoners calmer. Aside from housing the "General Population" of felons, CMC also had an extensive psychiatric hospital.

When Marcos arrived he was evaluated, medicated, and placed in a 72-hour *holding tank* with padded walls and a heavy wooden door. The only light came from the small observation window, which the guards were required to peek through once every hour, twenty-four hours a day.

At some point during the later part of his 72 hours Marcos woke up and became aware of both his surroundings and his future. Marcos looked around and realized he was no longer in his uncle's barn trying to find the strength to go on. After a while he figured out he was in some sort of hospital. Soon fleeting images filled in the gaps. Now he just wanted to die.

***

On Marcos' third day at CMC the psychotherapeutic team met and bestowed upon him the diagnosis of *clinically depressed*. This label enabled him to be permanently transferred to CMC. They made their decision based upon their collective belief that Marcos wouldn't survive at any other prison. They feared if they didn't brand him as such, he'd be returned to Stockton, which they concluded would be tantamount to converting his three-year prison commitment into a death sentence.

Once Marcos was released from the *holding tank*, he was transferred to the west wing at CMC. There he had his own small cell and was required, by state law, to attend several hours per week of *treatment*. Marcos wondered if this was the *treatment* his lawyer told him he'd hoped he'd get. If it was, then why'd he have to go through hell to get it?

***

Marcos quickly discovered CMC was very different from Stockton. At CMC the other inmates actually befriended him and they generally obeyed the rules. They did so because they didn't want to be transferred out.

Marcos soon realized he could survive at CMC. The cells were small, but at least he had one all to himself. Also, the place had a library, chapel, and large airy dining rooms with brightly colored expansive murals. Compared to Stockton, it was downright homey.

***

At the end of his first week in his new cell he was summoned to meet with his *Treatment Director* or T.D. His T.D. was Lieutenant Vallekamp, a former world-class swimmer with a master's degree in social work.

From behind his worn, photo-covered desk, Clark Vallekamp tried, as best as he could, to explain to Marcos what his life at CMC would be like. As a matter of course he always videotaped this meeting so the inmates couldn't argue later that they hadn't been warned.

"…Starting next week," Vallekamp advised him, "you'll be required to go to group therapy twice a week, and individual counseling once per month. If you don't go along with the program, you'll be transferred out. Marcos, you'll get exactly as much out of this place as you put into it. I know that doesn't mean much to you now, but hopefully sometime in the near future it will. My door is always open, but ultimately you'll have to look to yourself for the answers. Do you understand everything I've said?"

"Yes, sir."

"Well, that's fine. Then best of luck to you."

***

Marcos left having little idea what Lieutenant Vallekamp's speech was truly about, but what he did know was that he'd go wherever they sent him; because he now knew his remaining at CMC depended upon it.

***

On the first Monday in February Marcos walked down a barren, narrow hallway and cautiously opened a thick, noticeably soundproofed, door. Inside was a small room filled with a circle of prisoners who were being observed and taped by an obvious video camera. Once inside he immediately took his place among the dozen prisoners by sitting in one of the two empty chairs.

Soon each of the other prisoners nodded in his direction; then they returned to talking among themselves.

The room became silent the moment she turned the door's handle and entered. The first thing Marcos noticed was her height; she seemed to be just over 6 feet tall. Then as Dr. J. Abrams turned and closed the door behind her, he was struck by the way her long hair was braided with colorful fabric. He guessed she was about fifty, and thought she was beautiful. He especially liked her soothing blue eyes and smooth skin. To Marcos, in contrast to the rest of the prison, everything about her appeared soft, especially her smile.

"OK, let's get started," she said. "I see Marcos is here. Welcome, Marcos. In a minute we'll go around and make sure you know everyone."

Her no-nonsense voice stood out in stark contrast to her soothing looks. In response to her decree, Marcos nodded his head and offered a sliver of a smile.

"James, I know you're going before the parole board on Wednesday, and Stan, I recall you said you were expecting your wife to visit tomorrow. I'm sure both of you are anxious to talk about those things. And Pete, you wanted to talk about the book you're now reading on victimology and I'm confident we'll get to that too. Is there anything else that is pressing for anyone...?" She briefly looked into the eyes of each of her group members. "OK, then let's go around and introduce ourselves to Marcos."

Marcos sat there amazed as each prisoner gave his name, his charge, and the number of years to which he was sentenced. All of them were convicted child molesters. Two of them had been sentenced to life. None of them went into the details of their crimes, but the names of the charges alone shocked Marcos.

"Lewd and lascivious acts with a child under fourteen."

"Incest."

"Rape."

"Sodomy."

"Kidnap, sexual assault and infanticide."

By the time she came to Marcos he was too overwhelmed to speak. He was both frightened and disgusted by the crimes he'd just heard. Dr. Abrams bailed him out.

"Marcos was convicted of one count of child molestation. I'm sure in time, he will tell you all about it. What's more, he was only sentenced to three years, so we'll have to work quickly if we are going to help him."

Marcos was stunned, first upon hearing his charge announced, and then at being told he would, in time, tell this group of prisoners "all about it" and that *they* could help him. He couldn't imagine ever telling this group of dangerous perverts anything, or that they could ever help him in any way.

As the morning progressed he tried to look as if he was paying attention, but he was, in reality, consumed by terror. He was convinced one of the other prisoners would come after him the moment Group ended. Just before it did, Dr. Abrams asked him to remain behind while the others filed out.

"Marcos, how're you doing?" she asked.

"OK," he answered too quickly, feeling anything but OK.

"Marcos, you have to talk to me or I can't help you. You're pale and you were clearly some place else during Group. Where were you? What are you afraid of?"

What am I afraid of, he thought. I'm afraid of everything, but how could I possibly tell her that? He couldn't. She sat back down in her chair. He knew she'd just wait until he answered her.

"Everything," he finally said.

"OK, well good, that's a start," she said, as she both nodded and smiled. "Marcos, you're in a prison full of psychiatric patients surrounded by hyper-vigilant guards. If you weren't afraid, I'd be worried about you. Being afraid means you're aware of all this, which means you're probably not crazy, and that's part of the good news. The other part of the good news is that historically this has been a safe prison. The prisoners pretty much keep to themselves for fear that they'll be transferred out if they don't. And the guards tend to lighten up once they get to know you. I'm confident that in a relatively short time, you won't feel frightened anymore."

Marcos finally found the courage to speak, "But you told them I was a child molester—won't word get out? I mean even if those guys don't come after me, won't someone else?"

"No, I don't think so. Everything that is said in Group stays in Group. The guys don't even discuss it among themselves when they see each other out in the yard; it's just better that way. Even the name of the group doesn't say what these men are in for; it's just called *Group Therapy*. All of this will make more sense to you as time goes by, trust me." She looked into his eyes. He looked down. She went on. "But for your own sake, I think you should try and pay more attention in Group on Thursday; you'll be able to get a lot more out of it if you do. I hear your Psych. Eval. Team went out on a limb to keep you here by giving you a trumped-up diagnosis. I think they're all rooting for you, and so am I."

Her last statement surprised and comforted him.

"I've got to go now or I'll be late," she said as she stood up to leave. "I'll see you Thursday. Hang in there." She reached out and placed her hand on his shoulder. Her touch sent a pleasurable ripple throughout his body. "You'll be fine," she said, and then she gave him one of the best smiles he'd ever seen, turned, and hurried off to her next Group.

Walking back to his cell Marcos was trying to concentrate on what Dr. Abrams had just told him, but he kept thinking about her and the men in his Group. Some of them looked like child molesters, and some like regular guys. He knew his conviction fit into the same category as theirs, but he didn't think he belonged in their Group. They actually hurt kids, and he never hurt anybody. He knew he'd keep going to the Group, because he had to, and he liked Dr. Abrams, but he was sure it was just a waste of everybody's time.

***

Marcos arrived at Group on Thursday a few minutes early. James was already telling the others about his meeting with the parole board. When he finished, Stan started describing how things went during the visit with his wife. It didn't sound like either encounter had gone particularly well, still both men seemed thankful to be able to talk to the others about it. Marcos didn't join in, but he didn't feel left out either.

When Dr. Abrams arrived, she listened carefully as James, then Stan, brought her up to date. It seemed to Marcos that no one was surprised when James announced he'd, once again, been denied parole, or when Stan tearfully told the Group his wife still wanted the divorce. What surprised Marcos was how hard everyone else was working to keep James' and Stan's spirits up.

Eventually, Dr. Abrams turned the discussion back to the book Pete was reading on victimology and what he'd learned since their last session. Pete was a small white man with a bald head and a very narrow face.

"This week I was reading about victim empathy," Pete began. "Victim empathy is something I don't think a lot of us have, at least I don't think I have it. Victim empathy is not just when you know it's wrong to be messing with a kid, it's when you actually feel their pain, like it's happening to you—"

Dr. Abrams interrupted, "Exactly, Pete. Some of you were molested when you were kids, and you *know* the person who molested you hurt you, but when you molested children, you couldn't relate to the fact that they hurt, just like you hurt." She paused and leaned forward as if to see if she was getting through to anyone. "Most people on the outside don't understand that. They think you knew you were hurting the children and you wanted to hurt them. I know you didn't, but you need to understand most people don't know that, and so they think you're evil. What you've done *is* evil. What I'm trying to get you to realize is *why* you did it, so you *won't* do it again."

"Yeah," Pete remarked, "I'm sure it's the same thing, but the way the author says it, it kind of makes more sense to me. He says most sex offenders are like a three-layer cake; only we're missing the middle layer. That middle layer he says is victim empathy—"

"Precisely," Dr. Abrams jumped in again, "and I don't know whether you guys were born this way or if all the bad things that've happened to you in your life made you this way. I just want you to understand that critical middle layer. I want you to *get* that when you molest kids, *you are hurting them.* And if *that* doesn't bother you enough to make you stop, then we have to come up with other ways that will. This is just one way, but it's the thing that stops most people on the outside from hurting others—"

"I once saw an image on TV that looked like me," interrupted William. William was the prisoner convicted of multiple counts of sodomy. He looked both overweight and over-medicated. Marcos later learned that William rarely spoke. After everyone appeared to get over their brief shock at hearing William's voice, Stan asked, "Was that during your trial?"

Marcos had no idea why Dr. Abrams was allowing this obvious switch in topics, but he continued to listen.

"No, it was on the Discovery channel," William said. "It was a shark attack and I looked like the shark."

Maybe this guy, thought Marcos, is just flat out nuts.

William continued. "Just before the shark attacked the baby seal, his eyes rolled to the back of his head and when I saw him do that, I knew he didn't care about the baby seal. I cared about the baby seal because I was watching, but he didn't care about the baby seal; he was just looking forward to eating it."

Marcos thought he was now beginning to see the connection.

William concluded. "That's the way I was with kids. I didn't care about them like they were people, at least not at that moment, not when I was horny. During those moments, I didn't think about them at all. Sometimes I did later, and then I'd feel real bad, but not bad enough so that the next time I had the chance to have one of them I'd let those bad feelings stop me."

The room became silent; everyone looked down.

"What's happening right now," Dr. Abrams said, "is that most of you are busy thinking back to a time when you felt like the shark, and some of you are also thinking about times when you felt like the baby seal."

Marcos, however, wasn't thinking either of those thoughts. Nor was he sure he really understood the shark story, or the cake analogy, still, he was certain whatever those words were about, they weren't about him. He'd never hurt any child. He went into Sophia's bed because she begged him to. He knew what he did was technically wrong, but no one got really hurt, except him when they sent him to prison. These guys are a bunch of whackos, Marcos concluded. And I'm just here because my mother made me baby-sit and my half-sister was a whiner—

Dr. Abrams interrupted his thoughts.

"Marcos, what do you think about all this?"

"I don't know," he answered, in a clear effort to cut off any further discussion with her.

"Well, can you relate to what we've been saying?"

Marcos felt uncomfortable. His knee started bouncing. He didn't want to talk and he didn't want to be put on the spot. He just wanted to listen and do his time.

Clearly, Dr. Abrams was not about to let him get away with that. "Marcos, here's the deal. You're either a member of this group or you're not. If you are a member you must participate, which means you must both listen and talk. There are no observers here. So, I'll ask you again. Can you relate to what we have been talking about?"

"No," was all he could say.

"What do you mean, no?" Sid the child rapist jumped in and asked. "Did you know you were hurting the kid you diddled at the time you were diddling 'em?"

"I didn't hurt her and she wasn't just any kid; she was my half-sister and she begged me to come into her bed." The minute Marcos trumpeted his position he heard how ridiculous it sounded. Still he believed in what he was saying, so he stuck with it.

"How old was she, man?" asked Mick, the child murderer.

"Five," Marcos said, in a voice so soft they all had to obviously strain to hear him.

"Five? She was five years old?" Mick asked. "Man, you got to know that's bullshit. She was just a baby. She didn't know what she wanted; she was probably just trying to get by. Man, that sucks..." Mick was a redhead, and pale by nature, but now his face was beginning to turn crimson.

The others looked away and just shook their heads.

Dr. Abrams interrupted their silence. "Marcos, Mick, I think we should move on for now. This is only Marcos' second session and we've all got a lot of work ahead of us. Still, I think you should both be proud of yourselves, because you each said what you believed to be true. Marcos, please think about what you did and what was said here this morning. Everyone in this room is on your side and each of us knows just how strong a sense of denial can be."

The last thing Marcos wanted to do was "think about" what he and Sophia had done. What he wanted to do was to run out of the room as fast as he could.

For the rest of the session Marcos concentrated on the wall clock. He wanted to make sure he was the first one out the door.

As soon as the session ended, Marcos sprinted over to the open courtyard. Once he arrived, he ran laps until sunset when he was required to line up for dinner.

***

Dr. Abrams looked out her window and saw him running. She wanted to comfort him but knew better. He was now in his own private hell, a place he needed to go.

***

As Marcos ran, he started to cry. He thought he was crying because he was frustrated, because no one believed his version of what happened with Sophia, but somewhere, deep inside, he started to realize that perhaps he no longer believed it himself.

***

When Marcos returned to Group the following session, he arrived right on time. He didn't want to arrive early for the pre-session chat, nor did he want to arrive late and call attention to himself. He just wanted to blend in.

As soon as the session started, Dr. Abrams focused the group's attention on him. "Well, Marcos, did you do as I asked? Did you think about what the other group members were saying to you last time?"

"Yes, I thought about it." He still didn't want to talk, but she'd made it clear he had to.

"And what did you decide?"

"I decided that I didn't think so, but I wasn't one hundred percent sure. I mean I heard how stupid it sounded when I said she was five and she wanted it, but that's what happened." He looked around the room. No one looked back. He went on. "I'm just not the type of person that would hurt a five-year-old, especially not my own sister." He once again sought out a set of sympathetic eyes but none existed. He could tell they all thought he was bullshitting. "But I understand how someone else might see it that way, so I do get that all this stuff doesn't quite stack up…"

"Sort of like a three-layer cake without the middle layer?" Pete asked with a slight smile.

"Yeah," Marcos said softly, "sort of."

***

From that day forward Marcos began to slowly accept responsibility for what he'd done to Sophia. It was a long, arduous, and at times backward process, but once begun, he could no longer deny his culpability or his growing remorse.

As time went on he began to develop a keen interest in the other Group members' progress and why some of them seemed to benefit from their discussions while others remained aloof, unscathed and unchanged. He was interested because he was beginning to care about them and the children they might someday molest, but above all, he wanted to learn whatever he could in order to avoid a relapse himself. Eventually, he even began volunteering his time at the front desk at the counseling center.

Within a few months Dr. Abrams gave him the only funded inmate job they had. For $12.50 a day he kept the offices clean, answered the phone, typed, and ran errands. He very much appreciated working there, especially when he was able to overhear the clinical conversations between the various therapists.

After six weeks of being on the job Dr. Abrams asked him what he was doing with all of his hard-earned money. He told her he was sending some home and spending some at the canteen. She suggested he use it to continue his education, and advised him to go talk to Heather George, the librarian.

***

Heather was a petite, aloof, and somewhat skeptical woman in her early 60s. Having worked in the prison library for almost 20 years she had little tolerance for people who wasted their time. She felt at a minimum, they should at least be reading. Marcos got her attention when he told her what he was interested in doing.

***

"You know we used to have college classes right here in the prison," Heather said, "but that funding stopped. I guess the State of California didn't want to spend their money giving prisoners a college education. I personally think it would've been a good use of their money, but no one asked me." She looked down and began to stamp in some books. After a few long moments, she pushed a strand of her graying hair out of her face and continued. "The only way for you to earn a college degree now is through a correspondence school, and that's expensive." She looked directly into his eyes. "It'll cost you most of your salary," she kept her eyes locked on his, "but at least when you leave here, you'll be taking more with you than just bad memories."

Eventually Marcos convinced her he saw the wisdom in her words. In exchange for his enthusiasm, she helped him get the materials he needed to prepare for the GED exam and the college correspondence courses.

From then on, whenever Marcos wasn't working or in therapy, he was studying in the near silent library. What money he had left after paying his tuition, he immediately sent home. Life at CMC was now tolerable and occasionally, exhilarating. As time passed he felt more and more certain he would make it in the outside world.

While in the library, he would occasionally meet people who, knowing where he worked, would quietly admit to him that they were there on child molestation charges and they wanted to get some help before they got out. He continuously asked Dr. Abrams if they could join one of her groups, and she always told him that there wasn't any room.

One day, upon seeing his frustration with her negative response, she took him aside and explained how the system worked.

"Look Marcos, if you just come here on a child molestation charge and you're housed with CMC's *General Population*, you don't get a place in one of my groups, even if you want treatment. The only reason you got into Group was because you were declared *clinically depressed*. With that designation you were then *required by law* to get treatment services. Years ago there were treatment programs for all sex offenders, but the money for those programs has been cut off."

Marcos couldn't believe what he was hearing. "Do you mean, if a child molester comes in here, is placed within General Population and *wants* to get help so he can change before he gets out, he can't?"

"Right," she answered, "not unless he's been given a clinical diagnosis. And," she continued, "what makes the system equally flawed is that in some cases, Group is a waste of time for some patients; while for others, it's downright dangerous, because for them, actually talking about what they've done tends to excite them and makes them even more likely to re-offend. And for the others, it's a waste of time because, given their diagnosis, they are either going to re-offend or not, no matter what. Still for others it's a great tool. That's why a complete diagnosis by a competent

124

shrink is so damned important; and then, that *must* be followed by the *appropriate* therapy."

Dr. Abrams was clearly getting upset. She clenched her fists, turned, and briefly walked away. A moment later she took a deep breath, turned back toward him and continued in a calmer voice. "If our Groups only had in them the people we could possibly help, then we could take others in from General Population who could also really profit from it. I'm not saying it's impossible to get into one of my groups from GP, I'm just saying during the last two years I've only been able to admit three convicted child molesters from the hundred or so who have asked. In all three of those cases the prisoners wrote me in excess of twenty letters beseeching me to let them in. One of those men later told me he molested more than two hundred children and he was *not* serving a life sentence, which means he would have gotten out without getting *any* help. So, what do you think the chances of *that* guy re-offending would've been?

"There just isn't enough funding or interest," she said, "and what politician wants to come out publicly and say, 'Let's increase our funding for the treatment of sex offenders'? All they want to say is let's increase their prison time. Now don't get me wrong, I'm not opposed to that, but that just isn't enough!" Once again she briefly turned away and quickly turned back. "I hate it," she said, barely breathing between sentences. "It makes me crazy. How can we not provide treatment for those who can benefit from it and want it? *Most* sex offenders will be returned to the streets; *most* of them will live in neighborhoods with children, and without treatment *most* of them will re-offend."

At that point Dr. Abrams appeared so involved in what she was saying she seemed to have forgotten Marcos was there. She was now staring out the dirty cracked window. "With treatment," she continued, "at least we have a fighting chance with *some* of them. Ideally, it would be great to have a separate state prison facility, one where prisoners could avoid the abuse they endure in the General Population of most prisons and regularly get the treatment they need. How could everyone not want that?" She tuned around and looked pleadingly at Marcos.

He knew she didn't want or expect an answer. The room became silent; there was clearly nothing left to say. She shook her head, threw up her arms and went back into her office.

Marcos remained in the hallway. He was still in shock. He couldn't believe it. It made no sense. He always thought everyone in this country really cared about kids and that's why he was arrested, tried and locked up. It seemed to him now, that all the criminal justice system really cared about was getting a conviction and locking up the child molester. What Marcos didn't know was whether the Americanos actually *believed* just temporarily locking them all up would decrease their chances of doing it again, or whether they just didn't care.

***

After two-and-a-half years of group therapy, individual counseling, and countless conversations with prisoners and therapists, Marcos came to believe the criminal justice system was flawed, but he alone was in charge of his own destiny. By then, he'd come to grips with most of what he'd done; he just hoped that was enough.

***

Jordon finally closed Marcos' file. She stood up and stretched. She was exhausted, not just from her work, but from the tension she felt going through Marcos' life in prison. No matter how convinced she was that he deserved the conviction, she still felt guilty about his punishment.

Time was running out; she had to keep going. She sat back down and returned to Pat.

26

June 25, 1981
PAT

Mens rea—A guilty mind; a guilty or wrongful purpose.

When the jury announced their guilty verdict, the local TV station was there, and later repeatedly showed Pat's blank face and vacuous eyes. He looked crazed. It was the vision their community longed for; they needed to believe he was just an aberration, a monster in priest's clothing.

***

One month later, when Pat was sentenced to 10 years in state prison, his expression remained the same. His lawyer later told the newspapers he doubted whether Pat even heard the judge's pronouncement, so consumed was he with quietly singing, "Bringing in the Sheaves."

Two days after sentencing, Pat was put on the bus to La Crosse. He left without saying good-bye to anyone.

***

Pat tried to ignore the priest who sat across from him in a visitor's booth at La Crosse Prison, but when the priest asked him to join in prayer, Pat began laughing hysterically.

The priest soon left, and never came back. Pat was relieved; he didn't want to be disturbed.

Pat had decided on the night he was arrested, having failed at killing himself, he'd only allow his body to remain on earth. His soul, he resolved, would float freely about the heavens. He was sure he could continue with this illusion as long as he kept his eyes closed and sang. Hence, over and over again, he'd sing the hymns he sang with his boys, and, in so doing, he and his boys were never apart.

***

After four months of exhibiting this eccentric behavior Pat was finally referred for a psychological evaluation. When the day arrived for his interview, he kept his eyes closed and sang until the very last minute. However, when he walked into the psychiatrist's office, he looked her straight in her eyes and spoke. According to her notes, he spoke eloquently, with great clarity, authority and wisdom. He told her that he was doing what he needed in order to survive. "They can house my body," he declared, "but not my soul."

The psychiatrist was impressed with him and suggested they speak again. He respectfully declined and went back to his own world. Given their brief encounter, she felt he was sane enough. She was wrong.

***

Years later, after Pat had vacated his cell, the guards found horrific penciled drawings on his wall, which clearly showed Pat's world was one where demons lived and prospered.

***

Jordon looked closer at photographs taken of the renderings on Pat's cell wall. They were so graphic they made her wince. She quickly returned to Marcos' file.

27

October 15,1979
MARCOS

Parolee—One who gains his conditional freedom as a result of an exercise of discretion on the part of the Parole Board.

By the time Marcos arrived, sweat from his torso had already reached his belt line. He was now standing at the door to the room where the parole board was meeting. When a draft came through the frigid hallway, he began to shiver. He then sat down on a hard, institutional-green plastic chair. He felt as if he'd been waiting there an eternity, but the clock, with its incredibly loud, whirring motor, indicated he'd only been there 10 minutes, and then they ushered him in.

Once inside, they bombarded Marcos with questions. In general, they wanted to know what he'd learned while he was there, and what his plans were once he got out. He answered all their questions as best he could. Occasionally, he'd use his hand to wipe the corners of his parched lips or steady his sporadically quivering knee. He knew the most important question was yet to come.

Finally, one of them asked it, "Are you going to do this again?"

Marcos looked his inquisitor squarely in the eyes. "No, I will never hurt another child again."

***

After he left, the parole board unanimously voted to grant him early parole. Later that day he was told he only had about a week left at CMC.

***

As his release date approached, Marcos became increasingly anxious. For the first time in over a year he had trouble sleeping. He knew he'd done well in prison, but he feared he'd fail on the outside.

He described his fears during his last Group session. Dr. Abrams and the others were supportive. Just before he walked out

129

of the door for the last time, most of them told him, in their own way, that they believed in him.

That night, alone in his cell, he wished he had half the faith in himself that his Group appeared to have. Besides feeling apprehensive about risks on the outside, he was also sad to be leaving Dr. Abrams, the other staff, and some of his Group members. He'd grown close to these people, and he didn't have a single friend in the outside world. He was sure his prior high school acquaintances would want nothing to do with him, and he knew he still wasn't allowed to see Sophia. The only person in the outside world whom Marcos could see, and who'd want to see him, was his mother.

***

At first Margarita had come to see him often, but when she visited, it always made him uncomfortable. He was embarrassed for her and himself. He thought she looked poor and pathetic. After her third monthly visit he discouraged her from coming back. He explained the visits were hard on him. She told him she understood, and appeared relieved. Now Marcos was actually looking forward to seeing her.

Still, he continued to feel conflicting emotions about getting out. At CMC he felt safe, comfortable, at home, and was considered a success; in the outside world, he'd be considered— the worst kind of felon. Conversely, he was excited about experiencing many little things he'd missed during his two-and-a-half-years of confinement: the night sky, the feel of a soft blanket, and the smell of a bakery.

***

Shortly before his release, his parole agent, Dempsey Riley, notified him he was being paroled to Los Angeles. Initially, he was told he'd be required to live in a halfway house then, after 3 months, he'd have to find his own place. He was warned to start looking early, because it wouldn't be easy to find an apartment that was the required distance from a school or play area. Before Dempsey left, he reminded Marcos that his parole could last three years. "During the entire three years," Riley said with marked gravity, "you are forbidden to be alone with a child under the age of eighteen."

"I understand," Marcos said. At that point, he had no desire to go near children in general. The only child he wanted to see was his sister, and that wasn't out of lust; it was because Sophia was his sister, and he needed to make peace with her.

***

According to Marcos' prison file, his last day at CMC was a sad one for many, all of whom felt they'd miss him, but hoped they'd never see him again.

***

When he first walked out of the prison gates, Margarita was there to greet him, and her tears started anew. She wanted to bring him back to Santa Barbara, but he refused. She said they'd all been punished enough, and it was time for them to be a family again.

Marcos carefully explained the terms and conditions of his parole to her, as well as his hope that someday they could reunite as a family.

***

Marcos' first goal was to find a job and enroll in college. Having finished two years of correspondence school, he expected to earn a BA in psychology two years from his release. With that expectation in mind, he went to Westwood to see an admission assistant at UCLA.

As he walked on campus he tried not to be overwhelmed or deterred by UCLA's beauty and prestige. He kept his eyes forward and headed right for the door marked "Undergraduate Admissions."

As he walked in he saw rows of people looking down at their respective paper work. Only one woman, Darla Anders, looked up. Marcos stepped over to her desk, showed her his transcript and release papers, and said he wanted to enroll. She looked at the straight A's on his transcript, but didn't seem impressed. When she glanced at his CMC release papers, she looked horrified.

"Well, Mr. Estrada.," she pushed her chair back and shuffled some papers on her desk, "it's not simply a matter of enrolling; you must be *admitted*. To be admitted, you must fill out an application, request your official transcripts, and procure letters of recommendation. Given your, err, situation," she started reshuffling the same papers, "it would probably be prudent of you to take the SAT exams. I'm not at all sure that, even assuming you'd be admitted, it would be as a transfer student. You might have to begin as a freshman. Of course, it's not up to me, but you're probably not going to get credit for most of these psychology correspondence classes. The only way to get around that is to bring in some of your written work, the texts you used, and seek our Psychology Department Chair's approval, which, at best, is an uphill battle."

Marcos thought she looked very uncomfortable.

"Let me write down," she began to write quickly, "the names and addresses of some local community colleges; you might want to start there—"

He interrupted her, "That's OK, if you'd just give me an application, I'll be on my way."

She quickly opened her drawer, exposing barely enough of its contents to pull out an application. Then, using only the tips of her fingers, she slid it across her desk. He picked it up, thanked her for her time, and left.

***

Given where he'd been, Darla Anders was relieved to see him leave, and hoped she'd never see him again.

***

Marcos, however, was confident he'd fulfill all of Mrs. Anders' requirements, and return.

Several days later he started a day job at a bookstore, and a night job at a parking kiosk. While inside the kiosk, he studied. He liked studying for the SAT's, enjoying both the questions, and considering each possible answer. Three months later, he took the SAT exam. The day his results arrived he returned to see Darla Anders.

***

Darla remembered him. She was surprised to see him back, and shocked by his SAT scores: 730 in Math and 720 in English. Along with copies of these high scores, he also brought everything else she'd mentioned, including some of his written work.

She carefully flipped through it all, and then asked Marcos to sit down. She pulled out his admission's essay, and was hooked after reading the first sentence. Still, she tried to read quickly, knowing he was watching her as she read.

The essay was a brief discussion on the innocence of childhood. She was deeply moved.

"Marcos, I'd like to show your packet to someone. Can you come back after lunch?" Marcos promised to return at 1:00.

As soon as he left, Darla walked over to the Psychology Department and showed his essay to her friend, Dr. Stuart Koppell, the Department Chair.

Darla sat down and watched Stuart read. Stuart was clearly impressed. Next Darla handed him Marcos' grades, letters of recommendation, SAT scores, and other written work. Finally, she explained to him that Marcos was a parolee. Stuart seemed put off, but still offered to meet with Marcos sometime. Darla told him Marcos would be returning to her office after lunch. She asked Stuart to call her before 1:00 p.m., if he wanted her to relay any message to Marcos.

***

As Stuart shuffled through Marcos' paperwork, he came upon the name of an old acquaintance of his, Jaye Abrams. She was the writer of one of Marcos' letters of recommendation. He noted her telephone number on the file, and called her at once.

Jaye gave Marcos a glowing report, and told Stuart that UCLA would be fortunate to have him as a student. Stuart then asked the question that was really on his mind, "So, what was he in for?"

"Child molestation."

"Whoa, wait a minute. Was he guilty?"

"I assume so."

"So, is it safe for us to even have him here?" Stuart could hear how paranoid and judgmental he sounded, but, after all, this was his community.

"Define safe," she answered somewhat defensively.

"Well, is he going to re-offend?"

"Stuart, you know as well as I do, I'd need a crystal ball to answer that. What I *can* tell you is, I've never felt as confident in someone as I do in Marcos. He came to us at a very young age, and, relatively speaking, he quickly took responsibility for his actions. After that, he worked extremely hard at understanding why he did what he did, and how to avoid ever doing it again. Bottom line," Jaye Abrams continued, "I would not only let him baby-sit for my own daughter, if I had one, but I also consider it an honor to have my name associated with his, and I believe you will, too."

Same old Jaye Abrams, Stuart thought. "Well," he said, "coming from you, that says a lot. I'm looking forward to meeting this young Freud." Stuart smiled, "I'll give him your best."

"Please, I'd rather you didn't do that. I don't want him to think you had to be talked into admitting him."

"Fair enough." Stuart was struck by how protective she sounded. "Would you like me to keep you posted on his progress, assuming we admit him?"

"Yes, I'd like that very much… Meanwhile, changing gears for a minute, you don't happen to have any brilliant graduate students who want to consider working up here, do you?"

Stuart shook his head and smiled, "No, can't say that I do. You and I both know what you do, although worthy and necessary, is not appealing to most of *my* graduate students. They feel the pay up there is as low as the success rate." Stuart was sorry he said those last few words the moment they left his mouth.

"Well, it is a *Catch 22*," Jaye answered, once again sounding defensive. "Without more funding, I can't improve the success rate, and without an improved success rate, I can't get more funding. Who knows, maybe someday Marcos, or someone like him, will make a difference. I've got to believe in something, otherwise it would be tough to keep going."

Stuart heard her sigh. "Stuart," Jaye continued, "take Marcos under your wing. I don't think he'll let *you* down, just make sure *you* don't let him down. I suspect he's still very fragile."

"OK, well, you're starting to convince me," Stuart said with a smile, "or guilt-trip me, I'm not sure which. Either way, I'll give serious consideration to taking on your Marcos Estrada, and hope for the best. "

"Stuart," Jaye said quickly, "don't hope for the best, expect it; Marcos deserves nothing less."

***

After a few more minutes of catch-up chatter, Jaye hung up the phone. She hoped this universally-admired professor at UCLA would embrace this teaching opportunity, as well as Marcos himself. Over the last nearly 3 years she'd come to care a great deal about the beautiful young man who came to her in denial, but left with a dream.

***

As Stuart hung up the phone he was still smiling, thinking about a wide-eyed, fellow graduate student he met twenty-five years ago.

Stuart had first met Jaye Abrams when they were students at The Berkeley Graduate School of Psychology. Although they never became close friends, he always liked her. Unlike many other fellow graduate students, he wasn't intimidated by her self-righteousness, he admired it. Early on in their camaraderie, he became comfortable with the fact that she was far braver than he'd ever be. To no one's surprise, upon graduation Jaye went to work for the state prison system, while he slipped silently into the safety of his *ivory tower* at UCLA.

He sat back and looked out of his formidable office window at the expansive lawns, impressive buildings, and comely, clean-cut student body. Soon, he began to reflect upon some of the things Jaye had said. Moments later, he stood up and walked over to the window; he wanted to take a closer look.

I've been in this insulated tower for twenty years, he thought, and I'd say my life here is very comfortable, maybe too comfortable. I know in some ways I've sold out; I wonder if I've encouraged my students to do the same.

He walked over to one of his bookshelves and picked up an old photograph of himself sporting his version of an Afro haircut. When I left Berkeley, he continued to muse, I had greater aspirations than that.... Walking back to his desk, he thought, not for the first time, that maybe somewhere along the way, he'd lost his way. While Jaye Abrams was still in the trenches fighting, he was just—getting by.

Maybe, I'm just going through a midlife crisis, he thought with a smile, and then, just maybe, taking on Marcos would be good for both of us...

He picked up the telephone, and told Darla, "Hold on to young Marcos, I'll be there by 1:00."

***

Marcos arrived early. Moments after 1:00, he saw Dr. Koppell approach Darla's desk, and stood up. As he rose, he noted that Dr.

Stuart Koppell seemed tall and fit, but his most notable characteristics were his bushy eyebrows and luminous eyes.

Stuart immediately extended both a warm hand and a big smile. Marcos felt so drawn to him he froze.

"Marcos I'm Stuart Koppell. I just read your essay, and I think it's extraordinary. I've also read through the material you submitted, and from what I saw, it appears to me that you just might be extraordinary as well. Come, let's sit down in that empty office and talk."

***

Marcos' world was spinning; by then he'd been engaged in a conversation with Dr. Koppel for well over an hour, during which time he'd gone from giddy to inadequate, and back again. Just then he knew an important question had been asked, but he couldn't find the words to respond. A lump had formed in his throat. He decided to remain silent rather than appear foolish; fortunately Dr. Koppell asked him again.

Prior to that moment, Marcos had cried many times, but he'd never experienced tears of joy. Finally, after a few long seconds, he eked out a barely audible, "Yes, yes, I would, sir."

"Well, then it's settled. All we have to do now is pick out your classes. Can you meet me back here tomorrow at 9:00?" As Marcos nodded, Koppell concluded, "Wonderful, we'll work out all the details then."

***

Never before had Stuart Koppell become so personally involved with an undergraduate, but from what little he already knew about Marcos, he sensed all his efforts would pale in comparison to the Herculean efforts already made by Marcos.

***

When they met the next day, Marcos explained that, in part, his choice of classes would have to be governed by his work schedules. In response, Stuart insisted they walk over to the financial aid office at once.

As they walked through the campus it was clear to Marcos that Dr. Koppell was a very popular teacher. It seemed to him as if everyone they passed smiled and greeted him by name. Marcos felt proud just to be seen with him.

The financial aid administrator's name was Flota Wallace. Dr. Koppell had warned Marcos, prior to arriving, that he suspected Miss Wallace would not be as easily charmed by Marcos as he was.

As soon as they walked in Marcos could tell she resented Dr. Koppell for coming to see her without an appointment. When she briefly walked ahead, Dr. Koppell whispered, it was a well-known fact that inside Flota Wallace's office, ice would not melt.

True to her reputation, Miss Wallace spent as little time as possible in her office with them. After just a few minutes she handed Marcos reams of forms to complete and said good-bye. She never once looked him in the eyes.

Once they were outside, Dr Koppell offered, "Don't let her get to you, Marcos. No doubt you've already discovered that sometimes in life, you can find inspiration in someone's act of kindness and other times from an act of unjustified mean-spiritedness. I suggest you use her aloofness to your advantage. Let it drive you to do great things, and let it be a lesson to you of how *not* to interact with others, once you have."

***

Stuart could tell Marcos understood. He was sure Marcos had experienced his share of mean-spirited people.

"For now," Stuart said, "let me buy you some lunch—off campus. Once you've been fortified, you can conquer those papers, and maybe even her."

***

Lunch was in a busy, noisy, aromatic Italian bistro. Marcos enjoyed the food and atmosphere almost as much as Dr. Koppell's company. After lunch Marcos thanked Dr. Koppell repeatedly, and made his way back to campus.

When he walked into the library, he again felt like an intruder. It was hard to believe he'd ever feel at home in such a daunting environment. Finding a seat at a window table he longed to sit there for a moment and take it all in. Instead, he decided to tackle the financial aid forms.

By four o'clock, he was back in the financial aid office.

***

Miss Wallace saw him in line and gave him her customary glacial glare. I'll reject this one personally, she thought. Who does he think he is waltzing into my office with Dr. Koppell, and demanding financial aid? Something about this kid tells me he just doesn't belong here.

"Mr. Estrada," she said, "follow me." She swung open a wooden half gate, strode through, stepped behind it, and pressed the gate up against her protruding stomach; only then did she motion for him to walk through.

***

Marcos was sure she held the door that way in order to avoid any physical contact with him. Walking in, he felt as if he were entering a combination walk-in icebox and lion's den. He missed Dr. Koppell's protective warmth.

"Sit," she said, as she pointed to a metal chair. She took the papers out of his hands and over to her desk. She immediately picked up a red pen and appeared both ready and willing to annihilate everything he'd written. Marcos tried to breathe as quietly as he could.

***

A few minutes into her evaluation, Flota discovered, much to her dismay that he qualified, not just for basic financial aid based upon needs, grades, and SAT scores, but also for a rarely used scholarship available only to parolees. She still didn't want to give him financial aid, but felt she had no choice. Concerned someone might question her impartiality, she painstakingly explained to him all the aid he'd soon be receiving.

***

When Miss Wallace finished her explanation, she handed him more papers and turned her attention back to her other work. Marcos understood this was his signal to leave. He stood, thanked her, extended his hand, and waited to leave until she shook it.

As he walked away he felt her frosty scowl move from the base of his neck down to the bottom of his spine. He felt chilled, but not disheartened. Despite Miss Wallace's negative attitude, he'd had a great day. When he got home, he immediately called his mother.

She was still at her cleaning jobs. He'd never called her at work before, but now he just couldn't wait to share his good news.

***

"Mama?"

"Marcos, mi hijo, what's wrong?"

"Nothing, Mama, everything is fine."

"Are you sure?"

"Of course I'm sure."

"Well then, why're you calling me *here*?" Marcos could hear the embarrassment in her voice.

"I'm calling you there, because I have good news."

"What?"

Marcos could hear a loud vacuum cleaner in the background.

"I said, I'm calling with *good* news."

"What kind of good news?" she sounded skeptical.

"The only kind there is. The kind that makes you feel good after you've heard it." Marcos smiled. He could never have teased her before.

"Marcos, que pasa?" Now she sounded skeptical and irritated.

"Mama, I've been accepted at UCLA, and they gave me a full scholarship."

***

It took Margarita a few minutes to understand, but once she did, she too began to cry tears of joy. As soon as she could speak again, she asked him to call that night to tell Sophia his good news personally, but he declined.

***

"No Mama, I'm not ready to talk to her, and I doubt that she's ready to talk to me. She and I will talk, but only when it's right. Meanwhile, I'll see you in Oxnard on Sunday, and we'll celebrate! Mama," he cautiously added, "I think this is my beginning, my true birthday… Now, you drive carefully on Sunday. Remember, I love you."

***

Jordon later learned, even though he'd already hung up, or maybe, because of it, Margarita responded, "I love you, too, Son, and Happy Birthday. Who knows, maybe this time, things will turn out right." After that, she hung up the phone and went back to mopping the floor, but now, she too was smiling. My boy, my son, she thought; he has accomplished so much.

Moments later, her smile dissolved as she heard the voice inside her scream—he's not your son; you abandoned your son a long time ago.

Please, dear God, she thought, punish me, not him; let him have his new beginning, leave him alone, enough is enough.

28

**March 3, 2002—1:25 a.m.
JORDON**

Vicarious—To experience the joy or pain of another.

Enough is enough, Jordon repeated to herself, as she pressed redial on her cell phone.

"Hi, Sweetheart," she said, trying to sound up beat, "I know you're probably at some gig somewhere." She always felt disingenuous when she used his language, but she really wanted to sound hip. "I'm up at the cabin with Dad. It looks like I'm gonna have to pull another all nighter, and I figured you'd be the only person I knew who'd still be awake at this hour; but, I guess you're busy." Her throat tightened, "It seems like we never get to talk anymore." She hated sounding like a whiner, much less like her own mother. She chastised herself and went on, "Well, I hope things are going OK with your music and all. I know it's a struggle. I was just calling to tell you I love you and I'm rooting for you, but if you reach a point where enough is enough, that's OK too. Call me whenever you want to talk. I guess I already said I love you, so I guess I'll just say goodnight." Her eyes filled with tears.

She'd been leaving him messages for days. He left her messages in return, so she knew he was safe, but they never spoke. She was sure he was just trying to politely avoid her.

It had been three months since her son Anthony had moved to LA, confident he'd return a rock star. At the time she told him to follow his heart, but they both knew she wanted him back at UCSB by the end of the next quarter.

He was her second born, the darkly handsome one, the one she always feared she'd lose. Over the last 21 years, she'd often reflect upon her first thought at the moment of his birth—*And now it's time to let go….* but she never could, not then and certainly not now. She hoped he'd call again soon, she knew he'd at least leave a message; she wished he'd call when he knew she could answer. She missed him desperately, but she knew that was the last thing he wanted or needed to hear. He was trying to find his own way and she both admired him for that, and wished he'd come home soon.

Within moments of having picked up Pat's file, her focus shifted back to her job, and she stopped, at least for the time being, obsessing about Anthony. Work, Jordon concluded, was her greatest distraction—her drug of choice.

29

November 21, 1990
PAT

Good Time Credits—The credits a prisoner can receive toward an early release, if he comports with all of the prison rules.

Nine years went by slowly and uneventfully for Pat. Most of the time he just sat, sang, and stewed. Still, he never stopped thinking about his boys. Throughout the nine years, he neither feared death nor embraced life.

Despite his bizarre conduct, and lack of any behavior suggesting rehabilitation, he was paroled early. The parole board reasoned that since he was a former priest who'd avoided any trouble while confined, they wanted to reward him with "good time credits," and release him in time to celebrate Christmas. According to notes in Pat's prison file, when he was told about the parole board's reasoning, he threw his head back and laughed.

Ten days later, December 1, 1990, Pat was set free. Once again, he said good-bye to no one, and took nothing with him—except his rosary beads.

He was paroled to a halfway house in Platteville, Wisconsin, 60 miles west of Madison. His closest neighbor was the Lark Printing Company, owned by the Taft family. In the past, the Tafts had hired recent parolees. His parole officer, Ed Poire, arranged for him to meet with them the next day.

The Taft family was deeply religious and by their very nature, forgiving. They also needed Pat's help with the Christmas rush. Their biggest concern was where to safely place him. In an abundance of caution, they decided to give him a small office off the main corridor.

***

As far as Pat was concerned, the job suited him perfectly; everyone left him alone. What's more, he could fantasize and sing Christmas hymns all day, and everyone would think he was just embracing the holiday spirit.

***

At first, some of the employees were nervous because they knew he had *a record*, but, after a few days, they decided he looked harmless and contrite. Some even wondered if he'd been wrongly convicted.

***

On December 13, 1990 Pat came upon a church mailer from Mineral Way, Wisconsin. It was a print of a painting of an old church in Mineral Way, a place he was well acquainted with. It proclaimed that an all-boys' choir was coming to do a series of concerts in local rural communities. The boys would be singing at Mineral Way's Trinity Episcopal Church on Christmas Eve. The card declared, "Everyone is welcome!"

Pat sniffed the announcement, and then pressed it up against his chest. Finally, he slipped it into his breast pocket. It was the epistle he'd been waiting for.

***

Jordon knew she should continue reading about Pat, but, considering what she'd be reading about next, she decided she needed a break. She temporarily returned to Sophia.

30

May 23, 1983
SOPHIA

Overt Act—An open, manifest act from which criminality may be implied.

By age 12 Sophia no longer remembered much about "the molest," as she and her counselor, Craig, called it. She knew what Marcos had done, but had trouble reconciling that knowledge with her good memories of him. Every once in a while she wished she could see him again, but ever since she was a child she'd been told seeing him would be illegal. She didn't understand the prohibition, especially now that he was out of prison, but believing there was nothing she could do about it, she just accepted it.

***

Friday, June 5th, was to be her sixth-grade graduation. Both her mother and Craig, whom she now saw only on occasion, had promised to be there. She was excited about her graduation, but not about her dress.

Her dress was shiny and brown; it was a gift from one of the ladies whose house her mother cleaned. The lady had told Margarita it was the dress her daughter had worn to sixth grade graduation a few years before. Margarita told Sophia she wanted to make the dress special for her, so she added some white lace and a bow. Sophia thought it was nice, but not *hip*.

On the Wednesday before graduation, Sophia came home from school and discovered a large box in front of their door. The box had her name and address in bold print, but no return address. She quickly brought it inside and opened it.

Inside was a light blue satin dress, trimmed with delicate white embroidery. Sophia thought the dress was the most beautiful she'd ever seen or touched. Next to it was a matching pair of tights, shoes and a barrette. She was ecstatic. But who…?

She read the note inside:

Dear Sophia:

I have written this letter one hundred times on paper, and a thousand times in my mind. Maybe this will be the one I will actually send.

Let me start with I'm sorry. I hardly know the 18-year-old who hurt you, but with a lot of hard work, I have come to understand him.

I now know that what I did to you when you were so young, was *in part* because of what someone else did to me when I was a kid, but, I also know there are no excuses. What happened between us was all my fault, and I'm still learning how to deal with that.

Mama says you have been seeing a counselor named Craig. I'm so glad. I've been in counseling since my days in prison, and I think I will need to stay with it for a very long time.

You and I did not have happy childhoods, but that doesn't mean we can't be happy now.

I hope I haven't already said too much for a future 7th grader to handle. I guess I just wanted you to know that I have been working hard to figure it all out. Anyway, Mama says you're very smart and understand a lot, so I hope what I am writing makes some sense to you.

I love talking to Mama about you, because she always speaks of you with great pride, and that makes me very happy. Mama also tells me you are a size five, five feet tall, and wear size five shoes. That's a lot of fives, but it was also easy for me to remember.

My friend Dr. Koppell has a thirteen-year-old daughter, who he says is very "cool". I gave him a copy of *Seventeen Magazine* to give her, along with instructions that she should circle the coolest dresses and things. I bought what she picked out, and I hope you like them.

I picked out the barrette myself, because it reminded me of the color of your eyes; I hope I'm right about that.

If you like the dress and wear it to graduation, please have Mama take a picture of you for me. I'll be thinking of you on June 5th.

Sophia, I'm so deeply sorry, and so very proud of you.
Most Sincerely,
Marcos

Sophia wasn't sure she understood every word in the letter, or exactly how she felt about it, but she loved the dress, and the barrette *was* the same color as her eyes. She was glad Marcos hadn't forgotten her.

***

June 5th was also the day Marcos was to graduate from UCLA. He was to receive a B.A. in psychology, with high honors. Marcos didn't invite his mother to his graduation. He didn't want to put her in a position where, once again, she'd have to choose between the two of them.

He knew Sophia would be graduating about 10 a.m., and he'd be graduating at 1 p.m. He thought, if he moved quickly, he could see her ceremony and rush back for his own.

He left Westwood, at 7:30 a.m. and arrived right on time for Sophia's graduation. Wanting to go unnoticed, he stood some distance away. Looking through his binoculars, he saw her approach the stage to receive an award.

My God, he thought, she's gorgeous and she's wearing the dress, and, maybe even the barrette, although, with her long black shiny curls, it's hard to tell. His eyes began to glisten as he reflected upon how far each of them had come, and at what cost.

"What are *you* doing here?"

The familiar voice frightened Marcos before he even saw him. He turned around and gasped. Suddenly, his limbs became rigid, and he stood there motionless.

"I said, what are you doing here?"

"I, I came to watch Sophia graduate?"

"Aren't you still supposed to stay the fuck away from her, and elementary schools in general? Isn't that one of the most important terms and conditions of your parole?"

Marcos started to feel his heart pound against his chest, and he feared he might, once again, lose control of his bladder. This was becoming much too familiar for him. In a flash, the image of being returned to prison on a parole violation became a reality, and his world began to disintegrate.

"I, I, I don't think I'm on parole anymore."

"Oh, so you don't think so? Well, I do, so just put your hands behind your back. You know the drill. You're coming with me."

Marcos had already said everything he thought he could say. He knew Detective Alexander, the officer who played the *bad cop* to Greene's *good cop*, didn't believe him, and he was sure things could never be as good as they were a moment ago. He let his head drop down, and put his hands behind his back.

31

March 3, 2002—2:15 a.m.
JORDON

Threat—A verbal statement made by one person in an effort to get another to take, or avoid, an action by ensuring negative consequences if they don't comply.

Jordon put down the papers, leaned forward and rubbed her tired eyes. Damn, it's hard to believe how much Marcos went through...I've got to take a break. She got up and went into the kitchen to make some tea. While waiting for water to boil, she decided to do her nightly voicemail check:

"You have one new message. Press one for your new message."

Jordon pressed one.

"Yeah, Jordon, Bert here."

Jordon wanted to hang up immediately, and keep the District Attorney's voice out of her mountain retreat. Still, she knew if she did that, she'd just worry about what he'd said. She decided to keep listening.

"Yeah, well, I just got a call here, at my house, from the police department and a Sergeant over there; I forget his name. Anyway, he said there was a screw-up on their part, and they sent over a case for you to review. I don't even know the name of the suspect. I just know they sent it over late and so now, if we're going to file it, we have to do it by tomorrow. So, I called Betty up at home, and asked her to go into the office to look through your mail, and she did, but she couldn't find it. But she did find someone who said they might have seen you there earlier. So, I'm guessing you have it with you.

"For now, I don't want to deal with the fact you reentered the office in spite of my directive not to. *For now*, I just want you to take that case and get it filed. We have to get his ass in jail. For the moment, I don't give a shit whether he's guilty or not. We can't let another alleged child molester go. It's coming close to election time, and we need the good ink. So, tomorrow—I want you to sign off on the arrest warrant and tell the boys to get his ass in jail.

Later, we can decide if we actually had enough evidence to arrest him in the first place. No need for you to call me back." Click.

Jordon couldn't let go of her phone quickly enough. I hate that man, she thought. My old boss, T.W.S, would never have told me to do anything illegal or unethical, and Feller just ordered me to do both. Beyond that I'm quite sure he knows the name of the suspect...

The teakettle started to whistle; the piercing sound startled her. Concluding she now had no time to waste, she decided to forego the break and go back to reading the old cases in earnest. In just a few hours she'd either have to file the new case, or come up with some indisputable reason why not.

Jordon noted she hadn't read about Colin for a while, so she picked up where she left off—with Colin finally arriving at the rim of Bryce Canyon.

32

August 24, 1981
COLIN

Per saltum—By leap or bound; by a sudden movement; passing over certain proceedings.

"Son, that's just a little too close. Why don't you step back a bit?"

"Oh, come on, Dad. Don't tell me you were actually afraid I was gonna jump?"

"Please, Colin, just humor me and step back. Let's go throw our gear in the cabin and head out to Sunset Point. Sunset should be in about twenty minutes."

"OK Dad." Colin stepped back, and Dwight finally exhaled.

A short while later, they arrived at Bryce Canyon's Sunset Point. It was crowded with people from various countries, most of whom were silent. In between sporadic whispers of foreign languages, Dwight could hear the incessant sound of cameras clicking, especially Colin's.

After the sun went down most people left, but Colin and Dwight remained. They were too moved by the magnificence of the vista to leave before the first star came out.

***

Colin hadn't felt this safe since before the assault. Looking at the vast and radiant canyon helped him gain perspective; he was glad to be alive.

***

Dwight too was captivated by the beauty of the red gorge. There was something in its stark, dramatic contrasts and sheer dimensions that made him feel omnipotent, and their troubles less significant.

While Dwight was gazing at the stars, Colin moved one step closer and put his outstretched arm around Dwight's neck. The moment Dwight felt the imprint of his boy's hand he felt a ripple of joy and he sensed the trip had been a success.

Still, Dwight thought, I didn't accomplish the one thing Cathy asked for. I won't be bringing her baby back. I believe that trusting little guy is gone forever.

***

The next day, they began their uneventful trip home. They were sad to be leaving, but tired of being on the road and away from Cathy.

***

Once they returned to Madison, Cathy couldn't get enough of either gazing at them or listening to their stories. Since Dwight had kept in touch during the trip she knew in general how things had gone. She also knew Dwight was concerned Colin might be reluctant to attend their local public junior high school. In response, Cathy had looked for other alternatives.

***

After much discussion, Colin decided he wanted to go to the small private middle school on the east side of town. What made that particular school so appealing was its outward-bound type of program. This program purported to "integrate travel in the great outdoors with academic studies." So, he reasoned, in addition to getting back to nature, this program would also get him away from his old neighborhood. What finally sold him were the photos in the school's catalog displaying exuberant carefree teenagers as they biked, rafted, and climbed their way through multiple parks and wilderness areas. Each of the students looked the way Colin longed to feel.

***

Unbeknownst to Colin, his parents had to take out a second home mortgage for his school tuition. Again, Dwight's boss disapproved and said he should sue the Catholic Church, but Dwight told him that no amount of money was worth putting Colin back on the witness stand.

***

Shortly before school began, Colin sought out Tom. He wanted to tell him about his school change, but also to thank Tom for saving his life.

When they finally got together, Colin struggled, but still couldn't find the words. Eventually, Colin felt, through descriptions of his summer photographs, Tom understood. Colin believed Tom was ready to resume their close friendship, but he still wasn't. He still felt Tom was a living reminder of what Colin was trying desperately to forget.

***

Once at his new school, Colin made some acquaintances, but more often than not, he was alone. Although he was willing to take risks physically, emotionally he had shut down. Hence, he spent most days buried in studies or planning his next adventure. Ultimately, his first year at middle school went by just as he had hoped—nothing bad happened.

Toward the middle of his second year, his parents began to ask if he wanted to go to his local high school, or somewhere else. Colin chose the latter, but he didn't know where. From his guidance counselor he soon discovered that the closest outward-bound type high school was Springfield Academy, in St. Paul, Minnesota, a full four hours away.

Once he glanced at the photographs in Springfield's catalogue, he was again enticed. That very day, he brought the catalogue home, and enthusiastically reviewed it with his parents.

Clearly delighted to see him excited about anything, they promised to look into it.

That night, while walking past their bedroom, Colin paused in front of their door. He heard his mother quietly weeping. She was worried about the new school's high cost, and was agonizing over what they could do. "I just can't say no to him," she cried, "I can't let him down again..."

In the end, Colin heard them say they'd tell him they needed a few weeks to work it all out. He was surprised to find out they still felt guilty about what had happened to him, and he wanted to make them feel better.

The following morning, Colin took the catalogue and called the school's toll free telephone number.

***

Two weeks later, another official-looking envelope arrived for Colin. That evening, when Dwight came home, Colin, baring a wry smile, greeted him. His son handed him the letter. "Go ahead,

Dad, it's OK to open it." Dwight nervously took the missive out of the envelope. While doing so, he briefly flashed back to the time he'd come home to a catatonic Colin gripping onto another official-looking envelope, which turned out to be the subpoena. He quickly put that miserable memory aside and began to read.

Half looking up at his son, and half gleaning its contents, Dwight was suddenly overjoyed. My God, he thought, Colin did all this on his *own;* he'd been awarded a partial scholarship to Springfield Academy! In one swift movement, Dwight had Colin in both of his arms, and off the ground. "Easy, Dad, you're getting to be an old man, and I'm now a young one. You can't go around lifting me up all the time." Colin's eyes glistened with joy and confidence.

"OK," Dwight said as he put him down. "How about if I only do it on special occasions, like every time you knock my socks off... Tell me, how'd you do this?"

"I called up the school, and told them my parents couldn't afford it, but that we all wanted me to go. They told me to have my school send them my grades, two letters of recommendation, and for me to send them a letter telling them why I wanted to go. I did everything they asked, and, according to this, I guess they liked what they saw."

Colin's smile now filled his face, and for the first time in many years, he looked self-assured. "Hey, Dad," he suddenly looked serious, "did they give us enough money? Can you guys afford to send me now?"

Dwight started to get choked up and had to swallow hard. He couldn't speak, but managed to nod yes.

Colin placed his arm over his father's shoulder. As his arm rested there, Dwight remembered a poignant sunset they experienced almost two years ago, while standing on the edge of Bryce Canyon. He recalled how desperately he needed to hang on to Colin back then, but now it was time for his son to move on, and for Dwight to let go.

***

Jordon briefly closed her watery eyes and thought about Anthony once again. As soon as she could, she continued to read on.

***

Springfield Academy turned out to be almost everything Colin had hoped. One night, during his first winter there, he called his father from a pay phone in his dorm. He wanted to share his joy.

"Dad, this place is so cool. We're constantly going on amazing adventures, and I'm learning *so* much about environmental sciences and forest preservation. You're never going to believe what really grabs me. Can you guess?" Colin asked, but not waiting for an answer, he announced, "Forest fire prevention!"

***

As Colin excitedly described how one thoughtless act could affect all forms of life, the metaphor wasn't lost on Dwight.

At the time, Dwight was sitting in his den with his feet raised up on his old desk. His den was filled with the quiet light of dusk mixing with the smoke from his cigar. Framed photographs Colin had taken from their summer trip were everywhere.

"You know," Dwight offered, "you might want to consider a career in that. You'd get to hang out in some pretty cool places, and you'd be doing very important work."

Colin told him he thought that sounded like a great idea. During the remainder of their conversation Colin never mentioned any friends, and Dwight never asked; he suspected there were none.

***

Colin continued to enjoy his experience at Springfield, where he immersed himself in outdoor adventures and his newfound passion, forest fire prevention.

For college, Colin chose the University of Montana in Missoula, where he applied for and received a full academic scholarship. While attending U of M he continued to study Forestry and Forest Fire Management. During his first summer session Colin began doing research in the backcountry, working for the U.S. Forest Service.

***

One night, his father received another exuberant call. This time it was from a wind-blown pay phone, just outside a remote diner near Colin's field research site.

"Hey, Dad, guess what? Ken Sampson, the district manager I've been working for up here, said I could come back next summer and every summer while I'm in school. He also said if things continued to work out, they'd probably offer me a full-time job when I graduate."

"Colin that's great, just great." But Dwight was wary. He took both his feet off his desk and sat straight up. "Did this man by any chance say why he was willing to make this kind of generous commitment to you so early in the game?"

"Yeah, matter of fact, he did. That's weird you'd ask me that. He said he wasn't used to a man as young as me being so completely focused on his work. What do you think of that? "

"Worth giving it some thought," was all Dwight said, but it wasn't all he felt. His mind was spinning. What did this District Manager see in Colin? Was he also preying upon him; or did he see him as a hard-working young man who would be completely devoted to his job because he had nothing else? Either way, the offer worried him. Dwight had always hoped Colin would eventually *get over it* and come home, but neither of those things appeared to be on the horizon.

***

To Colin, the job offer was a perfect fit. He felt safest in the forest, and most vulnerable in his hometown.

***

After that summer, Colin only occasionally returned to Madison. Sometimes his parents would visit him, or they'd meet him in a National Park, but mostly they tried to let him live his own life.

Colin still hadn't formed any close friendships and never got involved with anyone intimately. Instead, he poured all his youthful ardor into his studies and his dreams of someday saving a forest from a fiery demise.

***

Upon graduating from college, Colin began to work full time for the U.S. Forest Service. Because of his previous work for them and his excellent grades, they wanted to put him in a District Office, but he respectfully declined. He said he worked hard to avoid just that. Instead he wanted to be in a forest, working out of a fire-lookout tower.

He felt he didn't need a lot of money or people, only peace of mind. He ultimately convinced his boss of that, who then begrudgingly sent him to a remote Alaskan location.

Once Colin arrived, he was assigned to a tower on Kodiak Island, a former World War II military base. There, he decorated what little wall space he had with pictures of national parks, especially his beloved Bryce Canyon. The rest of the wall space was glass, which was just the way he wanted it. He didn't want anyone to ever sneak up on him again.

***

Over the next few years, on several occasions, he both prevented small fires from growing larger and conducted successful controlled burns.

By the spring of 1996 he was finally living a life that brought him as close as possible to true peace of mind. Still, both during the day and night, he occasionally thought about what happened with Father Pat. Sometimes, he'd dream about the actual molestation, other times he'd think about being powerless in the hospital or on the witness stand. His recurring reverie was that he was being held down, but the perpetrator's face changed; sometimes it was Father Pat, other times it was the doctor, the DA or the judge. The effect was always the same—he'd be covered in sweat and rattled for hours.

At 27, he wasn't looking for a life full of happiness and joy, but rather an existence of reduced pain.

***

What a tragic waste, Jordon thought, and then she returned to Marcos' file. She had last left him in the back of Detective Alexander's patrol car.

33

June 15, 1983
MARCOS

PAL—Parolee at Large.

En route to the Police Department, Marcos finally found the wherewithal to say again that he really didn't think he was still on parole. However, when Detective Alexander asked if anyone had actually *told* him that, Marcos honestly answered "No."

"Well, then we'll just have to keep you here until we sort this out. You see, we don't like guys like you hanging out near elementary schools, and I especially don't want you standing around ogling your victim."

Marcos' stomach clenched. After years of therapy, he knew he was no longer ogling her, nor did he see her as his victim. Now, he just thought of her as his sister. He sat back and let his head drop. He felt powerless and overwhelmed.

When they arrived at the police station, Detective Alexander grabbed a hold of him, yanked him out of the car, and placed him in a holding cell.

The cell was permeated with sweat, urine, vomit, and disinfectant, odors familiar to Marcos. When he took his first breath, he was overcome by nausea, caused not so much by the stench but more by the painful old memories the smells evoked. This was the last place Marcos expected to be that day.

"Detective Alexander!" Marcos finally found the courage to shout out, "This isn't right. I'm missing my graduation."

"No you're not," Detective Alexander smiled, "today you graduate from merely being a parolee-at-large to a parolee-in-custody." Detective Alexander laughed; he was obviously having a good time.

"Detective," Marcos begged, "would you at least call my parole officer?"

"Oh, you can count on that, 'cause he's the only one that can officially place the parole hold on you. I just need to grab a little lunch before I try and reach him. Don't worry, I'll be back!"

Detective Alexander chuckled at his own choice of words, and left.

Marcos sat down on the bench and placed his head in his hands. He felt as if he were completely alone in his own private purgatory, knowing that in a matter of hours he'd either be heading back to UCLA or prison.

***

Three hours later, Detective Alexander returned with a sheepish grin and a sheet of paper. He began talking to Marcos, but wouldn't look at him.

"It appears you were no longer on parole. It's just that the, er, the ah, paper work hadn't quite caught up to you, but you, er, were officially off parole. Oh well, no one's fault really. Sorry for the inconvenience. Look, here's a copy of your parole release papers. You, eh, really should keep them with you at all times, so you don't get yourself in this kind of trouble again."

Marcos was speechless. *He* hadn't gotten himself in this kind of trouble *this* time. He thought he was off parole or he wouldn't have gone to the school. Clearly, his word wasn't good enough, and he wondered if it ever would be.

Detective Alexander let him out of the cell and handed him the paper. Driving back to Sophia's school, Marcos didn't say a word; he wanted Alexander to feel uncomfortable.

By the time they reached the school, both graduation ceremonies were long over. Now, only a few programs, empty boxes of film, and crumpled up tissues remained.

"No offense, Mr. Estrada," Detective Alexander called out as Marcos opened the car door.

Exactly, Marcos thought—no offense, therefore there should have been no arrest. But, what he said instead was, "None taken, Walter."

As Walter Alexander pulled away, Marcos noticed he wasn't smiling anymore. He was now biting down hard on his lower lip. He's probably worried that I'm going to sue him for false arrest, Marcos thought. Good, let him worry.

Now suddenly, on a day previously full of scheduling conflicts, Marcos had nowhere to go. He got in his car, locked the doors, and started it up. A song by singer "Sting" was playing on the radio. He began to drive.

Ten minutes later he was at the beach. He took off his shoes, got out of the car, slammed its door shut, and walked toward the sand. Within moments, his pent up emotions exploded. He took off running, thinking about the song he'd just heard, "...Every move you make, I'll be watching you..."

Fueled by conflicting feelings of anger and relief, he wept as he sprinted along the water's edge. He knew his pants were getting wet, but he couldn't feel it.

***

By sunset, he was back on the road and feeling somewhat better. With Santa Barbara disappearing in his rearview mirror, he began to concentrate on his life at UCLA.

Marcos wanted to go to graduate school and continue working with Dr. Koppell, but he hadn't yet picked a particular field of study. He hoped by taking some summer school classes he'd find it. But, what he really wanted was to run away, to take a vacation. He'd never been on a vacation and felt he needed one now. Still, with so little time off between graduation and summer school, and almost no money, a vacation would have to wait. By the end of summer, he thought, I'll have a lot of time and a little bit of money, and I know just where I want to go...

***

Marcos had first heard of the Grand Canyon while in prison. There he saw a photograph of it in *National Geographic*. He remembered thinking then, if he ever got out of prison alive, he'd go to the north rim, stand on its edge, gaze at the spectacular world around him, and know for sure he was free.

After seeing the article in the prison library, he'd frequently walk over to the magazine rack and pick it up again. Often, it was just the inspiration he needed to keep his dreams alive.

The day he turned in his final library book, Heather, the prison librarian, handed him that magazine and declared, "It's in your hands now, my friend."

***

Marcos now smiled, thinking of all the times Heather George had taken care of him. He still had that magazine with its picture of the Grand Canyon, and by summer's end, he promised himself, he'd go there.

***

Jordon never ceased to be amazed by Marcos' resilience. She knew she'd raised her own children to yell foul at injustice, but she wasn't sure she'd given them enough tools to deal with adversity. In trying to protect them, she now thought, she just might have spoiled them, or worse, rendered them "learned helpless."

She'd have to give that serious thought another day; for now, she needed to return to Sophia's file.

34

June 5, 1983
SOPHIA

Compensation—Making amends; that which is necessary to restore an injured party.

Even though Sophia didn't expect Marcos to come to her graduation, she looked for him nonetheless and was surprised by her disappointment when she never found him. Still, she felt comforted when she spotted Craig, and he mouthed the words, "You look beautiful."

Sophia also thought she looked beautiful. She loved her outfit and felt like a model in a magazine. Standing there, waiting on the platform with the other graduates, she remembered back to when she first opened the box, and her joy upon seeing its contents.

She also recalled how she'd cried when she re-read Marcos' note, and how she tried to send him a thank you note, but couldn't.

Moments after the graduation ceremony, Sophia sought Craig out and told him she had something she wanted to discuss with him. They agreed to meet the following Monday.

***

Once in Craig's office, Sophia told him about Marcos' gifts and note. Then she emptied a small bag of her wrinkled replies on his desk.

"So, can I see Marcos' letter?" Craig asked. After she handed it to him, he carefully read it, and then he asked, "OK, Sophia, what do ya want to do?"

"I want to see him," she said without conviction.

"Are you sure?" he asked.

"No, I'm not sure, but I also know I'm not one hundred percent OK; if I was, I could've written him a thank you note and been done with it."

Craig nodded. "All right, assuming he's off parole, let's consider meeting with him at the end of the summer."

Sophia's pulse quickened, as her thoughts mushroomed. She never, before that moment, imagined that day would really come.

Their next few sessions were devoted to talking about her anxiety, and considering the meeting's logistics. They ultimately agreed that the meeting should be in Craig's office, with just the three of them in attendance.

***

Craig's first call was to Marcos' parole officer, Dempsey Riley. Dempsey explained that Marcos was no longer on parole, and that, although he was a registered sex offender, they couldn't legally stop him from spending time alone with children.

"Off the record," Dempsey said, "I'm not worried about Marcos re-offending. He was perfectly behaved while he was on parole and has stayed in touch with me even after it ended. Although, now that I think about it, I haven't spoken to him for several weeks."

"Anyway," Dempsey continued, "I guess Marcos is just one of the lucky ones; he saw the light before another kid got hurt. But I think he's still working on it. Matter of fact, I think he's still in counseling with a lady named Karen Schwartz. Hang on a minute and I'll get you her number."

When Craig called Dr. Schwartz, she reminded him that, legally, she couldn't acknowledge whether Marcos was even her patient, and, certainly, couldn't release any information about him without his consent if he were. She did however tell Craig that, *if* she had any patient who she felt was a danger to someone else, she'd have a legal duty to inform a responsible party. However, she had *no* such concerns at this time about *any* of her patients. She ended the call by assuring Craig that, if she had permission from any patient of hers to talk to him about their mental status, she would.

Craig thanked her and asked her not to mention his call, so that no one would be unduly disappointed if things couldn't be worked out. Dr. Schwartz readily agreed.

***

Karen Schwartz was delighted that such a plan was finally in the works. As she reflected upon things Marcos had said over the years, she concluded, facing Sophia was both his greatest desire and his greatest fear.

***

Craig's final call was made out of legal necessity, rather than any doubt about the outcome. The call was to Margarita, who predictably jumped at the possibility of their being a family once again.

***

When Craig told Sophia about his calls, she sat up straight and spoke with animated excitement. However, a few minutes later, she looked exhausted, exhaled deeply, and slumped down in her chair.

By the time Sophia's appointment was over, Craig had helped her return to a more even keel. As soon as she left, he shut his door, put his calls on hold, and dialed Marcos' number.

Between the first and second rings, he prayed: Please God, don't let this be the biggest mistake of my professional career…

35

Know—To have knowledge; to possess information, instruction or wisdom. To perceive, or apprehend; to understand.

Just before his phone rang Marcos had been looking through a book purchased at the Grand Canyon. He was still profoundly affected by his summer experience there.

***

In the late evening of August 18, 1983, seven weeks after receiving his Bachelor of Science degree from UCLA, Marcos arrived at the North Rim. After rummaging around in the darkness for a while, he eventually found his cabin. It was hidden away in a grove of aspen trees. Once inside, he set his alarm for 5:00 a.m. and promptly fell asleep.

That night, he slept fitfully, worried he might miss the sunrise he'd read so much about.

At first light, even before his alarm went off, he awakened, grabbed water and candy bars, and found his way to Sunrise Point. There, he and a dozen other disciples wordlessly waited for the moment they'd all come to experience.

Softly, silhouetted beauty began to surround them. When the sun rose, the small assemblage gasped, as the magnificent gorge before them began to glow.

Minutes later, only a few of them remained. Most were making their way back to bed or breakfast. Marcos alone still had tears streaming down his face. He wasn't surprised he was crying, it was his reason for crying that surprised him.

He expected to be moved by the beauty of the canyon and his newfound sense of freedom, but what he didn't expect was that his thoughts would turn to his father, Julio. To his amazement, at the very instant the sun came over the horizon, he was deeply saddened by the fact that his father had died without ever having seen this sight.

Moments later, he began to think of everything he and his father had missed out on by Julio's untimely death. Overwhelmed, he sat down on a nearby ledge.

Marcos now missed his father for the first time in many years, but these sensations were different than any he'd experienced before. Previously, when thinking about his father, Marcos felt a sense of pining and abandonment, which always turned into anger as he considered the turn his life took after his father's death. This time, however, instead of anger, his yearning evolved into a completely new feeling, one Marcos couldn't quite identify. Unnerved by all he was experiencing, he stood up and began to walk.

Ten minutes later, he reached a trailhead marked *Bright Angel Trail*. From his *National Geographic* article, he knew this trail descended, "...precariously into the Grand Canyon, toward the mighty Colorado River..." That sounded good to him, so he began his descent.

By mid-morning, when he was most of the way down the astonishing trail, he reflected again upon the mysterious feeling he'd experienced at sunrise. Since his father's death he'd always felt weighted down by an underlying sense of betrayal and rage. From that point on, his hostility and resentment had been as much a part of him as his own skin. However, since this morning's sunrise, he'd begun to feel a certain un-weighting, an emerging sense of lightness. One word seemed to be surfacing—forgiveness. He now looked for a place to sit down.

When he found a large weathered rock by a small swiftly-moving stream, he dropped down and took a deep breath. His chest filled with moist pinion-scented air. He put his hand in the rivulet, and was surprised by its icy cold strength. When he could no longer distract himself with his immediate surroundings, he returned to his musing.

I've never felt like this before, he thought. I'm not even sure I've ever really forgiven *anybody* for *anything*. This is too weird, I mean, I don't want to forgive and forget. I *never* want to forget the effect all those things had on my life, they made me who I am, but still, this feels pretty good. Suddenly, I'm in control of my feelings, rather than their controlling me. Still, something's missing...

After a few more minutes of frustrating reflection, he finally figured out that what he needed to do was to forgive himself. But, just as sure as he was about the validity of that revelation, he was equally convinced *that* was something he should not do. He should *never* forgive himself for what he'd done, that was unthinkable. He'd worked hard in counseling to take responsibility for all of it, and now, he had to bear the burden of those heinous acts for all of the rest of his life.

More confused than ever, he got up, brushed himself off and hiked on. At the canyon bottom, Marcos started to roam along the banks of the Colorado River. Soon, his tired legs weakened and he stopped on a small deserted beach. He looked up and caught the sun's final glow as it lowered itself behind majestic cliffs. Moments later, he was distracted by the sound of swirling current as the river lapped against the shore.

"I've got it," he said out loud. More than I need to forgive myself, I need to be inspired and motivated to forgive myself. It's the motivation that's critical, not the forgiveness. What I *have* to do is work to end child molestation.

As soon as he considered his lofty and preposterous idea, he wanted to will it away, but couldn't; it was how he truly felt. I know I can't do that, but I don't think that's what's important. What's important is that I try.

Just as confident as he was of his newfound goal, he was positive if he shared it with anyone, they'd surely roll their eyes and laugh at him. Still, he rationalized, scientists have in the past found cures for other so-called incurable diseases or behaviors. Didn't he at least have a right to try? No, more than that, he concluded, he had an obligation to. Prior to this moment, studying child molestation was certainly not what he would have embraced as his life's work. He wanted to *get over it*, not *get in to it*, but now, he felt entering any other field would be cowardly and ultimately meaningless.

He squatted down on the sand. He let the river run between his fingers as his mind began to formulate a plan. Moments later, he stood, brushed off his hands, smiled, and headed toward camp.

***

Jordon tried to imagine what a stranger observing Marcos at that moment would have seen. Undoubtedly, she thought, they would've seen a lean, dark, handsome young man with a glowing smile, and they might've been a little envious. They certainly could never have suspected how difficult the trail he took to get there truly was.

***

By nightfall Marcos had been welcomed by other campers on the Canyon floor, and given what he needed to curl up and go to sleep.

The next morning, he awoke to the sound of hushed voices and the realization that, for the first time in memory, he'd actually slept through the entire night.

When he sat up, they offered him hot coffee, a slab of ham and cheesy scrambled eggs. Marcos felt blessed. Just before daybreak, the campers began their assent. At first he walked with them, but soon pushed ahead on his own.

Alone with his thoughts, he went back to thinking about his revelations of the evening before. Now certain he'd made the right decision, he was anxious to return to the rim and call Dr. Koppell.

***

Stuart Koppell listened as Marcos fervently told him about his time in the Canyon, and what focus he wanted his graduate studies to take. In spite of Stuart's own enthusiasm, he felt compelled to remind Marcos that his research would have to result in a scholarly thesis and represent more than a mere personal catharsis. Marcos agreed, but Stuart suspected Marcos knew that if he were successful, both could likely occur.

When Stuart hung up, he realized he'd been smiling during the entire conversation. He'd always hoped Marcos would recognize that he should use his own personal experiences and insight toward gaining a better understanding of this complicated human condition. Now that Marcos had made his decision, Stuart wanted to offer him a teaching assistantship to make it all feasible. This was something he normally did without consulting anyone, but, given Marcos' past, he decided to discuss it directly with the Chancellor himself. He called Dr. Lang's office immediately.

***

Because Stuart Koppell was a very popular teacher, and was responsible for bringing significant grant money to the school, Dr. Lang made himself available the next day. Once Stuart told him about Marcos' history and what Stuart wanted the school to do, Lang was astounded.

"Stuart, you can't be serious. You want me to make a registered sex offender a teaching assistant, essentially an instructor, at our school?"

"Yes, I do."

Dr. Lang stood up and began to pace. He was worrying about possible media coverage and alumni reaction, but he could tell Stuart was committed to convincing him, "I tell you Stuart, I just don't know. It seems that the risks to this institution, in this situation, far outweigh any possible gain. There are many talented graduate students out there. Why should we go out on such a potentially perilous limb for this one?"

"Because *he's* worth it." Stuart continued, "Academically speaking, he's sure to become one of my most outstanding graduate students. On a personal level, he's been in counseling many years and has overcome tremendous adversity. So much so that I have, on multiple occasions, confidently trusted him to be alone with my thirteen-year-old daughter."

Dr. Lang could hear Stuart's enthusiasm begin to mix with defensiveness and perhaps even anger...

"Finally, Dr. Lang, if you need another reason, let me be clear. If you don't give me your support, I might just find another college chancellor who will, and then I will take Marcos, and whoever and *whatever* else I can with me."

Dr. Lang stopped pacing and looked into Stuart's eyes.

"I don't mean to sound threatening," Stuart said, as he corrected his tone and lowered his gaze. "I know this is not an easy decision for you to make. Further, I hope you know I wouldn't be putting you in this awkward position if I didn't firmly believe that hiring him *was* in the best interests of this University."

Stuart leaned forward in his chair. "This University has always prided itself in exemplifying the concepts of forward thinking and tolerance, and you now have an opportunity to foster that splendid reputation."

As Stuart rose to leave, he thanked Dr. Lang for his time, shook his hand, and told him he hoped he'd hear from him soon.

Zhang Lang walked Stuart to the door, but gave no indication of what his decision would be. Since he'd been both threatened and cajoled, he needed time to think.

Throughout his adult life, Lang took great pride in always carefully considering all possible ramifications of every potentially high profile decision.

***

The next afternoon, Stuart received a handwritten note from Dr. Lang, supporting his request to hire Marcos. Stuart never knew which of his arguments ultimately prevailed, but he hoped it was Lang's innate desire to do the right thing.

***

That evening when Marcos returned to Westwood from the Grand Canyon, he was greeted by a note from Dr. Koppell offering him a teaching assistantship, instructing a section of an Introduction to Psychology class.

After a somewhat sleepless night, Marcos arrived early the next morning, and sat in front of Dr. Koppell's office. When Stuart arrived, he greeted Marcos with a warm handshake and invited him in.

"Marcos, sit down, you look a little bedraggled. What's up?"

"You talked to the powers that be, and they said it was OK to hire me?" Marcos asked with squinted eyes and a furrowed brow.

"Yes," Dr. Koppell answered with a cocky smile.

"To teach *here*, at UCLA and get paid?" Marcos inquired, beginning to smile back.

"Yes."

"*And* I also get to work on my Ph.D., focusing on the area of study we discussed?" Marcos now leaned forward in his seat.

"Yes! Marcos, why are you having such a hard time believing all this? This is what we typically offer our graduate students."

"Yeah, but you and I both know," he said, sitting back and clearing his throat, "I'm not your typical graduate student." He was now trying both to hide his reddening eyes and augment his quavering voice.

"No, you're not a typical graduate student," Stuart Koppell offered. "You're a particularly insightful one."

***

That night, as Marcos paged through his book on the Grand Canyon, and pondered over his good fortune, his thoughts were suddenly interrupted by the ringing telephone…

36

Begin—To come into existence; to start; to initiate.

The man on the other end of the phone introduced himself as Craig Petner, a marriage and family counselor.

"Yes," Marcos responded sitting up in his chair. "I know who you are, my mother told me, you're Sophia's counselor. Is Sophia all right? I mean, I know she's not all right, but did something happen to her?"

"Mr. Estrada, she's fine, but something did happen; she decided she wanted to see you and I think it's time."

Marcos felt a current charge through his body, which ended with a pang in his gut. He said nothing in reply.

"Mr. Estrada, are *you* all right?" Petner asked.

"I'm... I'm fine. Please call me Marcos. It's just—it's just that I'm a little surprised. I mean, I'd always hoped this day would come. I guess, I just didn't think it would come so soon... Do *you* think it's too soon? Do you think I'm ready? I'm sorry, you don't even know me, but do you think she's ready?"

"Yes, I think she's ready, and from what I've learned about you, I think you're ready, too. This, as I'm sure you know, isn't going to be easy on either one of you, but Sophia and I think it's time."

***

Craig could tell from Marcos' voice he was both scared and honestly concerned about Sophia's well being. Still, he remained cautious. Craig was well aware of all the past pain Marcos had caused his precious patient, and he didn't want to put her at risk of experiencing any more.

"She's an extraordinary young lady," Craig continued. "She's worked very hard, and wants desperately to come to grips with all of this, and at the same time hopes to rebuild her relationship with you." Craig paused for a moment; he wanted to give Marcos a chance to let some of what he just said sink in.

"I'm not at all sure," Craig cautiously continued, "if that can ever happen, but I do have a 'reunification plan' I'd like to go over with you. If you think it makes sense, we can start right away; I know that's what Sophia wants. So, if you are interested, I can put the plan in the mail, and you can call me in a few days after you've had a chance to review it."

***

"OK...Sounds good to me," was all Marcos could eke out. After that, he gave Craig his address, thanked him, hung up, and panicked. No longer able to sit still, he went out for a 2-hour run.

***

A few days later the plan arrived. Marcos' heart was pounding as he opened the envelope. After getting over the initial shock of seeing their names together on the same page, he eventually calmed down enough to study it.

Marcos ultimately decided the plan looked well thought out, but somewhat overly structured. He wondered why Craig felt compelled to put in so much detail, but then concluded, under the circumstances, maybe detailed structure was a good idea.

***

Marcos and Sophia finally met the following Saturday in Craig's office.

Marcos arrived first, at the appointed 9:00 a.m. Craig thought he appeared painfully nervous; he immediately took him into his inner office. It took an hour to calm Marcos down. By 10:00, the time Sophia was due to arrive, Marcos could at least sit still.

When Craig heard her enter the waiting room, he quickly walked outside and closed the inner-office door behind him. After greeting her, he told her how nervous Marcos was when he first arrived. Sophia responded by telling him she felt the same way, and had hardly slept the night before. Craig carefully explained to her where Marcos was seated and where he'd placed her chair. He wanted her to feel in as much control as possible. Just before they walked in, Craig reminded her, "You've worked very hard for this moment, and so has your brother. I have faith in both of you and the process. You *can* do this."

"OK, then," she said with a smile, "what are we waiting for?"

Craig smiled back, knocked at his office door, and together they walked in.

***

Marcos was startled, at first by the knock, and then by his sister. My God, he thought, as she walked through the door, she actually came, and she's wearing the barrette I gave her, which really *does* match her beautiful eyes.

"Hi, Sophia."

"Hi, Marcos."

They both stood frozen in time.

***

"Sophia, sit down," Craig said, as he gestured toward a chair. It was the chair he'd just told her about moments ago, but one which she appeared to have already forgotten. Craig began to worry.

***

Sophia sat down and looked directly into Marcos' eyes. She wasn't feeling so much anxious, as she was deeply emotionally invested and very curious.

***

"How's Mama?" Marcos asked, looking like he didn't really know what to say.

"Good, she's really good," Sophia replied too quickly. "She dropped me off and went for a walk. She really wanted to come in, but Craig told her she couldn't. He said this had to be just about us, at least for now."

Marcos energetically nodded his head. "Yeah, I think he's right, but I'll call her later. I'm sure she's holding her breath until she finds out we both survived." He then smiled a cautious smile, which, although small, still managed to light up his face.

An awkward moment went by.

"So, how are *you*?" he finally asked, appearing more subdued.

"Fine, I mean scared, I mean fine." Now, it was her turn to smile. "I mean, I'm both fine and scared. How are you?" She now leaned forward in an obvious effort to show she was capable of being serious and mature.

"Well, calmer than I was when I first got here, but more scared than I can remember being for a long time."

"What are you scared of?" Now, she looked fretful.

"I'm scared that this won't work out, and then I'll lose you again," he replied, with surprising clarity.

"I'm scared of that too," she said, and then looked down.

"OK," Craig interjected, "I'm just going to interrupt for a minute and give you my professional opinion. You *will not* lose each other again unless you give up, and I don't believe either of you will do that." Craig thought he sounded more confident than he really felt, but still he continued. "OK? So, with that said, let's get to work. I noticed when Sophia walked in neither of you got close enough to hug. Do either of you want to do that now?"

They both looked away and gently shook their heads—no.

"That's just fine; I don't want either of you to feel pressured in any way," Craig said. "Now, what about shaking hands? Is that something either of you feels like doing?"

They smiled, immediately extended their hands, shook, and then quickly let go.

Even that small amount of touching seemed to set off feelings in each of them. Sophia suddenly became very solemn.

"Marcos, I have questions."

"I know you do, Sophia, go ahead." Marcos leaned forward in his chair.

***

Marcos really wanted to get past this, but knew the only right answers would be the honest ones. He just hoped his responses wouldn't cause her any more pain.

Sophia's eyes filled with tears. "Why'd you do it?"

Man, Marcos thought, the hardest question first.... I really have *no* idea how much she can handle; I just hope Craig knows what he's doing—

As if he read Marcos' mind, Craig interrupted again. "Marcos, you have to be honest, direct, and thorough. Sophia and you deserve nothing less. Plus, remember I'm here, and if I feel I should jump in, I will."

"OK," Marcos responded, "but Sophia, you have to stop me if I say too much. Bottom line, I'm probably not going to say anything you don't already know, after all your work with Craig, but I just don't want to hurt you ever again." Marcos let out a big sigh, and slowly shared with her the conclusions he'd reached a very long time ago.

"I was young, lonely, angry, and had been abused myself. The last time I felt loved was eight years earlier, before my own father died. After that I was abandoned, assaulted, and treated like an outsider. When Mama sent for me, I had visions of America, of me finally being loved by my own mother, and becoming a successful Americano. I knew she had a little daughter, that I had a half-sister, but I didn't give you much thought. It was all about me, about how I was finally going to get mine." He was having trouble going on, but knew he had to.

"When I got here, the reality of America didn't fit my dream. America wasn't beautiful, at least not the apartment we lived in, and Mama didn't have time to give me the love and attention I'd dreamed of. Any love she had at the end of her long day of work went to you, and, once again, I was the outsider." Reliving that period of his life was painful for Marcos, but he knew he'd do anything to help Sophia, and so he continued.

"The one joy I had found in America was going to school. I liked the classes and friendships I was beginning to form, but I wasn't allowed to spend much time with my friends, because I had to pick you up every day right after school. I resented that, and especially resented that once I got home, I couldn't go out again at night with my friends. Every hour I wasn't in school, I had to baby-sit you."

He then flashed back to his frustration in those days. "Back then, Mama worked about 10 hours a day cleaning houses and small businesses. I never thought much about how hard she was working. I just resented her and," he cautiously continued, "you. But," he quickly added, "I also loved you, at least I loved you as much as I was capable of loving anyone in those days."

An image of a very young Sophia emerged. "I thought you were sweet and adorable, and, at times I actually looked forward to seeing you at the end of the day. But mostly, since I was eighteen, I thought *my* time had finally come, and you were in my way."

Marcos had to pause for a minute; he was now having trouble finding his next breath. So much of what he'd just said were painful facts that were still extremely difficult for him to relive, and even harder to articulate, especially to the one person he never wanted to hurt again.

He wanted to stop, take her in his arms, and beg for her forgiveness, but he knew he owed her much more than that. "I'm so sorry," he offered. "I'm sure some of the things I just spewed out hurt you terribly, but you asked, and you and Craig deserve the truth."

"Go on," she said, without any apparent emotion.

"When I got into bed with you... Craig, Sophia," he looked to each of them for direction, "are you sure you want me to go on? This isn't going to get any easier."

Sophia answered without looking at Craig. "I want you to go on."

Marcos looked over at Craig, who immediately nodded. Marcos continued, "OK, when I got into bed with you, it was still all about me. I never thought about your pain or the pain I'd cause Mama. I felt I was overburdened with too much responsibility. I had to take care of you, cook, clean, and do laundry. I thought, at that point in my life, I deserved whatever gratification I could get. So, I took it."

"But," she interrupted, "when you were sexually assaulted when you were a kid, that hurt you, right?"

"Yes."

"I mean, physically, that hurt you, right?" The volume of her voice increased.

"Yes," he nodded. He then stretched his head back, left it there and squeezed his eyes shut.

"And you did the same thing to me. So how could you not think about my pain?" Her voice got slightly loud. "You said you loved me at times, so how could you *not* think that what you were doing was hurting me?"

Marcos forced himself to look back into her eyes, which were now red and once again filling with tears. He was beginning to panic, but knew he had to respond. "I don't know," he finally admitted. He willed himself to think fast. "First of all, I didn't do the same thing to you as was done to me." He was afraid that sounded like a cop-out. "But, it might have progressed to that. And, as far as the physical pain I did cause you, as unbelievable as this may sound, I didn't think about it in those days." He feverishly added, "But I do think about it now; matter of fact, I think about it all the time..." Marcos wanted to avert his now reddening eyes; instead he swallowed hard and forced himself to look into hers. "Back then," he persisted, "like I said, it was all about me, and I had little or no, what I've come to learn is called, *victim empathy*. I just didn't feel it for you, Mama, or anyone else." He had to pause. A very familiar feeling, followed by a very bad taste in his mouth, now overwhelmed him. He was consumed by disgust for the young man he once was.

***

Sophia waited and then asked, "Was it in any way my fault? Was there anything I did that made it happen?" She held her breath, praying his answer would be no.

"No, no, nothing at all," Marcos said with unqualified earnestness. "And it's very important to me that you believe and understand that. Sophia," he paused again, as if to give what he was about to say more emphasis, "it was *always all my fault.*"

Still unconvinced, Sophia had to ask—"Mama said you told her I would beg for you to come into my bed. Did I? Did I beg for you to come into my bed?" Sophia was now shaking, but, at the same time, she was also feeling somewhat exhilarated by her own bravery.

"Yes," Marcos nodded, and looked at her with ever-saddening eyes. "Yes, you did beg me to come into your bed."

She knew she had, and, as painful as it was to hear it, she felt comforted by his telling her the truth. She hesitantly continued, "So, didn't you blame me for begging you to do that?"

"I did then, but I don't now. Back then, I blamed everyone but myself for everything. Now, I know better."

Part of her was ready to stop, but she was afraid if she did, she'd never find the courage to go on. "The police caught you because I told on you. If it weren't for me, you wouldn't have gone to jail. Are you angry at me for sending you to jail?"

"I was then, but no more." He began to look exhausted.

"Why?" She knew she was pushing him, but she hoped he'd say something that would rid her of her guilt once and for all.

"Well," he paused and rubbed his face with his hands, "first and foremost, I needed to be stopped by the police because what I was doing was terribly wrong. Then I needed to be tried, convicted, and punished, because I'd committed a crime. Once incarcerated, I needed treatment because I was messed up. Years later I learned that without all of that intervention, the likelihood of my re-offending would have been astronomical. So, not only would I have continued hurting you, if you hadn't told the police, but I probably would have hurt other children as well…"

***

A painful fleeting image from his past swept across Marcos' mind, but he willed it away and continued. "Sophia, you've got to understand, back then I could never have even imagined saying any of this. Back then, I was angry with you and I blamed you. Now, as weird as it may sound, I actually want to thank you. Because of your bravery in telling people, when you did, you probably saved both of our lives."

***

Sophia sat still for a moment, reeling from all Marcos had said. She now felt torn between admiration for him and revulsion for everything he'd done to her.

Craig turned to her. "Sophia, what's going on?"

She was fervently trying to put everything she was feeling into words. Taking a deep breath, she waded in, "Well, I'm hurting for Marcos and all he's been through, but I'm also hurting for *me* and all the stuff he put me through. But, I'm OK."

"Sophia, you never cease to amaze me," Craig declared. "So, do you want to go on, or shall we just call it a day?"

"I want to go on." Sophia felt as if she were watching an exciting, scary movie in which she was playing the lead role. She was terrified, but still, she wasn't ready for the movie to end.

"All right, then, if it's OK with Marcos, let's continue."

Craig turned his attention to Marcos. "Marcos, I can see you're upset, but, can you go on a little bit longer, for Sophia's sake?"

***

Marcos simply said, "Yes." But, what he thought was, I would go on, stop, or even cut off my right arm for Sophia's sake.

"All right," Craig said. "Let's give Marcos an opportunity to ask a few questions. Then we can plan for our next meeting, and decide how to end this one. Is that OK with you guys?"

They both nodded yes. "OK, Marcos, what do you need to ask Sophia?"

Marcos inhaled deeply, turned toward Sophia, but couldn't look directly into her eyes. "Sophia," he finally asked, "how much do you hate me?"

***

The question surprised her. She didn't remember ever hating him. "I don't hate you, I've never hated you. I was, and still am at times, angry with you. For years, that's what Craig and I were working on, my anger. First, I had to admit it, next, I had to understand it, and, finally, I had to get control of it. Marcos," she said, with some defiance in her still childish voice, "you hurt me and you made Mama very unhappy. Also, you did all this very soon after my own Papa left. There's no easy way to say it: I loved you and trusted you and you used those feelings to get what you wanted."

***

Stillness and sadness suddenly filled the room. Craig was taken aback by how direct each of them was, although brutally honest was maybe a better description. Even knowing they'd both been involved in intensive counseling for nearly six years, it was remarkable for him to witness such a candid exchange. Clearly, he thought, these were two remarkable young people.

Marcos interrupted Craig's thoughts by slowly asking Sophia, "So, I came from Guatemala in search of love, I found it, and then I destroyed it?"

But Sophia was quick to respond. "You didn't destroy the love, Marcos, just a few lives, and that didn't last forever. Right after that, I met some very kind and smart people, especially Craig, and from that moment on, I began my 'healing process,' as Craig calls it. And, Marcos, in case you haven't noticed, I'm pretty much healed."

"I did notice," Marcos said immediately, "and I thank God for that every day. Because, had I ever discovered that I caused you irreparable harm, I'm not sure I could have gone on…" Marcos let his head drop forward, and covered his face with his hands.

"OK, folks, that's enough for one day," Craig said, as he hastily jumped in. He had to interrupt; even if they could handle more, he wasn't sure he could.

He always knew Sophia was exceptional, but he had no idea that anyone nearing 12 years old could think and behave as she had that morning.

"So, shall we meet here again at the same time next week? Would that work for both of you?"

Each nodded yes, but Craig knew neither wanted to leave. Still, they'd both been briefed on the process, and knew that true "reunification" took time. They'd also been told they would need time in between counseling sessions to reflect and rebuild. Craig remained seated, as each reluctantly stood to leave.

Marcos held his hand out, and looked deeply into Sophia's eyes. Sophia took his hand and held on tight. Clearly, they still weren't ready to hug, but their handshake lingered.

Marcos left first; Sophia stayed behind to spend a few minutes alone with Craig. Once the door shut she collapsed in her chair, grabbed its sides, and extended her long legs in front.

"How are you, really?" Craig asked.

"Fine, really. Hey, you're a great shrink; you should have a little more faith in yourself. Now," Sophia said, firmly re-planting her feet on the ground and then leaning forward, "how about my brother, he's a pretty cool, huh?"

"He is now," Craig offered, "but his behavior years ago wasn't. Don't rush into forgiving him. Forgiveness, if it's real, will come in time. I know you're in a hurry to be close again, to make everything all right, but, if you rush, it might not be real. And if it's not real, it won't last."

Sophia stood up to leave. "OK, I understand, but I still think he's cool." She then flashed Craig a mischievous smile, hugged him, and left.

Gone, Craig thought, is the sad little girl who bit her nails and hid her eyes. Now, in her place, stands this exceptionally sophisticated young lady, who seems so much older than her chronological years.

***

Marcos drove home a happy man. He felt as if the fog he'd been living with for years was finally lifting. Suddenly, colors were brighter, radio music sounded more beautiful, and, when he rolled down the car windows, he could swear he smelled roses.

He had no idea how long these feelings would last, but at least for now, he was beginning to feel better, and was finally on his way home.

***

As Jordon poured over Craig's notes, she noticed that their next big emotional surge came during their fifth session, when Sophia and Marcos finally found the courage to hug.

***

While the first four sessions were generally warm and meaningful, there were rough moments. Craig fully expected these, but soon realized they were hard on Marcos and Sophia. Although he tried to end each session positively, that wasn't always possible.

Just before the fifth session ended, Sophia surprised everyone. "Marcos," she said, "I want to hug you, but I'm afraid to reach out to you. I want to ask for a hug, but I don't want you to think I'm begging—like I used to—"

Marcos interrupted, "I wouldn't think that now, and I shouldn't have thought that then. Wanting to hug and cuddle your big brother is normal, I'm the one who made it into something ugly."

"Then why do I feel so weird about it now?" Sophia asked.

"Because of what I turned it into," Marcos answered. "Look, Sophia, the way I see it, we've had a really weird past, where everything was upside down. I made you think your normal feelings of wanting to be close to your big brother were wrong; they weren't wrong, they were right. I was wrong."

***

Marcos was surprised at how good it always felt to admit to her he was wrong and that it was all his fault. He continued, "But, Sophia, despite my past atrocious behavior, I promise I'll never knowingly hurt you again." His eyes locked onto hers, "So now, I'd like to shake on that, but, even more, I'd love to hug on that."

Unsure of everything, including his own ability to remain standing, Marcos stood and opened his arms. Sophia stepped in.

***

Craig later learned, the second before they embraced, each secretly worried their hug would bring up his old erotic feelings or her old fears. But it didn't, both of them had changed. Sophia now felt safe in Marcos' arms, the way she'd always longed to feel, and Marcos felt like a protective big brother, the person he'd hoped he had become.

Eventually, Craig invited their mother to join them at their counseling sessions, and, slowly, they became a family.

***

After six months of family re-unification sessions, Marcos was finally at peace. His life had become his dream come true. His experience at UCLA was ideal; he loved both his graduate research and student teaching. Many students described him in their evaluations as "inspirational." Beyond that, he was also starting to develop an active social life. Although he hadn't yet fallen in love, he was open to it, and having a wonderful time in the process.

***

Marcos completed his Ph.D. in four years. This time his beaming mother and sister both came to his graduation.

***

Prior to Marcos' graduation, Dr. Koppell again approached Dr. Lang for a second request. This time, it was for approval to offer Marcos an assistant professorship on a full professor track.

It seemed to Lang that Marcos' classes had become very popular, and thankfully, his unusual background had never caused any problems. After thoroughly considering all possible ramifications, Dr. Lang gave Dr. Koppell his approval.

Marcos was slated to begin teaching on September 27, 1987.

***

Jordon then read a few letters Marcos had sent his parole officer that summer. She saw Marcos often wrote about both his good fortune, as well as his fear that it couldn't last. Marcos was right.

37

June 6, 1987
SOPHIA

California Penal Code Section 868.8 requires that The Court shall take special precautions to provide for comfort and support of minor witnesses.

During the drive home from Marcos' graduation, Sophia was so exhilarated she could hardly stay seated. "Didn't you think Marcos' friends were wonderful, especially Dr. Koppell and his daughter, Sally?"

"Yes," Margarita responded, "they all seemed like very nice people."

Sophia could barely wait for her mother to respond to her first question before asking another. "And didn't Marcos look just so handsome in that long black robe with its colorful sash?"

"Yes, mi hija, he did."

"And, Mama," Sophia asked, picking up the graduation program, "weren't you just so proud when they called him Dr. Estrada?"

"Yes, si, of course I was."

"Mama," Sophia turned toward her, "what's wrong? Why don't you seem excited?"

"I am," she said, grimacing. "It's just that it's all such a surprise for me. I never thought my boy could end up in prison, but he did. I never thought any child of mine could go to college, but now he'll be teaching at one…"

"Mama, are you going to cry again, because if you are, I'm going to drive."

"Can't a Mama cry on the day of her son's graduation?"

"Yes," Sophia said with a comforting smile, "but not also drive on an L.A. freeway. Mama, let's just stop and get a cup of tea, and then I'll drive from here. Marcos said now that I have my permit, I should help with driving."

"My little Sophia," Margarita said, shaking her head from side to side, "you always take such good care of your Mama. You and your brother, I give you nothing but pain and trouble, and you both

183

turn out so good. I don't understand." She exhaled deeply and dropped her shoulders. "I'll never understand."

***

In August 1987, Sophia began her junior year at Bishop Arturo High School, during which time she joined the Debate Club and was named a homecoming princess. She loved the excitement of the Debate Club, and the fanfare of being a princess, but her chief concern was always her grades. Marcos had often said that being academically successful would make her life richer and also enable her to become independent, which meant she'd be less vulnerable.

***

Two weeks after starting her junior year she met Senior Deputy District Attorney Jordon Danner for the first time. For Career Day Jordon had been invited by the school's counselor to speak about her life as a deputy district attorney.

A month later Sophia learned that it wasn't the first time Jordon had seen her…

***

On Career Day no students were introduced. Still Jordon, oblivious to who Sophia was noticed her right away. She thought Sophia was unusually beautiful, poised, and seemed older and more sophisticated than her fellow classmates. The only thing Jordon found somewhat annoying about her was Sophia's endless barrage of questions, which were very direct and moderately difficult to answer. Jordon didn't get the feeling Sophia was trying to embarrass her, only that she really wanted answers, and couldn't be bothered with phrasing her inquiries sensitively.

One week later Jordon received a call from Judith Willis, Assistant Dean at Arturo.

Ms. Willis explained the school had a program for students to spend a day in the workplace with someone whose career they might want to emulate. A student named *Sophia* had asked Ms. Willis to arrange for her to spend a day in court with Jordon. Once Ms. Willis described Sophia, Jordon was happy to have her along for the day. She still fondly remembered the pretty, spirited girl in the front row who had asked the difficult questions.

However, Jordon panicked when, a few days later, the confirmation letter arrived:

To: Senior Deputy District Attorney Jordon Danner
From: Judith Willis, Assistant Dean, Bishop Arturo High School
RE: Take A Student To Work Day
Thank you for your willingness to participate in *Take A Student To Work Day*. This is to confirm that Sophia Estrada will be brought to your office on September 20, 1987 at 8:15 a.m. by a member of our staff, and picked up by 3:00 p.m. She will have with her all necessary supplies and a sack lunch.
If this is no longer convenient for you, please do not hesitate to contact us.
Once again, on behalf of the Bishop Arturo High School community, I offer you our heartfelt thanks.
Yours Truly,
Judith Willis

"Convenient isn't the problem," Jordon said out loud. She picked up the phone, called the school, and asked for Sophia's home number. Jordon's hand trembled slightly as she dialed. After all these years, she thought, I still dislike this woman and blame her for the pain both her children endured.

"Si?"

"Hello, Mrs. Estrada, this is Deputy District Attorney Jordon Danner." Her announcement was met with silence. Jordon could almost feel Margarita's panic.

"What is it?" Margarita asked.

"Mrs. Estrada, this has nothing to do with Marcos or my prosecution of him. This call has to do with Sophia."

"Sophia is a good girl. She can't have nothing to do with *you.*"

"According to Ms. Willis at her school," Jordon continued, "she wants to spend the day with me at work." Jordon felt nervous, partly out of disdain for Mrs. Estrada, and partly out of guilt. "I don't know that she even knows who I am; *I* certainly didn't know who she was until I got the letter from the school today. I guess this all started about two weeks ago when I spoke to her class on Career Day. Now I understand she's thinking she might want to become a lawyer, maybe even a district attorney." Jordon thought she was beginning to sound like a rambling idiot.

***

Margarita didn't respond; this was a lot for her to take in. She was on the phone with the DA who'd sent her son to prison, but who also saved her daughter from having to testify. Now, she was hearing for the first time that her daughter wanted to spend the day with that DA, and might even want to become one herself.

***

Jordon continued, "She wants to spend time with me in court as part of her school's *Take A Student to Work Day*. That's OK with me, but I wanted to make sure it was OK with you. I didn't tell the school anything about our, er, prior history—"

"Well, Ms. Danner, thank you for that," Margarita interrupted. "I will need to think about it, and I will call you back tomorrow."

Margarita quickly and forcefully hung up. Jordon could tell Margarita hated hearing her voice as much as she hated calling.

***

When Sophia came home that night, Margarita told her she'd received a call from Deputy District Attorney Danner.

"You did, I mean, she did?" Sophia asked. "She called here? Isn't she the coolest lady you ever spoke to?"

"Mi hija, do you know what she does?"

Sophia had committed to memory much of what Jordon had spoken about on Career Day. "Yeah, she puts away the bad guys, and does it whenever she can without re-victimizing their victims. She believes a good prosecution is when you ethically prosecute the bad guys and empower their victims. She even does child molestation cases and sometimes gets the judge to let her show a videotape of the kid telling what happened, instead of bringing the kid into court."

"I know," her mother said.

"Really? How do *you* know, did she tell you?" Sophia stood there, wide-eyed and teeming with enthusiasm.

Margarita decided to be direct, knowing Sophia would tolerate nothing less. "No, she was the lady who prosecuted your brother, and when she did, she kept you out of court."

***

Sophia was taken aback. This woman had become her hero, but she was the one responsible for sending Marcos to prison. Her first instinct was to call off the meeting; her second was to call Marcos. "I have to talk to Marcos about this," she said, heading toward her bedroom.

Margarita grabbed her arm. "Sophia, wait a minute, if you talk to Marcos now, you might upset him while he's working very hard to get ready for his teaching—"

Sophia yanked her arm away, walked into her room, and slammed the door.

***

Sophia reached Marcos at his campus office. Upon hearing his voice she skipped the greeting, and went right into what she wanted to discuss.

"Marcos, I met Jordon Danner, the lady DA who prosecuted you. I mean I didn't *just* meet her, I met her a few weeks ago. I was thinking about going to spend the day with her, but that was before I knew who she was. Mama told me not to call you, not to bother you—"

"Sophia, hang on, wait a minute, slow down. I don't know what you're talking about, but your calling me could *never* bother me. Now, with that said, why don't you take it from the top?"

Sophia explained the whole story, in great detail, to her obviously astonished brother. She concluded with, "So, Marcos, what do you think? Should I go?"

***

"Yes, I think you should spend the day with her. I believe she deserves your admiration. I mean, think about all she did. She got me convicted, fair and square, of what I'd done, and did it without making you testify. I sat there for three days," he continued, "while she brought in experts to explain what you'd already gone through, and what you'd have to endure if you came to court. Then, for hours, she argued with my lawyer and the judge, all for you, a kid she only saw through the two-way mirror at the SART house." Marcos paused. "Sophia, without even knowing you, she took better care of you than your own family did."

Marcos shook his head in disbelief. "I remember, to this day, her incredibly powerful argument to the judge. 'We couldn't be there for Sophia when she was victimized by the brother she loved. But our legislators have seen fit to give you the power to see to it that she is not further re-victimized by our criminal justice

187

system. Your Honor, with all due respect, I believe ignoring that power today would be an of obstruction of justice and embracing it would be justice served.'"

"She knocked my socks off with that argument, so much so that when I got a copy of the transcript later, I kept reading that part over and over again. That's probably why I still remember it. Pretty amazing words, huh?"

As Marcos listened to himself quote the familiar lines from the transcript, it seemed as if it had happened a million years ago, but felt as if it were yesterday.

"Sophia, my advice to you is that you spend the day with her. If it comes up, tell her I think she and the cop who interviewed me did a great job in my case. You can also tell her how I turned out; I'm sure it will please her. As strange as it sounds now, I honestly felt, even back then, that she cared about me, too. Matter of fact, I remember what she said to the bailiff when he turned to congratulate her after the verdict was read. She said, 'Thanks, Deputy Duarte, but, just because it's right, doesn't mean it's fair.' When he finally escorted me out of the courtroom that day, I thought he was especially kind and gentle, and her words to him were the reason why."

Marcos leaned back in his chair for a moment; vivid images of that day left him speechless and a little bit drained.

"So, Sophia," he eventually continued, "when you meet up with her, hold your head up high and say thank you from both of us."

***

Sophia was stunned by Marcos' response, "Damn, it sure sounds like you've given her a lot of thought. How do you remember so much of what she said?"

"Because it was followed by nearly three years in prison where I had the entire transcript to read and little else to think about. At first, I blamed her and the cop, along with you and Mama, for everything, but, as my counseling progressed, I began to believe that they really saved us all."

"Yeah, I guess so." Sophia still had a hard time picturing Marcos in prison. "So, you think I should go to court and spend the day with her?"

"Absolutely!" Marcos re-emphasized.

"OK, well, I gotta go," Sophia said. "I gotta tell Mama what you said." She suddenly paused, "Hey, are you OK? I mean, after hearing her name, and thinking about all the stuff she said and did, I mean this call had to be kind of hard on you, especially with your trying to get ready for your first class as a real professor?"

"I'm OK, but thanks for asking. Meanwhile, take care, and give Mama a hug from me; also, tell her to be nice to Ms. Danner when she calls back. I've always had the feeling those two blamed each other for my mistakes."

"OK" Sophia quickly answered, "I'll tell Mama to be nice to her, but I doubt she'll listen, you know Mama. Bye, love you."

"I love you too." Marcos answered, but he wasn't sure she waited around for his reply.

***

Sophia triumphantly walked back into the living room. "Well," her mother asked, "what did Marcos say?"

"He said I should do it, and that he loved *me*, and that *you* should be nice to Ms. Danner when you call her back."

"Was that it?" Margarita looked disappointed.

"No, he also said I should give you a hug from him."

"So, where's my hug?"

"Right here, Mama, right here."

***

Margarita held onto Sophia clearly longer than her daughter wanted. A moment later, Sophia ran off to begin her schoolwork.

Margarita hated the thought of her baby girl having any contact with Jordon Danner. She was sure it could only end badly.

38

Victim—The injured party.

The day Sophia came to court, Jordon was planning to argue for the rights of another injured child. This 5-year-old child wasn't legally considered a *victim*, because she was a *mere* observer; she had witnessed her four-year old sister being molested through a crack in the door.

As they walked to court Jordon explained to Sophia that the child's legal status, as a *non-victim*, was both ridiculous and frustrating. Ridiculous, because when one child observes another child to whom she's emotionally tied, being abused, she too feels abused and responsible. Frustrating, because this preposterous legal gap makes it impossible for Jordon to use statutes that protect child *victims*.

Before they walked into the courtroom, Jordon added, "I'm trying to change that law, but, for now, all I can do is try to convince this judge to make testifying as easy as possible on this particular child." Jordon handed Sophia a copy of the 6-page brief she had prepared, and explained that the entire brief only addressed that single issue.

As soon as the judge took the bench, the defense attorney started to argue: "Your Honor, this is a court of law, not a preschool. Why should we jump through all the hoops that Ms. Danner is suggesting in her brief, just to make it easier on her witness? This whole thing is very difficult on my client, and he's got the presumption of innocence!"

"Ms. Danner," the Honorable Judge Slatier said, "is all this really necessary? Maybe you don't really need this witness. If you're so worried about her fragile state of mind, maybe you could just proceed without her. After all, if I go along with all these new ideas of yours and you win your case here, but it gets reversed on appeal, you'll have to retry it back here. That certainly couldn't be good for your fragile witness— "

"No, Your Honor, that would not be good for my fragile witness," Jordon interrupted, "but I don't think that would happen. With all due respect, I am concerned with my witness' fragile state, as well as the finality, legality and veracity of these proceedings. This is precisely why I am making these *lawful* requests. After carefully considering all the circumstances surrounding this case, I am confident of two things: One, that my requests are within codified boundaries; and two, that if you make testifying more comfortable for this child, it will be easier for her to tell the truth. Contrary to counsel's assertion, I have no intention of turning this court of law into a preschool. Quite to the contrary, I want to uphold this court's integrity by making it a place where this witness feels *compelled* to tell the truth. To do that, when a young child is a witness, adjustments must be made."

"Ms. Danner, what is it you want me to do?" Judge Slatier asked, sounding only somewhat annoyed.

"To begin with, before the child even enters the courtroom, I want you, Your Honor, to take off your robe and step down from the bench. Then, I'd like to swear the child in. *I* know her, and I'll be able to use words I'm confident she will understand. That way, she'll be swearing to something that makes sense to her, instead of merely nodding after your clerk reads the usual oath. When she testifies, I'd like her to do so, not from the witness box, but from a regular chair, with her sitting on her mother's lap and her father right next to her. Additionally, I'd like you to tell her it's OK for her to hold her favorite stuffed animal while she testifies, and reassure her that she can take as many breaks as she needs."

***

Jordon decided to keep going because the judge didn't cut her off, and appeared to be listening. "Beyond that, I'd like you to order the defense attorney to ask developmentally appropriate questions and avoid all compound and confusing ones. Finally, I'd like you to stop him from asking questions that, either directly or indirectly, suggest to the child that he thinks she's lying. He can save all that for his closing argument when the child isn't around."

Jordon slowed her pace down. "Everything I've asked for, Your Honor, is either embodied or suggested in existing statutes, ones I've cited in my brief. All I'm asking you to do is to use your vested power to serve justice rather than thwart it." Jordon thought her last comment went over the line, and decided she'd better stop.

"*Anything* else you'd like, Ms. Danner?" Judge Slatier asked, smiling wryly.

"Well, a cappuccino/hot chocolate bar for the breaks would be nice, not to mention world, as well as inner, peace," Jordon joked, feeling that, based upon his smile, she might have won.

"Mr. Fitzgerald," Judge Slatier said without smiling back, "what say you?"

"I think Ms. Danner's demands are outrageous and a waste of the Court's time. You, Your Honor, are, after all, the one in charge. The law *might* give you the power to do what Ms. Danner has put forth, but the people of this county have certainly vested you with the authority to reject Ms. Danner's requests and thereby allow this court's decorum to remain intact." Mr. Fitzgerald nodded at the judge, but Slatier didn't nod back.

"As far as I'm concerned," Mr. Fitzgerald carefully continued, "you have complete discretion in this relatively uncharted legal arena, but the appellate court could possibly overturn your decision if you use your discretion unjustly." Mr. Fitzgerald slowed his pace, undoubtedly recognizing he too was on shaky ground.

"To be just," Fitzgerald continued, "you must be fair to all parties, including my client, and I don't think it would be fair to my client if you engage in the antics Ms. Danner is suggesting."

"Thank you, Mr. Fitzgerald. I think I've heard enough. Anything else, Ms. Danner?"

"No, Your Honor."

"I must admit, I was hesitant to rule in Ms. Danner's favor at first. However, your argument, Ms. Danner, combined with your brief, makes good sense, especially the part about a child being more likely to tell the truth in a child-adjusted atmosphere. Therefore, I'm going to grant all of your requests, except of course for the cappuccino/hot chocolate bar and world as well as inner peace; for those things, you will have to contact your local Starbucks and a higher authority."

Judge Slatier smiled, appearing to enjoy both his ruling and his joke. "That's all for now. Thank you, Ms. Danner and Mr. Fitzgerald. Court is adjourned." As the judge turned toward his chamber, he winked at Jordon, as if to say she'd done a good job.

When Jordon and Sophia walked out of the courtroom, Jordon motioned to her not to speak; she wanted Sophia to learn to be respectful of courthouse decorum.

Once outside, where no one could see them, they celebrated Jordon's victory with a high-five. Jordon's first words were,

"Another win for the little people." That said, they walked on in silence, as Jordon reveled in her victory.

***

While still walking, Sophia was trying to find the words to tell Jordon she knew about the Deputy DA's prior role in her life. Finally, gathering her strength, she blurted out, "Ms. Danner—"

"Please, call me Jordon."

"Jordon, I was one of your little people, my mother told me."

Jordon stopped walking; she appeared shocked. "Oh, I wasn't sure she would. And I'm really surprised you came anyway. I thought, once you found out, you'd surely hate me—"

"Hate you? I don't hate you, I love you. I mean I don't love you, love you, I mean, I love what you stood for today, what you've been doing for children for years, and what you did for me and my brother years ago."

"Really? I'm not so sure your brother shares your sentiments." Jordon now appeared to be having difficulty resuming eye contact with Sophia.

"Well then, that's where you're wrong," Sophia replied, "and, from where I sat this morning, it seems like this is the first time you've been wrong all day. My brother *does* share my sentiments; matter of fact, when we spoke about it last night—"

"You spoke to Marcos last night?"

"Yep."

"Sophia Estrada, would you please join me for lunch and tell me all about your brother?"

***

When Jordon said good-bye to Sophia a few hours later, she told her to congratulate Marcos on his unprecedented accomplishments, and asked her to come by anytime.

***

Now, looking out her window at the night sky, Jordon recalled walking back to her office after lunch that day, hoping everything would continue to go well for both Sophia and Marcos, but presuming it wouldn't. By then she'd already become too cynical to believe in happy endings for victims or perpetrators.

Jordon put down Sophia's file and reached across the rug for Marcos'.

39

September 27, 1987
MARCOS

A prosecutor shall act in the furtherance of justice.

As Marcos stood in front of his closet on the morning of September 27, 1987, he felt everything he'd ever worked for was finally his.

After some last minute indecision, he ultimately decided upon a pair of khaki slacks, a denim shirt—a gift from Sophia, and a Brooks Brothers tie he'd ordered from a catalogue. Just before he left, he buffed his shoes one more time. Passing by his hallway mirror, he thought he looked handsome, or "mucho guapo," as his father used to say. Julio, he thought, would've been proud.

With that thought still in his mind, Marcos approached his classroom door. A sign on the door identified it as: *Psychology 101 (4)—Instructor - Assistant Professor Dr. Marcos Estrada.* That's *me*, he thought with unabashed enthusiasm.

However, his joy quickly disappeared when he read the small handwritten note attached below: *9/27/87 Section 4 of Psychology 101 has been temporarily cancelled. Please report to the Registrar for a new section assignment.*

Marcos was confused, and then frightened. What could've happened? What's going on?

Dazed, he began to walk in the direction of Stuart Koppell's office. When his confusion evolved into paranoia, his walk turned into a sprint. He hoped Stuart knew what was going on, but if he did, why hadn't he told him?

Finally, Marcos arrived at Stuart's office and heard him before he saw him.

"I don't give a shit who *he* is," Koppell barked back, with uncharacteristic vulgarity. "He is *not* going to tell me who I can and can't hire and *you* had no right going behind my back!"

Marcos walked in and saw Stuart pacing while still speaking on the phone. "It doesn't matter that you're putting him on paid leave. What matters is what you've done will humiliate him... Dr. Lang, that's just *not true;* make no mistake about it, this *is* going to destroy him."

Stuart turned to find Marcos standing frozen in his doorway.

When Marcos mouthed the words, "What's going on?" Stuart just looked back.

Marcos was terrified; he'd never seen his teacher look helpless. "Dr. Lang," Stuart continued, "I have to hang up; we'll talk more about this later."

"Stuart, what's happening?"

"A lot. Please sit down. You look like you're going to pass out."

Marcos sat down.

"All right, I'll tell you everything I know, but I might not know enough. It seems the daughter of the District Attorney for Santa Barbara County signed up for one of your classes. When he saw your name on his daughter's registration slip, he flipped out. Apparently, he recognized your name from when his office prosecuted you. Once he was sure you were the same Marcos Estrada, he called Dr. Lang and demanded he fire you. Lang, at that point, told him you hadn't violated any laws and that he wouldn't fire you. Lang did, however, offer to transfer his daughter to another section. Evidently, that didn't placate the county prosecutor, so he did some research on you. When that didn't turn up *much,* he searched for some law you might have violated and, apparently, found it. According to Penal Code Section 290, you were supposed to have registered as a sex offender—"

"I know, and I did, I mean I always have. I've been registered as a sex offender with the Los Angeles County Sheriff's Department since I got out of prison, and I have the paperwork in my wallet to prove it." Marcos began to reach into his back pocket, but Stuart reached out and touched his arm in an effort to stop him.

"According to the university's legal counsel, that's not enough. You're also to be registered with the University Police."

"That can't be true; all I was ever told was that I should register with the agency whose jurisdiction I live in. I live in the county of Los Angeles."

"Well, therein lies the problem. You actually live within the county, but you reside in faculty housing, which is technically considered part of the 'Campus of the University of California,' so, technically you violated the law."

"This is unbelievable; no one ever told me *that*!" Marcos stood up and started to pace. "O.K, what else? You also said when he did some research on me he didn't find *much*. What else did he find?" Marcos stopped pacing and looked directly at Stuart.

There was no mistaking the pain in Stuart's eyes. "He found out you were diagnosed with a mental illness when you were at CMC."

Marcos threw both his hands up into the air. "Well, of course, I was diagnosed with a mental illness. That's what they said so they could keep me there. Otherwise, they would've had to send me back to Stockton. Their conjured-up mental-illness diagnosis saved my life."

"Ah, well, that was another thing. They also found out that you had suicidal ideations."

Marcos began to pace again. Stuart remained frozen in one spot, bracing himself on his desk.

"Oh, give me a break. That should just prove to them how crazy I *wasn't*. I would've been crazy *not* to think of everything I could do to avoid going back to Stockton. I can't believe all this is happening." Marcos sat down and put his head in his hands. By the time he looked up, he was sure he appeared as shattered as he felt. "So, this hot-shot Santa Barbara prosecutor found all this so-called confidential information about me, shared it with the good Chancellor, and what does the fair-minded Chancellor do? Does he tell the prosecutor to pound sand? No!" Marcos stood up and began to pace in earnest. "Call *me* in to ask me about it? No! Call *you* in to ask you about it? No! He secretly cancels my class and ruins my career, no, not just my career, my life. By putting that note on a public classroom door, he has ruined me." Marcos was now both seething and tearing up. "Hasn't the reputation I've built or the work I've accomplished meant *anything* to *anybody* at this university?"

"Marcos," Stuart said, trying to calm him down, "you *know* it has. It's meant a lot to your colleagues, your students and me. It's meant a lot to anyone who has met you, listened to one of your lectures, or read your dissertation. Lang is just a coward."

"No, Stuart, he's not *just* a coward, he's a bully. And he's like all the other bullies I've met in my life, only he's got a suit on."

Marcos froze and looked pleadingly at Stuart, who twice tried to say something, but ultimately could only shake his head.

Finally, Marcos continued, "Well, I know there are laws that prevent him from firing me because of my prior mental status, but I suppose if they arrest me on this trumped-up charge, he'll have his excuse. Does he think I'm going to be arrested for this so-called crime right in the middle of my class? Have they *ever* arrested *anybody* for this?"

"I don't know the answer to either of those questions."

"Well, *can* they legally arrest me for this?"

"Lang thinks so, or, at least, that's what the University's lawyer told him. That's why he shut down your class, to avoid any possible negative publicity—"

"So, that's what it boils down to for him, avoiding bad publicity. Clearly, in his eyes, I'm nothing, and he'll do whatever it takes in order to get what he wants or keep what he has..." Marcos exhaled loudly and shook his head in disbelief. A moment later, his eyes started to redden, he looked down, and in a softer voice he added, "I thought the University would be different than my life in the barn or at Stockton. So I ask you, Stuart—how come I'm feeling raped all over again?"

Marcos looked at his friend Stuart, willing him to answer; when he didn't, Marcos collapsed back into his chair and covered his face.

Stuart walked over to Marcos and put a hand on his shoulder.

"So, what now?" Marcos asked, sitting up and running his hands through his hair and down his perspiring neck. "Is it all over? Everything I've worked for is gone, and I'm about to be sent back to prison for another sex offense?"

Stuart cleared his throat. "Well, apparently, *that's* still up in the air."

Marcos looked up. "Why? Why is *that* still up in the air?"

"It's still up in the air, because, according to Lang, in order to arrest you they've got to get an arrest warrant, which has to be approved by the *Filing DA* and then signed by a judge."

Marcos continued to stare at Stuart a moment longer. Suddenly, he slapped both his hands on his thighs. "I'm outa here."

"Where are you going?"

"I'm not sure."

"Marcos, wait. Let's talk to a lawyer friend of mine and see what he thinks."

"I'm sick of lawyers. The only one I ever really respected was the one who prosecuted me, and she works for the son-of-bitch who's now leading the charge against me. So, no thanks, I don't think I'll be calling any damned lawyers. I'm going to have to handle this on my own."

"Marcos, please reconsider letting me call a lawyer. Whatever it is you're thinking about, you could end up making this much worse on yourself."

"Well, that's a risk I'll just have to take." Marcos quickly looked into his mentor's hopeless eyes. "Stuart, I gotta go. I promise I'll keep in touch; trust me." He turned and stormed out of the office.

"I always have," Stuart called out, but he was sure Marcos couldn't hear him.

***

Marcos rushed out of the building in a blind rage and ran the 6 blocks to his car. By the time he got there, he was shaking so hard, it was a struggle for him to even get his key in the door. Once inside he locked the door, grabbed the steering wheel, and put his head down on it.

Soon the sound of his sobs resonated in the car. At first, his pain pooled near his heart muscles, but then spread like a swiftly moving cramp throughout his body.

Everything, everything I've ever worked for is gone, he thought, and I'm going back to jail. Now, covered with sweat, he was repulsed by his own familiar odor. It was the same way he smelled the night he ran from the barn to the church. Nothing, nothing has changed, he thought, I'm still the same pathetic, frightened kid whose only defense is to run away. Why can't I get a break? Why does it always turn out this way for me? All that counseling and education, it was a waste of time, it did me absolutely *no* good...

As he continued to wallow in the unjustness of it all, a feeling began to emerge—his last thought didn't sit right. He knew the counseling and education *had done* him some good. He also knew he wasn't the same person he used to be. Soon, he found himself defending himself, to himself. There were some things about the old Marcos that were alright, he thought. His sweat was one of those things. I sweat because I persevere; as a kid I found the courage to travel to safety, even though it was night and I was all messed up; as a teenager I found the guts to survive and ultimately thrive in prison. More recently I found the nerve to face Sophia. My sweat, he concluded, is something I should be proud of; it's a sign that I'm hanging in there in the face of adversity. I don't sweat like a coward, he concluded, I sweat like a warrior. I'm not a loser; I'm a survivor and a fighter. The big difference between the old Marcos and the new me is that, these days, I've got more sophisticated weapons with which to go to war—I have my education and everything that comes with it.

"I'm not the person I was," he said out loud, but I can take the best of that person with me. I'm no longer the abandoned kid in the barn, or the humiliated, *dissed* teenager. I'm now Dr. Estrada, and I became him because I took control over my life. I've gone from victim to survivor before, and I can do it again!

He sat up straight. This, he concluded, is unfair; he then struck the dashboard for emphasis. And any fair-minded person would agree with me. Marcos knew he'd met fair-minded people before, and hoped he could manage to meet one of them again today.

He started the car and headed downtown. His first stop would be the Los Angeles County District Attorney's Office, and, if things didn't work out there…

***

Upon arriving in downtown LA, he decided to park his car several blocks away. He wanted time to walk, calm down, and remind himself who he now was: I'm Dr. Marcos Estrada, Ph.D., UCLA I'm no longer a child molestation victim nor a child molester. Therefore, I shouldn't have to *beg* for mercy; I should *expect* justice.

When he entered the District Attorney's Office, he stopped in a nearby restroom. Once inside he washed his face, combed his hair, tucked in his shirt, and straightened his tie. Then he stepped up to the mirror and again reminded himself who he was. By the time he walked out and approached the receptionist, he was sure he looked like Dr. Estrada, a poised UCLA professor, a gentleman in search of some answers.

"What can *I* do for you?" Tina, the sumptuous receptionist asked, leaning forward just enough to make her double-entendre obvious.

"I'd like to speak with the Filing District Attorney for Westwood, please."

"Do you have an appointment?

"No."

"Is she expecting you?"

"I don't think so. Here's my card."

She looked at his card and appeared impressed.

"Dr. Estrada, are you an expert witness in one of her cases?"

"No."

"Well, Doctor, I have to tell her what this is about, or she won't see you."

"Would you please just give her my card?" Marcos searched her eyes for kindness. "I believe once she sees my card, she will see me. I don't mean to be evasive, it's just that it's private." Marcos remained steadfast, but now added a slightly flirtatious smile.

***

Tina wasn't sure what to do. She was confident he wasn't a defendant, or any other kind of person she was supposed to keep away from the DDAs. Still, she felt he wasn't being forthright about why he was there and what he wanted. Yet, he looked so aristocratic and handsome. I'm sure, she concluded, whatever the circumstances are, Paula would love to see him. "Dr. Estrada, let me see what *I* can do. Meanwhile, have a seat over there."

***

Tina winked at him and called Paula Grossman's extension.

"There's a Dr. Estrada here to see you."

"Who is he?" Paula asked.

"I don't know."

"Why does he want to see me?"

"He wouldn't say. He said once I gave you his card, you'd want to see him."

"Well, what does his card say?"

"It says Marcos Estrada, Ph.D. He's from the UCLA Psychology Department."

"Never heard of him. How does he look?"

"Cute."

"I didn't mean how does he *look*, look, I meant, does he look dangerous, as in, should I *not* meet with him?"

"I knew what you meant, I just thought I'd answer your question succinctly. The only way to describe him in one word is—cute, and if you want me to use two words, I'd say—very cute."

"Well, OK, Tina, put your tongue back in your mouth and send him in. I could use a brief conversation with a very cute mysterious doctor. But call me in fifteen minutes to give me an excuse to throw him out. I still have a lot more cases to review."

"OK. Excuse me... Dr. Estrada, Ms. Grossman will see you now. Go through those double doors, her office is the second one on the right."

***

"Thank you very much." Marcos then smiled at Tina, hoping to convey that he knew just how influential she was.

"You're quite welcome." Tina looked flattered.

Marcos pushed his way through the double doors, feeling her approving eyes checking him out. Her obvious interest gave him just the boost he needed. He found the door marked Paula Grossman, Senior Deputy District Attorney. He knocked first, and then walked in.

***

"Ms. Grossman," he said, extending first a beguiling smile and then his hand, "thank you for seeing me. Here's my card. My name is Marcos Estrada; I'm an assistant professor at UCLA. I'll try to be brief; I know how busy you are."

"No, that's quite all right," she said, with deliberate warmth. "Please, sit down and tell me how I can help?" What do you know, Paula thought, he *is* cute. Now, I wonder what brings him here...

"I was wondering," Marcos asked, "if you've had a chance to review my file?"

"I am sorry, Dr. Estrada, you have the advantage. I don't know what file you're talking about. Were you a victim of some crime?"

"Yes, but that's not the way LAPD appears to see it. Again, I'll try to be brief, but, since you haven't seen the file, I'll have to give you the five-minute history, if that's OK with you."

"Yes, that's fine." This, she thought, is getting more interesting by the minute.

Marcos took a deep breath and began, "I am a convicted child molester, a 290 registrant."

Whoa, I never would've guessed that, she thought.

"Upon my release from prison about eight years ago, I finished my undergraduate work at UCLA and continued there as a graduate student. Last summer, I received my Ph.D., and was offered both a job and housing at an off-campus apartment complex. As a 290 registrant, I knew I had to register with the local authorities, so I mailed a change of address form to the Los Angeles Sheriff's Department. My alleged crime is that I didn't also register with the UCLA Police Department."

"But how—" Paula began to ask.

Marcos interrupted, "Apparently, the father of one of my future students is the DA for Santa Barbara County. When he recognized my name, he wanted me fired. When he found no obvious legal basis to do so, he found a legal loophole. Now, his position is that my not registering with the UCLA police is tantamount to another felony sex offense, one which could cost me my job and a return trip to prison."

Marcos finally exhaled. Paula was captivated by both his story and how succinctly he told it.

Marcos continued, "Just about an hour ago I was told I was put on a paid leave of absence, pending your decision to seek an arrest warrant. That's why I'm here. I wanted to tell you my side of the story, face to face, and answer any questions you might have. My hope is to convince you to neither sign the warrant, nor file charges against me."

Paula was unnerved by all she'd heard, but felt she should respond calmly, with appropriate questions. "Besides that, have you committed any other crimes since being released from prison?"

"No."

"Did you ever violate your parole?"

"No, still I was once taken into custody on an alleged parole violation, but that was after my parole term had already ended."

"But, how? A screw-up by some relentless law enforcement officer?"

"Exactly."

"Oh, that must have been a real treat."

"It was bad, but what made it worse was that the screw up caused me to miss my own under-graduate graduation."

"Ah, LA's finest?"

"No, a detective in Santa Barbara."

"That was where the initial arrest occurred, right?"

"Yes, the initial one, and the only one."

"Boy, I guess those guys don't let up."

"Actually they're a pretty good bunch of professionals—just one rotten apple in the group, his name is Detective Alexander. *He's* a bit over-zealous, and *I* keep having to bear the brunt of his enthusiasm." Marcos smiled for the first time all day.

Paula shook her head and thought, he's remarkably calm and he's even got a sense of humor; more than I'd have in his situation.

Marcos continued, "I have no trouble registering with UCLA or anywhere else. I'd just like to be told that I won't be facing another charge, so I can return to work."

Their eyes met and held. The ringing phone startled them. It was Tina. Paula answered it in one ring. Tina said she was calling to save her, even though she was sure Paula no longer wanted to be saved.

Paula quickly replied, "No, but thank you for calling," and hung up.

"Was that the 'call-me-in-ten-minutes-so-I-don't-get-stuck' phone call?" Marcos asked.

"No, well, not exactly," Paula said, with a defiant, yet sheepish, smile. "I actually told her to call me in fifteen minutes."

Marcos nodded. "Been there, done that. Those UCLA students of mine can be rather long-winded. Hopefully, I haven't been that way with you."

"Not at all, you've been very concise. Just give me a few minutes. First, I've got to look up the charge. Then, I'll pull up the warrant request and your rap sheet on my computer. After I've done both of those things I should be able to give you an answer. It may not be the answer you want, but at least you'll know where you stand."

"Thanks, I came in search of a fair-minded person," he said, once again locking his eyes with hers, "and I think I found one."

"Well, like I said, you might not hear what you want, but I will give it a careful read. Just give me a few minutes."

***

Marcos sat opposite her, trying desperately to appear calm. He leaned back and looked around. Well, she's got all kinds of impressive honors and diplomas, he noticed, but, unfortunately, she also appears to be married with kids. Too bad, she's very attractive... I can't believe I'm actually checking her out at a moment like this. Marcos' thoughts were suddenly interrupted by her outcry.

"This is bullshit! My office has *never* filed these charges on anyone before, and the first case certainly isn't going to happen under these circumstances. You had no way of knowing about this requirement, did you? Your apartment complex though technically on campus, is actually *miles* from the nearest classroom."

"So, technically, I did commit a crime, a felony?"

"Yes, you certainly did. Because you were initially convicted of a felony sex crime, not registering with the UCLA Police Department is also a felony. Therefore, technically, you could be sent back to prison."

"But, if I technically broke the law, and could be sent back to prison, how can you legally not file charges? Doesn't a Deputy District Attorney have to file charges if they know someone broke the law?"

"No, they don't. Just because someone technically breaks a law, doesn't mean a prosecutor has to file a charge. We have to act in the furtherance of justice and not engage in what's called— selective prosecution."

"So, how are you going to further justice in this case?"

"First, by rejecting both the warrant application and the case itself; then by asking you to register with the University police right away; finally, by calling the Santa Barbara DA and telling him in vague and uncertain terms to—g*et a life*."

"He'll listen to you?"

"Hell no, he probably won't even take my call, but at least I can tell my boss I tried to contact him, out of professional courtesy, but I assure you, no courtesy will be intended."

"That's it?"

"That's it. I'm printing a copy of the rejection paper work for you right now. If UCLA doesn't give you your job back after they've seen this, call me, and I'll give you the names of a couple of good lawyers who'd like nothing better than to sue the bastards!" Paula smiled broadly.

"You've been wonderful."

She stood up and extended her hand, "Best of luck to you, Dr. Estrada, and thanks for coming in."

"I don't know how to begin to thank you." Marcos took her hand and for the last time, looked directly into her eyes. "You've given me my life back."

"No," Paula shook her head, "you came and took it back, and you gave me a chance to administer justice, something I don't get to do nearly as often as I'd like to. Here's your paperwork, and, I repeat, thanks for coming in." Paula smiled again while gently releasing her hand from his extremely damp, and trembling grasp.

Before now, he thought, she probably had no idea how truly terrified I was.

Marcos smiled back and left her office. On his way out he stopped by Tina's desk to thank her again. As he trotted back to his car, he thought—holy shit, I did it and now I can't wait to tell Stuart!

***

Stuart Koppell was still thunderstruck by the tale Marcos had just conveyed. "So, you did it?"

"Yep!"

"You're amazing." Although this wasn't the first time Stuart was awed by Marcos' bravery and competence, it was just the most recent.

"Why, thank you," Marcos responded, taking a small bow, "but really, it was the DA who was amazing. She showed guts and integrity this morning; makes you almost proud to pay taxes. She gave me this document as a going away present. I think it is a combination 'get-out-of-jail-free' card and/or my best piece of evidence, should Lang not reinstate me immediately."

"Here, let me see that."

Marcos handed the form to Stuart.

"It says here that the reason for rejection is 'In the Furtherance of Justice.' What does that mean?"

"I don't know. All I can tell you is that when she looked at the charge, the warrant application, and my criminal record, she said, 'This is bullshit!' Then in the column labeled "Reason for rejection," she checked the box marked —'In the Furtherance of Justice.'"

"So, when I hand Lang these papers, and he replies, 'what does all this infer?'" Stuart asked, imitating Dr. Lang's voice, "am I supposed to say—the filing DA from Westwood thought the charge was bullshit?"

"That," Marcos replied, "would be both an accurate as well as concise account of her remarks." Marcos and Stuart both burst out laughing, and, to Stuart's surprise, they embraced. Stuart held on tight, he needed to, he'd just experienced an emotional roller coaster, one he never expected to experience in his ivory tower. As he released Marcos, he cleared his throat and said, "*I* can't wait to see Lang's face when I tell him precisely what she said."

Stuart immediately turned and headed toward Dr. Lang's office. This time, he didn't bother to make an appointment.

Lang's reaction to the news was extreme relief. Now, he wouldn't have to fire Marcos, and he could keep everybody's name out of the morning paper.

***

The following day, Marcos returned to his classroom. The hand written note on the door was gone, but so were his students. He assumed word of his suspension, and the reason behind it, had made its way through the gossip mill.

The class was to be held from 9:00-9:50. By 9:10, he'd already concluded no one was coming, but he stayed until 9:50. He knew he looked ridiculous sitting alone in the empty classroom, but he was sure it was the right thing to do. At 9:51 he packed his books and left.

***

Only one person saw Marcos come and go. Watching from the building shadows, she was trying to find the courage to approach him. When she saw him drive away, she went back to her dorm, but returned the next day at precisely 9:00.

"Dr. Estrada," she said, walking into his deserted classroom at 9:45, "I'm one of your students. My name is Annie."

"Hi, Annie, thanks for coming. I'm afraid you're a minority of one. My other students appear to be boycotting my class. If you'd like, you may join them, I believe their next class meets at 1:00 in this very room."

"I don't want to join them, I want to apologize to them."

"Why?"

"Because of my father, they are being deprived of the best Psych 101 teacher UCLA has to offer."

Marcos was taken aback, but revealed nothing. "Your father must be the DA from Santa Barbara."

"Yes, and I want you to know, for the record, I hate him for what he did."

"Really, I'm sorry to hear that."

"Why are you sorry to hear that? I thought you'd hate him too."

"Quite honestly, I absolutely hated him about 48 hours ago, and entertained visions of driving to Santa Barbara and confronting him. But, I don't feel that way anymore, nor do I think you should hate him."

"Why?"

"Because he presumably acted out of love for you, and was probably trying to protect you. Undoubtedly, if more parents tried to protect their children, less children would be hurt."

"Dr. Estrada, with all due respect, I think you're giving my father way too much credit. I think he was just being a jerk."

"Maybe so, but he didn't know *me* when he made his move; he knew my label. From my past record, he didn't want me anywhere near his daughter or anyone else's. Can you blame him for that?"

"Yes, he pre-judged you."

"Yes, but from where I stand now, he seems like a pretty good Dad. He tried to protect you, but at the same time, he raised you to be an extremely articulate and brave young lady. It took a lot of guts for you to come here and tell me who you are. Do you know how rare that is?"

"Probably not, nor do I think my father's motives were as pure as you apparently do, but, you're the teacher and I'm just the student, so, I'm open."

"Well, thank you, and I want you to know I very much appreciate—"

Annie interrupted him. "Dr. Estrada, how could you appreciate anything about me? I'm the reason all of *this* happened." She turned around and gestured toward the empty classroom.

"Because," Marcos finally responded, "you are here, and so am I, and, hopefully, others will join us tomorrow." She doesn't have a clue about appreciation, Marcos thought. She's probably been extremely protected all of her life. It's easy to appreciate a lot more, when you've had a lot less.

"Annie," he went on, "have you ever heard the expression, *In life, what doesn't kill you, will make you stronger,* or something like that?"

"No," she responded.

"Are you open to learning that might be true?"

"Like I said, I'm open to learning anything you have to teach."

"Ah, music to a professor's ears," he smiled. "Well then, Annie Feller, I'll see you tomorrow."

Annie immediately put out her hand and Marcos shook it. "Dr. Estrada, it was a pleasure meeting you, and, if I have anything to say about it, you'll not only see me tomorrow, but several other students as well."

Marcos smiled, but remained unconvinced.

***

The next morning, every built-in seat was filled; beyond that, it appeared additional chairs had also been dragged into the classroom.

"Good morning," Marcos bellowed as he entered the room, "welcome to Section 4 of Psych 101." He searched for Annie Feller and found her, glowing, in the center of the front row. Focusing his attention on her, he said, in a softer voice, "Thank you all for coming." They all smiled back, but none as broadly as Annie. "I am your professor, Dr. Marcos Estrada. I see we have more students than expected, so, after class today, it will give me great pleasure to ask the administration for a larger classroom." Putting his materials on his desk, he took an extra moment to compose himself. "For now, let's begin with the assignment from Chapter I...."

***

Jordon put down Marcos' file and started reflecting upon the comment made by her fellow prosecutor, Paula Grossman. So do I, Jordon wondered, get to "administer justice" as often as I'd like to?

She stood up and walked over to a framed photo taken at her law school graduation. In the photograph she was flanked by 3 friends, none of whom were still practicing law. They'd all burnt out long ago, but she never would, not after what she'd been through...

40

*Welfare and Institutions Code Section 300—Any child...who has
suffered...serious physical harm inflicted upon the child...either
willfully or through negligent failure on the part of the child's
parent(s) to protect said child...may be adjudged to be a
dependent child of the court.*

Jordon was 17 the first time she knocked on the large wood and
stone door. To its left was a small bronze sign, with words in
fading letters: N.Y. Society for the Prevention of Cruelty to
Children—Foster Home # 5

The door was opened by a child in a wheelchair, and held open
by another child on crutches. Still a third child stood back, but was
clearly visible—she had healing burn marks on her face and arms.
Jordon had come to volunteer to teach dance, but, at that moment,
all she wanted was to run away. As the little girl in the wheelchair
rolled back, the boy on crutches said, "Come in." Jordon felt she
had no choice.

No adults were around. The facility was decrepit and smelled
as bad as it looked. More injured children came out to join them.
Jordon felt nauseous and wanted to leave now more than ever. A
moment later, an adult arrived.

"You must be Jordon Danner, I'm Ann Miller. Thank you so
much for coming. I see you've already met a few of your dance
students." Ann greeted her with a warm smile.

My dance students, Jordon thought, can't dance; they can
barely walk.

"Alison will take you into the auditorium." Alison smiled,
creaking her wheelchair back. Ann continued, "That room should
be perfect for you. You'll have to excuse me now, I must return to
my office. We're in the middle of admitting a new child, and the
police are still here. I'll be in the room around the corner if you
need anything. Thanks so much for coming, I'm sure the kids will
have a great time!" With that said, she gently tousled the burn
victim's hair and left.

"This way," Alison said. Jordon and 6 other children followed.

The auditorium was enormous and cold. Its floor was filthy, with grime so thick both footprints and wheelchair tire marks were obvious. The children waited; Jordon still hadn't said a word. She took a deep breath; the smells nearly overwhelmed her. She decided to breathe through her mouth.

"Hi," she said with her very next exhale, "my name is Jordon. I've been studying dance for ten years, and I'd like to share my experience and training with you." This was her rehearsed opening line, but, the moment she said it, she knew it made absolutely no sense.

Great," Alison said, "we're ready!"

***

Jordon returned every Friday to the NYSPCC foster home for the remainder of her senior year. Occasionally, she taught them dance moves, but, mostly, she listened. Throughout the year she learned about their horrendous childhoods and atrocities they'd endured either at the hands of their parents, or from others when their parents were absent or too drunk or stoned to do anything about it.

Jordon came to hate all their parents, but her young friends didn't. They loved them and desperately wanted to go home as soon as the court would allow them to. Jordon thought the foster home was dismal, but at least here they were safe. When she asked the children why they wanted to go home, their responses always amounted to the same thing—I want to be with my family, they love me, and I love them.

On May 27, 1967, Alison finally got her wish. The administration agreed to send her home to visit for the long Memorial Day weekend, but Alison never returned. Three days later, her raped and strangled body was found along FDR Drive. Her rapist/murderer was never brought to trial. Jordon was inconsolable. Her parents tried to convince her not to return there, but they knew she couldn't let the other children down. Still, Jordon saw Alison's face everywhere and from that moment on, there was no doubt in anyone's mind, what Jordon would do when she grew up.

***

Jordon closed her eyes for a moment. After all these years, she could still see Alison's face, and hear her words: "We're ready!"

"OK, pal," Jordon said out loud, "then I'm ready too."

Jordon sat back down and picked up Pat's file.

41

December 1, 1990
PAT

Parole—A conditional release of a prisoner who has served part of his sentence; such may be revoked if he fails to observe the conditions of parole.

Pat knew the parole-ordered counseling was a waste of time. He tried to convince Bob Katz, his mandated therapist, of that, but Bob was emphatic. He insisted Pat needed private and group therapy. Bob especially extolled group therapy as the means by which Pat would understand and ultimately change his toxic behavior.

Pat knew Bob was flat out wrong; he, unlike the perverts in his group, had never hurt a child. He was always gentle and kind with his boys, but the others, he believed, were worthless pond scum who belonged locked up forever.

The way Pat saw it, the little boys he touched had secretly, wordlessly, told him they wanted him. He specifically remembered Colin, waiting around that night in anticipation of being with *him*. He also remembered that children in all the other countries had come to *him* and rubbed up against *him*, trying to get *his* attention and affection.

***

Often, during private therapy sessions, Dr. Katz asked Pat about his sexual fantasies. Katz believed keeping track of an offender's fantasies was the best way to predict if they were on the cusp of re-offending. Since Pat always denied having such fantasies, Bob didn't explore the issue any further.

***

On December 23, 1990 Pat, knowing he couldn't be rearrested for merely having *bad thoughts*, decided to *mess* with Bob. He told him what he thought he needed to hear.

***

Bob cringed as he listened to Pat's fantasy. Fearing what Pat might do once he left his office, Bob decided to force him to remember excruciating details of his prison life. He hoped if Pat recalled the feelings and sensations he experienced while there, he would refrain from re-offending.

"Pat," Bob said, "I appreciate your honesty concerning your fantasy today, but, before you leave, I want to make sure you understand the consequences of your molesting another child."

"I understand."

"Well then, you tell me, what would they be?"

"*If* I got caught, I'd be sent back to prison." Pat made no mention of the effect his actions could have on a child; he never did.

"OK, and you remember what prison was like?"

"Of course, I do."

"You remember the sensation of handcuffs and the smells of your cell?"

"Yes."

"The taste of prison food and the way guards and other prisoners acted toward you?"

"Yes." Pat, now visibly upset with this line of questioning offered. "Remember it? I still can't sleep at night because of it."

"So, you know if you touch another child, you will go back there?"

"I'm never going back there!"

"But, you know if you even *touch* another child, you *will* go back?"

"I'm never," Pat said very slowly and deliberately, "going...back!"

Bob felt a chill go down his spine, followed by a brief wave of nausea. "Well, that's very good to hear. When you leave my office today, I want you to remember everything you possibly can about prison. I want you to remember how it smelled, sounded and felt, and I want you to remember that's where you *will* go if you re-offend. Will you do that, if not for your victims, then, at least, out of respect for me?" Pat nodded yes.

***

That was an easy commitment for Pat to make, because he had no respect for Dr. Bob Katz. Moments after leaving Bob's office, Pat wasn't thinking about prison anymore. Thinking about prison upset him. He wanted to be happy, feel good, and experience pleasure, which he hadn't for a very long time. He now felt as if he were due.

***

The next day, Katz received a call from Jim Van Dyke, Pat's parole officer. "Dr. Katz, has Pat been showing up for his sessions?"

"Yes, why?"

"Well, he missed his early morning appointment with me today."

"Hum, no, he's been here. In fact, he was here yesterday, and I was going to call you. I think he might be at risk for re-offending; he's just not getting it. He still feels all-deserving, and no one else matters. In other words Jim, I think you should keep a close eye on him. I did what I could yesterday reminding him of prison life, but I don't think I got through."

Jim thanked Bob for his counsel and advice and slammed the phone down. He was convinced Dr. Katz would never have called him. "Sometimes I'm sure," he said out loud, "that I'm the only moron who truly gives a shit." He shook his head, and in a softer voice asked, "What the hell am I doing working on Christmas Eve Day anyway…?"

But he knew the answer; after 22 years in the business he couldn't turn it off. He felt personally responsible for protecting his community, and could only leave his worries behind when he drank.

Jim next called Pat's place of employment. He not only wanted to talk to Pat, but also to hear from Pat's boss.

Mr. Taft answered the phone.

"So, how's Pat getting along?" Jim asked.

"Fine, he's such a nice quiet man," Mr. Taft offered. "Personally, I doubt he ever did what he was convicted of, and people say I'm a pretty good judge of character. Matter of fact, at his request, I even gave him today off."

Jim took a deep breath, and quickly asked where he thought Pat might be. His boss said he assumed Pat had gone Christmas shopping. After thanking Mr. Taft, Jim hung up, hurried out of his office, and drove directly to Pat's apartment.

***

Jim feared Pat wouldn't be home. One of Pat's parole terms was that he was on "search and seizure." This meant Jim could enter his residence, "Day or night, with or without probable cause." As soon as he arrived, he knocked only once and then kicked the cheap door in.

The room he entered was spotless; still he put on a pair of plastic gloves. The smell was unmistakable; the pungent odor of cheap lotion and ejaculate was everywhere. He soon found its origin—mounds of tissues in the trash by the side of the bed. Next to it was a small pile of papers. On the desk was a telephone and computer. Everything *looked* normal, which made Jim certain something very wrong had or would soon occur. Either way, his personal radar and panic level were both soaring. He was positive he had to find Pat before it was too late.

He looked around the room for clues. He decided to start by turning on the computer. Pat's screen saver was a picture of a quaint Mexican village at sunset. Jim assumed Pat chose it because it reminded him of the Mexican village he was initially sent to—the first place he ever molested a child. Jim gritted his teeth and continued.

Next, he found Pat's computer password taped to the bottom of the telephone. He gained access to his e-mail. Seeing and opening a suspicious attachment, he was horrified by what he found.

They were, without a doubt, the worst set of child pornography photographs he'd ever seen. The first set of photos made him shudder. When he looked at the second set, his eyes welled up with tears. What a sick fuck that photographer was, he thought. How the hell could any member of the same species as me, force children to do that? He wanted to press *delete* and make it all disappear. But knowing it was evidence to be preserved, Jim held back, and instead carefully turned the computer off.

As far as he was concerned, Pat was beyond the *risk of re-offending*, and was downright *dangerous*. The only thing Jim didn't know, and now had to find out, was where the hell Pat was.

As Jim approached Pat's bed, the images he'd just seen were beginning to mix with the increasingly noxious smells. He wanted to rush outside and vomit; instead, he forced himself to look through Pat's pile of papers. At that point, Jim had only an amorphous notion of what he was looking for; he just hoped he'd know when he found it.

"Oh fuck," he cried out. In the pile of papers, he found a receipt for a hunting knife purchased yesterday. "He's not just dangerous, he's armed and dangerous." Continuing to search, now at a furious pace, he found a slip of paper that terrified him. "Oh no. Oh Dear God, no…"

***

"Five golden rings…" Pat was driving along, singing his favorite part of the popular Christmas song. When he was choir director, he usually chose the sweetest looking little boy to sing it. He wondered if they'd sing that song in Mineral Way, and, if so, what their little choirboy would look like.

***

Jim's first call was to the Moro County's Sheriff's Department. He had to warn the Watch Officer of his suspicions. After doing so, he promised to be there in a half-hour. He then asked them to, if possible, merely observe Pat until he arrived. His next call was to the local Police Department; he needed someone dispatched to Pat's apartment to secure the evidence.

***

"Pa rump pa pum pumm…" Pat wondered if the choir would feature a little drummer boy with curly blonde hair and big blue eyes.

***

Well, Mr. Taft was right about one thing, Jim concluded, as he sped down the freeway, Pat had gone shopping. He knew as a felon he'd never get a gun. Instead, Jim surmised, he bought the most ominous looking hunting knife he could lay his hands on…

***

Pat could hardly wait. Images of beautiful boy angels with curly blonde hair and blue eyes were circling through his mind and causing his groin to stir. He took a deep breath and momentarily closed his eyes. Suddenly, he had to jam on his brakes; he'd almost rear-ended the car in front of him. He pulled over to calm himself.

Maybe, he thought, that was a sign to abandon my plan. Getting out of his car, he pulled the frayed announcement from his breast pocket. Rubbing it against his face, he closed his eyes and inhaled deeply. He once again became aroused. He knew he had to go.

Getting back into his car, he slowly and now methodically continued his drive to Mineral Way. The last thing he wanted was to be delayed or distracted from his mission.

Soon, soon... he thought, and then he resumed his singing. "Amazing grace, how sweet the sound, that saved a wretch like me..."

When Pat first arrived in the Trinity Episcopal Church parking lot, he continued to sit in his car; he wanted to think about it one last time....

A few minutes later, he stepped out of the car, he was now convinced a greater power was in charge. Putting his hand on his knife sheath, he headed toward the church, in the direction of the little boys' seductive songs. Soon, soon... he thought. In the distance, he heard tires screeching, followed by his Parole Officer's familiar voice.

"Pat, put your hands up, and slowly drop down to the ground."

Pat ignored him, and kept walking. Next, Pat heard: "This is the Moro County Sheriff ordering you to stop!"

Pat kept going. And there's the predictable hero-cop, he thought. He's standing straight ahead, right between me and the luscious little boys with their sweet, sweet lips... Suddenly, Pat pulled his knife out of its sheath, and ran toward the Sheriff's deputy.

"Pat," Jim screamed, "don't do this!"

"Shoot him!" the Sheriff ordered.

The deputy fired on command. Pat doubled over, dropping his knife and some other object as he fell to the ground.

Jim rushed toward him while displaying his badge and shouting out who he was. He then crouched down next to him. "You stupid son-of-a-bitch, why?"

Pat was bleeding from his stomach wound, still he whispered to Jim, "Come on," he concluded, "you and I both knew it *had* to end this way."

Jim was silent for a moment shaking his head in disbelief. "You had this whole damned thing planned, didn't you? That's why you left all those clues, missing your appointment with me, telling your shrink about your fantasies, bringing the announcement about this to your apartment, and signing up for kiddy porn. I should have realized it then; kiddy porn was never your thing. This wasn't ever about you hurting another child, it was always about us stopping you before you ever did."

***

Closing his eyes, Pat tried to hear the little boys sing, but all he could hear were sirens.

"Pat," Jim said, "it didn't have to end this way. "

"Oh, yes… this is exactly the way..." Pat was having trouble finding enough breath to speak.

Jim sat back, and rubbed his temples while wondering out loud, "What about the poor son-of-a-bitch deputy who had to shoot you?"

"Tomorrow's hero," Pat whispered.

***

Jim was surprised Pat had heard him. He said nothing in response; he knew Pat was probably right. Paramedics were now rushing toward them. Pat clearly had one more thing to say. Jim leaned closer.

"Hey, Jim, you didn't fuck up, I did." With that final absolution, Pat drifted away. His last words were: "Father Romero?"

Who's Father Romero? Jim thought, as he stepped out of the paramedic's way.

He then stopped briefly and spoke to the Sheriff. Walking toward his car, Jim surprised himself by starting to pray.

Dear God, this poor tortured son-of-a-bitch's last act was one of kindness. In his own sick mind he thought this was the only way he could stop. If there is a Hell, at least give that some thought before you send him there.

***

After the crime scene was cleared, a few sheriff's deputies remained to calm the community. As children were leaving the rehearsal hall, one of the smallest boys stood back and watched. He saw something shining in the bushes where Pat had been shot. He surreptitiously scooped up the rosary beads, and pocketed them.

***

Returning home, Jim called Bob Katz and told him what had happened. They both agreed that maybe it was for the best, but inside, Jim knew, and thought Katz did too, that they'd failed again.

That night, while lying in bed and reflecting upon his horrendous day, Jim realized he hadn't yet notified Pat's next of kin as he told the sheriff he would. As far as he could remember, Pat hadn't named anyone. Still, he felt unable to fall asleep without checking.

He dressed, returned to his office and removed Pat's file from his desk. He turned to the first page, "Emergency contact—*No One.*" Jim kept searching, somewhere there had to be someone...

He never found Pat's next of kin, but buried among Dr. Katz's notes he found the name *Father Romero,* the name he'd heard Pat reveal with his last breath. Jim read on. Moments later he realized Pat had died, on the same night of the year, as someone named Father Romero had nearly thirty years ago. Who the hell was this guy? Jim wondered. He kept reading, but Father Romero was never mentioned again.

When he finished reading through Pat's file, Jim was sure of two things: Pat's death wasn't as much of a tragedy as his life was and he now desperately needed a drink. Without looking, he reached for the bourbon bottle tucked under his file cabinet. He drank enough to calm himself, but not so much as to risk a third D.U.I.

Before leaving, he made his final entries in the file, closed it and secured it with a tattered rubber band. Across the top, he wrote—Case Closed—Died a Parolee-at-Large—12/24/90.

***

Just before midnight, Jim returned to his apartment. I guess tomorrow, he thought, I could try to find Pat's former victim. I've got nothing else to do, and this news could at least make Colin's Christmas a merry one...

***

Although Jordon had read reports and suppositions on Pat's final hours many times, they always got to her. What a tragedy, she thought; Pat never had a chance. If only his mother hadn't physically abused him, or his father hadn't emotionally abandoned him, or Father Romero hadn't died when he did, any one of those things could have made a difference. But with everything stacked up against him, plus the very real possibility that the physical abuse he endured had also caused permanent brain damage, he was doomed.

Jordon's eyes filled with tears, for Pat's victims as well as for Pat. It's downright dangerous, she concluded, to ignore any form of child abuse. She then reached for Marcos' file.

42

December 12, 1988
MARCOS

Res Ipsa Loquitur—The thing speaks for itself.

The idea of seeing Marcos again after all these years worried Jordon. She would never have planned such a meeting, but she knew it was important to Sophia, so she acquiesced when Sophia suggested it.

Sophia was then a senior in high school, volunteering at both the Rape Crisis Center and the District Attorney's office. Lunch was set for December 12th at Humphrey's, Jordon's favorite café. Humphrey's was a small homemade-soup-scented restaurant, tucked away just down the street from the courthouse. As soon as Jordon appeared at its door the owner, Martha, greeted her by name and showed her where Sophia and Marcos were seated.

Sophia had chosen a small table against the wall, near a pot-bellied stove. When Jordon first saw their profiles, with uncanny resemblance to each other, she was taken aback. Marcos stood the moment he saw her, and extended both a sincere smile and his hand. "Ms. Danner, thank you so much for joining us."

Jordon was speechless. He was as handsome as Sophia was beautiful, and clearly fit his title of Dr. Estrada. Gone was the skinny young man of 18, and in his place was a poised professor.

"The pleasure is all mine," Jordon said, while regaining her composure. OK, now what, she thought, but that question was quickly resolved. Sophia's pager sounded; in response, Sophia leapt up and apologetically went in search of a pay phone, and Marcos pulled out a chair for Jordon.

While Sophia was gone they discussed their mutual admiration for Sophia. Shortly into their conversation, Jordon had difficulty focusing on what Marcos was saying. Memories of how she berated him in her closing argument returned, and she began to perspire.

Unlike Jordon, Marcos appeared completely relaxed and focused. While Jordon was busy tapping her fingers on her thigh, Marcos sat perfectly still. As her mind was racing ahead, thinking about the next thing to say, Marcos looked comfortable, even with the periodic silences. Whereas it felt to her as if Sophia had been gone for an eternity, Marcos seemed unaffected by her absence.

When Sophia finally returned, she didn't stay long. "Sorry, guys, I was paged by the Rape Crisis Center. There's been a call-out for a teen-aged advocate and I've got to go, cuz I'm on-call. Darn, and I was so looking forward to this."

Sophia then kissed them both on the cheek, avoided eye contact with either, and ran off. Jordon's uneasiness increased, she felt she and Marcos had already discussed one of two things they had in common. Now, all that was left to talk about was the other.

Marcos appeared to sense her angst. He turned to her and gently asked if she had difficultly sitting opposite a man she'd convicted of child molestation.

"Yes," she answered honestly, "but probably not for the reasons you're thinking. It's hard for me because I've always felt guilty about your sentence. I wanted you to go to a lock-down treatment facility, in lieu of prison, but no such facility existed then—"

"Not then," interrupted Marcos, "and not now. Really, things haven't improved much. Sorry, I didn't mean to interrupt you or preach to the choir. But, even if such a place existed, I can't speculate as to how it might have affected me. I can, however, tell you, if you are interested, how being in prison did affect me."

"I am very interested." Jordon, now nervous and curious, leaned forward. Sophia had told her about his experience at Stockton and CMC, but she wanted to hear it from him.

Marcos paused a moment, seemingly wanting to put the final touches on his carefully chosen words. He looked into her eyes. "I suffered great pain and humiliation at Stockton State Prison. As a result, I had a breakdown. But the breakdown was my ticket to CMC where I ultimately got the help and guidance I desperately needed. Since then, I've concentrated on rebuilding my relationship with my family, and," he said, with a self-conscious smile, "working daily to mitigate the effects of, and ultimately end, child abuse."

Marcos looked down briefly. "I know that sounds lofty and maybe even a little ridiculous, but it's how I feel." Regaining his composure, he continued, "With that goal, each day when I awake I have clarity of purpose; I know who I am and what I need to do.

With both purpose and my restored family, I consider myself a very lucky man."

When Marcos paused, Jordon was sure she looked shocked and knew she was at a loss for words. Marcos continued, "Please understand, I would never have wished my earlier life on anyone; but, in spite of, or maybe because of all I've been through, I feel blessed."

He paused again, until she looked directly into his eyes. "And I have you and the cops to thank for getting the ball rolling." He briefly stopped to moisten his drying lips.

"When I first met you, I was oblivious. I either didn't know, or didn't care whether I was hurting Sophia. Now she is more precious to me than anyone," his eyes started to redden, "and she's recovering from what I did to her, instead of still experiencing it."

"Marcos," Jordon interrupted, "you're overwhelming me. What you've done with your life is remarkable. You succeeded where most have failed, and you've thrived in a world that had mostly shown you nothing but its ugly side. You, and what you have accomplished, are, quite simply, amazing."

Marcos blushed, appearing uncomfortable with her compliment. "I met some good people along the way... OK, enough about me. You must be starving. How 'bout we order some lunch? This place smells great..."

Jordon felt that Marcos had said all he planned to say about his past, and it was time to move on. Before she knew it they'd been there for over an hour, and she had to rush back to court. At 1:15, they said their good-byes, wished each other well, and agreed they'd see each other again at Sophia's spring graduation.

As they left, Jordon was sure of two things, she and Marcos had an extraordinary conversation, and Sophia had set off her own pager.

***

Jordon now leaned back and closed her eyes; that, she recalled, was the last time she saw Marcos.

43

June 6, 1989
THE ESTRADA FAMILY

Family—Immediate kindred, constituting a fundamental social unit in a civilized society.

Sophia graduated from high school with Marcos and Margarita in attendance. Jordon's son's emergency appendectomy kept her from attending. Later that same week with Jordon back at work, Sophia came by to show her the photographs. They both agreed the Estradas looked elated.

With her excellent grades and volunteer work Sophia had her choice of colleges, but decided to live at home and attend UCSB That way, she rationalized, they'd have enough money saved for her to attend University of Wisconsin Law School. For years, she'd heard Jordon talk about her involvement in developing UW's new child advocacy program, and she wanted to be a part of it.

***

Three years later during Sophia's senior year at UCSB, she applied to and was accepted at UW Law School. Jordon then contacted her old law school friend, Jerry, at the Dane County DA's office. Years before, he'd been the one who sent her Pat's file. After a few moments of extolling Sophia's virtues, Jerry was convinced he should offer Sophia a paid internship.

***

Sophia loved living in Madison. After spending her life in Santa Barbara, she was ready for a change, and cautiously hungry to try life on her own. During her three years in law school she worked very hard and thus graduated early with accolades and honors. After graduation, although offered several more lucrative jobs in private firms, she decided to continue her employment at the DA's Office. They were thrilled to have her. It was very difficult for them to find good lawyers willing to prosecute child molestation cases; most felt those kinds of cases were too time consuming and too sad. Since Sophia felt neither of those things, her career at the DA's Office flourished. Her social life, however, did not.

Although Sophia appeared open and friendly to everyone she worked with, she never spent time with colleagues away from the office. She didn't want anyone finding out about her past. She feared if they did, soon defense attorneys would whine to judges that she couldn't be objective because of her personal bias.

She knew she had strong feelings, but she felt that they made her a better prosecutor. As a result of her past, she was adamant that neither the alleged victim nor the accused should be on the receiving end of an unjust criminal justice system. As a result of her strong feelings, Sophia worked exceedingly long hours.

***

Although Marcos admired Sophia's zeal, he often worried she was working too hard. To belay his fears, he made frequent visits, but far too often, she only had time to join him for dinner and an early morning run the next day. Not wanting to intrude, he tried to time most of his visits with her infrequent vacations. When he did, they'd habitually rent a quiet cabin at a northern Wisconsin lake, and talk for days at a time.

By then Marcos was becoming very well known. Once the book, based upon his dissertation, came out, he was *hot on the lecture circuit*, as his agent called it.

In general, he loved traveling and sharing his ideas with others. The only difficulty he experienced was that wherever he spoke, there was a small group of hecklers who didn't want a convicted child molester in their town. So far, their numbers had remained small, and their only mission appeared to be to harass him. Still, understanding how dangerous his detractors could become, he never mentioned them to Sophia or Margarita.

***

Earlier that year, Margarita had become caught up in her children's passion of working for the welfare of abused children. After Sophia left for law school, her mother began volunteering at the same SART House she'd accompanied Sophia to many years ago. Her main assignment there was to greet and stay with victim's mothers while their children were being interviewed. Mothers benefited because they felt she understood their pain, and

Margarita profited because it helped her deal with her own anger, guilt, and loneliness.

Though it appeared to Margarita that her children had moved on, she often lamented about Marcos' trial and incarceration. In spite of all the good that came out of it, Margarita remained full of anger and blame and most of it was directed toward Jordon. She was convinced if only Jordon had shown some mercy, Marcos would never have been imprisoned and abused.

***

At that point Jordon, too, was still angry at Margarita. She believed that, if Margarita hadn't abandoned Marcos in Guatemala, and then brought him to the U.S. to baby-sit for Sophia, neither assault would've occurred.

Since neither Jordon nor Margarita wanted to upset Sophia or Marcos, they simply avoided each other; this worked out well for both until January 15, 1997.

44

Mother—A woman who has borne a child.

The sun had set an hour ago, it was long past dinner hour, yet Jordon and Margarita were still at the SART House. Margarita was there as a volunteer and Jordon in her official DDA capacity. Jordon had just finished listening to a 5-year-old describe how she'd been molested by her cousin, after she'd been left in his care by her mother. The victim reminded Jordon so much of Sophia, her resentment toward Margarita swelled. Hence, she decided it would be best to leave quietly, without having any further contact with Margarita. As she gathered her belongings she overheard the investigating detective's final words to the victim's mother and Margarita: "Don't worry, we'll find him, arrest him, and send him to prison, where he'll get exactly what he deserves!"

Shortly thereafter, everyone but Margarita and Jordon left. As Jordon started to leave, she yelled *goodnight* to Margarita, but heard nothing in response. Jordon then poked her head into the waiting room. Margarita looked up, clearly she'd been crying.

"How could you send him there?" Margarita asked.

Jordon had no idea what she was talking about. "How could I send who, where?"

Margarita, now looking angry, cried, "How could you send my Marcos to prison?" Jordon was dumbfounded; Margarita continued, "It's all your fault."

Jordon was now outraged. She'd always managed to hold her tongue out of respect for Sophia, but this was too much, especially after just having witnessed this latest interview.

"My fault?" She retorted. "My fault? How could *I* send him there? How could *you* leave him in Guatemala and how could *you* be so neglectful as to not even notice that one of your children was molesting the other?"

Jordon knew she'd gone too far. She shouldn't have accused Margarita of neglecting her children. Still, she'd grown to love

Sophia and admire Marcos, and felt both had flourished in spite of their mother, not because of her.

"Neglect them?" Margarita responded. "How dare you say I neglected my babies? Yes, I couldn't give them things because I was poor, but you don't know about poor, you're rich. You have no right..." Margarita's eyes were full of rage, but still she persisted. "You don't know about my life after Marcos' father died, or when Sophia's papa became a drug addict. You don't know what it's like to leave your babies so you and they can live—"

"I may not personally know," Jordon interrupted, now thoroughly riled, "but I lost relatives in the Holocaust. All my life, I've heard about painful decisions mothers had to make to survive, but I've never heard of a single mother who blindly left *both* her children so defenseless, they *both* ended up sexually assaulted by members of their own family! You, Margarita, are in a class by yourself."

Jordon knew she was out of control, yet she couldn't stop; even though she realized her bitter response to Margarita was the culmination of years of anger built up toward all mothers who'd been blessed with children, yet failed to protect them. At that moment, lacking the wherewithal to apologize, Jordon tried to turn and walk away.

"Wait a minute!" Margarita snapped back. Although appearing hurt, she apparently wasn't done. "I'm in a class by myself? What does that mean? That I don't care or hurt? I cared and hurt all the time, but I got pregnant so I had no choice. I had to have—"

"You *had* a choice. You could have given them up for adoption or had an abortion."

"Abortion?" Margarita recoiled and her back became rigid in an instant. "Abortion is the worst form of child abuse."

"Oh, bullshit!" Jordon responded. That was it, as far as she was concerned, Margarita had just literally quoted Jordon's least favorite bumper sticker, which now made it impossible for her to remain silent. "You want to know what the worst form of child abuse is? Go to the video library in back of this building. You'll find hundreds of videos of children who've been neglected or abused. Some have physical injuries; all are scarred for life. Many of the assailants were their parents who either injured the children themselves or left them unprotected." Jordon barely stopped to breathe. "These parents were in *no* position to raise their children and so they didn't; they just emotionally checked out." Although her throat was strangled with emotion, she spoke through it. "These mothers gave life to children, but gave their children no kind of life." Jordon looked directly into Margarita's eyes. Control, she thought, get control, but control was far from her reach. "Becoming pregnant may not have been your choice," she continued, "but being a mother was. And after you made *that* call, you should've been the best damned mother possible, but you *weren't*!"

***

Margarita had no snappy comeback. She knew she was no match for Jordon, and, furthermore, she agreed with most of what was said. But, Jordon was wrong about her having a choice; abortion, for her, was not an option. Still, instead of accepting that, or giving her children up for adoption, she'd moved through motherhood in a daze. Now, suddenly feeling depleted, she let her head and shoulders drop, and then her tears started anew.

***

Jordon's heart was still racing. She was sure speaking her mind so boldly had been wrong. Now, watching Margarita cry, Jordon knew she could never repair the damage or even end their conversation in a remotely comfortable fashion.

"Margarita," she said, "I'm sorry; it's been a very long, hard day. I don't know what possessed me. You're right; I don't know what it was like for you. I can't, my life has been very different." Jordon looked around for her purse. I've got to get out of here, she thought, before I make things even worse.

"Well," Margarita injected, in a barely audible voice, "maybe not *so* different. My Sophia told me that even though you have this big important job you've always been, as you just said, 'the best damn mother.'"

No, I wasn't, thought Jordon, I sure wasn't one of those mothers who naturally wanted to do what was best for her children. I often felt imposed upon, and regularly resented the outcome.

"No, I wasn't," Jordon said out loud. "In many ways, I was, and still am, a very self-centered mother." She finally sat down. "I'm gone a lot, and, even when I'm there, I'm not always there for them. When they were toddlers, I wasn't exactly the doting mother..." She was now remembering back to all the times she avoided playing with her own children, and instead, went to her room to read case files.

"Sometimes," she continued, "especially when my children were younger, I'm sure I was a better mother to the victims I worked with than I was to my own kids." Jordon had no idea how she'd gone from exhaustion to hysteria, and from lecturer to confessor-of-the-soul, but she knew she was running on empty. Still, she had one last confession to make.

Taking a deep breath, she added, "While they were growing up, and to this day, I come in and out of their lives like a hurricane. I'm really not sure how close they *really* feel to me..." Now, what am I doing? Jordon thought, I'm blathering, and saying things out loud that I haven't even admitted to myself.

Margarita interrupted her thoughts. "From what I hear, they feel very close to their Mama, Sophia told me. Sophia also told me that your oldest boy, he told her no matter how busy you were, your kids always come first."

Jordon felt relieved to hear that, but didn't believe it. Although exhausted and more than ready to go home, she desperately wanted to find the right words to end their roller-coaster conversation. Come on, Jordon, a part of her thought, you're a lawyer, and words are your business. But the other part of her thought, Danner, you've already said too much!

It was Margarita who finally brought their arduous encounter to a close. She stood up, walked over to Jordon, took one of Jordon's hands in both of hers, and said, "I blow it."

Jordon started to smile in spite of herself; she was surprised to hear Margarita use that phrase. "You blow it?" Jordon repeated.

"Yes. Isn't that the right saying?"

"Well, that depends upon what you're trying to say."

"I want to say I make some bad mistakes. And I want to say, thank God, my children live through my bad mistakes."

Jordon was taken aback; Margarita was freely admitting what Jordon was struggling to accept about herself. Jordon's heart, and then her arms, went out to Margarita.

As they hugged, Jordon knew, in that moment, each finally acknowledged their greatest disappointment—neither had turned out to be the kind of mother they'd hoped they'd be. Both had made mistakes they could never go back and fix. Jordon knew her mistakes were not nearly as grave as Margarita's, but neither were her circumstances.

As they stood there embracing, Jordon flashed back to something she'd read in *Ms. Magazine* decades ago. It was an article in which a sociologist concluded that there were only two things all mothers, regardless of their socio-economic condition, had in common: they all loved their children, and all felt guilty about not being better mothers.

Eventually, each calmed down enough to say their good-byes.

While driving home, Jordon thought she still wasn't sure she could ever completely forgive Margarita, or now even herself, but she vowed to try and do better.

***

When Jordon walked through her front door that night, she was thrilled to see all four of her boys. Now that Sam was 5, Ray 11, Anthony 13 and George 14, they were rarely all home at the same time. They were all sitting around watching a Lakers' game and grumbling about how hungry they were. They, of course, had no idea what she had just been through.

"Mommy, where were you? What's for dinner? We're starving!" Sam said, jumping up and down on the couch. The older ones knew better than to complain or jump on the couch. They probably thought it best to let *The Baby* do their bidding for them.

"Sorry guys, I was delayed at work. Sam, stop jumping on the furniture. Hey guys, you know I love all of you very much, don't you?" She said, with a discernable lump in her throat.

Anthony appeared to immediately pick up on his mother's mood, and momentarily looked worried. He reassured her, "Yeah Mom, we love you too...damn, I can't believe he missed that basket! So, Mom," he continued, "what's for dinner anyway? We are starving, yah know."

Instead of pointing out they should've gotten something to eat themselves, or running into the kitchen and frantically preparing something healthy, Jordon decided to join them. She had no interest in watching the Lakers' game, but desperately wanted to be surrounded by her boys. Swallowing hard, she asked, "How 'bout I order a pizza?"

"Sodas, too?" George finally spoke.

"Yep."

"And bread sticks?" Ray asked, looking away from the game for the first time.

"Yep."

"Thanks, Mom."

"Yeah, thanks Mom," they chorused.

"Love ya, Mom, you're the best," her baby said, as he got up to give her a hug, which Jordon appreciated for as long as he'd let her.

***

When Jordon got into bed that night, she wondered if anyone ever turned out to be the kind of parent they hoped to be. She considered asking Greg his opinion, but after a moment's thought decided not to. She already had endured all the intense conversation she could handle for one day. Instead, she put her head on his chest and fell asleep.

***

Now, having relived the experience of that day, Jordon knew the decision she was about to reach, would be all the more difficult. Still she was convinced she could remain objective, but thought now would be a good time to return to Colin's file.

45

Change—Alter; cause to pass from one place to another.

It took two weeks for news of Pat's death to reach Colin at his Alaskan residence. It came in the form of an e-mail from Tom: "Father Pat committed death–by–cop suicide last week. Good riddance to bad rubbish is what I have to say. Hope it gives you comfort, old pal. Take care, Tom."

"Hope it gives you comfort?" Colin asked out loud. Does it? Does it give me some comfort? He didn't know.

He paced from one side of his tower to the other. Well, he thought, with Father Pat dead, at least there's no chance of my ever seeing him again, or of him ever hurting anybody else. So, I guess I'm glad he's dead, but it doesn't give me any real comfort. Matter of fact, he thought, suddenly stopping his pacing, I'm sorry Tom even told me.

Moments later, he stood up and wrenched the Velcro strap off his binoculars. I'm sorry, he concluded, to even be reminded of that sick bastard. My parents probably knew I'd feel this way, that's probably why *they* didn't tell me…

Beads of sweat started to form on his top lip, as painful images of the past came rushing back. Suddenly, his arm began to tremble. He held up his binoculars, trying to steady his hand, as he looked out at his forest and beyond the horizon. He then forced himself to take a deep breath. He desperately wanted to ward off the reaction he feared was coming. He didn't want Father Pat to have control over him any more! In spite of his best efforts, the tears still came, but armed with this new information, he hoped his nightmares would finally stop.

***

But the nightmares never stopped. Even years after Colin had found out about Father Pat's death, the priest still thrived in Colin's dreams and Colin remained uneasy everywhere, except within the confines of his lookout tower, a place he now rarely left.

When Colin wanted companionship, he would e-mail his parents or Tom, but even that was becoming infrequent. Through it all his parents continued to visit, but they didn't stay long. No matter how gracious he tried to be, Colin wasn't comfortable around people, and everyone around him knew it.

Tragically, the more time he spent alone, the more he began to fade away. It was as if he were turning into a thin gray cloud that would someday evaporate.

***

Seeing this metamorphosis in Colin weighed heavily upon Cathy and Dwight, but they felt helpless, and so remained a little bit in denial. Whenever they were traveling to see him, they secretly longed to be greeted by a grown-up version of the little boy whose energy and joy once filled their hearts and their lives. But each time they arrived, that little boy was nowhere to be found, and in his place was a broken recluse. Embarrassed by their continuing dream and devastated that it wasn't coming true, they didn't mention their heartache to anyone, not even each other.

As the years wore on, Dwight developed a heart condition, making his traveling to Alaska too difficult. To accommodate his parents, Colin made occasional brief trips back to Madison. Even though Pat was long gone, Colin still hated returning to his hometown.

***

On July 11, 1997 Colin received a frantic call from his mother. His father had fallen and broken his hip, could he come home right away? Colin was on the next plane out.

When he arrived, Dwight was awake in his bed at the University of Wisconsin Hospital. Colin thought Dwight looked pale and vulnerable. "Hey, Dad," he said, approaching his bed with forced cheer and a feigned smile. "How are those Badger doctors treating you?"

"Fine Son, just fine," Dwight answered without conviction, but full of warmth.

As soon as Colin reached the bed, they gently embraced and Dwight's eyes filled with tears. "Good to see you," Dwight whispered. Then he cleared his throat and asked, "Your mother called you in a panic, huh?"

"Yep, same old Mom, but, since you've always been the voice of reason around here, why don't you tell me how you're doing?" Colin watched Dwight briefly struggle in an attempt to sit up. He reached over to help, and was shocked to feel just how frail his father had become.

As soon as Dwight regained his breath, he began, "Well, it looks like I'm damned if I do, and damned if I don't. They say my heart may not be strong enough to survive surgery, but, if I don't have it, I'll never be able to walk on my own two legs again. Son, I've been thinking about this all day, and what I want and need is your permission to have the surgery."

Colin was shocked. "My permission? Why do you need my permission, Dad?"

"Because I might not make it, and if I don't, I won't be here for you and your mother anymore. It's a risk *I* want to take, and would take, if I didn't have you two to worry about."

Colin immediately reassured his father. "Go for it, Dad," he said with more bravado than he actually felt. "I can take care of myself, *and* I can help Mom, too."

"Are you sure?"

"Yes," he said clearly, but without certainty.

Dwight looked disappointed. "Oh Colin, I love you so much, big guy, but, in many ways, you're still so young; more like a boy stuck in a man's body… Still, I can see you're trying so damned hard to sound grown up."

"I *am* grown up, Dad." Colin replied, starting to feel defensive. "After all, I work for the Forest Service and have an important, responsible job. Maybe you're just underestimating me."

"Maybe so," Dwight nodded, but then slowly added, "you still think about what happened when you were a boy, don't you?"

Colin glanced at the floor. "Yeah, sometimes," he eventually answered.

"And the fact that he's dead isn't much help to you, is it?"

Colin kept his head down and gently shook it side to side.

"I hated that man!" Dwight blurted out.

Colin looked up. "Me too, Dad." Then he added, with a flurry of renewed assertiveness, "But I don't just hate him. I also hate the others who invaded my life after he assaulted me. That includes the cops, the doctor, the nurse, the lawyers, and the judge. Any one of them could have made it better; all of them made it worse." Listing them all upset Colin, but he was instantly distracted by what his father asked next.

"I wasn't much help either, was I?"

"No, Dad, that's not true." About this, Colin was clear. "I've thought about that a lot too. You actually saved my life and gave me back my sanity. You turned me on to the healing power of nature, and I am doing OK, really I am."

Dwight interrupted, "But you're not healed, you're still suffering…. Maybe being this sick has loosened my tongue, but it looks to me like you've created your very own prison, and you're afraid to step out of it."

***

Dwight hated to continue, but knew he had to. "At first, I thought that was OK, but you're a grown man now, and there's no end in sight." Dwight could no longer keep his feelings of guilt inside. "I know I should have sent you to counseling and support groups, and we should have gone to family counseling, but I learned all this too late."

"Dad, whoa, slow down. What are you talking about? Where are you getting all this from?"

"I heard this guy speaking on a local radio show. What he said made sense to me, so I bought his book." He pointed toward the book on his rolling bedside table. "I think he's got a sister in town, so that's why he came here. Anyway, I guess he's pretty famous, but I'd never heard of him before. I haven't had a chance to really read the book yet, but I did look at it. That's his picture on the back cover. It says he lives in Crested Butte, Colorado. Have you ever been there, Son? It's a beautiful place; promise me you'll go sometime."

Colin thought his Dad was rambling; probably tired, or out of it from the medication they'd been giving him. Colin decided it was time for him to leave; he'd already spoken more words in the last few minutes than he had in a very long time. Still, he wanted to leave on a positive note. "Hey, Dad, how 'bout I promise that you and I will go to Crested Butte together sometime? How does that sound?"

Dwight was not optimistic about his hip surgery, and shook his head. "That's not likely, Son. Even if I do survive, I'll probably never be able to go to the Rockies' high altitude with this old heart of mine."

"Dad, that's no way to think or feel. I want you to picture you and me, together in Crested Butte, Colorado, bopping around like we did when I was a kid. If you're gonna make it through this ordeal, you've got to have a goal, so make *that* your goal, and I'll make it my business to get us there."

Colin reached over and deliberately placed his hand on Dwight's cheek. "Remember, Dad?" he asked. Each recalled the story of Cathy and Dwight touching Colin's cheek, the moment after he was born. They both smiled.

Dwight hated being confined to a hospital bed, and he knew Colin hated to see him there.

Just before Colin left, they went back to talking about Dwight's health. They decided if Cathy agreed, they'd let the doctors proceed with the surgery as soon as possible.

***

On the way to his parents' home, Colin passed by some of his familiar haunts, and almost smiled thinking about how appropriate that word was.

When he arrived, he saw his mother intently focused on a book she was reading. Not wanting to frighten her, he gently called her name. As soon as she noticed him, she put her book aside. He then took her in his arms, and held her there. He needed a few extra seconds to regroup.

When Colin finally let go, he thought she appeared both relieved and delighted to see him. Still, sensing how exhausted he knew she was, he encouraged her to sit back down next to him.

"How was your father when you saw him?" She asked.

Colin gave her the details of their discussion, and told her of the risk his father wanted to take, but wouldn't without their support. Ultimately, Cathy and Colin agreed, if Dwight wanted the surgery, he should have it. Throughout their conversation, Cathy appeared stoic; this confused Colin.

"Mom, what's going on with you? Dad seems to think you're so fragile you can't live without him, yet you come across so strong with me. Which is it, Mom?"

"Well, I've always thought of myself as strong," she began to recount, "but until you were hurt and almost died I had no idea how very strong I was." She paused and looked away, while Colin listened intently. "However, I do get rattled," she continued, "when people I love are in danger." She nodded slowly and sighed deeply. "But I've learned over time that it doesn't do any good for me to carry on about it." Tears began to roll down her cheeks. "The hardest time in my life was right after you went through everything, and I didn't know what to do." Once again, she stopped talking. Moments later she continued as if she hadn't paused at all. "The strongest I've ever had to be was when I decided *not* to go with you and your father when you went off that summer." She looked past him and out onto their driveway. Colin waited patiently for her to continue.

"More than anything," she said, still gazing out the window, "I wanted to be there with you, put my arms around you, and never let you go, but I knew that wasn't what you needed. What you needed was to feel your own strength again, and for you to do that, I had to stand back."

She picked up the book she'd been reading. Colin noticed it was the same one his father had shown him. "After reading this book, I realize there was a lot more I could've done. Back then, I had no idea what to do, and no one to turn to."

Colin took her hand in his, and, once again, patiently waited for her to continue.

"In the past, I would've turned to the church, but the day you were violated by Father Pat, so was my belief in God." Cathy dropped her head; she couldn't go on. Between her husband's illness, seeing her son, and divulging her deepest thoughts, she was spent. Colin took her into his strong arms, and she wept.

In time, he released his grip, repositioned her, and tried to respond. "Mom, Father Pat was not God, nor was he the Catholic Church. Father Pat was a deranged man, who found his way into the Catholic Church." Colin surprised himself by sounding so clear and strong. "Our family was betrayed by Father Pat, but Mom, let the tragedy end there. Don't allow what Father Pat did to me destroy your faith in God or the church."

Once again, Colin reached out for her hand and continued. "If the church no longer has any meaning for you, stop going. But Mom, if the church does still have meaning, don't turn your back on it now when you need it."

***

Cathy could feel perspiration surface on his hand, as he continued, "Mom, I've thought about this a lot. If you never return to the church because of what Father Pat did to me, you're giving him power, and you're keeping his wretched spirit alive. We should have done this a long time ago, but now that he's been dead for a while, it's time we both try and forget it."

Cathy looked at her son with emerging awe. "You know, Son, there was many a time that I wanted, more than anything, to go back to church and pray. But, I always thought if you knew I did that, you'd feel I had, in some way, betrayed you—"

"Mom," Colin interrupted, "the only person who betrayed me was Father Pat, never you, and never Dad." He looked lovingly into her eyes and went on, "Go back to your church, go back to your God and pray. I'll take you over there tomorrow morning, if you'd like, that way you can pray for Dad."

Cathy leaned forward. "Colin, is it too much to ask you to come with me? Then we can pray for Dad together—"

"No," Colin stopped her before she could say another word. "I will *never* enter that church again. Part of the reason I've been able to survive, aside from all I've gotten from you and Dad, is because I don't put myself in situations that will upset me. I haven't been back in that church since that night, and I *never* will go there again!"

Colin stood up and walked over to the fireplace. He grabbed hold of the mantel and paused. Moments later, in a calmer voice he continued. "But, Mom, keep in mind, I never found God there. I went there mostly for the music and to make you and Dad happy. You found God there, and *that's* where you belong. I found my God in nature, and *that's* where I belong."

Cathy thought he looked as exhausted as she felt. Now obviously overcome by the day's events, he walked toward her, gave her one more hug, and said he was ready to go to bed.

***

As soon as Colin got upstairs, he lay down and promptly fell asleep. His final thought was, as brave as he tried to appear for his parents, he was completely ill-equipped to deal with what he knew would happen the very next day.

***

Jordon put down his file and pushed away her tears because she couldn't push away the memory of her own father's death...

46

Mensh—Yiddish for an upright, honorable, decent person.

Jordon had always considered her father to be a "real mensh." The spring he was diagnosed, Jordon was a senior in college, and Saul was only 54 years old.

When she first found out about his fate, she was leaning against a wall in a hospital corridor. The doctor was directing his comments to her mother and older sister, who was at the time, a medical student interning at that hospital. Doctor Bates said Saul had cancer, and his tumor was the size of a football. Jordon froze. Doctor Bates concluded by forecasting that Saul would only live for another 6 months. Jordon gasped, and slid down the wall to the floor. Her sister chastised her and demanded she get up; her mother didn't say a word. Jordon felt incapable of moving. Of the three of them, she'd always been closest to Saul. She instantly felt completely alone in her anguish and grief.

Over the next several months she woke up each morning with a pain in her gut. Her reaction was always the same, she wanted to rush to the hospital and make the cancer go away. Often, she'd dream about putting him on the back of a motorcycle and driving too fast for the cancer to catch them.

At least once during the week, and always on weekends, she'd drive 2 hours to the hospital to be with him. She didn't go there out of obligation; she went there because that was where she wanted to be.

Through it all, Jordon continued to relish their time together, and he remained the same warm, loving, and compassionate man he'd always been.

While at the hospital they talked endlessly; long after nurses had turned out the lights. Jordon desperately wanted his thoughts and advice on every dilemma she presently had, or might ever possibly encounter, and he just as obviously wanted to be there for her. Each night, when he no longer had the strength to stay awake, she'd bring her chair next to his bed, take hold of his hand, and quietly cry. She wanted to feel his warmth as long as she possibly could.

Often, she'd wake up in the morning, her face still damp with tears, still holding his hand. Sometimes, even though she was fully awake, she kept her head resting upon his failing frame, wanting to prolong the feeling of him silently stroking her hair.

Nevertheless, all the synergy, passion, and love in the world couldn't keep Saul alive. He died almost 6 months to the day the doctor had projected.

***

Now, 30 years later, Jordon still thought about those conversations and how much she continued to miss him. She once considered therapy as a means of ending her grieving, but decided the hole his death left in her heart was too precious to mend.

With her tears starting anew, she was sure it was time for a break. She walked onto their deck and looked at the sky.

After finding the inspiration she needed to go on, she came back inside, and returned to Colin's file.

47

Change—Alter; to make different.

Much to everyone's amazement, Dwight didn't die. His heart remained strong and the surgery was a success.

"I can't explain it," Dr. Sullivan said, shaking his head, "I know the results of the stress test we gave him yesterday, and, quite frankly, I'm as astounded as you are. All I can tell you," he said in complete bewilderment, "is somehow, between yesterday and this morning, either his heart strengthened or," he smiled playfully, "his stress was magically reduced. Either way, he's got a new hip and is very much alive." They all smiled. "And," the doctor concluded, "as improbable as this may sound, I think he'll be just fine. However, his recovery and rehab will be long, and he's going to need lots of help."

***

Cathy finally found her voice. "Thank you so much, Doctor."

"No doubt about it," Doctor Sullivan said, continuing to shake his head, "he's a very lucky man. It's the damnedest thing, really."

***

As soon as the doctor left, Cathy and Colin embraced. Holding on to his mother, Colin humbly reflected upon the conversation he had with his father yesterday and wondered if that might have reduced Dwight's stress. "Mom," he whispered, "I'm gonna stick around and help you guys out for a while."

Cathy pulled away. "But, what about your job? Your forest?"

He took her back in his arms, and smiled again. "The forest will probably survive without me, and anyway, I'm sure they can get a substitute to take over my post. Dad took a leave of absence from his job when I needed him…" Colin's hug intensified as he felt his throat tighten. When he could speak, he added, "Now, it's my turn."

***

Cathy kept her face pressed against his chest. Finding her voice again, she whispered, "He'll like that."

***

Dwight remained in the hospital for another week. One day while Colin was there, Tom paid them a visit. By then, Colin hadn't seen Tom for years. Sadly, he still viewed Tom as a living reminder of the worst days of his life, so he couldn't greet him with the warmth Colin knew was deserved.

***

Tom understood, he'd just come by to offer his help and to tell Colin, the guy he still considered to be his best friend, his good news. Tom had wanted Colin to know he'd finally fallen in love, but he quickly sensed now was not the right time to tell Colin.

***

Having committed to stay in the Madison area for as long as his parents needed him, Colin contacted his supervisor Ken Sampson, to see what his options might be.

Sampson called back later in the week and offered Colin a job he could perform in Madison. He asked him to become editor of the *Forest Service Technical Newsletter*.

Within weeks articles were sent to him from all over the country, which he would first edit and then compile. Once the first few issues of the newsletter were under his belt, Colin started including some of his photography. Among them were photos taken during his trips to various National Parks. Before long, he was also contributing brief articles to accompany his photographs. Within months he began hearing from several colleagues telling him they now looked forward to receiving the previously disregarded circular.

Once Cathy could manage Dwight's care, Colin moved out of his old room to Coulee Ridge, a small rustic cabin located thirty miles outside of town. Dwight's family had purchased it decades ago along with forty acres of old-growth forest. Furnishings were little more than an old stove and bed. Given Colin's proclivity for living simply in nature, it was the perfect place for him to stay for as long as his parents needed him.

Within months he'd settled into a fairly comfortable life at Coulee Ridge. Two or three times a week he'd go into town to help his parents, the rest of the time he'd stay working on his newsletter.

***

One afternoon as Colin was walking along the streets of downtown Madison a flier caught his attention. It advertised a lecture offered late that afternoon entitled: "Empowering Adult Victims of Child Molestation." Colin didn't understand the title; how could an adult be a victim of child molestation, and why would they need empowering now? Colin wasn't even sure he knew what empowering meant; still, the title intrigued him. The presentation was to be held inside Bascom Hall.

Bascom was a beautiful old stone structure, located near the center of the university campus. Colin had always loved that building. He remembered with fondness going to events there as a child, and staring at the glow emanating from the lecture room's high stained-glass windows. He decided to hear the speaker, rationalizing that even if the presentation was boring, he'd still enjoy sitting in that room at dusk.

***

As soon as the speaker approached the lectern, Colin recognized him as the man whose picture was on the back of the book he'd seen his father reading at the hospital, a book he never felt inclined to open. Now he was no longer certain he wanted to stay, but neither did he want to draw attention to himself by walking out. Why can't I just get *over* it, he thought for the thousandth time. Sometimes I still feel like that eleven-year old kid and being in Madison only seems to make things worse... Unexpectedly, his thoughts merged with what Dr. Estrada was saying.

"Adults who were molested as children," Dr. Estrada professed, "on some level, remain stuck in that same time period and are doomed to remain child victims unless and until they get the right kind of counseling."

Dr. Estrada then went on to describe the psychological and sociological makeup of a typical adult victim of child molestation. Colin was aghast; my God, he thought, he's describing me.

All too quickly the lecture ended, but Colin, anxious to hear more, uncharacteristically waited around until he could speak with

Dr. Estrada alone. After twenty minutes, most of the crowd had dispersed, except for the woman Colin kept noticing. She was sitting alone in the back of the lecture hall.

He'd first noticed her when the lecture ended and he turned to look toward the back of the room. There she was, bathed in the remembered light emanating from the stained glass windows. He instantly thought she was one of the most beautiful women he'd ever seen. But now, in spite of her loveliness, he was eager for her to leave, he wanted to talk to Dr. Estrada alone. However, as time went on, it became clear that she too wanted to speak with Dr. Estrada, and wasn't going to move until she did.

Colin knew he'd have to summon up the courage to approach Dr. Estrada while she was still there, or he'd miss his chance forever. He stood and bravely, albeit reluctantly, approached the front of the hall. While doing so, Colin looked at her again, both to see if she was approaching, and because he couldn't take his eyes off her.

Colin had, for most of his life, avoided women altogether. But now, much to his amazement, he felt drawn to her. Feeling pulled in two very different directions, he was temporarily motionless. Suddenly Marcos solved his dilemma.

"Good evening," Marcos said, "did you want to talk to me?"

"Yes, ah, um," Colin was struggling to find the right words. He hadn't yet considered *what* he wanted to say; he just knew he wanted to connect with him. Colin looked down, put his hand on his forehead, and rubbed his eyebrows. "I really don't know where to begin; I guess I just wanted to hear more."

"Thank you, those are the very words every lecturer longs to hear," Marcos said. "More often than not, I have no idea if I've bored people to death, or said something that struck a chord. I obviously struck a chord with you, so do you mind if I ask you a very personal question?"

Colin looked up. "No, I mean, that is, no, I don't mind."

"I'm just going to assume someone hurt you when you were a child, right?"

"Right," Colin said, astonished that he'd answered without delay or embarrassment.

"How old were you?"

"Eleven."

"Who was it?"

"My priest."

"Ouch, that hurts. So, you lost your childhood and your religion all at once?"

"Well, I was never a big believer in organized religion anyway, but I did love singing in the choir, and he was the choir director." Beads of sweat began to form on Colin's forehead, as he averted his eyes. "I also thought he was my friend."

"Boy, that's tough. Did you ever have a chance to confront him?"

"No." Colin couldn't imagine doing that. "He committed suicide, actually death-by-cop suicide, shortly after he got out of prison."

"Oh, so he was caught? Did you have to go through a trial and all that?"

"Yes, and I'd certainly emphasize the *all that*; it was gruesome."

"Yes, I know. In the hands of the wrong people, that process can be a living nightmare."

"Tell me about it," Colin said, shaking his head in disbelief, "sixteen years later, and I'm still living with the nightmares."

"Were you in therapy at the time?"

"No, I've never been in therapy, not then, and not now. Before tonight, I didn't know how important it was."

"Listen, it's never too late. Come with me to my hotel, and I'll give you names of some local people who I think do good work. Then, if you'd like, join my sister and me for dinner."

"I guess it's no surprise to you," Colin responded, "this is when I usually bow out. But after listening to you tonight, I will take, what you referred to as, 'the emotional risk,' and join you. Where are you meeting your sister?"

"Right here, matter of fact, that's her in the back of the hall." Marcos smiled and waved at Sophia; Sophia smiled back.

Oh no, thought Colin, not her! Now there's no polite way to get out of it. I just wish she wasn't so damned pretty. Shit, what've I gotten myself into? Boy, I'd give anything to be anywhere but here right now, and my first choice would probably be my lookout tower in far away Alaska, but I guess I'm stuck.

Having resigned himself to being completely ill at ease, Colin followed Marcos toward the back of the room. After his barely audible "Nice to meet you," the three of them walked to Marcos' hotel.

***

Marcos was staying at The Edgewater, a stately old renovated mansion located a few blocks from Bascom Hall. When they arrived, he briefly ran up to his room for the promised list of counselors.

During Marcos' absence Colin felt scarcely able to keep his part of the conversation going. He'd never been so drawn to someone in his life. Within moments he thought Sophia was as bright as she was beautiful, as stimulating as she was charming, and as caring as she was confident. He felt as if he were falling through space, but she was so engaging, he never wanted the fall to end.

So affected was he by Sophia that after Marcos returned Colin was hardly able to concentrate on what was said. Compared to gazing at Sophia, Marcos seemed downright boring.

***

Sophia was also drawn to Colin. She was particularly attracted to his vulnerability, warmth, and gentle good looks. Many of the men she encountered at work were brash and self-absorbed. Compared to them, Colin seemed all the more appealing.

***

None of this went unnoticed by Marcos, who jokingly thought, this is the last time *I* take someone impressed by me to dinner with Sophia. With a bat of her eyes and a quick smile, she completely stole my audience. Still, Colin seems like a nice enough young man, one who definitely has some things to work out, and yet, capable of doing it.

Marcos continued to watch them and ruminate. Given what they've both been through, he may actually be very good for her. If only she'd take the initiative and the time away from her job to get to know him. God knows he'll never find the courage to pursue her. Well, maybe I can help this thing along.

"Colin," Marcos suddenly interrupted their eye-locked conversation, "I'm exhausted. I was wondering if you'd mind taking Sophia home?"

"No," Colin said too quickly.

"No?" asked Sophia and Marcos simultaneously.

"No, not no, no. No, I wouldn't mind, it would be a pleasure. I mean, sure that's fine with me, I mean—I'd be glad to."

Colin thought he sounded like an idiot, and wished he could be beamed back to Alaska. Instead, he tried again, "What I'm trying to say is, if it is OK with Sophia, it's OK with me."

At that point, they all started to laugh.

"Oh sure," she said, "I'd love to hear more about your life on Kodiak Island."

That, Colin thought gratefully, is something I *can* talk about.

After saying goodnight to Marcos, they headed back to get Colin's car.

To their dismay, they reached his car too soon. Undaunted, Sophia suggested they walk around a bit longer.

The *bit longer* turned into nearly two hours. At various points it became perfectly clear to each of them they were walking around in circles, but neither mentioned it to the other.

***

After two hours passed, Colin couldn't help but notice Sophia was trembling from the cold. Since he didn't have a jacket, he reluctantly suggested he take her home.

Once they got in his car, both became quiet. Colin was hoping he'd somehow find the courage to ask for her phone number, but by the time they reached her apartment, he still hadn't. Overwhelmed by his own fear of rejection, he simply said goodnight.

She thanked him, and suddenly she was gone.

Colin sat alone and dejected in his abruptly emptied automobile. "Colin, Colin, Colin," he said aloud, feeling like a coward and an idiot.

"Colin?" He heard his name repeated again. This time, it wasn't him talking, it was Sophia. She'd come back outside to his car.

"Colin, I hope you don't think I'm being too forward, but I'd love to see you again. Here's my telephone number. If you feel like it, call me. Thanks again for a great evening, I really enjoyed meeting you." She then briefly smiled and ran off.

All Colin could say, and it was long after she left, was, "Thank you, I will."

***

When Colin got home, he did a Gene Kelly-style dance around his cabin. Stars were out, the moon was aglow, and he'd just met the most incredible woman in the world. "What's more," he shouted to the heavens, "*she* gave *me* her phone number!"

***

Jordon later learned that as Marcos fell asleep that night, he too was thankful, appreciating the fact that no hecklers had showed up. No matter what, he never wanted Sophia to find out just how aggressive they'd become.

Jordon knew she should go back to Marcos' file, but really wanted to keep reading about Colin and Sophia. Following her heart, instead of her head, she went to the couch, reset its pillows, unfolded a quilt, and reentered their world.

48

March 23,1998
COLIN & SOPHIA

Find—To come upon by seeking or by effort.

In spite of experiencing a sleepless night of conflicting emotions, Colin called Sophia at 7 a.m.

"Too early?" he asked.

"Nah, I've been up for hours. By six a.m., I'd given up all hope of you calling."

"Really? No, not really, you're just teasing me, right?"

"Wrong, Colin, I'm really glad you called."

"I miss you," he said, shocking himself.

"Well, that's because you don't really know me very well," Sophia said, with a slight tease to her voice.

"I can fix that. What're you doing right now?" By then he'd hardly gotten any sleep, and was subsisting on pure adrenaline, mixed with a serious case of infatuation.

"Besides sleeping?" she asked sheepishly.

"I thought, you said you'd been awake for hours, waiting for my call?"

"I lied. I just said that so you wouldn't feel bad about waking me up."

"Did I wake you up?" he asked, with sincere concern.

"Yep."

"I'm sorry." He suddenly felt embarrassed and insecure. "Do you want to go back to sleep?"

"Definitely not! I want to see you."

He felt a surge of energy. "Do you want to meet me for coffee or a run?" He was astounded by his own assertiveness.

"How about coffee and then a run?"

Now feeling a little bit cocky, he offered, "You're my kind of woman!"

***

I hope so, Sophia thought, as they made plans to meet.

They met in front of the Student Union, within feet of a favorite running path. Once they grabbed their coffees, Sophia led him to a wooden booth in the Paul Bunyon Room, a small chamber off the main hallway. The room was covered wall-to-wall with a colorful mural, depicting scenes and characters from the famous fable. Between its vibrant colors, low ceiling and flagstone floor, it gave Sophia just the festive, intimate environment she was looking for.

Colin drank his coffee black; she used lots of cream and sugar. From the moment they met, they never stopped talking. At some point Sophia reminded Colin about his proposed jog. An hour later, they were running along the University's northern border, heading toward Picnic Point and the pristine banks of a shimmering Lake Mendota.

When they got to Picnic Point, he wanted to stop for a moment to reflect upon its beauty. She wanted to keep running out to the point, so she ran and he sat. When she returned, they sprinted back to campus together.

***

Colin was becoming intensely aware of his attraction to her, and it was beginning to terrify him.

***

Although they hadn't yet talked about it, Sophia assumed he'd also been molested, and feared that their similarly dysfunctional pasts would ultimately collide... I can't believe I'm worried about this now, she thought, but I really want this to work. Still, if I bring it up too soon, I could scare him away. But, if I don't, and we weren't meant to be together, it'll hurt a lot more later...

Sophia decided she had to talk to Colin about it, but still wasn't sure how.

Although Marcos freely admitted in his book that he was a convicted child molester, he never told anyone who his victim was; he'd always wanted to protect Sophia's privacy. Previously, Sophia too had kept that part of her life concealed, but she now wanted Colin to understand. If he can't handle it, she concluded, I want to know now, before I get any more involved.

"Colin, I was about to ask you what brought you to my brother's lecture last night, but let me tell you something first."

She took a deep breath. "I was molested by Marcos when I was five."

Colin stopped running. "What? Did I hear you say what I thought you said?" He looked into her eyes.

"Yes."

"Should we stop here and talk?"

"No, not on my account, I prefer to keep running. I can think more clearly when I run." She looked away. They ran on in silence for a few minutes, until Colin finally asked, "So, do you hate him?"

"Funny you'd ask me that; that was the first question he asked me a long time ago. But, to answer your question, no, I don't hate him, I love him. Matter of fact, after years of hard work and counseling, I've actually forgiven him."

"If you were five, then he must have been very young too."

"Yeah, he was only eighteen." Sophia launched into her past, and surprised even herself by how easy it was for her to disclose her history, thoughts and feelings to Colin.

***

Colin listened carefully to everything Sophia had to say, and stole an occasional look in her direction. She seemed sad, but confident. He was in awe. When they arrived back on campus, they sat down on The Terrace, an outdoor extension of the Student Union. This time it was Colin who led the way. He took her to his favorite table, the one perched closest to the lake's edge.

"I know we just sat down," he said, "but would you mind if we got up and walked around a bit? I have something to tell you and it might be easier on me—"

***

"Sure," she interrupted, and they both stood. She knew what he wanted to say, and felt relieved and exhilarated that he felt comfortable enough to say it.

"I, too, was molested as a child. You probably already figured that out when you saw me talking to your brother last night, but my experience was nothing like yours. My assailant was a priest, my choir director, and it only happened to me once, but it was devastating. I was eleven at the time."

Sophia was glad he'd found the courage to bring it all up, but she ached for him now, and for the little boy he once was.

***

Colin decided to get the hardest part out first. "I'm still not over it, even though he's been dead for many years. Unlike you, I had to endure a miserable physical exam right after it happened, and a torturous experience in court months later." As the familiar nausea began to return, he swallowed hard to continue. "I never went to counseling, not then, not now, not ever; I didn't even know how important it was until I heard your brother's presentation last night. I did, however, have the support of two very loving parents and my best friend, Tom..."

He looked over at Lake Mendota and the sunlight glinting off its rippled surface. "If it weren't for them, I wouldn't have survived..." He squeezed his eyes shut, thought about shutting down, but decided instead to keep going.

"I must warn you," he continued with great trepidation, surprising himself with every word he spoke," I've never had a girlfriend. In fact, I've spent most of my adult life avoiding people. I rarely go to lectures. But yesterday, by chance, I saw the flier of your brother's lecture and I knew I had to go. After hearing Marcos speak, I felt compelled to wait around and talk to him. I had no idea that would lead to dinner with him or meeting you, but I'm glad I got to do both. Beyond that, I have no idea where I found the courage to call you this morning. Before last night, I've always considered myself to be painfully shy."

***

He looks painfully shy, Sophia thought, and I'd love to touch his hand, but I'm afraid it would scare him away.

***

"Your and Marcos' secret is safe with me," he continued, "but I'm not sure you are. I'm a nervous wreck. Every cell in my body is telling me to run away, but I can't go anywhere. Truthfully, Sophia, I feel like damaged goods. But after listening to your brother last night, and to you today, I'm committed to begin counseling as soon as possible. I want to get past this for my sake, and I hope, for ours as well. Whether you decide to stick around me or not, you and your brother have already had a profound effect on my life."

Colin couldn't say anymore, having already said more than he'd ever told anyone. He waited for her response; he didn't have to wait long.

"Colin, I don't think you're damaged goods. I think you're wonderful, and very brave, and I think we've got a lot to learn from each other. I suspect both of our more frail instincts are telling us to run away, but I'm so tired of running... and of being alone."

"Me too," he said, clearing his throat. He reached out, took her hand, and held it as they finished their walk in silence.

***

Colin and Sophia spent the next few weeks running, dining, and going to the movies. They were falling in love, and their only remaining fear was that it might not last forever.

One night several weeks after they'd met, Sophia suggested they cook dinner at his place. At first, this worried him, because he understood what it meant, but he also knew it was time.

The next afternoon he came to town and picked up both Sophia and the makings for a romantic Wisconsin dinner, bratwurst and beer. After they arrived at his place, they cooked and stayed outside until the stars came out. When it grew cold, Colin spoke first. Fortified by the beer, he softly confessed, "Sophia, I've never done *it* before."

Sophia wasn't sure how she should respond, so she tried humor. "Is that supposed to be some sort of excuse?" she asked, with a very warm smile.

"No, that's supposed to be my great and meaningful revelation to you," he answered, only somewhat defensively.

"So, OK, are you done?" she asked, still smiling.

"Yeah," he said, beginning to smile back and sounding slightly more comfortable.

She got up, walked behind him, and threw her arms over his shoulders. First, she kissed him gently on the ear, and then she whispered, "Let's go to bed." Sophia released her hold on him as Colin stood. Next, she took his hand and led him into the cabin.

***

Colin's head was spinning as he lay down on his bed. Sophia quickly put her head on his chest. "Could you just hold me?" she asked. He sighed outwardly. Moments later, for the first time in a very long time, they both felt completely safe and happy. Lost in their happiness, their breathing completely synchronized, they fell asleep.

***

It was close to midnight before Colin woke up. What a glorious feeling, he thought, waking up with this incredible woman resting on my chest. He stirred and woke Sophia up. In response he caressed her breasts. At first, he touched her gently, and then he quickly began to move with great fervor. Before long, they were undressed.

***

Sophia felt dizzy, and somewhat uncomfortable. He was moving rapidly and purposefully, making sure he touched all the *right places*. She didn't care where he touched her, as long as they connected emotionally. Not wanting him to feel inadequate, she kept up with his furious pace.

Finally, he wasn't a virgin anymore and she held him very close.

Colin spoke first. "That wasn't very good, was it?"

"Define good," Sophia replied.

"Sophia!" he said, sounding only somewhat frustrated.

"Do you mean," she responded, "was it technically the best ever? Answer, no. Did I come? Answer, no again. Did it feel great to have sex with the man I love? Absolutely, yes!"

"You love me?" he asked.

"Yes" she said very seriously, "I do."

"Since when?" he asked.

"Probably from the moment you first looked at me at Bascom Hall. But, it could have ended then, if you didn't turn out to be the incredible person you are."

"Not so incredible just now though, huh?"

"Colin, that's just not true," she assured him again. "Hey, wait a minute, I just told you, for the first time, that I love you and you didn't say, 'I love you,' back. Don't you love me?"

"Matter of fact, I do," he said, taking her into his arms again, "but this is all a little bit much for me. It's two in the morning; I've just lost my virginity, and, for the first time in my life, I've told a woman, other than my mother, that I love her. Now, all of this might be a nightly activity for some, but I'm a little freaked out, a little freaked out, but a lot a happy." He brought her closer to his chest and continued, "Sophia, I'm new to this, but I think I can catch up and keep up, if you just give me a little space."

Sophia sat up and pulled away. "Space? Does that mean you want me to go?"

"No, that's not what I mean." He gathered her back into his arms. "I don't mean physical space. Matter of fact, what I need is to stay very close to you for a very long time. Sometimes, I might not be your emotional equal, and I may not know exactly what to say, or do. Above all, what I don't want to happen is for you to reject me, or think I'm rejecting you just because I'm being weird. Is any of my rambling making any sense to you?"

"Yes," she said, but knew she sounded unconvinced. "So, do you want me to go home now or wait until morning?"

"Yes and no," he answered playfully.

"What?"

"Yes, I want you home, but as far as I'm concerned, you are home. And, no, I don't want you to go anywhere in the morning. Sophia, if you left now, or anytime soon, I'd be miserable, wondering when I'd get to see you again. I know this isn't the traditional thing to do at this point in our dating relationship, but you and I aren't conventional people with normal pasts. Stay until it is time for you to go, OK?"

"OK," she said, but thought, I hope that day never comes.

***

When they awakened, it was just before dawn. This time Sophia guided Colin, and together they made warm and passionate love.

Later that morning, Colin drove her to town. That afternoon she returned in her car with some personal belongings. They agreed she wasn't really moving in; she was just *staying* with him.

A few days later she *moved in*. She'd suggested he move into her apartment in Madison, but they both knew that wouldn't happen. She'd fallen in love with *Nature Boy*, as she tenderly called him, and in nature they would stay.

***

Once Sophia took up residence in Coulee Ridge the rest of Colin's life seemed to fall into place. He'd been working with his counselor, Diane Kaufman, for several weeks, and thought she was terrific. Initially, Colin started with Diane alone, but later he invited his parents to join. By then both had read Marcos' book and understood the importance of individual and family counseling. They just felt guilty they hadn't done it years sooner. In time, Diane persuaded them that all the love and devotion they'd shown Colin after he was molested and testified was what had sustained him. Now, to get beyond mere sustenance, they'd have to go back in time and rebuild what had been broken. Ultimately, she assured them all they'd get past the raw pain and incorporate this tragedy into their life experiences; moving, as Diane phrased it, "from being victims to survivors." After all, she maintained, they'd already physically survived, now it was just a matter of fine-tuning.

At times Sophia also went to the counseling sessions with Colin. He liked having her there; it made him feel even closer to her.

***

Within a few months Colin decided since counseling was going so well, and the love of his life enjoyed working in Madison so much, he would just stay in Wisconsin.

His supervisor, Ken Sampson, told him he could continue to work on the newsletter, but should also consider enrolling at the University to get an advanced degree. Colin agreed.

By late summer, he returned to Alaska and retrieved a few remaining personal possessions. Sophia went with him. He wanted her to gain further insight into both who he used to be, and why he'd loved it there so much.

That fall Colin began graduate work in the Institute for Environmental Studies. No longer feeling personally responsible to save earth from a fiery demise, he changed his field of interest from fighting fires to Water Resource Management. He now wanted to protect rather than defend. This time the metaphor wasn't lost on anyone close to him.

Sophia continued to work as hard as ever at the DA's office; though each night, instead of coming home to law books and files, she also came home to Colin.

Both felt blessed. By then, they'd come to know each other's families, and Tom was once again part of Colin's life.

Soon after he decided to move back to Wisconsin, Colin met Tom's life-partner, Jake. Colin thought Jake was terrific, and felt

Tom and Jake's commitment to each other was contagious. By spring, Colin asked Sophia to marry him.

***

Early that fall, they married on the edge of Picnic Point. Triumphantly standing on the spectacular shore of an autumnal Lake Mendota, Marcos gave Sophia away, while Tom and his partner became Colin's *best men*.

Their private reception was held in the Paul Bunyon Room. It was a small gathering, with only an ecstatic Cathy, Dwight, Tom, Jake, Marcos and Margarita in attendance. The fare was bratwurst, steaming with grilled onions and ice-cold Miller beer. For dessert, they ate bountiful scoops of ice cream from the University's creamery. The ice cream was so rich it made Margarita purr, which in turn made everyone especially Margarita, laugh.

***

The night of their wedding, as Sophia lay in Colin's arms, she finally felt the sense of comfort she'd once begged for, but had never, until that moment, found.

49

Comfort—Contentment, ease or satisfaction, however short-lived.

Marcos returned home the day after Sophia and Colin's wedding. He hated leaving his family, but loved returning to Colorado.

He'd been living in Crested Butte for over two years, having left UCLA a few years after his experience with the cowardly chancellor. At first, he missed his daily contact with students, but after time had passed, he found he preferred guest lecturing and writing. He now believed those two means of communication were the most effective way to get his message to those who needed it most. Although the occasional hecklers, at times, became downright threatening, they were never violent. When he left UCLA, he realized that between royalties from his book and additional money earned as a guest lecturer, he could support himself comfortably and live anywhere he wanted. Crested Butte was his first choice.

He'd discovered Crested Butte when a colleague he'd been dating took him skiing there. Atop the chairlift, he instantly fell in love with both the sport and the spot.

"...This place is amazing," he'd written to Sophia, "it's nestled in the Elk Mountains, 30 miles over the range from the glitter and glitz of Aspen. But, unlike Aspen, Crested Butte has managed to preserve its old Victorian buildings and hold out against relentless development pressures...

"Winter nights look like a glass snow globe after one quick twist of the wrist. In summer kaleidoscopes of wild flowers grow everywhere. In the fall golden aspen leaves quake and shimmer throughout the mountain slopes. Spring is lovingly referred to as *mud season*, so I plan to travel as much as I can during the spring months...

"I can't wait to share this place with my family, so do come soon..."

Whereas in prison, Marcos had to learn to shut down his senses in order to survive, in Crested Butte, he had to be ever vigilant against becoming blasé to his glorious surroundings.

***

When Marcos returned from the wedding, he was working on his second book. Although progress was slow, his agent convinced him to stick with it, being certain it would become another bestseller.

***

The following Christmas Sophia, Colin, and Margarita joined Marcos in Crested Butte. The beauty of the area was not lost on Colin or Sophia, but his mother was uncomfortable with the snow, ice, and extreme cold. She preferred staying indoors, where she got the chance to get to know Marcos' live-in housekeeper, Edith.

Like Margarita, Edith was born in Guatemala. She and Margarita spent endless hours talking about their lives in the old country. They were both glad to live in America now, but there were still things about Guatemala they cherished and loved sharing with each other.

For Christmas the fare was a traditional Guatemalan dinner, pollo en pĩna, carne en jo͞con, arroz, and chojin. The spicy aromas alone had everyone salivating during the two days it took to prepare.

Sadly, the holiday ended too soon for all of them. Colin and Sophia had to get back right away. Colin would be taking exams within days of their return and Sophia was about to begin another challenging trial.

***

Colin and Sophia's life in Madison was both frenzied and fulfilling. Although they were strongly focused on their careers, they still found time to rejoice in the love and friendship they'd found in each other.

***

Jordon knew she should continue reading about Marcos, but she wasn't ready to read about what happened next; especially knowing what was about to hit Colin…

50

April 1999
COLIN, SOPHIA & MARCOS

Misrepresentation—Any manifestation by words or conduct that amounts to an assertion not in accordance with the facts.

To no one's surprise, Colin passed his exams for his Master of Science degree. Eventually, and after much prodding from Sophia and Ken, he ran several excerpts from his Master's thesis in his newsletter. Shortly after his third excerpt appeared, he received an unexpected call from Dr. Dave McCoy, Assistant Director and Principal Engineer of the National Forest Service's New Mexico Office. Dr. McCoy invited Colin to apply for a job with his agency.

"What exactly would I do?" Colin asked.

"Primarily, work as a consultant and researcher. You'd only have to come into the city two to three times a week; the rest of the time you could work out of your house. I understand from my conversation with Ken Sampson, that's what you've been doing for quite a while now."

So, he's checked up on me already, Colin thought. He must really want me, and it sounds like Ken's supportive...

"When you come into town, it would mostly be for meetings," Dr. McCoy continued, "and some lobbying with the state legislature. Ken tells me you're self-motivated and require little or no supervision, and that's exactly what I'm looking for."

This job sounds ideal, Colin continued to ruminate, and it definitely sounds like Ken's on-board.

As Dr. McCoy described the position in more depth, he mentioned Colin's office would be in Santa Fe, the capital of New Mexico.

While still on the phone with Dave, Colin looked up Santa Fe on the Internet. The pictures on his PC were of brilliant desert sunsets and howling coyotes. Colin thought it looked both exotic and exciting. Still, he felt certain he could never get Sophia to leave her job or Madison.

After a few more minutes of discussion, Colin thanked Dr. McCoy for the call, said the job sounded great, but that he doubted he could sell such a move to his wife. As Colin hung up, he decided he wouldn't even discuss it with Sophia, unless his parents were comfortable with the idea. Colin called their house and reached his father.

***

Dwight could almost hear Colin trying to contain his excitement. Although fully recovered, and no longer needing Colin's assistance, he still cherished the times he spent with Colin and Sophia.

Both he and Cathy had grown very fond of Sophia. They believed that she, even more than counseling, had brought their old son back.

As Dwight listened to Colin, his throat started to constrict. He knew it would be hard to see them leave, but he would never stand in their way. After asking a few fatherly questions, he gave Colin his heartfelt blessing.

***

Now comes the hard part, thought Colin, convincing Sophia. Deciding he was far too excited to wait until she got home, he called her at work.

Sophia's receptionist, Debbie, said Sophia wasn't there. When pressed, Debbie reluctantly admitted Sophia wasn't in court either. Colin now openly persisted in knowing where she was, but Debbie would only tell him she had checked out on *personal time*.

"But, what does *personal time* mean, Debbie?" Colin asked, with mounting frustration.

"Well," she answered, "it means different things to different people. Some people use it for errands, others doctor's appointments, others ... well, whatever they want to use it for, that's why it's called *personal time*. But, she did say she'd be back by noon. "

"OK, so she said she'd be back by noon?" Colin interrupted.

"Oh yes, yes, she certainly did."

Colin knew Debbie had a reputation for being very loyal to those she worked for, and never rude to those trying to find them, even when her co-workers didn't want to be found.

Colin decided he was no match for Debbie. "Well, please ask Sophia to meet me at the Brat House at 12:15."

Debbie promised she'd give Sophia the message; Colin thanked her and hung up. *Personal time*, Colin thought, I wonder if anything's going on that I should know about? I can't imagine Sophia would keep any secrets from me, but I can't be sure...

Suddenly, a part of him he thought was long gone, reemerged. He was consumed with self-doubt, and his mind began to race through the *Parade of Horribles*.

Could she...would she? Is she having an affair—an affair with another lawyer? Why else would Debbie be so secretive? Clearly, she knows what's going on, *and* where Sophia is. Why wouldn't she tell me? Could she be protecting Sophia *and* some other lawyer in the office? Could Sophia be having an affair with another DDA? His insecurity was burgeoning... Not that I could blame her, he continued torturing himself, I'm sure I'm not the best lover she's ever had. I'm so inexperienced and predictable. I'll bet the other guy is experienced and exciting. And, if he's another DDA, she could talk to him more about her work...

Colin started pacing and finally concluded, I'm totally screwed! What if she's fallen in love with someone else? I *knew* this kind of happiness would never last for me. His pacing increased in earnest. "Wait," he said out loud, "I can't do this to myself. I can't jump to any conclusions. I have to see her, and hang on until then."

But, he couldn't *hang on* around their home any longer; he grabbed his keys and left.

It was the most protracted, lonely drive of his life. What started out as his mission to try and convince Sophia to move to Santa Fe had suddenly changed to his desperate need to simply try and convince her to stay with him. He no longer cared where they lived, as long as they were together.

At 11:00 he arrived at the restaurant, picked up a copy of the college newspaper, and sat down at their favorite table.

He never opened the paper. Instead, for over an hour, he stared at the front door and waited.

***

Lunch was the last thing on Sophia's mind. At that moment, she was lying down, staring up at a stork painted on the ceiling. Her legs were dangling over cold stirrups.

"But, how could I be pregnant? *Colin* and I have always used birth control."

"Well, I'm sorry to say, birth control doesn't *always* work. And, there's no question about it, you're pregnant. Still, we need to run more tests."

Dr. Tanner looked worried. "Hey," he asked Sophia, "are you OK? You're looking a little pale. Why don't you just sit up a bit and drink some water?"

"I'm not sure…" Sophia answered softly.

Dr. Tanner sat her up, and handed her a half-filled cup of water. "Drink this," he ordered. Sophia took it with a trembling hand.

"Does this have something to do with Colin?" Dr. Tanner asked.

"Yes," Sophia nodded, looking down. They'd never talked about having any children.

"Are you afraid he might, er, hurt your child?"

"*What*?" Sophia looked up; she felt disoriented and confused.

"I mean," Dr. Tanner said, "are you afraid, given Colin's, er, history, he might molest your child?"

Sophia knew the doctor had lived in Madison long enough to know the story of the little boy who'd been molested by the priest. Still, she didn't respond.

Dr. Tanner went on, only somewhat defensively. "I mean, you know as well as I do—after all, your own brother wrote the book on it—children who've been molested, are more likely to molest."

Tanner could tell Sophia was getting increasingly upset, but he wasn't sure of the source. Knowing Sophia was a very private person, and sensing he'd already stepped over the line, he thought it might be best to give Sophia a break before going further.

"Look, Sophia, I'm going to give you a few minutes to re-group, and then we can finish up those tests. Why don't you sit up for a minute, drink a little more water, and use this phone if you'd like. I'll be back in a few, OK?"

"OK," Sophia said, in a barely audible voice.

By the time the doctor left, Sophia felt as if she were experiencing a full-blown panic attack. *Pregnant*, she thought, but *Colin* and I have always used birth control. Use the phone? Yeah, I'll use the phone, but who'll I call? She knew the answer to her question immediately, and started dialing his familiar number.

She finally tracked him down at a hotel room in Indianapolis. The moment she heard his voice, she started to cry.

***

Hearing her sobs, Marcos thought at first she might've found out about the threats. He soon realized his mistake.

When she regained control, Sophia told him everything. Through it all, she could tell,by his reassuring words and sounds he was there for her.

"Well," he said, "it sounds like you only have another minute or two before the doctor comes back in, so how can I help you right now?"

"Tell me what to do."

"That's the one thing I can't do."

"Why?"

"Because you have to live with whatever you decide, and only you know what's best."

"I'm in over my head."

"No, you're not."

"I never meant this to happen."

"I know."

"Oh, God, what am I going to do?"

"You're going to do whatever's in the best interest of your child, and a big part of that is giving your child a mom who is ready to embrace motherhood and everything it entails."

"It's not that easy, can't you give me any assurances?"

"No, but I remind you of your great instincts, and that you should trust them."

"And that's it?"

"That's it for now, but there's still plenty of time."

"OK, well, obviously, I've got a lot to think about, and I don't have to decide today. However, I do have to decide today what, if anything, to tell Colin. Oh, poor Colin, what's *he* going to say?"

Sophia's eyes filled with tears, but before starting to cry again, she said, "OK, look, I gotta go. Where will you be this evening? I'll have to call you back."

"Right here, waiting for your call."

"Thanks, it was good to hear your voice. I knew I could count on you, if not for the answer, at least to point me in the right direction. I love you."

"I love you too, and listen," he momentarily wanted to stop her before she hung up, "you don't need me to give you the right answer. You just need to have as much faith in yourself as I have in you."

"OK, thanks, and good luck this afternoon, knock 'em dead." The doctor knocked at the door. "I really gotta go now; I'll talk to you later. Bye."

***

Knock 'em dead, Marcos thought, interesting choice of words. As soon as he hung up, Sergeant Mark Grove of the U of I campus police asked him again, "Well, Dr. Estrada, what've you decided to do?"

Marcos was told Grove had years of experience, but he had the muscular torso of a young man. As he stood there, waiting for a reply, Marcos thought he looked a little like Superman, and secretly hoped Grove was. "I'm going to go out there," Marcos finally answered.

"Even after everything I've told you?"

"Yep."

"But don't you believe me when I say I think you're in *serious* danger?" Sergeant Grove was clearly becoming frustrated, but they both knew he couldn't stop Marcos if he wanted to give his lecture.

"Yes," Marcos nodded slowly, "I do believe you."

"Then why on earth have you changed your mind? It seems to me, before that phone call you were leaning toward canceling."

"You're right, but I heard the advice I gave my sister and decided I had to follow it too."

"Do you mind if I ask what that was?"

"I told her she had to do what was in the best interest of her child, and now I've got to do the same. If I cancel the lecture, the good people who've come to hear me speak, the ones who are still hurting, or are working with those who are, will be disappointed, and I simply can't do that." Now resigned, Marcos just shrugged his shoulders. But Sergeant Grove wasn't ready to give up.

"Even though we think whoever wrote that death threat means it?" Grove asked.

Marcos saw Sergeant's Grove's eyes change from warm to menacing.

"Yes."

"And even though those zealots picketing out there are carrying some pretty nasty and explicit signs?"

"Yes. After all," Marcos injected, trying to lighten things up, "what is it they say about sticks and stones?"

"Dr. Estrada," Sergeant Grove interrupted, "this is not a laughing matter, and this group may just throw those sticks and stones."

"I understand and I apologize. I didn't mean to cast aspersions on your concerns." Marcos placed his hand on the Sergeant's shoulder and gave him an appreciative smile. "You guys have been terrific but now it's time to go."

Mark Grove looked at him with a combination of frustration and pleading. "Dr. Estrada, is there anything I can say to convince you what you're about to do is too damned risky?"

"No, not anymore." Marcos took his hand off the sergeant's shoulder and retrieved his sports jacket.

Even though he'd just met Grove earlier that day, he already liked and respected him. Marcos had met many law enforcement officers over the years, and although he thought most treated him fairly, he felt few saw beyond his label of *convicted child molester*. Sergeant Grove, he concluded, was one of the few. Sensing the sergeant actually cared about him as a person, rather than just an assignment, Marcos turned back to give him a more complete explanation.

"Sergeant, do you know what the word *diss* means?"

"Yeah, it means to disrespect someone."

"Do you know what happens to someone in prison, once they let someone 'diss' them?"

"Yeah, I've heard tell."

"Well, I've experienced it. I let people in Stockton diss me and it was as bad as you've heard. So you see, I've got to go out there tonight, I can't be intimidated. If I am, then I haven't changed as much as I think I have."

Marcos could see respect return to Sergeant Grove's eyes. Still, he wasn't the least bit surprised when Grove gave it one more try. "But, if you go out there, you know they just might—"

"I understand," Marcos stopped him from finishing his sentence, "but I still gotta go."

Grove exhaled deeply, and nodded, "All right then, let's go. I'll call backstage and let them know we're coming. And, Dr. Estrada, I *will* do whatever I can to protect you."

"Thanks, but please don't put yourself in harm's way; this is my battle."

Shortly before noon, Sergeant Grove ushered Marcos through the picket line. Someone yelled, "Once a mother-fucking child molester, always a mother-fucking child molester. Get the fuck away from our kids, and get the hell off our campus!"

At 12:00 exactly, Marcos stepped onto the stage. He was immediately pelted with an egg. In response, several U of I campus police approached him from three directions.

"Back off," Marcos said, as forcefully and unobtrusively as he could. He then continued to approach the lectern while nonchalantly brushing off eggshell. The next thing he heard was gun fire.

Marcos' last conscious thought was regret that he wouldn't be there when Sophia called back.

***

Colin watched Sophia walk through the door at 12:15. On the surface she appeared happy to see him, but he could tell she couldn't look directly into his eyes. Seeing her behave this way only increased his anxiety.

After they'd been there several minutes he thought, we've been here a long time and she *still* hasn't stopped talking, or asked me why I drove into town to have lunch with her. Paralyzed with fear, he was too anxious to ask directly where she'd been, so he continued to listen.

That's another thing, he worried, although often extremely enthusiastic, she's rarely this talkative, and still she hasn't said *anything* of *any* consequence. She's just rambling, and obviously nervous and preoccupied. But I'm not sure really which one of us is feeling that way. For all I know, I could be reading her all wrong, but I don't think so. I think she's trying to hide something…

***.

In truth, Sophia was trying to hide everything. Following Marcos' advice, she considered the matter, and decided what was in the *best interest of her child* was to embrace him or her and never tell Colin she'd doubted him. Whatever Dr. Tanner's concerns were, they didn't apply to Colin. Her husband was incapable of hurting any child.

By the time her tests were completed, Sophia left the doctor's office confident she'd made the right decisions. But, it wasn't until she called her office, and got Colin's message, that she became downright excited.

By the time she entered the restaurant she couldn't wait to tell Colin the good news. Still, she felt she had to wait until just the right moment...

*** .

Colin couldn't take it anymore. He either had to ask where the hell she'd been, or tell her his news. "Sophia!" He blurted out.

"What?" Sophia looked as if she were lost in thought and was suddenly taken aback.

Colin continued, "I've been offered a job in Santa Fe, New Mexico." He decided to bring up the easier issue first, thinking it would give him insight into the other more difficult one.

"What?" Sophia squinted her eyes and tucked in her chin.

"The Assistant Director of The National Forest Service called me this morning. I haven't actually been offered a job, but it seems to be mine for the asking. He's talked to Ken and everything, and he wants me to fly to Santa Fe next week for an interview."

Sophia, in true prosecutorial-like fashion, began to ask him a million questions, and he, in true scientific parley, responded to her as carefully as he could. Finally, she asked, "So, you said you were interested, right?"

"No, I said I'd talk to you about it."

Sophia scooted back in her chair. "Well, now you have, and you simply *have* to go for it."

"Sophia," he said, leaning forward on both forearms, "I'm not going to Santa Fe without you."

"Well, of course you're not, don't be ridiculous. We'll have to move to Santa Fe, or any other place you'd like. God knows, Santa Fe may be too much of a big city for you, and we'll probably end up having to live in the boonies somewhere, but we can adjust. Thank God you'd only have to come into the city two or three times a week. You do think we could live outside Santa Fe proper, don't you?"

Something *is* very wrong, he thought. She's still going a mile a minute, but everything she's saying is confusing the hell out of me.

"Sophia," he said, not answering her last question, "you do know if we move there, you'd have to give up your job, *and* leave your friends at the office right? I mean, am I missing something? I thought you loved your work?"

Well there it is, Colin thought. I've laid it out, but she didn't react to leaving her job *or* her office mates; maybe my suspicions were all wrong...

Sophia interrupted his thoughts by answering his question. "I do, but this sounds like *just* what the doctor ordered."

Colin didn't like the way *that* sounded at all.

Doctor, what doctor, he wondered. All his internal alarms went off. He knew she usually chose her words very carefully and he was certain he'd never heard her use that particular expression before. Maybe she wasn't having an affair; maybe she's sick, maybe she's really sick....

Suddenly he recalled what Debbie had told him, "Some people use personal time for doctor's appointments." Colin started to panic and couldn't breathe properly, but still he managed to ask, "Sophia, are you OK?" If anything ever happened to her, he thought, I'd die.

"Hey, don't look so crestfallen," she responded with a big smile, "I told the kids you were a happy guy."

"Kids, what kids?" He was lost, what with his job offer, his suspicions about an affair, then something about a doctor, and now something about kids....

She interrupted his thoughts again, "Our kids!"

"Our kids?"

"Yeah, our kids, as in more than one!" Sophia's smile encompassed her entire face.

"Sophia, *what* are you talking about?"

"I'm talking about twins, Colin, twins!"

"Whose twins?"

"Our twins! Haven't you been paying attention? Colin, our twins, as in yours and mine, as in you and me, as in Mom and Dad; as in no birth control method is 100%, and our kids are clearly one in a million!"

He progressed from sheer panic to cautious elation.

"So, the doctor's orders you were talking about, that doctor would be—"

"My obstetrician!"

"I assume you just heard, this...what, this morning?"

"Yep."

"Why didn't you tell me you were going to see a doctor? I would've gone with you."

He felt like a complete idiot for doubting her and decided to never tell her what he'd feared.

***

"I wasn't really sure what was going on." She paused and reconsidered telling him everything she'd been through, but once again decided it was best left unsaid. "Anyway, I wanted to surprise you, sort of like an *I Love Lucy* thing. I had it all planned to tell you tonight under the stars, over steak and champagne; that is, champagne for you, milk for me. I had all these romantic notions about how I wanted this conversation to go, but over our favorite brats, at the Brat House. Well, I guess, that's OK too."

***

Colin's mind was reeling. "So, what did the doctor say, and what's this about twins?" Colin was trying desperately to catch up.

"What can I say?" she responded. "With this newfangled prenatal equipment, the Doc thought he could hear two heart beats."

"Well, how'd they sound?"

"Glorious! Actually I couldn't quite hear them, but, from what little I did hear, it sounded as good as that New York Philharmonic Orchestra album of yours."

Colin's heart and mind were racing. He felt as if both jubilation and consternation were erupting in every body cell but then, kerplunk, both emotions landed in his heart at the same time. He knew he had to say something. "OK, I'm starting to get this now, you're pregnant with twins. But, why did you say the move sounded like just what the doctor *ordered*?"

"Well, the doctor also told me I was anemic and, being pregnant with twins, he thought I should be extra careful and plan on leaving my job sometime before summer begins; that is, if we can afford to—"

"You're anemic?"

"Yeah, but that's no big deal, it's just best if I take it easy. So, now do you see why this move is just what the doctor ordered?"

"Yea, but you are OK, right?"

"Yes."

"And the twins, they're OK?"

"Absolutely!"

***

Seeing Colin's concern and his reaction to the news that his children were safe were all the reassurances Sophia needed. Now she was certain she'd made the right decision.

Colin interrupted her musings, "And you're OK with leaving your job?"

"Definitely."

"Sophia," Colin asked slowly, "won't you miss fighting the good fight for the little people?"

"No, because I'll still be doing that. It's just that for a little while, I'll be doing it for two very special little people. I can always go back to work later, but if we can scrape together enough money for us for a short time, I'd like to stay home with them. My mother couldn't afford to stay home with me and I think we both missed out because of it."

***

Colin was trying hard to follow her lead, but she was giving him an overwhelming amount of important information. And true to form, he didn't think he was processing it very well. They'd never talked about having any children, but now they were suddenly having two. He was thrilled, even while needing a minute to sort it all out. At the same time, he knew he had to convey his happiness to Sophia right away.

Reaching across the table, he grabbed both her hands, brought them to his lips, and said, "Thank you." His vision started blurring as his eyes reddened. Still, he wouldn't let go of her hands, or stop gazing into her eyes. This beautiful, amazing woman, he thought, is *my* wife and now she's pregnant with *my* babies.

***

Sophia loved seeing him so happy. The look in his eyes was more than even she could've hoped for. When Colin could speak again, he assured her that between his newsletter and new job, they'd have plenty of money, as long as they didn't live extravagantly. This of course, made her laugh.

"Nature Boy," she remarked, "I think I can handle it."

"Sophia my love, I don't think there's anything you couldn't handle. I only hope I didn't let you down just now by my slow response."

"Hey, I married a scientist, and a very cute one at that. My idea of telling you later was a silly one. I should've known better than to try and keep a secret from you, and the look in your eyes, once it all sunk in, well that was all I could've hoped for."

***

Colin was glad he hadn't disappointed her and beseeched her to take the rest of the afternoon off. He wanted time with her to grasp it fully and to celebrate. It didn't take much prodding to convince her, and together they walked to a phone booth.

"You wait here." She stepped inside the phone booth and closed the door. Colin kept pressing his lips on the glass of the phone booth. Shaking her head, Sophia turned away and called her office. Once she stepped back out, and the phone booth door closed behind her, she smiled triumphantly. "OK, Papa, I'm all yours. How would you like to celebrate?"

"Well, I actually gave that some thought while you were on the phone. I'd like to buy the babies University of Wisconsin T-shirts, so they'll know where they came from. Then, I want to call our families, and then, only if it's safe, I'd like to make love."

"Of course it's safe. So, do you want to do those things in *that* particular order?"

"No, I'm flexible," Colin smiled, "but I figure, while we're out, we should get the T-shirts. Once we get home, well, then I can't be responsible for my behavior." He took her hand firmly in his and together, they walked in silence toward the UW bookstore.

By the time they crossed the street, Colin put a hand on each of her shoulders and turned her toward him. Sophia saw his eyes were again filled with tears and he was having trouble speaking. She waited a few long seconds until his voice returned.

"Sophia, if someone would've asked me this morning when I woke up, 'Is it possible for you to love your wife any more than you already do?' I would've said 'No way!' But, I would've been wrong..." He was clearly having trouble continuing, but did. "Because I've never been more in love with you than I am at this very moment. You are, without a doubt, my guardian angel. First, you gave me my life back, and now, you'll be giving life to my children. I just can't figure out what I did to deserve you, and my greatest fear is that some day I'll lose you."

Sophia reached up, grabbed his hands, brought them to her mouth, and kissed them, one at a time. "Colin, please look into my eyes. What you see there is love. You are the love of my life. I may at times temporarily wig out, because of my past or the sadness I see at work each day. But, what I've come to learn is that even those two things can never touch the love I feel for you, or the underlying faith I have in us."

When she finally let go of his hands, he promptly drew her into his trembling arms. His breathing was deep but halting. A few more tears rolled down his face, onto her neck. She held him until he began to breathe normally.

"Hey," Sophia finally said, "how 'bout those T-shirts? I'm thinking they should have a big picture of our mascot, Bucky Badger, smiling and kicking up his heels. What do you think?"

Colin cleared his throat and swallowed, "I think that'd be perfect."

***

They walked to the bookstore locked in each other's arms. They were, at that moment, inseparable, which made walking through the front door together difficult, but not impossible.

Along with T-shirts, Colin found little footed pajamas, replete with tiny coyotes howling at the moon. "We've *got* to get these," he said, with great enthusiasm. "This is like Santa Fe's mascot."

"OK," Sophia said, smiling sheepishly, "but then, let's go. You've got me all excited about the other things you suggested!" Colin paid for their purchases and they swiftly left the store. With the tiny pajamas and T-shirts placed firmly under one arm and Sophia on the other, Colin was ready to leave the Badger State and conquer the coyote frontier.

During the drive home, Sophia made lists of all the things they had to do in preparation for their new life. But when they walked into their front door she threw her list on the dining room table, and he left their packages on the floor.

Later that afternoon, as Sophia rested her still flushed face on Colin's chest, he asked, "Whom, my darling, should we call first?"

"Marcos, of course," she said, as she reached for the phone.

51

April 12, 1999
MARCOS

Extraordinary risk—One lying outside the sphere of normal.

Marcos lay on the stage floor with a rolled-up jacket under his head. Sergeant Grove was sitting right next to him.

"What happened?" Marcos asked.

"Someone got a shot off."

"Then why aren't I dead?"

"Because when I saw the gunman approach I knocked you down."

Marcos was slowly beginning to understand. "Sergeant, do you mean that, contrary to my request, you put yourself in harm's way?" Marcos smiled and discovered even that small movement increased the pain in the back of his head.

"Yeah," Sergeant Grove replied. "After listening to you back there in the hotel room, I realized we're both after the same thing. We both want to make the world a safer place."

"Thanks," Marcos was deeply touched by Mark Grove's sentiments and actions. "Hey, are *you* OK?"

"Yes. I'm OK."

"A hundred percent OK?"

"Yes," Sergeant Grove assured him, "I am one hundred percent OK."

"So," Marcos finally asked as he struggled to sit up, "did you catch the guy?"

"Yeah, matter of fact, we did. He's a known local parolee, whose sister was molested by his father when he was a kid. I guess he thought this was *payback*. Anyway, since he's on parole, and merely possessing a gun is a violation of his parole, he'll probably just be sent back to prison without your even having to testify."

Marcos' head was still spinning. "Sounds pretty sad all the way around," he finally responded.

Marcos understood the gravity of what had just occurred, but it was impossible for him not to also recognize that his shooter was yet another victim of an act of child molestation. Marcos decided not to share these last thoughts with Sergeant Grove. Instead he simply asked, "Is everyone else OK too?"

"Yeah, but *you* better lie still here a minute. I think my over-zealousness gave you a pretty nasty bump. Do you want to go to the hospital?"

"No, no thanks. If all I've got is a bump, I'd rather go back to the hotel. I'm expecting an important call."

"Got you covered Doc." Mark Grove smiled at his double entendre. "Now, just give me another minute and I'll get you out of here."

***

Soon after Marcos returned to his hotel room the phone rang. It was Sophia and Colin; they called to share their incredible news.

Marcos could tell by Sophia's voice she felt good about her decision. He could also sense by her choice of words she hadn't told Colin about their previous conversation. Now he just hoped and prayed she'd never come to regret her optimism.

For his part he was delighted, not just about the twins, but also about Colin's potential job offer. Soon he'd not only have Sophia and Colin hours away in Santa Fe, but he'd also have their children.

By the time Marcos finally hung up he was exhausted. Halfway through their conversation he decided not to tell them what had happened to him. He didn't want to re-live it, worry them, or in any way put a damper on their joy. At that moment, all he wanted was a refill on his ice pack, room service, and a good night's sleep.

The next day he woke up early with a dull ache and a burning desire to go home.

***

By the time he got back to Crested Butte his headache was gone. Now, feeling he had much to celebrate and be thankful for, he decided to take himself out to his favorite restaurant.

The restaurant was called Bon Soir. It served unique, exquisite European food in a French country atmosphere. Its entrance too was exotic, requiring all its patrons to park on a side street and crouch down as they found their way through a small, dimly-lit, covered alley. Marcos loved this part of the experience; it always made him feel as if he were entering Wonderland.

Tonight he was feeling particularly affluent, so he ordered an expensive bottle of French Bordeaux, escargots, and filet mignon.

***

While he ordered, someone was looking over at him. Her name was Charlene Morton or Professor Morton as she was known professionally, or Char as her friends called her. Char had recognized Marcos from the jacket of his book.

Dr. Charlene Morton was a psychology professor at Williams College in Williamstown, Massachusetts. She taught abnormal psychology and used parts of his book to teach the section on obsessive-compulsive behavior. She always thought he was brilliant, but now she thought he was also extremely handsome, in fact even more attractive than he appeared in the photo on his book jacket.

Char Morton was not a particularly patient or shy person; hence, she had to use great restraint to not intrude upon Marcos' supper.

When she saw the waitress deliver his after-dinner coffee, she decided her opportunity had finally arrived.

"Excuse me," she announced as she walked over to his table.

***

Although Marcos held the steaming cup of coffee up to his lips, he hadn't yet taken his first sip. Suddenly, he looked up; slowly he put his cup down. Before him was a very attractive woman with a dazzling smile and glorious green eyes.

"Excuse me," she repeated, "Dr. Estrada, I just had to tell you how much I loved your book."

Marcos stood. "Well thank you fair lady." Between the effects of the alcohol, the sumptuous meal and his recent good fortune, Uncle Marcos was feeling uncharacteristically bold. "I am very pleased to make your acquaintance, but I apologize, I haven't yet done so."

"My name is Charlene Morton," she responded. "I teach psychology at Williams College."

"I'm honored Professor. So, you've seen my book."

"Seen it? I've not only seen it, I've read it, and I've put it on my students' required reading list."

"Well then, thank you again, and I suppose I should also thank the fine students of Williams College for my being able to afford this extravagant meal."

"Well then, on behalf of the students at Williams College, you are quite welcome; although, I think your book was on the bestseller list long before my students purchased their copies. It is," she said in all seriousness, "quite an astounding book and your personal history is, to say the least, compelling. What a life you've had."

"Yes, and as a matter of fact, my life and my personal history are the reasons I'm here tonight." After a very brief reflective moment, Marcos resolved not to tell her about his life threatening experience, but rather to focus instead on Sophia's announcement. "I am celebrating my sister's good fortune. She has just found out she and her husband are pregnant with twins and they're likely moving from Wisconsin to Santa Fe. The upshot of that is, soon I will have my dear sister, her terrific husband, and their two enchanting children a mere stone's throw away." For a brief moment Marcos disappeared into the future where he pictured himself proudly strolling his nieces and/or nephews down the streets of Crested Butte. "Prior to this moment, the only thing wrong with this paradise I live in is that, at times, I get very lonely."

"Oh, so there is no Mrs. Estrada?"

"No, I'm single, very single. And you?"

"Very. I mean, yes, I'm single too."

"Well, single and very delightful woman, would you please do me the honor of joining me for coffee?"

"Thank you," she said, "I thought you'd never ask."

Marcos then asked for atonement for his rudeness, and with great ceremony pulled out a chair for her. He then stood by until she was comfortably seated.

Once he had settled back down, they began to speak. They never once took their eyes off one another.

After a while the owner of the restaurant, Mrs. Russo, brought their conversation to a halt. She came over, apologized for the interruption, and informed them the restaurant would soon be beginning its eight o'clock seating.

After only a moment's hesitation, Marcos asked, "Madame, do you have any reservations left for your eight o'clock seating?"

"Oui... Monsieur..." she said, with some hesitancy.

"Dr. Morton—" Marcos continued.

"Please call me Charlene."

"Thank you, Charlene. Will you do me the honor of joining me?"

"Well then, Madame, please reserve a table for us, and by the way, this one would be just fine."

Mrs. Russo looked perplexed. "But will you both be dining again, Monsieur?"

"Maybe. Can I get you anything, Charlene?" he asked, turning his attention back to her.

"No, no, thank you. I've already eaten."

"Madame," Marcos said, returning his attention to Mrs. Russo, "do you have a dishwasher back there in the kitchen? I mean somebody who actually washes the pots, pans and dishes?"

"Bien sur, of course we do. His name is Robert."

"Fine then, would you please pack up our eight o'clock dinner for two and give it to Robert?"

"I'm not sure I understand Monsieur," Mrs. Russo answered.

"I'm sorry, I didn't mean to be obtuse," Marcos replied. "I just want to be able to remain here with this lovely woman, ensure you are being fully compensated, and give your Robert a treat. Please just put whatever Robert orders for dinner on my bill."

"But Monsieur, that's not necessary—"

"Please Madame, I insist." He left no question in his voice that he did.

Mrs. Russo stepped back and walked away. She appeared flustered, but as she pushed open the kitchen door, she finally smiled.

A moment later Marcos and Charlene heard a non-discernable, animated conversation, which culminated in a youthful voice yelling, "No shit?" which caused Charlene and Marcos to burst out laughing, but not for long. Soon they were again oblivious to their surroundings.

Just before closing, they looked around and realized the restaurant had emptied.

After walking Charlene to her car, Marcos wouldn't let her leave until they made firm plans to spring ski together the next day.

***

From the following morning on they were inseparable for the remainder of Charlene's vacation. They skied, snow-shoed, shopped, dined, and above all else talked. Much to their surprise, they never tired of each other, or ran out of things to say.

Fearful of disturbing what they had just created, they didn't make love until her last afternoon in town.

By the time they finally got into his bed, they were both hungry for each other and couldn't imagine a single part of the other's body they didn't want to touch and explore.

They made love with the ardor of adolescents and the intimacy of old friends. Their lovemaking lasted for hours. Their desire and enthusiasm slowed down only long enough to look deeply into each other's eyes so each could make sure the other was comfortable and satisfied.

Afterward, they feasted on a meal catered by Bon Soir.

The next day, as she dressed to leave, Char told Marcos she wished she never had to go. In response, Marcos asked her if he could join her in Williamstown the following weekend. In response Char's eyes filled with tears and Marcos pulled her back to bed.

As they began to make love again, they both silently hoped they could painlessly wait that long.

***

Marcos finally arrived on Friday, right after her last class. In spite of all of her planned activities, they spent most of their weekend in bed. Neither had ever been so happy.

***

Although Charlene had dated occasionally, she generally filled her time with work-related events because she'd never, until now, found anyone as absorbing or as emotionally safe, as her work.

***

Months wore on; they spoke on the phone each night, e-mailed each other constantly, and spent as much time together as they possibly could. The more they got to know each other, the deeper their love grew.

As the Thanksgiving holidays approached, he invited her to meet his family.

Colin and a very pregnant Sophia agreed to drive up from Santa Fe and he flew his mother in from Santa Barbara.

Though Margarita visited frequently, having developed a real sense of camaraderie with Edith, this visit would be special; this time the big draw was Charlene.

***

The family finally met her the Tuesday before Thanksgiving. What they appreciated most about her was her assertiveness and her complete adoration and devotion to Marcos. None of them had ever known a woman that forward, but they all understood, knowing how insecure Marcos still felt around women, it was Charlene's temperate aggressiveness that brought, and kept, the two of them together.

***

On the Wednesday evening before Thanksgiving Margarita and Sophia found themselves silently sitting on a couch in the living room. They were gazing at Charlene and Marcos as they folded cloth napkins in his dining room.

Marcos whispered something in Charlene's ear and she playfully hit him with one of the newly folded napkins. They laughed and then she nuzzled into his neck. Marcos held her there, closed his eyes and pressed his lips against her cheek.

Margarita leaned closer to Sophia. "In all of his life, mi hija, I have never seen your brother so happy."

Sophia just nodded.

During Thanksgiving supper Margarita rose to make a toast. "To begin with, please everyone, lift up your glasses to Charlene... I mean Char. Char, you have brought so much—"

Margarita's eyes filled with tears, she shook her head; she couldn't go on, but Sophia could... "love back into our family." Margarita nodded and sat down. Sophia stood and continued, "Marcos always deserved love and tenderness..." Sophia's eyes began to well up, she paused and looked over at her brother. In a glance, Marcos acknowledged her struggle. Colin reached out and gently put his hand on top of the one she left on the table to maintain her balance. She drew strength from his touch and continued. "And, at last," she looked at Charlene, and swallowed hard, "he's found it, in you." Through unabashed tears Sophia concluded with, "God Bless you Charlene Morton."

"Here, here," said Marcos with a face-lighting smile, whereas everyone else was rendered silent and tearful. Still, through their tears, they blissfully clinked glasses.

***

The Sunday morning after Thanksgiving everyone returned home, except Margarita, who stayed on to enjoy more time with Marcos and Edith. That evening, as she sat curled up on Marcos' overstuffed couch, right beside his spectacular stone fireplace, with its now glowing and crackling fire, she readied herself for what she knew she had to say. Finally, she looked over at Marcos across the room, deeply exhaled and bravely offered, "Marcos I'm sorry, I couldn't finish the toast on Thanksgiving. I guess I still feel so guilty—"

***

Marcos could see the pain in her eyes. He stood up and came toward her. As he approached he said, "Mama you need to just let the past go."

"Marcos, tell me truthfully, do you think you ever will?" She looked down and continued, "Do you think you'll ever really be able to forgive me for leaving you behind?"

Marcos sat down, took her hand in his, looked straight into her eyes and said, "Mama, I already have. I can't believe you're still so concerned about it. Look, I'm going to try to make a few things clear to you, once and for all." Marcos positioned her so she could look right into his eyes. "I would never have wished my childhood on anyone. It was miserable, but that's not an excuse for what I did to Sophia and the pain I caused you. I and I alone am responsible for that. Once I came to grips with that painful realization, instead of wallowing in all of my guilt or rushing into forgiving myself, I used my feelings of remorse to fuel my passion to continue my work." Marcos smiled. "Look Mama, I don't mean to lecture you. I just want you to understand, I have no desire to look back anymore, unless it is to continue to motivate me to go forward. Now, all I want is to be able to concentrate on my work and spend time with the people I love... I just wish Papa was still with us." He looked down.

Margarita reached out and laid her hand over his. When he looked back up at her, he knew his eyes were red. He still missed Julio, he hoped he always would; he never wanted to forget him or their bond. "You Mama," he continued "through no fault of your own, became our only parent and over time we've all grown to understand your pain, as well as your pride." Marcos took hold of her other hand and declared, "I am, as I sit here today, very thankful to have you as my mother. And, I am thrilled you liked Charlene so much you thought to raise your glass to her. The fact that you couldn't finish the toast isn't what matters. What matters is that you started it."

***

The next day Margarita returned home and Marcos left to give a lecture in Des Moines, Iowa.

52

November 28, 1999
MARCOS & CHARLENE

Assumption of the Risk—When a person, knowing the risks
involved, still chooses to take an action.

When Charlene returned to Williamstown late the Sunday after
Thanksgiving, she was plagued by loneliness. Just the day before
she felt so at home, and now felt completely alone.

Overcome by these feelings, she impetuously, in the middle of
the night on Monday, sent Marcos a very brief e-mail—"Marry
me?" She then went back to bed, but she couldn't fall asleep.
Every few minutes throughout the night, she got up to check her e-
mail; but Marcos didn't respond.

By seven the next morning she thought about calling him, but
by then she was too embarrassed. She knew he checked his e-mail
every morning at six o'clock no matter where he was. She was
sure he was just busy trying to find the right words to say, "It's too
soon" or "I'm not ready" or worse yet, "I'm not sure I love you
enough."

By nine o'clock she had to leave or she'd be late for her
classes. That's it, she decided, he's not writing back and I'm an
idiot for sending that ridiculous e-mail. Confident she'd made the
worst mistake of her life, she dragged herself out of bed. After
brushing her hair and teeth, she pulled on a turtleneck, jeans and a
blazer and left for class.

By the middle of the afternoon, she was completely
despondent. She'd already gone home twice to check her computer
screen. Each time she did so she found the dreaded words: "You
have no unopened messages."

By the time she left her apartment, en route to teach her last
class of the day, she was inconsolable.

A cold wind blew as she slowly trudged across campus. Under
a rapidly graying sky, her next chilling thought was: What if I've
blown it all? Why did I have to be so pushy? Why couldn't I have
just left well enough alone…?

Suddenly her focus shifted again. I hope, she now worried, nothing happened to him...Oh God, please just let him be safe...

Meanwhile, her four o'clock lecture was, to all in attendance, uninspired. Her heart just wasn't in it. Her heart was in Crested Butte and her students looked restless and bored. Many, she now observed, were just outright ignoring her and simply looking out the window.

As she followed their stares, she saw, through the first snowstorm of the year, an image of what appeared to be Marcos, but she knew she was just hallucinating. Still, she took a step closer to the window. She opened the window. She couldn't believe her eyes. Was it Marcos...or was her mind playing tricks on her? She continued to stare...

It is Marcos, she concluded, but what's he doing? He's standing in the middle of the courtyard. He's putting something in some kind of machine... maybe some kind of tape machine? And now he's looking around. He has to be looking for me.

Charlene tried to call out to him and wave, but she couldn't. She felt as if her hands were stuck, cupped in front of her mouth.

When Marcos caught sight of her, the music started, and he began to sing along with Stevie Wonder.

"For once in my life, I have someone who needs me,
Someone I've needed so long..."

Charlene couldn't believe her eyes or ears. She briefly looked at her students; they appeared dumbfounded. She remained speechless and completely overwhelmed while Marcos continued singing *her* heart out.

"...For once I can say this is mine, you can't take it..."

When he finally finished singing, he yelled out, "Yes, Professor Charlene Morton, I will marry you, and then I'll spend the rest of my life trying to deserve you."

She briefly remained stone still and stunned. Then, with a burst of energy, she ran from the classroom and down the steps to join him.

Meanwhile, her students, along with many others, were now leaning out of their classroom windows, cheering and applauding wildly.

When the two finally met in the middle of the courtyard, they grabbed on to each other with such force, they almost slipped and toppled over. Once they regained their balance, they stood firmly, and held each other silently, as snow whirled all around them.

Finally, Marcos settled down enough to speak. He whispered into her ear, "I would have asked you, but I didn't think you really wanted to marry an ex-felon, and a registered sex offender to boot."

"Well you were wrong," Charlene managed to eke out, "because those are two of the things you happen to be, and I fell in love with the whole package."

"But Char, what about children?"

"I will always trust you with children, but I don't know about us actually having any. Can you live with that?"

"Yes," he nodded. Then he nuzzled deeper into her neck and said, "but there's something I couldn't possibly live with. I couldn't possibly marry you, unless you promised me, that you'll never let go. I've been through a lot and I've survived, but losing you would be the one thing I'm sure would break me."

"Oh Marcos, I can't imagine ever leaving you. I love you with all of my heart."

***

Marcos knew by then there were no guarantees in life and what she'd just said was the best anyone could hope for.

***

Later that evening, they agreed they wanted to be married as soon as possible and decided to do it in Santa Fe during her Christmas break. By now Sophia was too pregnant to travel, and Marcos couldn't imagine his wedding without her.

They married at the Loretto Chapel, a picturesque church built in the 1800s, situated in the heart of Santa Fe. Their brief ceremony was followed by a gourmet meal at the Anasazi Inn. Second only to Bon Soir, the Anasazi Inn had become their favorite restaurant. It housed a particularly spectacular private room. The room was a refurbished wine cellar, which still had within its recessed walls some of the finest wines from around the world. The centerpiece of the room was a large ornately-carved wooden table, which comfortably accommodated their group of fourteen.

On the night of their wedding Charlene and Marcos sat at opposite ends of that grand table, but they rarely took their eyes off one another. Along side of them were Sophia, Margarita,

Colin, Edith, Dwight, Cathy, Dr. and Mrs. Koppell, and four of Charlene's friends from Williams.

No one from Char's family was in attendance. Char's parents had been killed in a plane crash when she was very young. After that she was raised by her loving grandmother who later died when Char was in graduate school. The people who now sat at this table had become all the family she had, and all the family she felt she ever needed.

After the wedding, the group spent the next week enjoying Santa Fe. Some went skiing while others explored museums, galleries, and the finer restaurants. Still, whenever possible, they spent as much time as they could together.

Char's favorite experience was the evening they spent walking along Canyon Road.

It was Christmas Eve and by the time they arrived, the sun was beginning to set. Candles inside paper bags, called luminarios, lined the paths to people's homes, while small open-pit fires, called farilitos, were lit in front of these same homes. At each residence visitors were offered coffee or cider and invited to sing Christmas carols while standing around the farilitos.

Margarita and Edith were clearly entranced by this tradition and joyfully joined in the singing whenever the time-honored songs were sung in Spanish. Margarita appeared particularly gratified whenever she could coax Marcos or Sophia into singing along.

***

As Charlene watched the four of them singing in the glow of the farilitos and luminarios, she was deeply moved.

***

After Christmas Marcos and Charlene returned to Crested Butte to pack. Marcos was going to move to Williamstown and leave the house in Edith's good care. Although they planned on coming back as often as they could, Williamstown, at least for now, would be their home.

Despite the fact that Marcos didn't find Williamstown as breath taking as Crested Butte, he still thought it was beautiful and quaint. He especially appreciated the way it was tucked seamlessly into the middle of the spectacular Berkshire Mountains. Still, as he and Char walked hand-in-hand throughout the meandering, amicable campus, they longed to return to the dramatic beauty of the Colorado Rockies.

For Marcos, the up side, as he thought of it, of living on a college campus in the middle of nowhere, was he was much more productive. After only being there a short while, he completed his second book and began his third.

His second book, A Treatment Plan, had, just as his agent predicted, become a great success shortly after it was released. He could now afford to take Char with him on any speaking engagement she chose. Whether he was comfortable doing so was another question.

Although Marcos had, for the most part, put his U of I experience behind him, he feared for Char's safety. When he knew she'd be accompanying him, he surreptitiously hired private security to protect her. He kept these calls a secret because he hadn't told her, or anyone else in his family, what had happened to him. He didn't want them to either worry, or worse yet, try and stop him from lecturing. Aside from that concern, he loved bringing Char with him, not only for the pleasure of her company, but also because of her insight.

Often, while lecturing, once he knew the room was safe, he would invite her up on the stage to contribute her acumen. Marcos took tremendous pride in sharing the spotlight with her. He thought she was not only brilliant but also, beautiful. Sometimes, when she spoke at length on a subject, Marcos beamed at her and thought: There's no doubt about it, she's magnificent; the astonishing thing is that she's married to me...

One night after a particularly successful co-lecture, he asked her to consider co-authoring his third book. Char said she'd be honored as long as he didn't expect her ideas to take a back seat to his.

"Char," he said, as his smile widened, "you should know by now, one of the reasons I'm so madly in love with you is that you never let your ideas take a back seat to anyone's."

"Well then," she said throwing her arms around him, "let's get started." Then she whispered in his ear, "Thanks for wanting me."

Later that night, they made tender and passionate love.

The next day they began work on their first book.

***

After three exhausting, but exciting months of writing and lecturing together, Char felt also teaching in a classroom was too tiring, so, she decided to quit her job at Williams College. From then on, she promised an overjoyed Marcos, she'd devote most of her time to writing and lecturing with him.

***

By then, both of them were amazed they'd gotten along so well, each fully expected at any moment one of their *intellectual disagreements* would explode into an insurmountable problem, but that never happened. Charlene assumed it had to do with how much respect they had for each other, while Marcos presumed it was just because they were so madly in love.

With her teaching life behind her, they were free to leave Williamstown and return to their beloved Crested Butte. By then the twins, Malana and Alani, were six months old, and Charlene and Marcos were frustrated at not being able to spend more time with them.

Once having settled back into their home in the Rockies Charlene longed to have their entire family there for the Christmas holidays.

***

Jordon now remembered that Christmas there simply was no choice, everyone *had* to gather in Crested Butte.

53

December 24, 2000
THE FAMILY

Commingling—To put together in one mass.

By Christmas the twins were fast-moving toddlers and looked like two perfect little dolls. They were the consummate combination of their parent's diverse ethnic backgrounds. Both of them had olive skin, big brown eyes, and an abundance of curly blonde hair.

Sophia still hadn't gone back to work. She had however, been reviewing some study guides in preparation for taking the New Mexico bar examination. She knew in time she'd want to step back into the arena and continue *the good fight*, but for now it was Christmas and all she wanted was to enjoy her family.

By then Colin was fully engrossed in both his new job and his dynamic family. He thought living on the outskirts of Santa Fe, spending four days a week at home and three in the city, created a perfect work environment for him. Although dealing with government administrators was at times extremely stressful, he reveled daily in the thought that he always had Sophia as well as the girls to come home to, and Tom and Jake to call whenever he longed for a male's perspective. Colin was particularly looking forward to this Christmas, when he could spend more time with his ever-expanding family.

Christmas morning found the twins playing in the snow with their parents, while their grandparents were content to watch them from their window.

Age was catching up with both Dwight and Cathy, but seeing their darling granddaughters rolling around in the snow with their father gave them immense pleasure. They now knew Colin would be fine. He'd grown so much over the last few years and these days he had so much to live for.

Upstairs in the kitchen, Edith and Margarita were again cooking and singing their favorite Guatemalan Christmas songs, while blissfully rejoicing in their recent new addition.

In the living room sat Marcos, Charlene and Julio. Charlene was completely exhausted and had finally fallen asleep as little Julio sucked intently on her breast.

***

How can she sleep through that? Marcos wondered. But he knew it was because she was completely worn out. Prior to inviting everyone, Marcos had repeatedly cautioned her that having a house full of people and a newborn would be taking on too much, but she wouldn't listen.

"This," she pronounced, "will be our greatest Christmas ever, and I want us all to be together."

Thinking about all the efforts everyone had made to make it to this, their "greatest Christmas ever," inspired Marcos to turn to his son and whisper, "Little Julio, you are indeed a lucky little boy. You have two parents who love you with all their hearts and an extended family that will always be there for you. My commitment to you, little guy, is that I will always take care of you. Beyond that, I'll continue to work hard to protect children everywhere. My hope and dream is that someday people will look back on these times as the dark ages, a dark period in our modern day history when we didn't yet know what scholars would eventually discover regarding what makes adults hurt children. Maybe," Marcos began to smile, "they will even view child abusers, as we know them today, like we now view dinosaurs— extinct but not forgotten."

Imagining child abusers as extinct dinosaurs made Marcos' smile broaden.

"Hey Papa," Charlene said barely waking up, "what are you smiling about?"

"Everything," Marcos answered, as he cautiously leaned over their child and kissed his radiant wife.

54

Justice—The constant and perpetual disposition of legal matters, or disputes to render every person their due.

The last piece of paper in Marcos' file was a photograph Sophia had sent Jordon in January 2001. It was a family picture taken that Christmas around a lopsided snowman. Everyone was in it, including little Julio. The old adage, Jordon thought, that one picture is worth a thousand words, was never truer. Sheer joy and contentment registered on each of their faces.

The last piece of paper in Pat's file was a newspaper article describing his suicide. It was entitled *Deputy Saves Christmas*. She didn't bother to read it.

OK that's it, she thought. Time is running out. It's almost 7:00 o'clock, time to re-read the sergeant's note, take another look at the new police report, and make a decision.

Jordon reopened the large brown envelope; on top was the crinkled memo she'd already read from Sergeant Agnew. As she read it again she thought, all of my career I've prided myself on aggressively prosecuting child molesters and now I've got a *fileable* case right in my hands and I'm still not sure what I should do with it. By law, the only two questions I really have to ask myself are: Would filing these charges be *in the furtherance of justice* and, if I don't choose to file them, am I engaging in *selective prosecution*? Jordon stood up and went back to the window. The sun was beginning to light up the sky from behind the mountain peaks. It's a hell of a standard, she thought, and a troublesome question. She was exhausted, and feared she couldn't think straight. She wanted to lie down, but knew she couldn't, she had to keep going.

After rereading those files, she thought, there's no question in my mind, if Pat were the alleged perpetrator, I'd file the charges in a heartbeat, and then fight like hell to convict him, but I'm not so sure how knowing *that* should affect my decision today. I'm going to take one more look at the desk clerk's Probable Cause Statement:

> "Victim, Emily Scott age 31, reports having been molested at age six by a teenager who she believes was Marcos Estrada.
>
> "According to the victim (herein, victim 2), she was at the time, a neighbor and playmate of the young child who was identified as the victim (herein, victim 1), in case #75-659543, Sophia Estrada.
>
> "Victim 2 now claims she recognized Estrada from today's newspaper, in which there appeared a picture of him, his wife and their baby. Her claimed reason for coming forth at this time, was that she'd been urged to do so by her counselor who wanted her to "seek closure," after what he described to her as a "repressed memory" came back to haunt her.
>
> "Victim 2 does not seek prosecution, but would cooperate if it is pursued.
>
> "Note to the File: In my opinion, Victim 2 gave a very credible and detailed account of the sexual assault, one that was very similar in nature to those given by Victim 1. (See attached Victim 1 and Victim 2 statements.) All reports will be forwarded to the Investigative Division for further evaluation."

Well, Jordon thought, except for expressing his personal opinion in a law enforcement report, he did a good job, although God knows how long the report lay around. This system is so damned inefficient. But in truth, I would've agonized over this decision no matter when it arrived..."OK, enough," she said out loud, "it's crunch time."

She got up, stretched out her body, and walked outside. The sun had just come up over the mountains. She began to pace and thought again about all the people she'd just finished reading about.

No question about it, she considered, if the new report related to Pat, I'd file it, even though Pat, like Marcos, had already served his time. Yeah, but it's how he served his time, she began arguing with herself. Pat came out, even after serving a longer sentence, no better. Matter of fact, he came out worse.

In the *furtherance of justice*, the Penal Code says, but what the hell does that mean? I suppose it means that I'm supposed to figure out which would best serve justice, filing charges against Marcos or rejecting them. Here it is over twenty-five years later, and Emily is apparently still suffering. No doubt about it, prosecuting her perpetrator would serve justice in her mind, but then there's Marcos. Would punishing *him* now for something he did twenty-five years ago serve justice? Would taking him away from his young family and his life's work serve justice?

"Shit," she yelled, banging her hand on the railing. She was completely worn out. She rubbed her eyes. Feeling lightheaded, she sat down on the nearby bench. Why the hell did I think comparing Pat's file to Marcos' would help me find my way in all of this? She put her head in her hands.

You didn't, she heard a voice inside her say, you never wanted to file the charges to begin with. You were just looking for an excuse not to. You knew if you compared Marcos' file to Pat's, you'd just feel less guilty about doing what you wanted to do in the first place...

Maybe that's true, Jordon concluded, but that's not what I'll do. I cannot in good conscience let an *act* of child abuse go unpunished.

She walked back into the house, picked up the police report and headed toward the kitchen phone.

***

"Emily Scott?"

"Yes."

"This is Jordon Danner. I'm a Deputy District Attorney with the Santa Barbara District Attorney's office. I'm sorry to call so early. This is about the report you filed awhile back."

"Un huh." Emily was mystified; she had no idea why this woman was calling her now. After all, she'd already talked to the sergeant two days ago, but, whatever it was, she just hoped it wouldn't take long. She was already late for work.

"Well," Jordon continued, "I was calling you because I had some additional questions."

"Well what is it?" Emily was getting annoyed. She'd already discussed this twice with law enforcement, and that was two times more than she wanted to.

Jordon quickly explained the importance of her call. "…So you see I'm calling now because I'm the one who has to decide whether or not to file these charges."

"Un huh." This is definitely getting old, thought Emily.

"So, I wanted to talk to you about that."

"I already told Sergeant Agnew," Emily responded without hiding her annoyance. "I don't care whether *you* file the charges or not. I just felt *I* had to make the police report."

"But why? Why did you feel you had to report this to the police?"

Emily could sense Jordon felt awkward about pressing her. Still, she couldn't keep the edge out of her voice. "I went over *that* with Sergeant Agnew too."

"I know you did, I guess my question is why now? Why didn't you report it at the time?"

"Because," Emily said, "no one asked."

"What do you mean—no one asked?"

"I don't know. All I do know is that I was five and no one ever asked. I remember telling our teacher that Sophia was bleeding, but she never asked me if *I* was OK, she just ran off to talk to Sophia. At the time, I didn't have any idea that what Marcos had done was such a big deal. I didn't realize *that* until many years later. And by the time I figured it out, I didn't want to discuss it with anyone but my shrink."

Emily was starting to feel better about talking to Jordon. It sounded as if Jordon actually cared, and it felt good to explain to someone in law enforcement what had happened.

***

Jordon knew, as hard as the investigators tried, they sometimes missed other victims. Still, she had to get to the crux of her call. She had to know if there was more; she pushed on.

"But I guess my question is, what made you finally report it that day?"

"His picture was in the morning paper," she answered. "Prior to that moment, I hadn't seen him since before he went off to jail, but that morning I recognized him right away. Then, when I saw he had a baby, I panicked. I just couldn't stand the thought of him doing to another child what he'd done to Sophia and me, so I decided to do something about it. Anyway, my shrink had been after me to report it for quite some time. I guess I just wasn't ready to do it for myself, but when it came to an innocent baby…"

So that was it, Jordon thought. She did it because of Julio. Still Jordon sensed there was more. "Do you mind if I ask you another question?"

"No, go ahead."

"You said at first you didn't know that it was such a big deal and then later you figured it out. What happened to you later that helped you figure it out?"

"Does this have anything to do with whether or not you file the charges?"

"I don't think so, but it might. For now I'm just asking because I care. You see, I work with victims of these types of crimes all the time, and the more I understand how children react to being abused, the better I can help them."

"OK, well if that's your reason, I'll tell you. To understand how all this affected me, I guess you had to have known me about a year ago. You see, I was an aerobics instructor and I kind of flaunted my body. On top of that I always dressed very sexily, but I didn't *feel* very sexy. Once I got into bed with a man, I felt kind of cold."

***

Emily was amazed she was being so forthright, and as hard as saying all this was for her, she felt she should go on. "Around that time, I started dating a doctor I really liked, but when he started to see how cold I was in bed, he didn't end our relationship, like all the other guys did; he just told me he thought I should talk to a counselor about it, so I did. Then what happened was, once I started counseling, I began to *feel* that Marcos had abused me too and then I started getting these fleeting memories of what he did."

"And so that was your *repressed memory*?"

"Yeah, well at least that's what the counselor called it."

"Well what'd you think it was? I mean, do you think he molested you?"

"Yes, but, I guess what's more important," she said trying desperately to control her emotions, "is what do you think? I mean, do you think he molested me? Do you believe me?"

"Yes, yes I do believe you," Jordon said, without apparent hesitation.

"Whew," Emily said, finally exhaling. A moment later she added, "That's something."

"What?" Jordon asked.

"I didn't realize, until now, just how important it was to me that someone in authority understand me."

Emily thought back to the day she'd filed the report. "When I first went into the police station, and told the cop it happened twenty-five years ago, I think he just thought I was nuts. Also, I could tell when that Sergeant Agnew called me a couple of days ago all he really wanted was for me to say that it was OK to forget the whole thing. But now, hearing you say you believe me, well, that actually feels pretty good...So, I guess that means you'll be filing the charges then, right?"

"No."

"No?"

"No."

"Why not?"

"Because, after carefully considering everything you've said and comparing that to everything I've read I don't think filing these charges, at this time, would be in the furtherance of justice."

***

The ambivalence was finally gone. Jordon paused to see if Emily would protest. Hearing nothing she continued. "But that doesn't mean I don't ache for you, because I do. Have you by any chance read any of Dr. Estrada's books?"

"No, have you?" Emily was feeling confused again.

"Yes, I've read them all."

"What are they about?"

"Well, the first one was about the devastating effects of child molestation. The second was about treatment programs and the third focused on the possibility of prevention."

"You're kidding? I had no idea. Are they any good?"

"I think they're terrific," Jordon responded. "I believe Dr. Estrada really understands this problem from the inside out and can write about it in a way that grabs people *and* makes a difference in their lives. His books, and what he's done with his life," Jordon slowly continued, "are part of the reason I think prosecuting him again would just be wrong."

"I didn't know that's what he wrote about," Emily said. "I didn't know anything about him until I saw his picture in the paper that day, and once I saw his picture I didn't read the article."

Emily thought again about the picture. "But what about his baby?" She asked.

"What about his baby?"

"Aren't you worried about him? I've always heard child molesters can't be rehabilitated. Isn't that true?"

"No." Jordon replied. "I don't believe that's true in *all* cases. What's more, after giving this some careful consideration, I've decided I firmly believe in Marcos, and my faith in him is rooted in the decisions he's made and actions he's taken. Of course," she continued, "there are no guarantees."

***

Jordon decided she also wanted to tell Emily something about Charlene, thinking that might help reassure her.

"And, besides, these days Dr. Estrada writes and lectures with his wife, the mother of his baby, who is also a psychologist." Jordon paused to give Emily some time to consider all she'd just said.

A moment later Emily responded. "Well then, I guess that's that."

"Officially, yes, but personally I'd like to know how you feel about my decision not to file the case?"

"I feel fine about it, really. And I do feel better having talked to you."

"I'm glad, but listen, just because I'm not filing these criminal charges doesn't mean you can't. You can still file civil charges against Marcos and sue him for damages—"

Emily interrupted her, "I'm not in the least bit interested in that. I filed the police report for my own psychological well-being and because I was worried he might hurt somebody else. Now that I've spoken to you, I feel as if I've accomplished what I needed to do publicly, and now I can continue to work on my own stuff privately."

"Well, OK, but if you change your mind, call me, and I can give you the names of some good civil lawyers." Sensing some hesitancy on Emily's part, Jordon asked, "Emily, is there anything else I can do for you, or anything else you want to say to me before I contact my office?"

"Yeah, I guess there's something else I want to say. I want to thank you for calling and for doing the work you do. I'm sure it can't be easy and it sounds like you work really hard at it."

Jordon smiled. "Oh, I think you just caught me on one of my good days, but thanks for your kind words."

By the time Jordon hung up the phone she felt confident that under no circumstances, even under threat of being fired, would she file these new charges against Marcos.

To file these new charges against him now, she concluded, wouldn't be in the furtherance of justice, it would make a mockery of it.

Convinced she'd made the right call, Jordon headed toward her bedroom.

***

Once she crawled under the covers, Greg began to wake up.

"What time is it?" he asked.

"Morning," she replied.

"Have you gone to sleep yet?"

"Nope."

"Did you make a *just* decision?" he smiled.

"Yep."

"So, are we going back to Santa Barbara today?"

"No, definitely not."

"So you've decided not to file the charges. Are you OK with that?"

"Yes," she nodded slowly, "yes I am."

"So do you think you can get some sleep now?"

"Probably not."

"Well, let's consider the options," he suggested as he sat up. "We can make love or I can cook you bacon and eggs or we can just head out on a morning hike."

"Yes, yes, and yes," she said, as she started to fall asleep.

Greg stroked her forehead and then up into her hair. "I love you Jordon," he whispered, "and thanks for working so hard. I know you really anguished over this one, but I'm sure that's exactly what this one needed. No doubt the next one will be easier."

Jordon heard him, but acted as if she'd already fallen asleep. She didn't want to assure him of something she knew would never be true. These kinds of cases would never be easy; each would be difficult in its own painful way...

***

Jordon woke up to the smell of bacon. "What time is it?" She had no idea how long she'd slept.

Greg sat back down on the bed with a plate of steaming scrambled eggs, crisp bacon, and buttered toast. "About eleven."

"Mmm, smells good, thanks." Jordon reached for the warm plate, and immediately took a bite of the toast. With her mouth still full she asked, "I guess I fell back asleep, huh?"

"Yep."

Now, wiping away stray crumbs on her lips she inquired, "So, are those other two options still available?"

"Yep," Greg answered, smiling what she considered to be his sexiest smile.

"OK, then, I choose both. Just give me a minute; I have to forward a call."

"You have to *forward* a call?"

"Yep."

"What's that about?"

"I'll tell you in a minute."

She got up, walked back into the kitchen, lifted the phone off the receiver, dialed her voice-mail and listened again to Bert Feller's message:

"… I don't give a shit whether he's guilty or not. We can't let another alleged child molester go. It's coming close to election time, and we need the good ink. So, tomorrow—I want you to sign off on the arrest warrant and tell the boys to get his ass in jail. Later, we can decide if we actually had enough evidence to arrest him in the first place…"

"Perfect," she said out loud. Then, with the push of a few buttons she forwarded his crude and highly incriminating words to the Board of Supervisors and the Public Defender's office.

Once Greg joined her in the kitchen, she explained what she'd just done.

"…So you see, if I just didn't file the case, Feller would've, so now I've done more than that. I've exposed him for the unethical, unjust, self-centered man that he is."

What she didn't tell Greg was that if she didn't just ruin Feller's career, she'd ruined her own.

55

*Equitable or moral consideration—Considerations which are
devoid of efficacy in point of strict law, but are founded upon a
moral duty.*

Jordon, no longer employed as a Deputy District Attorney, was
now busy introducing her youngest son Sam, age 12, to another
potential donor.

She felt Sam, more than anyone else, worked tirelessly to help
her raise the funds she now desperately needed to become the next
District Attorney for Santa Barbara County.

She stood back, took a sip of her watered-down wine and
listened, as she watched her *baby* effortlessly *work the room.*
Motherly pride, mixed with the knowledge of just how important
his schmoozing was, made her smile and sparkle.

Jordon was sure Sam had a future in politics. He was willing to
put himself out there and he knew how to use his ocean-blue eyes
and long thick eyelashes. Besides his looks, he was also smart and
had a genuine concern for his community. Senator Sam Danner,
she thought, that sounds pretty good....

Consumed with her own private musings, she suddenly felt
mildly annoyed when someone tapped her on the shoulder. When
she turned around and saw who it was, she felt an instant chill and
sudden nausea.

She hadn't seen *him* since their last encounter in court months
ago. Doubtlessly sensing her angst, Sam rejoined her and stood
close by his mother's side.

"Ms. Danner, how nice to see you again, and this must be your
boy." He put out his hand; Sam instantly took it.

Jordon's nausea increased, and now she was momentarily
speechless. She hated seeing him touch her baby, matter of fact,
she was shocked to see him there at all.

"Nice to meet you, Sir; my name is Sam Danner. I'm working
on my mother's campaign."

Marshall Riverstone spoke again. "Well, young man, it's a pleasure to meet you too. I've always admired your mother's sense of fairness and I think she'll make a fine District Attorney. Why don't you just step over here with me for a moment and I'll write out a check to help support her candidacy."

Riverstone walked away to a nearby table. As Sam turned to follow him, Jordon reached out and grabbed her son's hand. She needed a moment to consider the taking of Riverstone's blood money.

Finally, in hushed tones, she instructed Sam, "Take his check, but stay away from him. He thinks his money can buy me, but we'll show him it can't. In fact, if we win this thing, I'll use his money to hire an expert witness in child pornography, one whose testimony will be strong enough to put Riverstone away for good."

Moments later, as Jordon looked at Riverstone's check for $10,000, she smiled. You, Mr. Riverstone, have just made it possible for justice to finally be served.

The End

Joyce is eager for your feedback. You can contact her at Joyce@dudleybook.com or check out her website: www.dudleybook.com. She is available for speaking engagements, and will make special arrangements for not-for-profit organizations.

Epilogue

Based upon my educational and personal experiences of working in this field for over three decades, it appears the sad truth is that an unknown number of child molesters will re-offend no matter how much intervention they receive. Some will do so because they don't want to stop, others because they can't, and no amount of therapy will change that.

Those who want to stop, and can, under most circumstances must seek out and commit to long-term mental health treatment. A successful mental heath treatment program usually requires a <u>minimum</u> of three to five years of individual and group therapy and in many instances a lifetime commitment, similar to A.A. meetings. Further, it is crucial for therapists treating this type of aberrant behavior to be specifically trained in working with sex offenders or more damage than good can occur.

Chemical or pharmaceutical therapy may also play an integral part in a sex offender's treatment plan, but very little is known about this. More funds must become available so that additional pharmaceuticals can be formulated and produced. Further, reliable delivery methods need to be developed in order to ensure that the necessary medications are successfully administered.

For the child molesters who want to stop and can, there are some programs presently being run by trained individuals which can make a difference. However, these programs are grossly under-funded and are in desperate need of high quality research studies to both quantify and qualify their long-term effectiveness.

Presently, there are few treatment programs available to convicted child molesters incarcerated in state prison systems throughout the United States, most of whom will be released from prison within a matter of years of their initial incarceration. Without therapy, many professionals believe there is a significant chance that these child molesters will re-offend. With appropriate therapy and treatment, most believe these numbers can be reduced, but no one knows by how much. Still, many mental health professionals believe that these programs must become available within the prison system in order to allow for the *possibility* of rehabilitation while inmates can still be monitored and controlled.

Historically, many child molesters claim to have been physically, emotionally, or sexually abused when they were children. Many of them later claim their perpetrators were women. For a variety of reasons sex crimes perpetrated by women are rarely reported, and therefore even more infrequently prosecuted. One of the tragic results of this omission is that their victims are not identified until some actually become perpetrators themselves. To stop this cycle intervention therapy must be available to these highly vulnerable victims soon after they are assaulted.

Most child victims who testify in court today are in some manner re-victimized by the criminal justice system. In the late 1980s the California Legislature passed legislation which amended these courtroom procedures in an effort to avoid or diminish these negative effects. Still many California courts, as well as other courts across the country, are hesitant to apply these non-traditional procedures, and children continue to be revictimized.

In some parts of the country forensic specialists such as doctors, nurses, law enforcement officers, social workers, and psychologists are trained to examine children who've allegedly been molested. As a result of this training, these dedicated individuals have reduced the traumatic effects on these children of both the physical exam and the initial interview. When these forensic exams are properly conducted, not only are children rarely re-traumatized, but the evidence itself is collected in a scientifically defensible manner, which promotes due process of law.

In some parts of the country, untrained *professionals*, are used to conduct these highly specialized investigations and exams. If these "professionals," no matter how caring, remain untrained, they can unwittingly cause irreparable harm to the child, the accused, and the integrity of the criminal justice system.

Those who enter this specialized area of criminal investigation must be both highly motivated and highly educated. That this is so is because they are charged with the daunting task of righting an intolerable wrong, be it a crime that has occurred or the clearing of a name of an individual who has been falsely accused.

Most of us find it abhorrent to consider issues surrounding child molestation and abuse, so we don't. If we continue to remain complacent, our children will continue to be molested and abused. However, if we instead confront this grave problem head on, we increase our chances of ensuring that justice will be served.